AFTER ARIEL

It started as a game...

by Diana Hockley

After Ariel
Published by
Diana Hockley 2014
www.dianahockley.webs.com

Book layout and cover design
by Publicious Pty Ltd
www.publicious.com.au

Printed in Australia by
SOS Print+Media
www.sos.com.au

International printing by
Lightning Source
www.lightningsource.com

Catalogue-in-Publication details available
from the National Library of Australia
ISBN: 978-0-9941900-0-0

DEDICATION

For Andrew and our sweet Inky,
now at the Rainbow Bridge.

ACKNOWLEDGEMENTS

Retired Detective Senior Constable Melanie Mather, Friends and fellow writers: Mar Preston, Gillian McKee, Susan Fleet, Martin Line and , Photographer Peter Truer, Retired Senior Sergeant Pat Ritter. Also Senior Sergeant Peter Boyce, Doctor Nat Sheehan, friends – Pam, Jo, Andrea, Felicity and Margaret, all who have put up with my whining at some stage. My sincere thanks go to Nigel Munro-Wallis for all the invaluable information. And a special thank you to my friend, Barbara Dykes, who went through this book for typos and dramas!

Thank you to Kings River Life Magazine for allowing your title to be used in this novel.

NOTE

This book is written in 'Australian English' which, of course, is a slightly bastardised version of Queen's English! We use 's' instead of 'z' 'our' instead of 'or' and in the case of one of those things which moves your car – 'tyre' instead of 'tire' ☺

We also have a plethora of 'Aussiespeak' which we use with impunity and a certain amount of smugness. Here is a dictionary for those of you who think we are quite mad. Of course, we are not.

GLOSSARY OF
AUSTRALIAN/BRITISH SLANG

4WD: four wheel drive vehicle, SUV.

Arvo: afternoon

Arse: butt, bum, ass

Awesome: this word is frequently used by teens indicate that something is pretty good.

Berk: fool.

Bikies: bikers.

Bloke: man, guy.

Boag: dude.

Bolshie: cranky, feisty.

Bollocking: scolding.

Bonkers: mad, crazy.

Boot: when related to the car, this refers to the 'trunk.'

Brick wall you-know-what: The person is built like a very large, indestructible toilet block. Usually said in a coarser manner!

Bull-dusted: Bull dust is a fine red dust out west of NSW in NT, QLD and Western Australia.

Bum/Arse: bottom, fanny, butt & ass

Bung: put

Cattle grid: nickname for the turnstiles inside the foyer of police HQ in Brisbane.

CBD: Central Business District.

Chateau Cardboard: wine in a box with a tap attached. Natural habitat: backyard barbecues.

Chooffed (off): went away, trundle off – a slang term for someone walking away.

Chooks: chickens

City Cat: Catamaran connecting points of the city via the Brisbane river.

Classic Drive: Program of classical music played in the afternoon, about the time people drive home from work.

Cobbler's Peg: a small single sticky burr which drives you crazy picking millions of them out of your socks before the wash. Also known as Farmers Friend, Beggars Ticks, Spanish Needle, Black Jack and formally, Bidens Pilosa.

"Could have fooled me": Sarcastic Aussie saying, meaning you *haven't* fooled me one little bit!

Cop shop: police station.

Cracking hardy: pretending nothing is wrong, being stoic.

Cranky: irritable/ angry but not toweringly mad.

Docos: documentaries.

Doolally: mad, crazy, bonkers.

Doona: eiderdown, duvet.

Driz-a-bone (dry-as-a bone): a heavy duty, almost canvas, oiled all-weather coat.

Drongo: idiot

Drop of a hat: do something immediately without planning.

Dymocks: major booksellers.

Fisted: bunched hand into a fist.

Flat: unit or apartment.

Galah: a pink, grey and white parrot who doesn't mind making a fool of himself. A term also used for youths who are doing just that.

Go mental: get really angry.

Granny Smith: a large, green crunchy apple used copiously in pies and crumbles. Used in this context as "the apple of his parent's eye" meaning he can do no wrong.

'Hairy one': difficult or dangerous one.

Hunk: handsome man.

Kip: nap, sleep.

Kipling's Bandarlog: In Hindi, *Bandar* means "monkey"

Knock off: kill, or leaving work, e.g. "knock-off time"

Knocking off: Youths or uncouth oafs referring to having sex. "Jeez, I'd like to knock *her* off, mate!"

Lift: elevator

Lift: ride as in picked a person up to give them a ride to somewhere, e.g. "Do you want a lift to work?"

Lorikeets: brightly coloured (red, green, blue and yellow) small Australian parrots. Nasty, greedy, noisy little thugs, much given to chasing other birds away from the seed feeders.

Lug: drag

Macca's: McDonald's eateries.

Manky: scruffy, ill-kempt

Message stick: USB stick

Mobile phone: cell phone.

Mock Orange: sweet smelling blossom.

Muso: musician.

My bad: sarcastic acknowledgement of wrong doing accompanied by sanctimonious eye rolling, expertly performed by teenage girls.

NAFIS: National Automated Fingerprint Identification Service.

On about: what he or she means when they're talking about something incomprehensible. E.g. "What are you on about now?"

Parka: anorak, puffy waterproof, hooded jacket.

(A) pretty good fist of it: a very good effort.

Pub-light: the gleam in the eye of a thirsty man heading off to the pub for a beer after work.

Pud: pudding, dessert.

Red Ned: red wine, quite often an inexpensive brand of Shiraz, Burgundy or Rosé.

Rooster: in this context, a young, lusty man.

Ruckus: commotion.

Scallywags: naughty. If a bloke or a child is a "scallywag" then he or she is naughty but not really bad. (Scottish)

Scoffs: eats rapidly, like a wolf!

Scrub up: tidy up, to make oneself look nice.

Scrubber: a 'loose' woman.

Shearwater: medium-sized, long-winged seabird.

Shire Council: local government body, e.g. county.

Shonky: suspect, suspicious.

Sig Event: Significant Event Report. Cop speak.

Sig other: significant other – lover, man friend.

Size twelves: the size of his shoes.

Skellums: Idiomatic Shona term for minor criminals.

Solicitor: No, he's not trawling for business – well – a lawyer! May I refute that first statement? J

Spot on: accurate, correct.

Sprung: caught.

Super: Superintendent, as in police rank.

Sussed out: discovered/cover blown as in undercover investigation.

'Talked for the Olympics': A saying which means the person talked so rapidly and copiously that he or she was Olympic standard.

Tanti: short for 'tantrum'

Takeaway: a meal 'to go'.

Thick: in this instance, 'stupid.'

Tubby: chubby, a little overweight.

Unit: apartment or flat.

Vanity: bathroom cupboard, frequently a repository for the washbasin and if wide enough, makeup and miscellaneous clutter necessary to women!

Wanker: idiot, fool.

'Who's who at the zoo': Australian police term for the villains in the community.

Witter: babble, talk nonsense.

Wonkus: faint, wobbly.

Wonky: wobbly, skewhiff.

Yabby: freshwater crayfish.

Yonks: ages, a long time.

Music mentioned in this novel.

Gluck: Dance of the Blessed Spirits from Orfeos and Eurydice.

Haydn: Concerto for Flute and Piano

Mozart: Concerto No 20 in D Major.

Mozart: Clarinet Concerto, First Movement.

Schubert: Shepherd on a Rock.

Contents

Jeffrey finds the Shoe

Saturday, 8am

'Jeff-rey!'

He shook his head and tugged harder.

'Jeffrey? Jeffrey, where *are* you! Here, boy!'

Jeffrey, who had failed Obedience School abysmally, ignored his master's call. He pulled harder. The object, caught under a sharp twig, suddenly freed from the pile of branches, landing on the grass in front of him, sending Jeffrey back onto his haunches. The call came closer. Torn between his natural inclination to disobey and a vestige of training left in his frivolous Labrador brain, Jeffrey hesitated.

'Jeff-reeeeeeeeeey!' The voice rose to a screech.

Jeffrey stood, staring at the pile of branches and weeds, yearning to investigate further – the smell was so enticing – then picked up his prize and galloped the twenty metres separating him from his master. His tail wagged furiously. *Look what I've got!*

'Not again, Jeffrey, you stupid animal! Why did I have to get a dog with a "shoe fetish?"'

His master reached down, grasped the sandal and twisted. Jeffrey resisted until the shiny leather straps were decidedly the worse for wear, before surrendering his trophy. 'Let's hope the woman who owns this isn't looking for it, mate, because it's ruined now.' His master turned the sandal around, frowning at the teeth marks marring its red patina. *Some silly drunken cow playing in the park...*

Sighing, he tucked it into the pocket of his parka and headed for home. Jeffrey paused to glance back toward to the pile of branches, gave a mental doggy shrug and followed. He would get breakfast when he got home and maybe investigate the pile of branches on his evening walk.

CHAPTER 1

The Pickup

Friday, 3.51pm.

He shouldn't have squeezed the baby. He had known that for his adult life, an eight year- old's recollection. His mother's voice returned, a fragment from a radio play – 'You must always be gentle, darling,' – words imprinted on his mind to surface when he least expected, bearing no relationship to any of the bizarre events which regularly coursed through his REM sleep.

He jerked into wakefulness, momentarily disoriented until he got his bearings. The plane bounced in an air-pocket. Piercing ring tones flared from the seat opposite. His brow crinkled in momentary annoyance.

Her clear, bell-like tone took him by surprise; he hadn't figured her for refined. He closed his eyes, allowing her words to wash over him before he focused on her face. Small, dainty and dark-haired, with "Bailey's Irish Cream" complexion and velvety skin, she personified all that he was attracted to. He wasn't too charmed by the ring in her nose, but the multi-coloured beads shimmering in her ears reminded him of glow-worms. He wanted to skim his fingertips over the bright buttons, to glide across the soft, milky skin of the back of her neck. Her spicy perfume wafted across the aisle.

'I missed the bus, so I decided to fly... No, they don't know. Dad would go mental if he knew...Yes, on my way home ... No, I'm going to be on my own tonight, because they want me to be there to look after the house and answer the phone, but thanks lots. I'll see you tomorrow.'

The elderly woman sitting next to him by the window hissed disapproval, but he'd caught the most important part. She'd be home alone.

She snapped off her mobile and thrust the plug of her iPod past the dangling trinkets into her ear, then pulled a lurid-looking paperback from her tote bag. She stuck her little pink tongue out, moistened the tip of a forefinger and flicked the pages until she found her place. He watched through half-closed eyes as she became engrossed in the story, her foot tapping in time to a silent rhythm. *Wonder if she'd like company tonight, but would she want to play the games he had in mind?* He was on for play anytime, anywhere...

Had he spoken his thoughts aloud? He shot a sidelong glance at the fat man sitting in the window seat shuffling to get comfortable. Perhaps, like himself, he'd had to get somewhere at the last minute and copped "cattle class." His attention snapped back to the dark-haired girl who had taken her iPod plugs out of her ears and was speaking on her mobile again.

'Hi, it's me, Ariel. Doing anything tonight?' Her face scrunched as she listened. 'Oh, well it's like, I can't go out. Have to be home ...yeah, it sucks.' She listened for a moment or two more, then trilled, 'Okay, by-ee.'

Snapping her mobile shut, she sensed someone watching. She turned her head and smiled. A thrill shot through him. Heat spread throughout his body, pulses of excitement flooded his limbs, chasing prickles of perspiration out to the tips of his fingers and toes. He clenched and unclenched his hands and shifted in his seat. *'Don't be so ready to assume, love. Not everyone wants to play.'* The stricture was angrily dismissed. *Get away from me, Mum. Onetwothreefour...*

Exhaling slowly he allowed his gaze to wander back to Ariel, intending to make an opportunity to talk to her when they arrived in Brisbane. He glowed with anticipation. *'Don't get excited, love. You're too impetuous!'* *Shut up, Mum.* Leaning back into his seat, he allowed his eyelids to drift shut.

The announcement over the address system to fasten their seatbelts jolted him awake. He leaned forward and gazed out of the window, counting the airport buildings and as they taxied to the terminal, including the planes parked along the side of the paved access roadway. Once the seatbelt light went out, he got to his feet and reefed his backpack down from the overhead locker, stepped across the aisle and dragged her faded tote bag out of the locker. Ariel's hazel eyes, framed by long lashes, met his. 'Thanks. It's like, too high for me.'

'I'll carry it for you.' He cast a husky tone into his voice. *Girls like that.*

'Thanks, like, millions.' She threw him a flirtatious glance as she stuffed her iPod and the paperback into her tote bag, picked it up and got into line to edge down the aisle. Shrugging himself into his parka, he pulled the hood up and led the way to the luggage carousel, studying Ariel as she stood beside him, chattering into her phone. Her denim jacket partially covered a white camisole top. Her long legs were encased in "skinny" jeans with sexy, high-heeled ankle boots. A line of bags came into view and he tapped her on the shoulder.

'Which one's yours?'

She snapped her phone shut and looked at him through half-closed eyes. 'You gunna help me with it?' Her lips twitched.

'Sure. No problem...'

'That one!' she squealed, pointing to a pink, soft-zipped bag wending its way toward them. He lunged for it and whipped it off the carousel, followed by his own plain black case. Ariel laughed up into his face, clutching his arm. 'Hey, cool!'

'How're you getting to the city?'

'Catching the train in and then a cab,' she said, grinning. 'You coming?'

'Sure. Let me carry these...' He settled his backpack over his shoulders, handed her his music case and picked up the large bags. 'Lead the way!'

A chilly breeze swirled around the platform for the air-train. The girl dropped her backpack, dragged a denim jacket out and struggled into it, giggling as he tried to help her. He heaved their luggage into the carriage and up onto a vacant rack.

They didn't speak as the train raced toward the transit centre. Ariel stood close and texted her friends while he hovered, inhaling her scent, so engrossed that he even forgot to count the people in the carriage, the stations or the buildings zipping by below.

As they left the station, the girl introduced herself as Ariel Maxwell, announced that she only lived fifteen minutes away and then kept up a steady stream of chatter as they headed for the cab rank. Hefting her case into a taxi, he confided that he needed to find somewhere to stay overnight, a pub or motel. *Easier to keep her away from my unit.*

'That's all right, there's a good pub just near us. The

Commercial on Grey. It's pretty posh,' she chirped. The jewellery in her ears flashed. 'We'll share a cab if you like?' She gave her address and settled back into the corner.

'How about dinner later, then? We can eat at the pub, or we could go somewhere else if you like. Perhaps to the city.' His gaze skittered away from hers and then, almost reluctantly, back to her.

'Maybe. What's your name?'

'I have a nickname.' He told her, watching as she put her hand up to her face and giggled. 'You're joking! That sounds like someone's dog! What's your real name?'

Warmth spread from his neck into his face. 'You don't want to know. A nickname's more fun!' *It's better I remain anonymous.* Who knows where this game will end? It mightn't be worth it anyway. 'I'll go on to the pub after this.'

Ariel didn't want to appear too eager, but she couldn't help regarding him with keen interest and growing excitement. His lightly bronzed skin set off his handsome features. She wondered how much time he spent on the beach. His glossy, longish hair and small gold stud in one ear gave him a rakish, unreliable appearance. She wondered what it would be like to run her fingers through those silken strands. What would Deanna say, when she heard what a prize she, Ariel, had discovered on the train, a gorgeous, tall, broad-shouldered hot guy? Not the usual 'ocker.' *No, this one was a man.*

From Ariel's perspective things were looking up. Her parents were away for the weekend and she had the house to herself.

'This it?' His gaze flicked over the neat house with its pretty garden as he guided her from the taxi. His beautiful, full lips moved as though he was counting.

'Yeah.' She paid the driver, who grunted, stuffed the

note into his cash bag and embarked on a barrage of coughing as he waited for his remaining passenger.

'Shall I come back for you about seven?'

She smiled. Tonight dinner and who knew what would be next? Caught up in the excitement of her unexpected date, her parents request that she stay at home had flown her mind. 'No, I'll meet you. Seven in the lounge bar.'

He gestured to the bag. 'Shall I carry this in for you?'

She thought quickly. What if they ended up back there? The house would be a tip; she had two hours to get it sorted. 'No thanks, I'm good.' For a moment, doubt crept into her mind but was swiftly dismissed. They'd be in the pub, surrounded by the Friday night crowd.

What could possibly go wrong?

CHAPTER 2

Reunion

Pamela Miller

Friday, 4.30pm

My mother, Rosalind, stands on a river bank holding a baby. It is early autumn and the trees are changing colour. Tears trickle down her cheeks and drip off her quivering chin to soak her chambray shirt. Sunlight glitters on her sequin-splattered denim skirt. As I watch, fascinated, willow trees appear from behind to shroud her from the world but just as her image fades into the cool green fronds, a man's tall figure looms behind her with folded arms. She turns and clasps the baby tightly to her as he turns away from her and slowly vanishes from sight. Her pain fills my heart.

My eyes snapped open, shaking off the recurring dream which I believe symbolises the loss of my father. As always, a feeling of emptiness engulfed me but faded quickly this time. I have at last a surrogate, in the form of my much loved stepfather, John. *I want this concert done with and I want my mum!* Not necessarily in that order.

My fellow passengers were gathering their belongings, bumping hips with each other as they struggled for luggage in the racks above. Thank goodness I got the last seat in Business Class. My long legs are not designed for "cattle."

I didn't have to wait too long at the carousel, though I was entertained by the little beagle checking our luggage. I watched, laughing silently, as a young man with revoltingly large earrings set into his ears like an African woman's decoration, was led away after an enthusiastic response from the dog.

My laughing, noisy cousin, Marigold Humphries ran up to me as I wheeled my bag away from the carousel where I stopped to load my backpack over my shoulders. 'Is this all you've got, Pammie?' She gave me a big hug, almost knocking my spectacles off and then looked for what else I may have secreted about my person. 'Got everything? How was the tour? Are you ready for tomorrow night's concert?'She snatched the handle of my big case out of my hand and wheeled it toward the exit. I slung my backpack over my shoulder picked up my precious flute case and laptop, then trudged after her.

Tired out, I answered as economically as possible. She nodded in approval, chattering over her shoulder – the family are fine and waiting eagerly for me to arrive and yes, she is off again on a new assignment! By the time we reached her car, I was reeling with information overload. She slung my case into the boot and climbed behind the wheel. I carefully placed my flute case and laptop in the back, shoved my backpack down behind the passenger seat and scrambled in. Goldie gunned the motor and lurched out of the parking lot, cursing as we reached the boom gate. Marigold – Goldie to her family and friends – is one of the two women with whom I can bitch about errant boyfriends, corporate sponsors, arrogant conductors, lack of time and currently, sex.

We're both tall, fair-haired and slim, but her bold and classically beautiful face marks the difference between us.

She's used to being approached by scouts for modelling agencies and other 'would-be, could-be's' who back off pretty smartly when she delivers her standard reply: 'Listen, Cuddles, I've had better wet dreams than what you're offering!' Her responses to hopefuls who approach her in bars don't bear repeating. She's an internationally renowned free-lance photo-journalist who's much in demand, fiercely ambitious and will let nothing stand in her way of reaching the top of her profession.

I took a long swig of water 'So how have you been?'

Goldie flicked the indicator for left and turned into the stream of traffic. 'Oh fine! Fine.' *Oh yeah? Could have fooled me.*

'So what's the latest on the 'sig other' front? You were pretty cagey when we spoke on the phone yesterday. What aren't you telling me?'

'Nothing, really nothing.' Her face closed, her eyebrows drew into a frown. *Something's wrong...*

'Goldie, I know you too well.'

She laughed and blew a kiss to a male motorist, who besottedly allowed her into the line of traffic.

Men adore her. 'I know you have someone in tow, you always do!' Goldie goes through men like a lioness through a mob of gazelles.

'Did, you mean.' She chewed her lip briefly and then informed me that she has just dismissed her latest suitor two days ago and is ready to frolic.

'For God's sake, what was wrong with *this* one?'

'He was a dickhead, love, but apart from that, nothing.'

'So, what's next?'

'Well, I have to get back to Sydney earlier than I planned. KRL mag wants their photo-spread a lot faster than we thought. Apparently someone has let them down, so it's all a bit complicated, Pammie. The bottom line is I can finish up the river shots tomorrow morning, and then meet up with Jack Boode, the TV bloke, to plan for the Africa job and fly back to Sydney late Sunday night.' She looked at me, guiltily. 'I know we planned to have a few days together, but I'll be back in a few weeks and we can do something then. I am coming to your concert tomorrow night, though!'

I'd hoped that we would have a little time together. She appeared to have forgotten that I'm going overseas for a couple of weeks shortly, but of course work has to come first.

'Pam?'

'Sure, no problems.'

'So what about tomorrow night's concert? You're all set, then?' She threw a twinkling glance at me, as she swung the car around a corner, nearly taking out a cyclist.

'As ready as I'll ever be.'

While I have been somewhat successful in the world of classical music, stage fright has been the bane of my life and until a short time ago, actually prevented me achieving anything like a sizzling career. 'Puking Pam twelve o'clock' is the favourite, a stage hand's cruel catch-cry, as they bring out a bucket with great ceremony and place it behind the curtains at the entrance to the stage. I want to kick them up their well-endowed or otherwise, crotches. This tour, however, things are looking up.

When I turned twenty six, I realised that if I didn't overcome my affliction and get a grip on myself, I may as well toss in the towel and settle for a life in front of waist-high future stockbrokers, CEOs, lawyers and possible apprentice criminals. Not so you'd notice the difference.

I decided stage fright would not – *could not* –get the better of me. Three years later and I'm all good. Literally hundreds of hours of practice and hard work with tutors have seen to that. A musician's life is not the easy one people seem to imagine.

'How's the tour been so far?' Goldie's voice is a flat, Australian outback twang. Educated in one of the foremost private boarding schools in the country, one could be forgiven for wondering how she ended up with an accent like that. When asked, her reply is classic: 'This is the result of screwing a shearer for three fucking years, darls.' Her voice remains steady, but her eyes tell a story of grief and loneliness.

The photographic record of their travels in the red, bull-dusted outback has won her accolades and countless awards, as has her stints in Iraq and Afghanistan, the last almost ending her life with a stray bullet in the chest, but in Goldie's own words, she wouldn't give the Taliban 'the satisfaction of knocking off a Western journalist and a *woman* at that!'

'The hypnotism worked, but I have to keep working at it. So far, touch wood, I haven't had a problem this whole tour, so let's not tempt fate and talk about it.'

'You said you were doing a number with a pianist. Who is it this time?'

'Vladimir Rezanov.'

'Oh my God, Pammie, he's *hot*!!' She turned to stare at me, narrowly missing oncoming traffic. I reached out to grab the wheel, but she recovered herself just in time. The blare of a horn pursued us down the street. 'He's *so* photogenic. I want an introduction!'

Strangely, I have never met Rezanov who had studied at the Queensland Conservatorium a couple of years ahead of me. A somewhat Godly figure, he had been revered by all, surrounding himself with the most attractive of the students. Then he began to make a name for himself by winning the Sydney International Piano Competition which enabled him to enjoy the more glamorous aspects of what society had to offer and it wasn't long before he headed off permanently overseas to further his career. By the time I arrived in London, he had established himself on the international stage, and since then his fame had grown. Recordings, concerts – he'd played for the highest in every land.

'We're supposed to be rehearsing the Haydn tomorrow morning. If you can't come then, there might be a chance after the concert, but from what I've heard on the grapevine he'll be crotch-deep in groupies.' My sarcasm drew a startled glance from Goldie as we pulled up in front of her parent's house.

'I have things to do in the morning. What a bummer!' She shrugged and turned off the engine.

'You can come backstage after the concert and I can introduce you then, if we can find the bugger.' If Goldie accompanies me to the concert, I don't like even *her* chances of storming his citadel. My agent, Ann, said: *'He's a sexual predator. You girls should keep a safe distance from that young man,'* When I told my friend, Ally, she screamed with laughter. 'Thirty centimetres would be about right! Anyway, eighteen to twenty year old teenies are his preference. We're too old, Pammie!' *Twenty-eight is too old for another twenty-eight year old?* In this case, apparently it is!

Rezanov tends to remain in his dressing room until the last possible moment before his performance and vaporizes immediately the curtain falls on his last bow, if his agent and the management don't catch him and haul him out to meet his fans. No doubt the sponsors get a tad restless from time to time. I must admit I'm curious about this woman-magnet who apparently dispenses his favours liberally. From his publicity photos, I can see what they're raving about. Gorgeous, two metres tall and brilliant, from all accounts he's a sexual hurricane. I promise Goldie I will do my best to introduce her.

'Please God, the idiot won't bring another artist along with him,' I muttered, remembering a celebrity percussionist who spent all his free time frolicking with his partner, a blonde clarinettist whose boobs had the eyes of all the men in the orchestra – even the gays – sticking out like the proverbial organ stops. We women couldn't figure out how she managed to get her arms in front of her to play, but the unkindest cut of all was the undeniable fact that she is a fine musician.

'Now you're talking!' Grinning with anticipation, Goldie leapt out of the car, slung her handbag over her shoulder, snatched her exotic shopping bags and headed for her parent's front gate. 'Mum's expecting us to have coffee and then we can go home or out to the pub. Whatever you like! We'll leave your things in the car for now.'

I retrieved my flute case and laptop before some weasel stole them. The front door opened and my uncle and aunt surged out to greet us. All talk of Rezanov and the concert was put on hold while we had coffee and scoffed the cakes for which Goldie's mum is renowned. Comfortably round, my mother's younger sister fits neatly under the armpit of her husband. Every time I look at her face under strong, dark brows, hazel eyes and thick, fair hair, I see my mother staring back at me.

'Pam...*Pam?*'

'No more, thanks, Fiona,' I started to gather up crockery, which she took from me with a no-nonsense wave of her hand.

As Goldie and her father argued amiably about nothing in particular, I took the opportunity to look around. It was a long time since I had visited and nothing had changed. The wall was still covered with decorative plates painted with everything from portraits of the Royal Family, to flowers, landscapes and kittens. I am reasonably sure the curtains over the windows were the same lace rose-embossed ones. A huge urn of dried leaves stood in a corner.

Millicent, Fiona's beloved cat slept on a footstool, her long tabby legs dangling over the side. From time to time, she half opened her eyes, flexed her front paws and looked toward the kitchen. When my aunt came back, Millicent, who always has an eye to the main chance, staked her claim to a comfortable lap.

My mind returned as always before a concert, to the program I am to perform. Haydn's Flute Concerto would be my major work, but the Schubert – Shepherd on a Rock – was to be performed with Rezanov. Hopefully, the audience would call for at least one encore, and for that I'd chosen Dance of the Blessed Spirits, a huge favourite not only of mine but audiences as well. Fiona returned and interrupted my thoughts by joining in with my cousin and her father's discussion about Goldie's next job and whether she will ever go back to a war zone. It was not long, however, before their attention turned back to me.

'So, you're ready for the concert tomorrow night?' Alex fished out a massive handkerchief with which he proceeded to clean his spectacles. Millicent turned around in Fiona's aproned lap, puddling her paws while her mistress waited for her to settle.

'Yes, I have to go over there in the morning and rehearse. It's only a matter of running through the program and rehearsing one piece with the pianist.' I hoped no one would ask me about him.

Fiona looked concerned. 'You really *are* over your stage fright, aren't you, Dear?'

'Yes, it doesn't bother me anymore. Of course, I'll always be nervous before a performance, but at least I can get onto the stage without throwing up.'

'Fancy being able to fix something like that!' For my aunt, hypnosis comes under the heading of witchcraft. 'Who's on the program with you? I know you told me, but my memory isn't what it used to be.'

After I mentioned Rezanov, she looked at me with concern. 'You mean the one who's always on the tellie and in the paper with models hanging off him? Only last week, he had that Princess who was over here opening something – whatever her name is – besotted with him.' She waved her hands, as she tried to remember the name of some minor royal.

'Yes, Fiona, but don't worry, I'm too old for him. He only likes teenagers.'

'Oh dear, one of those is he?' Alex chimed in. The expression on his face said he was not sure whether to be relieved that I am too old or disgusted because the man in question likes younger women.

'He's not a dirty *old* man; he's a dirty *young* one! He's only the same age as me.'

'Have you spoken to your mother lately?' Fiona changed the subject. Something in her voice alerted me to a hidden agenda. 'Er...no, not for a week or so.

Why?' I knew mum was about to undergo an operation for cancer.

'Well, you should because I think she's sicker than she's letting on. It's not what she said, more what she didn't say. I know my sister and when she's covering something up.'

'We know she's having the op on Monday, but could it be worse than she's saying? Or is something wrong with John?' My mother married a widowed, retired Senior Constable only six months previously and had never been happier.

'I don't know, but the sooner you get home to her the better, dear. Are you two coming back here for tea, Goldie?'

My cousin glanced at me. 'Want to come back for tea or shall we go to the pub?'

I let the idea run through my mind. Knowing Goldie's capacity to hold liquor, I decided discretion was the better part of valour. 'Thanks for the invite, Fiona, but I need to get up early and I'm rather tired.' I turned to Goldie. 'Perhaps we could get a takeaway and knock off a bottle of 'Red Ned' at your place?'

She lived a few streets away from her parents in a refurbished workman's cottage. I would be staying for a couple of nights until my own unit became vacant on Saturday morning.

* * *

Goldie's 1930s cottage was more of a two-storeyed home, painted a pale lemon, topped by a dark grey roof and with leadlight windows, behind a small lawn surrounded by tall shrubs. Because she is gone for months at a time, she prefers to keep her garden simple, knowing that her parents will be looking after it. She opened the glossy dark grey front door, stepped over the threshold and hurled her keys into a wide, shallow pottery dish on a side table. The natural light of a summer evening showed that nothing had changed since my last visit.

Goldie's decor revealed her penchant for all things big and garish – like herself, but in a comfortable way. The snug lounge room was, as always, strewn with newspapers and books, her small piano stood in the corner near the window next to a desk on which her laptop sat open, surrounded by papers and piles of what appeared to be photographs. A few crudely carved souvenirs of donkeys and camels decorate the tops of bookshelves. Of her numerous awards, there was no sign. Family photos adorn the walls and the top of a dresser. On the wall above the fireplace is a stunning portrait of Parry Reynolds.

He was large enough to make my cousin appear petite, and I knew him to have been beautiful outside *and* within. My heart ached for her, as I tore my gaze away from his twinkling dark eyes and smiling, perfect mouth. Their love for each other was supposed to keep them safe. Goldie's gaze travelled to Parry's photo then swung back to me. 'I'll never find what Parry and I gave each other, Pammie. Sometimes I wish I could just lift that slab and melt down into the coffin with him.' Great tears tumbled down her cheeks, falling to her shirt front.

The old adage 'Time heals all wounds' flitted through my mind, but for once, I managed to keep my big fat mouth shut. 'There's nothing I can say to lighten the load, Glory, but I'm always here to listen and give you a hug when you need it.'

Our hands entwined. We stayed motionless for a moment or two, before she pulled gently away. 'Come on, let's get you settled.'

We lugged my backpack and case up the narrow winding stairs to the guest room. Nothing had changed in the year or so since I last stayed there – the bedspread screaming red, the sheets black. The prints on the walls embody all that is animal and mineral; original wildlife paintings hang from the walls. The bathroom will be totally stark white and the black claw-footed bath deep and comfortable, and no doubt the towels would match the bedspread!

Resisting the impulse to throw myself onto the queen-sized bed and stare at the ceiling, I grabbed a change of clothing and my toiletry bag.

There was no premonition, no feeling of urgency – nothing, in fact, to warn me that a chain of events had been set in motion that would change my life forever.

CHAPTER 3

Detective Inspector Susan Prescott

Wifely Suspicions

Friday, 4.30pm.

Grant Winslow went down in a shower of Kevlar vests and testosterone with a police dog hanging off his bum. We congratulated our hairy colleague as he swung joyfully on a wad of white cotton held by his grinning handler, after which my partner, Detective Senior Sergeant Evan Taylor, and I prepared to head back to Police Headquarters. We'd been down the street talking to an informant when the excitement broke out, and stopped to admire the capture.

Some people never learn and Grant, the shiny little Granny Smith of his wealthy parent's eyes, is an excellent example. Having started his career in primary school roaming the streets after dark, stealing whatever he could get his hands on – car parts, hardware, from convenience stores – dear Grant graduated through partying, drunken brawling to 'minor' assault. No doubt he was into his fair share of drugs as well. The paramedics loaded him into an ambulance with an economy of long practice, ignoring his screaming invective, to cart him off to hospital where he would, no doubt, jump the never-ending queue of the honestly afflicted and be ushered immediately into the care of emergency doctors.

Weariness and a deep feeling of futility swept over me. It had been one of those afternoons when you know you're middle aged. How do you convey to idiots like Winslow that the path they have chosen will haunt them for the rest of their lives? He'd been given every opportunity, including numerous interventions and a prolonged spell at boot camp for juvenile offenders. The courts sympathised when they heard how a perceived lack of love from his devoted parents had twisted his tiny mind, so with the help of their money which hired a Rottweiler of a lawyer, and Grant's ability to melt the hearts of magistrates with his angelic face, he had gotten away with his crimes because he was still technically a juvenile. One day he would go too far and kill someone and then Grant would be *my* team's problem.

Robbery of a bottle shop was not going to be as easy to skim over. The un-sporting owner had put up a fight and in the process, fallen and hit his head on a chair. Grant grabbed as much of the money as he could and fled through a nearby park into a shopping centre. Such was his arrogance that the Dog Squad caught up with him strolling nonchalantly through the alley to the rear. Finally realising he'd been sprung he'd bolted up the side of a dumpster. Big mistake.

'What do you reckon the little shit'll get this time?'

Apart from the TV News vans, the mêleé in the alley had attracted quite a large group of office workers and retail staff. Many had paused on the overhead bridge, from whence they had a good vantage point across the main street. Mobile phone cameras recorded the drama, texting fingers flew; life had never been so exciting.

Evan rolled his eyes. 'With any luck, a hundred years, but when have they ever had any success with that little drongo? A hundred days'd be better than nothing.'

'Well, let's see how Sinclair gets him off this one. Grant'll be seventeen soon, so he won't be able to get away with it for much longer! Let me out at the front of the shop, please Evan. I want to see Amanda before I go up.'

Evan pulled into the curb at the front doors of Police HQ and drove off to stash the car in the car park. I threaded through the myriad of workers bustling for the railway station, dodging to avoid those vigorously texting, and scurried up the steps. The usual crowd of police and public had thinned. I had no trouble spotting my good friend, Amanda Sinclair, coming toward me through the 'cattle-grid' As she slapped her ID on the scanner and pushed through the turnstile, her eyes lit up. 'Susan! I was going to ring you!'

'Hey, how are you?' I noted the circles under her eyes. Amanda, a youth counsellor probation officer, was heavily pregnant and should have been on leave some time ago, a fact which appeared to have escaped her husband. Aloysius insisted that she needed to stay on a *bit* longer, 'to keep her busy.' *More likely he wants to pick up gossip from here...*I held my tongue with difficulty because Amanda has a tendency to shoot messengers.

She smiled wanly. 'You'll be happy to know I'm on leave from today. Don't know what Loy will say though.'

'He'll just have to wear it.' *Suck it up, Al, you prick.* 'So, you want to have lunch one day next week?'

Her face brightened. 'Love to! By the way, I heard they got Winslow again.' Word travelled fast in the Force. Amanda rolled her eyes and her shoulders slumped. As

Grant's court-appointed counsellor, she knew his life of crime would escalate, as would her workload.

'Yep! Zeus got him by the backside.'

'How come?' Police dogs normally go for the arm.

'He scrambled up the side of a dumpster and they thought he was going to jump onto the wall behind it. So did the dog.' Reluctantly, she laughed.

A thunder of corporate-looking 'teenage' detectives swept past, pub-light in their eyes. Amanda watched them go, shifting from one foot to the other. Getting the message, I made a move. 'Okay, I'll phone. Better get upstairs and fill out my report, then get home. David might be there before me tonight.'

The CIB room, normally chaotic, was pretty much deserted. No recent murders, but we all knew that could change in the flick of an eye. Evan had beaten me upstairs and I could hear him scuffling around in his corner at the far end. He was taking up a position in a couple of weeks as Senior Sergeant at a country town and looking forward to it. Genevieve, his wife, made no secret of the fact that she hated the city and wanted their four children to be brought up in a rural town.

Anxious to leave work before I got caught up by another case, I dived into my miniscule office, booted up my computer and commenced my Sig Event. There were few things which I could thank my mother for when I was young, but insisting I learn to type –'You'll always have a job, Susan'– was one. It didn't take long to fill the details in and sign off. Gathering up my handbag and briefcase, I made to leave.

Evan is a comfortably-padded, great bear of a man with kind brown eyes and a shock of receding dark brown hair. He straightened a pile of papers in his hands. 'I'm going to miss you a lot –' he glanced around the cluttered room – 'and the rest of the team. How's Anthony Hamilton shaping up?' He dumped the papers on his desk and grabbed his jacket off the chair.

'Good, and looks the part, too.'

Evan had been on short leave and hadn't yet met his replacement. I knew he felt guilty at what he saw as desertion after so many years of our working together. 'And how old is he?' Evan asked, as we turned for the lift.

'Early thirties, built like the proverbial brick you-know-what. He looks like a Russian assassin – in fact "the Assassin" is his nickname already.'

Evan laughed. 'So, able to leap tall buildings at a single bound, then? Glad *he's* watching your back then! I can't wait to get home. It's Genevieve's birthday and I'll be in the doghouse if I miss it again.'

'Well, you've no excuse this time. We're both going home early for once!' I pulled a gaily wrapped gift of perfume out of my bag. 'Here's a little something for Gen. I'm so sorry I can't wish her a happy birthday in person this year.'

He took it with evident pleasure. 'Gen knows you're On Call, Susan. No worries!'

'Hope we don't get a job. I would have loved to have gone to Pamela Miller's concert tonight, but *them's the breaks!*

I swung onto the road, heading for the western suburbs where David, my husband, and I were living. Around me the desperate evening traffic mounted up. I turned on the radio, humming along with Classic Drive. I couldn't wait to get back to the large, old double-storey house which David and I rented in lieu of our home in the country.

Some people thought I was mad when we announced that we were getting married to each other for the second time. 'It didn't work the first time. You're a glutton for punishment, aren't you?' said friends, trying to caution me without overstepping the mark. My Edwardian-raised mother of Irish descent – which made her more Irish than the Irish and who doesn't know there *is* a mark – snorted and said she hoped none of her friends would find out about it. 'Really Susan, how will it look? 'and 'If he left you once, he'll do it again and this time you won't find anyone else. You're no chicken you know. Holy Mother of God, girl, you must be quite mad!'

My father, rigorously trained not to say too much, discreetly pressed a one hundred dollar note into my hand, saying 'Get yourself something pretty,' out of the side of his mouth. He could have had a career as a ventriloquist. My younger sister, Melanie, waved a glass of wine under my nose and shouted 'Go for it, Susan. No forty-three year old man has a right to look as hot as he does, so you'd better grab him back while he's between wives.' *Thanks, Mel. Good one.*

I slumped in my seat, letting the music wash over me, happily anticipating my arrival home and being with David. A sudden movement in the car next to mine startled me. The driver – a gormless city type – was making moués at me, while talking on his mobile phone. Realising my plain clothes disguised my calling I fumbled for my wallet, snagged my ID out and held it up for him to see. The phone vanished as he snapped his gaze back to the front.

The sun was going down in pink and orange glory, leaving soft dusk to soothe the final few kilometres to home. I turned into the beautiful, tree-lined street and then in by our letterbox, looking for lights glowing at the end of the long, narrow driveway. If he was home first, David would pour me a large glass of wine as soon as he heard my car pull into the garage.

The scent of Mock Orange greeted me as I struggled from the car, gathered up my bag and briefcase and closed the roller door. Our dogs and two cats made walking across the verandah difficult, bumping my knees and looking for pats. I pulled up short at the kitchen door. Something simmered on the stove. Mug in hand – *no wine*? – David stood watching the back door, a bulging duffle bag on the floor beside him. Cold flickered throughout my limbs. Thus had Harry stood, surrounded by his luggage the morning he left for good.

'David? What's happening?' My voice came out in a squeak.

He stepped toward me, a concerned look on his face. 'What's the matter, Susan?' Words froze in my throat. David is nothing if not intuitive. 'Did you have a déjà vu moment there?' Without waiting for me to answer, he swept me into his arms. 'I'm not leaving you, sweetheart. Well, not forever.' He kissed the top of my head.

I pulled back and looked up at him. 'What do you mean you're not leaving me forever?'

'I've been seconded to Toowoomba. Start in the morning.' It was then I realised he was dressed in his oldest jeans, T-shirt and work boots. His favourite black leather jacket lay on the chair nearby.

My heart sank. Before I could comment, my mobile phone rang. I was tempted to ignore it, but David gestured to my bag and took a sip of tea, watching me steadily over the rim of his mug. Sighing with frustration, I up-ended my vast shoulder bag, a repository for many superfluous things, onto the kitchen table. *I can't go back to work right now, I just can't.* I caught my mobile before it skittered off the flat surface and onto the floor.

'Hi Ros!' The relief in my voice must have been evident.

'You sound very pleased to hear from me!'

'Yes, I thought I might be called out on a job.'

'I'm glad it's me then,' she countered with a smile in her voice, 'and how are you and that luscious David?'

I glanced at David and then down at the bag by his feet. 'He's still luscious and fine and so am I.'

I was about to pull out a chair and sit down when he glanced at his watch and then looked at me with a, 'Make this quick, I need to talk to you,' expression.

'How are you both?' I couldn't just bundle my friend off the phone before she had time to tell me what she wanted.

'We're okay, but that's what I need to talk to you about, but I don't want to intrude on your free time...'

Guilt flushed through me. My job constantly prevented me from keeping up with family and friends. 'What's wrong? Is everything all right? Is it Pam? Or the cows?'

'Don't worry, nothing's wrong with Pam *or* the cows, Susan. Is there any chance of you getting down here in the near future?'

Bearing in mind David's obvious travel plans, my first instinct was to say 'No, I'm sorry,' but something in her voice alerted me to trouble. Suppressing a sigh, I replied as brightly as possible. 'Actually, I've got tomorrow off, as long as nothing urgent comes in. I can be with you for morning tea.' The relief in her voice made me glad I had stifled my longing for a day at home.

David stepped to the sink to rinse his mug, glancing significantly at me as he towelled it dry. I refused to be hurried.

'How can I thank you? Will David come too?'

I swung around to face the wall. 'No, David can't come, I'm afraid. I didn't have anything planned beyond some gardening, so I can get there about ten. Will that do?'

Amid a flurry of 'Thank you's,' Ros said goodbye.

I closed my mobile and turned to face David. A waft of his aftershave engulfed me as he stepped close and wrapped his arms around me, crushing my nose into his sweater. He held me tightly and rested his cheek on my hair. We stood like that for some minutes before he put me away from him and gazed down into my face. 'You surely didn't think I was actually *leaving* you? Not a chance!'

Tears welled in my eyes, but I put on my "I'm just fine" woman-face. Not noticing anything untoward, David continued. 'Well, as I said, I'm seconded to Toowoomba, me and Peter Moffatt. He's picking me up at midnight because we start early tomorrow.'

'Peter Moffatt? From Covert Ops? David, just what are you getting into here? Are you going undercover?' Fear flashed through me.

' Just secondment, Susan, nothing more. It's all organised.' He ran his hand through his hair in a familiar gesture that showed he was excited, damn him. He wouldn't say – wasn't allowed to tell even *me* – but like a police wife, not to mention, a police officer, I *know* when my husband is keeping something from me.

'Just how long do you think you're going to be up there?' I'd bet he was putting himself in danger and he didn't seem to give a damn for his safety. For all I knew, he could be infiltrating of anything from animal abusers to drug dealers. "Furious" didn't begin to describe how I felt.

He frowned. 'Probably a week or so.'

'What squad are you seconded to?'

'Filling in at Major Crime.'

I stroked his arm to soften my stance, but fear crept through me. 'Filling in, eh? Pull the other leg that whistles. How are you getting wherever it is you're going? Are you driving up?'

'Driving with Pete. I'm going to miss you!' He wriggled his eyebrows, but his naughtiness failed to divert me. No one knows better than a cop that things can go awfully wrong within minutes on the street and even more so if undercover. I had only a few hours to keep him close to me and so help me, I wanted to kill him. What if the worst happened and I lost him just as I had found him again? And the girls had just gotten to know their father. How would they cope if...?

David is nothing if not an experienced husband; after all, our second marriage to each other is the third try for both of us! 'So what does Rosalind want to see you about?' As a diversion, it worked for the moment.

'She wants to talk to me about something personal. The house and the animals are fine, so that's one worry off my mind, but there's something wrong, I can feel it.'

'Is John going to be there?' John Glenwood, widower and retired policeman married our friend six months previously and we have never seen her so happy. 'I expect he will be,' I answered absently, as I took a box of Chateau Cardboard out of the fridge and poured myself a glass of white. David shook his head when I gestured with the cask, apologised for not getting me one and sat at the table, twirling his thumbs. He's nervous and knows that I know what he's up to.

'Say hi to him for me, will you?'

'Yes.'

'So, hold the fort and give my love to the girls.'

'Of course But aren't you going to keep in touch with them yourself?'

'No time. I'll ring them when I get up there.' He stepped forward and took me in his arms again. 'We've only got a few hours,' he muttered into my hair. I held him tightly as a wave of love and terror swept over me. I wished I could actually climb inside his skin, trap him there, and feign illness – anything to keep him with me.

CHAPTER 4

A Little Night Music

Friday, 6pm

If someone had asked her what she would do on her last night on earth, Ariel may well have rolled her eyes, giggled and said, 'Listen to Miley Cyrus while, like, kissing red hot abs!' In one respect, she would have been spot on.

Ariel's parents always said they could read her like a book and trusted her implicitly. Why wouldn't they? She'd never given them any reason to doubt her word and all nefarious activities were carefully hidden. Streetwise and game for anything, she knew her parents would be shocked if they realised what she and her friends got up to when she went clubbing, but she could do anything she liked with her own money, couldn't she? Working at Macca's was hard and the money not much good, but she'd put her name down for Woolworths until the start of next years technical college courses started.

Calls were always forwarded to her mobile while she was clubbing but this time she was meeting a bloke, moreover one she didn't really know. She felt just a little bad about deceiving them, but it was the only way. Then it came to her. They would buy fish and chips and come back here so she wouldn't *have* to lie!

She hummed as she rushed through her parent's house, tucking newspapers under the sofa cushions, washing the dishes piled beside the sink. Cleaning the bathroom was a novel experience, as she contributed generously to the mess, but was invariably less than diligent in clearing it up. Losing interest at the halfway mark, she bundled the cosmetics on top of the vanity into the top drawer of the unit, kicked the waste basket behind the clothesbasket and headed for the kitchen, calling her friend on her mobile as she went. 'Come on, answer, sod you, Maggie!' she yelled. The 'Switched off or out of range' recording played again. *I'll bet she's shagging Hamish. Stuff it!* There was nothing so frustrating as not being able to tell her latest news to her friends, after all that's what a mobile was for! *'Mags, I've got the most amazing thing to tell you. Ring me back.'* She was so excited that she didn't notice that the battery level was almost non-existent.

She tore sheets and towels out of the linen press and raced to her room to change the bed. Just in case. Then she gathered up piles of clothes and stuffed them into the wardrobe, kicked shoes under the bed and threw books and papers into a basket in the corner of the room before making the bed up.

Finally, she showered, slithered into a black lace thong and donned a matching black bra. A miniscule black skirt and a pair of black tights teamed with a gold cammie and black boots completed her ensemble. The pretty face, with hair piled artlessly on top of her head, glowed with excitement. She pressed her gleaming red lips together to set the lipstick and turned sideways, looking at herself from the corners of her eyes, all the better to gauge the length of her lashes. Her nose ring glittered in the light.

'*Coooool! Like, amazing.*' She pursed her lips and took tiny dabs at her pencilled eyebrows pausing to look between each stroke of the pencil until she was satisfied. *Good one.*

A faux fur coat around her shoulders, Ariel threw the front door key into her bag and swung out of the house.

* * *

During his two-week break, Dingo had found few normal, everyday girls he felt like asking for a serious date. Pickups in hotels and bars didn't count. He only wanted to play with *them*, but then, remembered Ariel's lithe body...after years of performing, the high-flyers bored him and nine times out of ten, sometimes even *their* games gave him pause for thought.

He smoothed aftershave over his cheeks, examining his reflection in the bathroom mirror; white shirt, black leather jacket, jeans and boots, casual...not a slob but not too rich, a good disguise. He went to the window and gazed on the cars parked below, knowing he should take his medication, and that he hadn't taken it for a month. *No way. I don't need it anymore.*

'Two blue, two red, a green...oh no, where is the other green...ah, there's one, but it's not stopping... yes it is!' Relief flooded him. Thank God, it was going to be a good night; the numbers were even for every colour! If one car didn't fit, something awful would happen. Reassured, he left the room, unaware of a white car slipping into the space at end of the line. At the last moment, he turned back and picked up his medication, hesitated, then plonked it back onto the shelf.

Spurning the lift, he edged his way down the staff stairs which creaked under his feet, and down the hallway. He tried to tread lightly and almost furtively stepped into the beer garden at the bottom. He didn't want anyone to stop and talk to him though several people looked up.

'More creaks in them stairs than a monkeys got tits!' joked a man, sitting with his companion at the table nearest the bottom of the stairway. His companion giggled. Trying to appear smaller, Dingo wended his way through the empty tables to the outside door, glad he was getting out before the evening rush. He wanted to take Ariel somewhere quiet for dinner. Put her in the mood.

The evening air had turned nippy and despite the lingering light, a breeze had sprung up. He hovered close to the door, not wanting to look too eager or like a right wanker if she didn't come. Music danced through his head; calm settled over him.

The trees in the park opposite the pub swayed gently. A low branch, just begging for someone to swing from it, caught his attention. He crossed the street, hurried to the tree and dropped his backpack on the park bench nearby. Glad there were no other people around to distract him or to stare, he sat down and opened it to check his possessions.

Firstly, he laid his notebook on the bench and placed a pen alongside it, then his wallet against that to form a T-junction, keeping exactly 3.2cms between each item before counting them twice. Having satisfied himself that all the items were arranged correctly, he put his comb at right angles to the group.

The only people visible were two men entering the front door of the pub, absorbed in their conversation. Dingo grasped the branch and swung himself up. The view from his perch encompassed the direction of Ariel's house. *All the better to see you coming, gorgeous!* He locked his knees around the branch and dropped his torso down to watch for her, upside down, then swung backward and forward a few times before cocking his head to look at his watch. Seven o'clock. Where was she? He looked back at the street, but there was no sign of her. Disappointment flooded through him, but as he prepared to pull himself upright, a movement caught his eye.

Ariel! She was smiling as she trotted toward the pub, taking little skips as though she could hardly wait to get to him. Excited, he swung his body again. Just as she reached the entrance, Dingo stuck his fingers in his mouth and emitted an ear-splitting whistle, causing her to jump and swing around.

'Hey, Ariel! Over here in the park!' She peered around and then spotted him. Laughing, she shook her head, checked for traffic, ran across the street to the tree and gazed up at him. He breathed in her perfume and reached out a playful hand to grab hers. She dodged his grasp and danced around, pretending to box with him, laughing.

'Hey, your face's all red! All the blood's running to your head, you idiot!'

'I'm overcome with love for you!' he shouted, dragging himself upright to sit on the branch. 'Are you hungry?' Suddenly he felt free, able to do anything – fly if he wanted.

'Oh course I am,' she chided, swinging a small black dillybag over her shoulder. The diamantes on the clasp twinkled in the last rays of sunshine. He jumped to the ground, straightened his shirt and gathered his things into the backpack. Ariel watched his methodical movements. 'Do you always carry a notebook?'

'Yeah, never know when I might want to write things down, like *your* phone number!' He grinned, as he swung the pack over his shoulders. 'Want to eat in the pub or do you know somewhere better?'

Ariel's gaze lingered on his handsome face, wandered down his broad shoulders, strong arms and huge hands, imagining them touching her. She shivered. This bloke was all hers. 'What say we get fish and chips and go back to my house? I forgot Mum and Dad are ringing tonight and I'm supposed to be at home. My brother's motorbike broke down in Mackay and they've gone to pick him up.' She wrapped her small hands around his arm and gazed up at him.

'Can't they ring you on your mobile?' *How old is this girl?* He wondered whether he was about to pluck a baby out of her virgin cradle. Perhaps he should slow this down, but a glance at Ariel's gleaming pink mouth and knowing eyes reassured him.

'They ring me at home on the old phone to make sure I'm all right.' Ariel pouted, annoyed by the parental restrictions. She knew she looked at least twenty and besides, she would be eighteen in a week's time.

He shrugged, not caring where they went as long as he could be alone with her and the parent's home was as good a place as any. 'Where's the shop then?'

'Just there by the corner.' She pointed to a building down the street, where light spilled through an open doorway. A chill wind swirled along the street, sending autumn leaves rustling along the pavement. He reached back and flipped the hood of his jacket over his head. Ariel stared. 'Are you cold?'

'Nah. Come on, I'm famished.' He took her small hand in his and they started down the deserted street, peering into the shop windows as they passed. When they almost reached the shop, he stopped. 'Get a load of that, will you?'

'What?' Ariel peered into the window. 'It's just music stuff! What's it to you?'

'It's my job – my career. I can play anything – piano, trumpet, clarinet...' He leaned close to the store front to shut out their reflection in the window. She slithered in front of him and, repressing a spurt of anger, he slipped his arms around her waist and pulled her small rounded bottom against his burgeoning groin. She giggled and twisted around to stare at him. 'What? Like, in a band?'

He debated putting her straight, but the effort of explaining was suddenly too much. 'Yeah, something like that.' Anxious to change the subject, he glanced around. A large poster on the back wall of the shop caught his attention. He pressed his face against the glass and squinted at the shadowed image of a fair-haired, sweet-faced woman holding a flute. He focused on the print. Pamela Miller. The concert tomorrow night...suddenly he wanted to go home to his unit and practice his music. He was in two minds to call the date off, when Ariel tugged his arm impatiently.

'*Truly?*'

'Something like that.'

Ariel looked at his closed expression and let it go. 'You stay here and look at the gear. I'll get the fish and chips.' She held out her hand for the money. Resigned, he dug into his back pocket for his wallet and without counting, handed her a fistful of notes. Her eyes widened. 'Hey, that's too much!'

'Get some drinks too,' he muttered, twisting his head sideways to look at the price tag on a clarinet just inside the window. Ariel swung away and hurried to the shop.

He dropped his backpack on the footpath and leaned against the wall of the shop, hands in pockets. One. Two. Three blue cars...the next one would have to be white... yes...then red...yes! His irritation vanished. This was going to be a fun night.

Clutching hot bundles of fish, chips and coca cola, they hurried back to the house. Ariel could hardly wait to get inside, open the succulent parcels and get to know her handsome prize. She sat him down at the kitchen table and chatted as she prepared drinks.

'Where are the plates?' he asked, staring at his parcel of food.

'Uh...we always eat it out of the paper.' Something felt off-kilter. For a moment, she felt as though there was a hidden agenda.

He looked apologetic. 'We always ate on a plate with cutlery, but you can use the paper and your fingers if you want.' *Don't you ever let me catch you eating like a vulgar peasant...no mum.*

A hot wave of embarrassment flooded her face. 'No, I'll get stuff,' she replied. Of course someone who spoke like him would, like, eat posh!

'So, tell me about yourself?' he asked after a few minutes. Ariel, who normally 'talked for Queensland,' didn't know what to say. She looked up, met his twinkling eyes and relaxed. He was just used to eating properly, like her mum was always harping on about. There was nothing more to it than that. Dredging up past lessons, she watched from under lowered lids as he ate slowly, carefully placing his knife and fork in the correct position on his plate and then moving the salt and pepper shakers equidistantly on each side. She wrinkled her brow and opened her mouth, but some instinct cautioned her not to comment.

'How many in the family?' he asked, glancing around the room, his eyes roaming over the photographs on the sideboard.

'Well, I've got two brothers, Jamie and Anthony. Ant's the one with the stuffed motorbike –and Jamie's up in Townsville. I work part-time at Dimmies.' Seeing his puzzled expression, she added quickly, 'Dymocks. The bookstore in the city and I'm at college.'

It was no time before he knew all about her penchant for shoes, movies, celebrities and One Direction, the five boy pop band currently the worldwide craze. Had she but known it, the latter placed Ariel in her age group. For a moment, Dingo faced the realisation that he, at twenty eight, shouldn't be hanging around a teenage girl, but then, looking at her smart face and nubile body, he dismissed the notion. After all, nothing was about to happen and he wasn't a rapist. If she was willing, well... He smiled as he read the message in her eyes.

He had no intention of following up with Ariel after that night. He'd play around tonight and then head home to his unit in the morning. He had rehearsals next day, the concert that night. The new young conductor leading could be interesting. He didn't know Lancelot McPherson, son of the mighty Sir James, but from all accounts, a bit of a 'Jack the Lad' underneath his sophisticated exterior. *Could be fun!*

He glanced around for a serviette and Ariel, flushing, dived for the paper ones her mother kept in a drawer and held out the box. He took a couple and leaned back in the chair. 'What are you doing at college?'

Ariel almost rested her elbows on the table, but laid her arms along it instead. 'I'm doing Animal Care. I always wanted to be a vet. My uncle was a vet, but he was, like, doing horses and cows, big animals, like, you know?' She laughed. 'He ended up working at Taronga Zoo and he did everything.'

Dingo realised an apparent absence in the household. 'You haven't got a pet?'

Ariel swallowed hard. 'Our dog died a couple of weeks ago. He was sixteen and mum won't get another one. I had pet rats a few years ago, but after they died, I wasn't allowed to have anymore.' She pouted. 'I always looked after them and everything, but I had to keep them away from everyone else.' Memories chased Ariel's play-girl persona away, revealing the thirteen year old she'd been once and deep down, remained.

Turned on by her gorgeous complexion, soft expression and full lips, Dingo speculated how far he could go with his plans. Long dark eyelashes swept her cheeks, hiding the tears he guessed were pooling in her eyes. His eyes swept over her full breasts, then up to her face. The scent of her perfume drowned his senses; he fought the urge to pounce. It was too soon. Perhaps later they could play a game... 'Your food will get cold.'

She flushed, and forgetting to use her utensils, picked up a piece of fish and held it between her hands. He pushed down the surge of anger, reminding himself that it was not his place to correct her. He looked down at the remaining fish and chips on his plate and flicked the chips around with his fork, panicking. *Odd number! Seven chips left...* Surreptitiously, he cut one in half. *Phew, now eight.* 'Can you bung this in the microwave, love?'

Her dimples flashed as she picked up his plate and flitted across the room. 'Only be a minute. So tell me about yourself? Like, what about the muso stuff?'

He paused, remembering the screaming, the wooden spoon slapping around his head and shoulders, the whiff of rum and bared teeth. *Practice. You'll practice eight hours a day or you know what'll happen!* A locked door, no food or water for as long as she felt like it. School lessons into the night. Anger surged through him. He fisted his hands under the table, *willing* himself to calm down. One, two, three... as he reached ten, something pinged behind him. He came to and realised Ariel was staring at him, eyes wide, as she brought his plate back to the table.

'Sorry.' He reached out and rubbed her arm gently. 'Bad memories.' He smiled despite his pain, as she put the plate on the table and picked up his fork to spear the last of his chips.

'She was strict then, your mum?' Ariel carefully placed her utensils together and rested her chin on her hands, gazing at him sympathetically.

'Yeah, you could say that. I got a beating if I didn't practice long enough.'

'That's sad. So where do you live?'

'In Sydney,' he lied. 'I'm only up here for a short time, so I'll stay at the pub for now.' He dabbed his lips with the serviette, folded it and placed it on his empty plate. Ariel leaped to her feet, swept their plates up and carried them to the sink, where she rinsed them and put them into the dishwasher, before examining the contents of the refrigerator. 'We've got red jelly and ice cream!'

'No thanks, Ariel. You have it if you want.'

Not wanting to appear greedy, she closed the fridge door. 'Coffee?' She flung a saucy glance at him over her shoulder. A delicious thought curled. Perhaps her mum and dad might like a boarder? After all, since the boys left home there were two spare rooms in the house. Remembering how her mum was always telling her not to blurt out the first thought which came into her head, she forced back the impulse to broach the subject.

'Got any wine?'

'Yep. White or red?' Ariel opened the fridge door again. He stood up, moved over to stand behind her and wrapped his arms around her waist, pulling her back into his powerful body. Her neat, rounded bottom nestled neatly into his thighs, rocketing his penis to attention. She froze; the soft skin on the back of her neck turned rosy.

Slowly now. *They always came quicker when he played hard to get.* He let her go and stepped away. She picked up fresh glasses and an unopened bottle of white wine. 'Let's be comfortable!'

In the lounge room, she invited him to sit, carefully poured the wine and then plopped down beside him.

'Cheers!' They clinked glasses. 'You haven't said a lot about yourself! What's the matter? Tell me more?' She grinned and, greatly daring, stroked the side of his face with a gentle finger.

He caught her hand and tucked it into his. 'What else do you want to know?'

'Where you were born, have you any brothers and sisters – are you parents still alive? All that sort of thing.' She snuggled closer, a thrill shooting through her as he angled his body toward her and leaned close.

41

'I was born in New South Wales. My parents had a property in the country – sheep and cattle. They're dead now.'

Ariel looked at him thoughtfully. 'Who taught you to play music? You *said* you could play anything?'

A flicker of anger played at the edge of his mind at what he perceived as an accusatory tone. He shifted away from her, and picked up his drink. 'I was about four when I got a drum kit for Christmas and I went on from there. I had to practice every day – clarinet, trumpet – you name it. I had to do hours on the piano too – classical.' He paused, surprised that he had actually told her all that.

'What? That stuff? I hate classical. It's booooring!' Ariel bounced up and went to the family stereo-system where she rummaged around, before holding up a CD for him to check the title. 'Mozart! *My mother's* CD.' She rolled her eyes, unaware of his expression hardening.

'There's nothing wrong with Mozart. He's the greatest composer who ever lived.' *Fourthreetwoone…keep your cool.* 'Put that on and come over here and listen to something decent for a change.'

Ariel, pouting, put the CD into the slot and came toward him as the glorious notes of Mozart's Clarinet Concerto soared through the room. Ariel's eyes widened momentarily, before she hastened to adopt an expression of indifference.

Dingo forced a smile and moved to the end of the sofa. 'Let me give you a foot rub!' *That always got them in.* She hesitated a moment, then slipped the CD into the player and came back to the sofa, grabbed a cushion off a nearby chair which she placed at the other end of the sofa and settled herself, half lying. He smiled, picked her legs up and took her bare feet in his lap where he proceeded to massage her toes, her arches, then heels and ankles, working along her legs, his beautiful, powerful hands stroking, soothing.

Ariel purred.

CHAPTER 5

Dingo

Games

Saturday, 4.30am.

Her arms and legs lashed at him. '*No, no! No don't!*'
'Come on, play with me! You said you would!
Remember what we planned...' His voice came out high-
pitched. He forced it lower. 'Hey baby, come on, you
know you liked it back at the house!'

'*Get off, you're hurting*...' She pushed her hands again
his chest, as he knelt on her chest, terrified when she
realised he was oblivious to the fact that she couldn't
breathe. She was vanishing into the earth under his
weight. He felt something give deep inside her body. She
tried to scream, but only a stifled grunt came out.

'Hey, not 'til you let me –'

Dingo took her face in both of his hands and
squeezed until her lips pouted, then angled his head,
swooped in and starting kissing her. Ignoring her
increasingly feeble struggles, he tightened his hands
around her face, pressing into her cheeks, grinding his
mouth down, down, uncaring of his own cheek cutting
off the air supply to her nose. Strangled sounds emerged
from her throat. Oblivious to anything around him,

flushed with anger and sexual desire, he tried to pull her jeans down with one hand, sliding one leg back between her thighs. She wriggled her left leg up to flail uselessly at his body. His hands slid, as though by their own volition around her throat. Slowly, Ariel's struggles weakened, but still he kept his mouth clamped down, her nostrils blocked by his cheek.

She stilled.

In the half-light, her face looked crumpled, as though a vacuum pump had sucked the air out of her.

Something about her lips alerted him to...he pushed his body upright, realising that he had been kneeling on her, hunched over like a gigantic insect, sucking the lifeblood out of her body.

'Ariel?' She didn't move. 'Ariel? Speak to me!'

He leaned back on his hands, horror slowly seeping through him.

'Ariel? Are you all right?'

Silence.

'Ariel? Come on, get up. It was only a game.' He waved his hand in front of her eyes. There was no response. Slowly he got to his feet, tried to pluck the wet denim away from his knees and then stretched a trembling hand to help her up, but Ariel stayed flat on her back, legs crumpled, gazing sightlessly at the rapidly lightening sky.

The trembling took him by surprise, like on the documentaries, when the lions had caught their meal, the survivors shook for awhile before they settled down and returned to grazing. Fear trickled through his limbs, paralysing his thought processes, rendering him helpless to work out what to do next. What to do? Tears pooled in his eyes; he dashed them away with an impatient hand.

Suddenly aware of his surroundings, he looked around, expecting to see a row of accusing witnesses pointing fingers at him. He felt like the last person left in the world, but he had company at his feet. Maybe... his heart turned over as he bent to gather her into his arms. Her limbs flopped. The muscles in his arms trembled uncontrollably under her weight, so that he was forced to set her back down and squat uselessly by her body, gasping for oxygen. Now he knew that grief was a colour, not the purple so beloved of religion, or the demented black of Central Europe but a wild, searing agony of red, digging deep no matter how hard he tried to shut it out. The tiny flame of hope which sprang to life with Ariel, flickered and died and left him alone in the bleak morning light. *They'd been having fun. Just minutes ago, we were laughing and chasing each other. How had it happened?*

A flash of a baby's face, so long ago and far away, limp in his hands, and the screaming broke over his mind. Adults all around, the baby being wrenched from his hands, the hush of shock before the sky fell in. *I didn't mean to hurt her! I didn't meant it – I didn't mean to hurt her...*the beating from the demented woman, slamming him to the floor, the heel of a shoe cracking against the side of his face...his hand went to his head, involuntarily feeling for the scars under his hair, as it had done so many times. *You don't know your own strength!* His mother's voice so clear, the shame branded into his soul that day overwhelmed him with his mother's constant refrain, so loud that he could swear she was standing nearby.

Dingo wanted to lash out, to wipe the unctuous expression plastered on her face like the cosmetics she applied so lavishly. He knew she was dead because he'd seen her in her coffin – watched the undertaker screw the lid shut. Even *she* couldn't have escaped her fate.

He snapped back to reality, hunched over Ariel who, like the baby, would never move again. What to do. Branches and tree trunks piled nearby caught his attention. A piece of sacking lay in the grass nearby, half buried in the long grass. He dragged the sacking out, shook it and laid it flat beside Ariel. Trying not look at her face, he rolled her into the middle, shocked by the wetness beneath her.

A bulge in her tight pocket attracted Dingo's attention. Metal met his probing fingers and something else. Her house keys! He slipped them into his pocket and then eased a piece of thick paper out, opened the front flap and squinted at the print. Ariel's used airline ticket from the Sydney to Brisbane flight. What was she doing with it in her pocket? It was then he realised she was probably wearing the jeans in which she'd travelled the day before. He quickly stuffed the ticket into his own pocket, grasped the sides of the sack, partially folded them and dragged the burden over to the pile. He pulled enough branches back to accommodate the bundle underneath and hauled it into the centre.

Horrified, he gazed for a moment on the lovely, cheeky face on which he had rained kisses only minutes ago and then folded the edge of the sack over it. He reached down, gently ran his hand over her still-warm ankle and pushed her bare, grass-stained feet out of sight, remembering her laughter as she'd shucked her shoes off and danced in the wet grass. *'Race you to the boatshed!'*

He gathered up her sandals and tucked them underneath the edge of the sacking. Why she wanted to wear such delicate footwear for a dawn walk, he hadn't bothered to enquire; now they just looked pathetic. Moving quickly, he placed the branches back over her, letting the leafy ends flop down. Finished, he moved back and stared at the pile. There was no sign of anyone underneath, but the furrows scoring the grass clearly indicated that something heavy had been hauled across it. He scuffed his joggers over the tracks, trying to obliterate the signs. If someone came along before the grass dried, they'd see them immediately.

His hand was shaking so badly that he had to hold his wrist still in order to read the time on his watch. Had only ten minutes passed since – his mind refused to acknowledge what had happened – *how it had happened* – but some vestige of self-preservation niggled at his tumbling thoughts. He had to get out of there! Behind the trees, the sky was growing lighter by the moment. Splashing downriver sent his heart into overdrive. *The rowers!* He peered through the overhanging branches of a tree, thankful for its canopy hiding him from the world.

The calls of the coxswain echoed across the water; the slap of oars sent his heart rate into orbit. The ramshackle boatshed nearby, Ariel had assured him, was no longer in use. 'No one ever comes down this far – at least not often,' she'd said with a sly grin.

A movement in the distance drew Dingo's eye. A group of walkers were charging through the park toward him – no, they'd turned up the street at the bottom of the green belt. Slowly his pulse slowed; safe for now. His backpack – where was it? Terrified, he turned full circle before he saw it lying on the grass near a fallen branch. He lunged and swooped, breathing heavily as he looped a strap over his shoulder. *Safe.*

He pulled the hood of his parka over his head, hoisted his canvas pack onto his back and cast a glance around before turning to leave. Something white attracted his attention; a small piece of paper almost hidden in the grass. He picked it up – a note to Ariel from her mum with a phone number to call and a reminder to pick up the milk from the corner shop. It took several tries before he could stuff it into the pocket of his jeans. Then he noticed Ariel's mobile phone lying in the grass nearby. What else had he forgotten? He picked it up and wiped it dry with the hem of his T-shirt. *Sixty, fifty-eight, fifty-six...*Ariel's parents would call and there'd be no reply! When they came home and found her missing they would start looking for her and they'd find *him*. All the crime shows on TV showed the cops tracing people through their phones.

He flipped the lid and checked out her Sent Box, reading her text messages to her friends – and her parents. A desperate plan materialised. Copying Ariel's mode of phrasing, he sent a text message to her mother's mobile phone purporting to be from Ariel, saying that she was going into the city for the day with friends, would stay with one of them and wouldn't be home until – what would be believable – Tuesday? His fingers sped across the tiny keyboard. How could he finish it? Ah, yes. He scrolled until he found a name he thought he could use, then finished: 'Gone 2 Heathers, c u tues luv Ariel xxxx' *That should do it.*

Dingo closed the phone with shaking hands, polished it thoroughly on the soft lining of his parka, and then walked down the short slope to the water. After checking there were no rowers in sight, he hurled it as far out into the river as he could, and then took the key out and threw it after the phone. Satisfied that neither would be found, he turned to leave. With one last glance at the pile of foliage up the bank under the trees, he headed back the way they had come, counting his steps as he went, trying not to draw attention to himself by hurrying. He pulled the hood of his jacket over his head and down so that it obscured most of his face.

His vision blurred with tears which he dashed away, trying to clear the lump of grief in his throat. *Stupid, stupid*...he shouldn't have allowed himself to feel for her that fast. He knew better than that, but what red-blooded male wouldn't take what was offered so willingly and sweetly? But after all they'd been to each other she hadn't wanted to play again...tears continued to trickle down his cheeks. He swiped them away angrily with the back of his hand. It was her own fault this had happened...one minute they were laughing and kidding, the next she'd gone limp like a tiny, double-barred finch with her chains around her neck. *How had it happened? Mother, save me...*

Dingo could hardly see the lines on the pedestrian crossing. He stopped and turned back to count them... twenty three. Why not twenty-four? It wasn't *right*. A pale streak of morning light peeped through the trees, throwing a line across the road at his feet. Twenty four! Nothing could happen now that the numbers were even. He took a deep breath, pulled the hood of his parka down to obscure his face and hitched his pack higher onto his back. He couldn't return to Ariel's home. They'd cleaned the house up, washed the dishes, cleaned the bath where they'd spent a very happy time and changed the sheets on her bed. 'Like, mum's got eyes like a hawk, Doobs. She'll know straight away I've had someone here.' So he'd left nothing there which would link him to

Ariel...the hotel! All his things were at the hotel, but he couldn't remember in which direction it was.

Instinct led him toward the West End CBD, striding along, just a man out for an early morning walk, perhaps going to work or off to university, but then his stride got faster as the memories came battling into his mind.

She disengaged her feet from his persuasive hands, and hoisted herself onto her knees. Laughing into his face, she leaned over the back of the sofa and hauled up cushions which she pitched onto the floor, then slithered down into the nest, pulling him down beside her.

'Seven cushions, why seven? What are they there for?' He had to make sure the numbers were even before he could concentrate on her. 'Don't you have another one?'

'What do you mean, another one? We're gunna play of course!' She laughed, noticing his expression, leaped to her feet and plucked another one from a nearby chair. 'There you are then, if you insist!' Laughing, she threw herself over his body, pressing her breasts against his chest, seeking his mouth.

A deep shudder went through him, as he remembered how he'd ripped her shirt open and slipped his hands inside to cup her soft, firm breasts and brought her down to his mouth, and how they'd laughed, naked in the half-light, gazing at each in wonder. He'd cupped her cheek in his hand and softly stroked down her throat, following the track of his hand with kisses.

Even now, he was getting hard, striding along the pavement, avoiding the cracks – one pace per paver – trying to look as though he knew where he was going, but his mind refused to co-operate. He couldn't remember the name of the hotel. Then he realised it would be on the receipt in the pocket of his parka. He paused to drag it out, squinting to read it: The

Commercial on Grey. He looked around. A dog barked in a yard nearby, startling him and then he realised he was standing at the alleyway leading to the car park belonging to the place, and the sun was coming up. Early morning Saturday workers trundled past toward the city. The sound of a dump truck collecting garbage bins came from just around the corner.

Faint with hunger and exhaustion, Dingo stumbled up the back steps of the building, hoping no one would see him coming in. He couldn't collapse. He had to be at the Concert Hall early; there was so much to do before the evening performance.

Voices and the sound of clattering dishes came from the kitchen nearby, alerting him to the fact that breakfast would be served early for the business types who were in the bar the previous evening – well, if any of them stayed. He recalled noises coming from behind nearby doors as he had gone out to meet Ariel. *Okay, so just go upstairs to the room, have a shower and get dressed and come back down with no fuss, no fear.*

One, two, three, four...he walked lightly up to the top landing and along the hallway to his room. Quietly sliding his key in the lock, he had the door open and whisked inside just as the door opposite started to open. It was vital that no one knew he had been out. He quietly closed his door. *Thank God...thank God...I'm so sorry, I'm so sorry.*

It was then Dingo remembered the photographer.

CHAPTER 6

Susan

Into Darkness

Saturday, midnight.

David always marvels when my internal clock awakens me when I need to, but this time there was no pleasure in my life-long skill. David was leaving, goodness knows for how long and doing God knew what. I made coffee and toast, as he stashed the final bits and pieces he was taking with him into a battered gym bag which reeked like the proverbial footballer's jock strap. Probably the whole department had used it at some stage.

We stood just inside the back door leading to the garage, invisible from the street. He pulled me against his hard body and we kissed as though for the last time. I could feel tension in his muscular frame. I *knew* – not just *suspected* – my husband was going into a place of darkness, where men brutalised each other, a world where an undercover agent, or an informer, could be found shot or worse. Undercover means you immerse yourself into the part and think like your opponents – your prey.

David, as always, picked up my thoughts. 'Susan, you're not to worry. Nothing's going to happen to me. It's just a secondment, nothing more – the usual murder, mayhem and drug dealers.' He drew back and cupped his hands around my face. 'I'll keep in touch. Just hang in there and I'll be home before you know it.'

Even though I'm a cop, David couldn't tell me where he was going or what he was doing, but he knew that the less I knew the better and safer for me. Behind us, our dogs whined, sensing my distress. He turned to fondle their silky ears and then opened the door. 'I promise you that the moment I'm on the way home, I'll call you. No matter what time it is.'

'Three in the morning?'

'Yes, whatever time. Now, go back to bed and think about me!' His eyes crinkled with mischief. Fear licked at my heart. I hung onto him, savouring the last seconds we would have together for heaven only knew how long – or forever.

Someone coughed. We broke apart and turned to see the tall, burly form of DSS Moffatt of the Drug Squad standing on the steps leading up to the verandah. 'Nice to see you, Susan. Sorry to interrupt, folks. Dave, it's time to go.'

Grinning, these responsible husbands and fathers glowed with the excitement of leaving on a 'Boy's Own Adventure.' I couldn't keep my feelings from showing. Peter Moffatt eyed me warily, as though I might bite him and he was right.

Fighting the urge to cling, I relinquished my hold as David gently put me aside, picked up his bag and stepped through the door. The dogs tried to follow, but I restrained them and watched as the two men slipped across the back lawn, ducked under the hydrangea bushes along the side fence and vanished without a backward glance.

Fat Albert brushed against my ankles. I sprinkled some cat nibble into his bowl, made a hot drink and trailed into the lounge room unable to face the bedroom, now empty of David's life-force. I switched on the table lamp, placed my cup on the coffee table and slotted a Bach cantata into the stereo. As I listened to the glorious music, my sister, Melanie's voice crept into my head: 'You've been a cop since you were twenty, you are now forty-one years old, raised your kids and gotten them off your hands, so what's next? Are you going to remain in CIB? Stay in the police force until you're sixty?'

'What else can I do? *Security*?' Even though occasional lassitude sets in, I couldn't imagine being anything other than a police officer. My career has been good to me. Satisfying completions of cases and some not, had propelled me to Detective Inspector, a rank which doesn't have quite as much physical activity attached to it. However, in spite of jogging most nights of the week and lifting weights, I find it harder to keep fit and leave leaping fences to my young troops and their dogs.

Now that I had a secret, which for the moment I've kept from David, even more so.

* * *

Saturday, 10 am

After restless hours, divided into times where I read and others when I wandered throughout the house, I fell asleep, as you do, just before dawn and awoke shivering, with a crick in my neck. Trying not look at the empty side of the bed, I heaved the cats off my legs. Genevieve – foisted onto me by Lady Ferna Robinson, now triumphantly widowed, Sir Arthur having fled to whatever Just Reward had been allotted him – hefted a fat paw, claws extended and missed my leg by a centimetre. Restraining myself from buffeting the fat furball with the pillow, I staggered to the en suite, showered and dressed, slapped on some make-up, bundled my hair into a scrunchy and headed for the kitchen

Sometime during the night, I made a decision to push David's "secondment" to the back of my mind, this being the only way I could cope. I would imagine him where he was *supposed* to be, in Toowoomba doing routine Major Crime jobs, filling in for someone or other, instead of being 'sussed out' by criminals. That didn't bear thinking about.

The overcast morning lured me to the window to watch the native shrubs in our garden and a line of gums along the south fence bending in the wind, leaves fluttering in distant supplication. The grass was longer than it should have been, because for my teenage lawn-mowing contractor who was sitting exams, tending to business was the furthest thing from his mind.

Overnight temperatures of 13 deg and 37 during the day – and 'they' say global warming is a myth? I slid the glass pane back and sniffed the air; rain coming, with any luck. The tinder dry bush was irresistible to the twisted arsonists who delighted in the misery of others. I went to the laundry, carefully avoiding the pile of washing lurking in the clothes basket, let the dogs out and headed for the kitchen.

Both cats wreathed themselves gracefully between my ankles, swatting each other spitefully from time to time. Marli's pet rats rustled in their cage in the family room. Kids leave home for university, but their pets don't!

I paid a neighbour's fifteen-year old daughter to clean the cage and feed the occupants. She spent far more time playing with them, which meant I had to check the cage every night in case she had forgotten to empty the litter tray. I didn't begrudge the chore. The more animals I have around me at night, the safer I feel, especially with David gone. *A tangle of limbs and whispered love seared through my memory...he promised he'd ring as soon as the job was finished.*

Breakfast, as always, was yoghurt and pears, followed by toast and coffee taken out on the side verandah. Time stretched endlessly ahead of me, with little prospect of respite from paperwork. Pitiful crime scenes – those of women and children horrendous – the misery caused by uncaring scum crowded my day. My aunt Beryl once said, 'Susan, believe me, life can be hardest when there is nothing to look forward to. When a crisis occurs, we rise to the occasion, no matter how drastic or exciting it can be. It's when the future stretches ahead of you without any chance of change, that's when you need your strength, girl.' Well, she was right.

I pulled the back door closed, flicked the cat flap to make sure it was swinging freely and checked the water bowls on the back verandah. Heaven only knew what time I would be home that night. The weather, reflecting my mood, had turned cold and rainy, the trees doing their level best to throw their branches around the surrounding paddocks. The ones by the house dipped and swayed. I envied the cats who had retired to my bed to curl up in the doona. The dogs, quivering with joy, leaped into the back seat of the car, fussing over who was going to sit which side, until I roared at them.

We reached the Valleys of the Scenic Rim in just over an hour and as I turned up the driveway to the house, my spirits lifted. No matter what my friend had to tell me, the sight of our country house always made me feel better. The main through-road was almost buried under the jacaranda petals stripped from the trees by heavy rain. I saw a few cars which I recognised, but hoped their occupants wouldn't see *me*. I didn't want to talk.

Our large, strawbale house was five kilometres out of town, nestling on ten hectares in a fold of the pastures under a massive mountain, one much beloved of climbers who swan-dived off its craggy rock face and had to be rescued on a regular basis. Ros Miller – now Glenwood – moved in with her daughter Pamela's spoilt marmalade cat, Fudge and their border collies. She and her new husband, John, rent from us and look after the Scottish Highland cows and the chooks which Eloise bequeathed to David and me. It was a few minutes before the house came into view bringing with a feeling of ambivalence foreign to me.

I pulled up before the broad, stone steps leading onto the verandah, grabbed my umbrella, climbed out and opened the back door of the car. The dogs burst out and took off, bouncing across the lawn to roll in the wet grass with evident enjoyment. *They can have it!*

The door whipped out of my cold, wet hand and slammed shut as Ros and John came out to greet me. At first sight, I was shocked. She had lost so much weight, her face looked translucent; when she smiled and threw her arms around me the frailty of her form sent a shaft of fear through me.

They hustled me up the steps and into the house. 'Come and have morning tea,' Ros urged. As always, the lovely sitting room enveloped me in the warmth and comfort of its ochre walls, the fire blazing in the hearth and the comfortable furniture. I was happy to see that Rosalind's music was set above the keys of the grand piano. At least she was well enough to play..

As Fudge leapt into Rosalind's lap, I sensed rather than saw her cringe. He butted his huge marmalade self into her chin; she wrapped her arms around his portly body. I settled myself into the couch beside her and reached out to stroke him. There was no point in beating around the bush. 'You're looking tired, Ros. Are you not feeling well?'

She lifted her face and I saw tears welling in her eyes. 'Susan, I've got cancer.'

'Oh no, where?'

'Inside my left cheek. We only found it two days ago, and they want me in the Royal Brisbane on Monday morning. I had the pre-op checks when I had the MRI.' She smiled weakly. 'I'm trying to be positive, Susan, but it's scary. A sort of ulcer actually, but very small.'

Cold spread through my body. *A sort of ulcer?* I knew my fear mustn't show; Rosalind had enough for all of us. 'How is John coping with the news?'

'He's bereft, but he's being so strong. What did I do to deserve him?' The cat settled into her lap, leaving her hands free for tissues and eye wiping. 'You know, it's ironic. Here I am, all these years without *anyone* decent in my life –'I know she's thinking of Tommy Esposito, a criminal who conned his way into her life and who is now in gaol.

I finished for her. '– and now you've finally found your soul-mate and this happens.'

Ros nodded, sniffing.

Just then, John arrived with a tray of cups and pots, so we cleared the coffee table and settled in for a cuppa. He adjusted the cushions behind his wife's back, every move showing his devotion. His face revealed the stress he was under, but as a retired senior constable, I knew he would never allow her to know the extent of his concern.

'So what can I do to help?' I asked, after I had taken a sip of tea, wincing because John always makes sure the water is *boiling*.

'I wondered if you would keep an eye out for Pam? She's coming down tomorrow. I know she's going to be horrified at just how big this operation is going to be as soon as she lays eyes on me. All the tubes and things. She'll get all worried and she still has to get through her major concert tonight.'

'That's at the Concert Hall in Brisbane?'

'Yes.'

John passed me the program.

'Yes, that's it. She has to finish her tour no matter what, and do the UK concerts as well!' Rosalind folded her lips in a thin line. *No matter what*...that meant even if she didn't come out of the operation... I put my hand on her 'sparrow-leg' thin fingers, aware that Ros' cancer may well be further advanced than she was letting on. I caught John's eye and we shared a terrible moment. 'Do you want to talk to me about this? I know you're going to be fine, but I'll get into contact with Pam and perhaps we can meet up for coffee if she has time. '

Rosalind sighed. 'The House Organisers should have her unit ready for her by Sunday afternoon, but she's planning on coming down here to see me on that morning. She had tenants, but they move out Saturday.'

Over the years, I have encountered victims of every age, sex and social strata, and criminals both vile and petty. Body language is second nature to me and I knew my dear friend was very worried indeed. Perhaps there was something she was not ready to tell me.

With David off up on the Darling Downs and Rosalind facing a life-saving operation, I really felt that nothing more could go awry.

CHAPTER 7

Pam

Rehearsal with a Swine

Saturday, 3.45am

No matter how long I've been awake staring into the darkness or reading, I always lurch into wakefulness with heart-pounding shock when the alarm clock goes off. I fumbled for the switch until the buzzing stopped, squinted at the dial and cringed. Someone had set the alarm for 3.45am.

When I was about twelve and staying on Masters Island with my best friend Ally and her mother, Aunt Eloise, we used to sneak the alarm clock into our room, set it for three o'clock and stow it under one of our pillows. When it was my turn, I always woke up, stabbed at the "off" button with shaking fingers, scared that Ally's mother, Aunt Eloise, would hear it and come to investigate.

Quivering with excitement, we would get dressed and sneak out into the moonlight – it was always a full moon the nights we went prowling – and roam at will on the island. It never occurred to us that we might come across someone who would hurt us, even though the island had lots of holiday makers most of the year round, for didn't we always take our dogs along on our adventures? Fortunately we didn't come to any harm, the most punishment incurred being the delicious secrets – neighbours being in places they shouldn't, for example – that we couldn't tell for fear of getting into trouble ourselves. Our mothers were horrified when we confessed years later of the scams we got up to at night.

A vestige of light shone through the window; I glanced around the room remembering I was Goldie's guest and the major concert of my tour was tonight! I yawned, hauled myself out of bed and headed for the bathroom feeling like a squashed beetle. Downstairs the sound of the electric jug coming to the boil indicating Goldie was up, getting ready to go out early on a photo shoot. I would join her for a cup of coffee and then get back to bed.

Doing a tour is exhausting as well as exhilarating. Perhaps there would be time for a nap after rehearsal with a Russian wolf and a run through with the orchestra. My reflection in the mirror, drowned in toothpaste and tangled hair didn't inspire confidence in my ability to 'scrub up.' When I got downstairs, Goldie was downstairs drinking coffee, her camera and tripod nearby.

'Help yourself, love. I'm going to nick off and take some shots of the river at the bottom the park and the ferry terminal.' She jerked her head in the general direction of the park. 'I've got to do an article and get some photos of the river and the rowers for KRL magazine in California. Only a small job, but it all helps and it won't take long. It'll be light soon. There's eggs and bacon in the fridge, so just help yourself.' She nodded at the dress which I had slung over shoulder. 'The ironing board's in the laundry and the iron's in the cupboard.'

She poured the dregs of her coffee into the sink, went to the backdoor and pulled on her boots. 'Okay, see you in a coupla hours!' She gathered up her gear.

'Oh Goldie, have you a spare message stick I can use later today?'

'I haven't got a spare one on me, but I'll get one from the office while I'm out this morning and give it to you this arvo. I'll leave it in the fruit bowl.' She pointed to the all-purpose shallow bowl on the counter, filled with bits and pieces. 'Do you want to borrow a camera?'

Goldie went to a cupboard and took a professional-looking camera off the shelf. 'You can take my Nikon 2. I left it in the car the other day and I've got my new 4 here, so I don't need it!'

'Crikey, Goldie, this looks too good for me!'

'Don't be silly, it's my old one. If you lose it or break it, it's insured.'

'Well, thanks so much. I'll look after it, believe me. I need to be at the concert hall early for rehearsal. I should be back here by two. How do the buses run around here?' I sold my car before I went overseas last spring. *Note to self: get car ASAP.*

Goldie shucked her keys over to me. 'Here, take my car. I'll catch the bus into town later and walk. I don't have to be anywhere else this morning.'

Gratefully, I put the keys on the bench beside me and hurried upstairs to put the camera in my carry bag to leave in the car for later. Goldie disappeared down the back garden to the laneway. I picked up my coffee mug and turned to go back up to bed, eyeing my basic, stand-by navy draped over the back of a chair. *Boring, boring –* but it would just have to do.

* * *

10.30am

I hunted out the musician's swipe card sent to me by my agent and headed through the morning traffic to the Concert Hall at Southbank. The river air was fresh; I drew a deep, appreciative lungful. Shopkeepers were running up the shutters and putting out merchandise; people bustling to work. Saturday was as busy as any other day in Brisbane. I pulled into a vacant space near the lift, gathered my flute case and briefcase. Unaccountably, nerves struck. Could I "cut it" after two years away?

Vacuum-wielding cleaning staff made a maroon path for me, as an anxious-eyed young woman of about my own age popped out of a doorway, carrying a sheaf of papers. Her eyes widened when she saw me. 'Hello, you must be Ms Miller. I'm Joan Hamilton, the admin assistant. I'll take you down to Mr Seymour. He wants to introduce you to Vladimir Rezanov, and Lance MacPherson will be in to rehearse the orchestra's item with you after that. We're at sixes and sevens here this morning because they've all just come back from short breaks. Mr Seymour has been away for a couple of weeks, Vlad – er – Mr Rezanov, well I'm not sure when he got in to Brisbane, and Lance has been here since early this morning.'

Grateful for a friendly face, because meeting a well-known musician for the first time is always stressful for me. What is it about ourselves that we can't recognise when we are worthy of being in such hallowed company?

I allowed Joan to usher me back into the lift. 'So, has Rezanov arrived for rehearsal yet?' I asked, hoping to elicit gossip.

She blushed, rolled her eyes and giggled. 'Oh yes, he's here. Have you met him before?' *Hm, I fear you're too old, Joan.*

'No, I haven't.' I was also curious to "suss out" the manager of the Concert Hall and the conductor.

We stepped into the lift and headed down to the dressing rooms. Somewhere in the distance, I heard the clatter of dishes, presumably in the canteen. Voices echoed along the corridor to the dressing rooms; I became aware of a brawl in progress. Although I speak reasonable French, Italian and German, this could only be Russian. *Rezanov's throwing a tantrum – or perhaps he's just discussing the soccer.* I didn't have to sneak up on them, the noise he and whomever he was bellowing at were making enough for an army. Joan slowed and grabbed my arm. 'Hang on, Pam.'

I disengaged myself and went to the door. Wondering whether to knock before stepping inside, I was riveted by the words 'Puking Pam' followed by more tirades. Russian didn't have to be a language I understood. The contemptuous snarl with which the words pronounced my nickname revealed what Rezanov thought of *me*. Curling my hands in the 'kill' position, I charged into the room. Two men were watching while the third strode back and forth. Dark-eyed, totally gorgeous and sporting designer stubble, Rezanov swung around.

I'm known for my laid back demeanour. The white-hot rage which surged through my body shocked *me* to the core. *'How dare you?'*

The Russian stared at me, speechless.

'Who the hell do you think you are, insulting a fellow artist? I'm supposed to work with you. Well, I've got news for you, mate, forget it! I wouldn't allow you within spit of the stage with me!'

He started to say something, but I hadn't finished. 'You're totally unprofessional. It wasn't *my* idea to play flute to your piano, believe me!' I swung around to the one I thought could be the manager. 'Get someone else to play with this drongo.'

Leaving Joan waving her arms, I swept out of the dressing room and charged along the corridor to the canteen, the only possible place of sanctuary on the floor. The canteen ladies greeted me with smiles as I stalked into the dining area. The way I hurled myself at the counter pretty much showed them the way the wind was blowing. A cup of coffee and a slice of iced banana cake were produced in record time. As I sat at a table forcing myself to hold hot, angry tears at bay, footsteps sounded behind me. 'You needn't bother oiling your way around here. I want nothing to do with you!' I snarled.

'Er...Ms Miller, I'm sorry you had to overhear Rezanov...'

I turned to find one of the combatants, a tall, well built, extremely good-looking man standing behind me. He introduced himself as the Concert Hall manager, Bill Seymour. Conceding he wasn't to blame, I invited him to sit with me. Looking relieved, he pulled out a chair and sat down. One of the ladies brought him a cup of strong, black tea. We faced each other, neither wanting to be the first to speak. Finally, he sighed, took a sip and grimaced. 'They always make it too hot, bless them,' he confided, 'but they're so good to me I can't say anything.' I remained silent; he could make the first move. 'Ms Miller – '

'Pam.'

'Pam, I heard you've overcome your stage fright and I can't for a *moment* imagine you'd undertake a concert of this magnitude if you felt you couldn't perform.' He smiled and I almost reached over to pat his hand. What he had to put up with would have made me choke the living you-know-what out of most people.

'I used to have a problem with paralysing stage fright, Mr Seymour, but I'm over that now. Oh, I still get nervous, but nowhere near the debilitating terror that used to overcome me.'

'Please call me Bill. I used to have a problem with stage fright – yes, I'm a musician too, pianist actually – though I don't get much chance to play with an orchestra anymore. Sometimes I play with the Gordon Trio as a quartet.' He laughed, and blew on the top of his tea to cool it down. 'I've been hearing great things about you. The critics are raving over your work but presumably, Rezanov hasn't been reading the papers! Unfortunately, you're contracted to play the Haydn with him, so we have to come to some sort of arrangement. Hopefully, his agent is giving him a good bollocking.'

I dissolved into giggles. Bill stared at me for a moment and then joined in. It was a few minutes before we could control ourselves. 'The thought of anyone scolding Rezanov is ridiculous!' I chortled. 'He's a law unto himself! And all that Russian crap is just that. He's as Australian as you and I, albeit with parents of Russian descent, but I've heard he only uses it to get his own way. He does speak the language, but I don't know how fluently.'

'I've had some royal battles with Russian performers over the years. We know all about Vlad's tantrums, but when you get to know him, he's a pretty good bloke. You'll get on with him when he's settled down.' Bill Seymour eyed me appreciatively. *Uh oh, no, down boy!* I've no time for dalliances.

'Okay, so what can we do?' I had to get our relationship on a business-like footing.

'Would you be prepared to go ahead with the item if I can broker a deal with,' he smiled, 'the 'drongo'?'

'Well, I'm being paid for it, so really I have to shut up or put up,' I replied, 'and I've never reneged on a concert in my whole life, but it did feel good to throw a tantie for once.'

Bill grinned. 'I think I know just what to say to that young man. Let's go and talk to him. Don't say anything, just follow my lead.'

Loud voices boomed down the corridor as we neared the dressing-room. It was impossible to tell who had the upper hand, but when we stepped into the room the two men fell silent. Rezanov scowled at me from the easy chair on other side of the room. His agent, an unassuming man with a more than adequate nose, looked enquiringly at Bill Seymour who presented an expressionless face. Only I saw him wink at the agent, before he confronted the Impaler. I took a chair near the door and sat down to watch the show.

Bill lowered his tone to a sympathetic croon. 'I fully understand how you must feel, Mr Rezanov, being paired with a woman whose concert tour has been lauded by the critics. What if she outplays you! Now, I don't know if you realise this, but Ms Miller is also a highly accomplished pianist, so if you feel you have to cancel out of the concert, I am sure she is more than able to take your place. Right, Ms Miller? And we can easily announce a change to the program for her to do a piano item as well.'

Oh no! I couldn't – he turned to me, carefully shielding his face from the pianist and winked again. The agent became engrossed in a painting on the wall.

'Oh yes, I could do that!' I replied with a smile, quaking inside. What if Rezanov told us to get on with it then and charged out of the concert hall? The silence lengthened. I didn't dare look at him, but kept my eyes on the poker-faced manager.

'It's not good enough! This woman can't play the work!' Rezanov leaped to his feet, sending the chair crashing onto its side. 'Ridiculous!' He reached me in two strides and thrust his face into mine. 'You can't play the Mozart. You're not a bloody pianist!' He'd forgotten to be Russian in his angst. I almost laughed aloud. *No, of course I'm not, you berk, but that set you back a peg or two.* I leaned back in my chair and met him stare for stare. 'Sez who?'

His nostrils flared; as a turn-on it was spectacular. 'I do. I, Rezanov, am booked for this performance. I will play! But not with you.' *You've remembered to be Russian now have you? Too late!*

'Oh yes you will, Mr Rezanov, you're contracted and we'll sue if you don't. Get over it. Pam hasn't had any problems throughout her whole concert tour. It's lasted six weeks and the critics have gone wild over her. No problems, *right?*' The last word clanged like the hinge on a steel strap.

A silent communication took place between the mad pianist and his agent. Something must have been decided to their satisfaction, because the agent faced the manager. 'He will play. Everything is alright.' He turned to glare at the pianist. 'And he apologises to Miss Miller.'

Rezanov's mutinous expression indicated that he no more wished to apologise than fly to the moon. Still, better to quit while we were ahead.

'We'll just have a look around. There've been some changes since you were here last.' Bill raised his voice. 'Give *Mr* Rezanov time to cool down.' As he put his arm around my back to guide me from the room, someone growled. *Don't laugh for God's sake, Pam...*

Suppressing a grin, Bill looked at his watch. 'Let's go and look at the river.' He took my arm and tucked it under his own, snug along his ribcage. Startled, I was about to pull away, but before I could, we were headed for the front of the concert hall. I allowed him to lead me through the concrete maze, down past the restaurant and across the grass to the edge of the water. 'See here, you don't have to put up with that, Pam. He's just pulling rank because he thinks we can't do without him!'

'But we can't! He's under contract for this concert, same as I am.'

Bill picked up a small stick and lobbed it into the water. 'Yes, but we all know he has to front up or lose a stack of money. I just wanted to stick it to him that we can pull the rug out from under his size thirteens. Actually, we *can* sue, but I would have to contact the directors first. I can't do that my own and really, it's a little late with the concert tonight.'

A chill wind came off the water. I shivered and my companion put his arm around me. By common consent we started to walk along the path beside the water. Ducks bobbed in the backwash from a passing City Cat – one day, I thought, I must have a ride on one of those – the sun was shining and in the distance the city went about its Saturday business. *No matter what happens, Rezanov is not going to ruin this concert for me.*

'So where do you go from here, Pam? I know you're joining the orchestra for the outback tour.'

Bill's voice startled me. 'My next concert is in Ipswich, and then I do a short tour in the UK. Oh, and the Outback Tour with the Pacific!'

Bill turned and put his hands on my shoulders, miraculously, a man the same height as me. 'Can you make some time for dating?' he asked, his eyes shining with mischief.

I looked back at him. 'Possibly. What did you have in mind?'

'Well, how about after the shindig is over tonight we go and find some supper in the city?'

I already had plans, but would it be a good idea to bring my social life so close to my professional? I liked him immensely, although he didn't pack the sexual punch of Rezanov...where did that come from? Disappointment flashed across Bill's face and he withdrew his hands, obviously thinking I wasn't going to respond.

'I've already made an arrangement to go with friends, but perhaps another time? I'm looking forward to winding down afterwards, though I might have bashed His Maj over the head with my flute by then and be under arrest.' In the distance, the town hall clock chimed. I looked at my watch. 'OMG, I really must go back and see if that twit will rehearse with me.'

'No problems. We'll go out to dinner one night next week if you're free, and Rezanov'll have to work with you because I'll make sure of it!' Bill replied grimly. We didn't speak much as we almost trotted back to the concert hall. The fact that there were no shouts coming from the dressing rooms was a good sign. The door to Rezanov's room was closed and Bill knocked quietly.

A cleaner thrust the mop-head into his bucket and grinned. 'If you're looking for 'his nibs,' he's gone upstairs.' Obviously they all knew what was going on, which was more than I did.

'Right. Thanks, John.' Bill turned to me. How about you grab your gear and I'll go ahead and test the waters?' He ushered me into a nearby dressing room, straightened his shoulders and winked before striding off to battle.

Someone had prepared the room – the air conditioner was running and my music and flute cases had been placed on the makeup bench. The room was small but comfortable with two easy chairs, coffee table, makeup bench and on the side, next to an open cupboard with hanging space and hangers, was an en suite complete with shower.

I nipped in and freshened up, then took a moment to deep breathe, allowing my mind to float to a space recommended by my hypnotherapist. A kaleidoscope of colours and memories swept through my mind... the audience, smiling at me...the orchestra approving... the conductor – the face of Sir James' Macpherson's precocious son, Lance, danced into my vision. Lance was a bit of a hunk; anticipation stirred within me. Things were shaping up to be interesting.

The years I'd worked for my career, always striving to give of my best, I felt deeply privileged to carry what I believed were messages from the great composers to my audiences, giving them the beauty from the brilliant minds of men such as Mozart, Beethoven, Handel and Bach. No one, certainly not a Russian thug, was going to disrupt my concentration and jeopardise my performance. I picked up my flute case and turned the air-conditioner and light off before I left the dressing room – my mother taught me frugality – and headed for the concert hall stage.

Rezanov was talking to his agent as he softly played the opening bars of the second movement to his major work for the night. Neither of them acknowledged my presence, so I walked over to the music stand beside the pianist and placed my case on a nearby chair. A waft of his after shave came to me and I stepped back a little. They stopped their conversation and turned to look at me. 'Well, are you ready to start?' I snarled.

A wee smile played around the agent's mouth; with a wave of his hand and a muttered salutation, he toddled off, business bent. Rezanov looked me up and down and then parted his lips in a sour grin. '*I* was waiting for *you*, Princess.' The heavy Russian accent had given way to pure "Ocker."

How am I going to keep my cool around this character...? If we got through the concert without strangling each other, it would be a triumph of patience and my hypnotherapists counselling.

'Are you ready or do you want to daydream the time away?' Rezanov's voice cut through my reverie.

I frowned. 'Which one did you want to do first?'

'The Haydn.' Turning back to the keyboard, his murderous expression shone back in the gleaming patina of the grand piano. Gritting my teeth, I opened my flute case and took out the precious instrument, vowing to show him what I was made of. I gently blew into the instrument to make sure the pipes were clean, catching the eye of a stagehand with whom I'd had acquaintance with some years previously. Smiling, he mimed a retch into a bucket. Rezanov, who didn't appear to have noticed the pantomime, counted me in and away we went. If it was the last thing I did in this life, I would show them all that Puking Pam was a person of the past.

I was exhilarated after two hours of rehearsal. Demanding I call him 'Vlad,' he'd thawed somewhat after the first twenty minutes. We side-lined our differences as we played phrases over and over, working on nuances and even my past problem was discussed in between swapping gossip about fellow musicians.

'When I first started out I was the same as you, only I saved my throwing up for the dressing room. I'd clear out anyone who was hanging around – including the birds'– he laughed – 'If there wasn't an en suite I'd try and wait until the coast was clear before rushing for the bathroom.' Noting my surprised look, he added, 'I wasn't always given my own dressing room, you know. I've played in some pretty manky places.'

Most artists, including musicians get to perform in draughty church halls, conference rooms, outdoors under the stars, in fact anywhere there's someone willing to pay the money. 'I know what you mean!' I replied. We shared a moment of accord. Just then the stagehand came back and, catching our eyes, gave a merciless grin and mimed puking into his hands. Vlad leaped to his feet and charged at the man, whose eyes widened in shock.

Bearing down on the hapless man, Rezanov roared so loudly that even I, who realised what he was on about, cringed. Down in the auditorium, staff cleaning and preparing for the evening performance, stopped what they were doing and watched the show. Backing away, the stagehand waved apologetically at me and scuttled for his life. 'Sorry, mate. I didn't mean anything. I was just having a bit of fun.'

Vlad strode back and snatched his music off the piano. 'If anyone ever does that to you again, I'll get them sacked.' His eyes bored into mine and I was lost to everything. His 189cm actually towered over me – oh, the novelty of looking *up* to a man – but spoiled the moment, by snapping, 'I can't have you collapsing before the concert.' With that, he turned and stormed off.

A slow hand-clap alerted me to a man standing at the back of the stage. 'Rezanov's full of shit, isn't he?' Lance MacPherson, as tall as his father and built like a Rugby front-row forward – *is being tall, hefty and good-looking a job description in this place?* – moved to the piano, leaned over the keys and played a quick trill. A shiver went down my spine. I knew MacPherson was a pianist too, but I hadn't realised how good. Perhaps he could stand in if Rezanov refused to play tonight? I had a feeling the Russian's tantrums were over for the time being.

A shadowy figure moved in the background and another man walked away from the stage. I looked after him, surprised he hadn't stayed to be introduced. Lance shrugged. 'Oh that's the new bloke. Doesn't talk much, but he can play like the devil himself. Now let's get down to business.' We went through the score, Lance emphasising phrasing. A few minutes later, the orchestra started to trickle in and we soon got down to rehearsing the Haydn, followed by Schubert's Shepherd on a Rock, the two pieces I was playing with full orchestra. Dance of the Blessed Spirits was set for an encore if required.

It was almost two o'clock before I could pack my flute away. I wasn't really looking forward to working with the Russian in spite of his apparent change of heart.

I am rarely affected by men, though I've had my share of relationships which had crumbled to dust, along with my emotional confidence, but here I was, ready to kill Rezanov and we hadn't even performed together. Oh, he had actually gone in to bat for me with a snide stagehand, but only because he didn't want me too upset to play.

I didn't have anything to pick up from my dressing room, so I headed for the outside world. As I arrived in the foyer, Bill, who was signing for a delivery, hailed me. 'How did it go? Did he behave himself?' I thought that it would be far safer if this kindly and eminently suitable man could accompany me instead of the mad Russian.

Blessing Goldie for lending me her car, I returned toward her cottage. People and their dogs were out and about, Saturday markets flooded with shorts and T-shirted couples while children wrestled and chased each other on the lawns abutting the river. The main street, littered with small boutique shops, was narrow, making it necessary to stop for kamikaze pedestrians. I looked around as I waited at the crossing for the lights to change and there it was! Hanging in the window of a nondescript dress shop halfway along the shopping strip was the most fabulous dress I had ever seen and one I wouldn't have bought in a fit.

'*No, you already have your outfit for tonight, you don't need another one,*' said Sweet Reason.

'*Of course you do!*' oozed The Devil, nestling in my wallet.

Tucking the car into a vacant space nearby, I practically ran up the street, skidding to a halt as I got to the door. The interior, cool, quiet and blessedly incense-free, lured me on. A young girl of about sixteen with dark brown curling hair, sporting nose rings and a stud in her lip – *ouch* – and a name tag, *Tia* – hopped out from the back room. 'Are you right?' she chirped, and tripped over a vacuum cleaner cord. Her light hazel eyes twinkled as she untangled herself from it.

I smiled an acknowledgement and charged to the window, running into an artfully placed, gilded, pink-padded chair. 'Have you got that in my size?'

She looked me up and down. 'Yes Ma'am, we've got larger sizes too.'

Now, I am not a 'big' woman, just tall, but I let it pass. She went to the rack, rummaged through and suddenly there it was, the dress in the window and in my size.

Dressing rooms are the very devil for changing. I jack-knifed to get my shoes and jeans off – plenty of practice in aircraft toilets – and dragged my sweaty t-shirt over my head. Hoping I wouldn't leave wet marks on the fabric, I carefully slid the garment down and smoothed it over my hips.

'Come out so I can get a look at you!' shouted Tia. She was standing so close to the door, I was surprised she didn't fall through it.

I faced the mirror at the end of the shop.

For a long moment we gazed at my reflection. 'It looks amazing with your hair,' she whispered. I swayed from side to side, sending the fabric swirling. The tiny amber beads scattered across the golden handkerchief skirt caught the light, shooting shards of fire around the walls. 'Does it wear me or do I wear it?' The last thing I wanted to do was look as though I was trying too hard.

Tia laughed. 'Oh no, it's awesome!' She reached up and pulled my long rivulets of hair gently back into a careless knot. 'Going somewhere special tonight?'

'Yes. I'm performing at the concert hall. I have a navy dress which would do, but...'I narrowed my eyes and turned side-on trying to pull my stomach in.

'You're Pamela Miller!' Tia's shriek almost sent me into orbit. 'My girlfriend and I are going to your concert for my birthday.' Her face fell. 'Grant – he's my boyfriend – hates classical music.'

'I'm playing a couple of items with Rezanov and two with the Pacific.'

'Oh my God, isn't he *gorgeous*?' Her face turned bright pink; her grin left the Cheshire cat's in the shade. 'What's he like?'

'Well, he's just like his photos and he's a bit of a handful.' I wasn't sure what else to say about him; I didn't want to burst her bubble. *He's a bit mad, actually.*

Tia's eyes grew dreamy, but then she snapped back to sales-girl mode. 'You'll need special earrings to go with this.' Her gaze roved across the glass-topped counter under which was a glittering mass of costume jewellery. In my excitement, I hadn't realised the shop also stocked handbags and shoes. She opened the back of the display, paused for a moment, hand hovering over the contents, then, like a Shearwater diving for fish, swooped on a pair of earrings. 'Try these! What size shoes do you wear?' Hardly waiting for me to say 'Ten,' she scuttled to the back wall of the shop where she proceeded to open boxes, peer inside and reject the contents after a second's glance.

I moved close to the mirror, took out my current pearl studs and replaced them with sparkling Citrine flowers. 'Awesome!' Tia appeared beside me holding a pair of golden high-heeled sandals. 'Come on, try these!' she instructed enthusiastically, holding out her hand to support me as I slipped them on. We turned to face the mirror. A glowing, fiery column of *woman* looked back at me. I knew that if I presented this well without my hair and makeup done, then just how – I looked at a grinning Tia – "awesome" would I look that night?

Carefully, we packed the dress, shoes and earrings into carrier bags and I paid an amount which could have covered a Shire Council debt. 'Tia, have you got your tickets yet?'

'No, we're buying them at the door.' *Oh dear, why hadn't they thought to book?*

I opened my shoulder bag and groped around inside. 'Here's a couple of complimentary tickets. ' I signed the back of them, then scribbled in the back of my diary and tore the page out. 'This will get you backstage and if we can drag Rezanov out of his cave, I'll make sure you get to meet him.' *A lump of raw meat should do it.*

I passed over the tickets and the note. 'Oh, my God! Awesome!' Tia screamed, almost squeezing me to death.

'Just get there in plenty of time as the queues can be horrendous. It's better if you come early. After the concert I'll be busy, but show the backstage doorman the note. See you tonight.'

Tia was texting before I got out the door.

CHAPTER 8

Dingo

The Concert

Saturday, 7pm

Flushed with excitement, the pulsing crowd of well-fed, cashed-up music lovers flooded the foyer. The bar staff's arms and hands worked like threshing machines as they served everything from beer to Squashed Frog, a risky choice if the ladies weren't used to it. Most of them regarded it as mother's milk.

Dingo stood off to the side of the stage as he looked at the rows of carefully placed seats for the orchestra – particularly where he would be – and the podium for the conductor, Lance McPherson. Tremors fluttered through him. Were Ariel's parents back from Mackay yet? How long would it be before they realised she wasn't at home – or anywhere? He'd never been in this position before and in spite of his OCD, had always coped without anyone knowing. Until, now, no girl had made him lose his composure. His heart ached as her lovely face sprang into his mind. *I'm sorry. I didn't mean it.*

There'd been nothing on the six o'clock news about her being discovered. Perhaps the cops were keeping it quiet for a while. He was surprised that someone's dog – or a council park attendant – hadn't found her. The undergrowth was pretty thick near the edge of the river; he remembered catching his parka on something. A chill swept through him as he pondered the possibility of having left a thread behind. Too late now...a member of the orchestra passed by, looking at him strangely. Had she spoken to him? She must have, because she shrugged and kept going. *No, breathe, that's it breathe. Don't draw attention to yourself.*

The orchestra filed in, took their places and sat to tune their instruments on the note, *A*, from the First Oboist. The conductor walked to the podium to enthusiastic clapping; the concert was underway.

Motionless, he absorbed the glorious sounds into his mind and body, forcing his fear into oblivion. By the end of the symphony which opened the evening performance, he had managed to thrust the horror of dawn and the memory of the photographer who had been taking shots of the park and the river banks. Instead, visions of his holiday burst forth...the surf breaking on the sand, the early morning sun warming his skin...dogs snuffling excitedly past, out with their jogging owners...

Clapping brought him out of his thoughts. He was close enough to spot a young girl in the audience looking at him. 'Having a kip were you?' she mouthed, grinning. He smiled back, his eyes alighting on her soft, red mouth. *Juicy.*

The audience coughed and rustled with anticipation then burst into applause as the young conductor came back. Dingo resisted the urge to hold his hands over his ears as a wave of clapping thundered throughout the auditorium. *One, two, three four...sixseveneightnineten.* The conductor raised his baton for the music to begin.

The lead in from the orchestra heightened the tension as the glorious notes of Mozart's Piano Concerto No 20 in D Minor filled the vast hall. Overwhelmed by the beauty of the music and performance, he forgot everything that had happened on this terrible day. His subconscious mind counted every beat, anticipated every note – but though numbers were his obsession, he forgot even that.

The second movement, the Romance, brought him back to the here and now and as the movement ended and the third and last started, suddenly he became impatient for it to finish. Why did they have to have an interval? Couldn't this lot sit on their arses for a bit longer? Anger and exhaustion surged through him; the day's events would no longer be denied...

Her lovely face, laughing and chatting. 'So Dingo, tell me your real name? Come on, you owe me!' She brought out a bottle of diet Coke and proceeded to pour him a glass. Gratefully, he took it and made a laughing reference to being a mystery man – for how could he tell her his real name? Sometimes he was glad he didn't have friends when he was young, because the bullies would have mauled him in the playground. Then he would remember watching, through the upstairs window of the music room, the other kids go by for school, laughing and hitting each other with their schoolbags, longing to join them. Surely anything was better than the loneliness of his life...her beautiful face changed from laughing to a grimace...

The applause brought him back to the present. Had he made a fool of himself? Apparently not! The acknowledgement from the audience went on and on – endless bowing and smiling – when would it ever end? He had never wanted to escape so badly.

When interval came, he scurried backstage and moved to the plate glass window looking out over the steps where people, wrapped in stylish coats, braved the night air. Beyond the expanse of lawn, the water rippled all colours from the city lights. *Have they found her yet?*

The bell for the second half rang through the foyer. He watched his fellow musicians take their places. *What would they do if they knew they were playing alongside a murderer?* He forced down nausea.

The rustling and coughing ceased. Tension filled the hall and before he realised it, a column of flame stood on the stage in front of them. Tall and slender, blonde hair upswept, her earrings pinpoints of light igniting the glowing dress, glittering lights flashing from the bodice and skirt. The audience gasped; thunderous applause ensued. Mesmerised, his gaze dropped to where the sexiest golden shoes he had ever seen flashed fire on her feet.

Pamela Miller, flautist.

A wave of Ariel's perfume reached him and suddenly he was transported back to the park. His heart started to pound. Sweat pricked under his suit coat and his collar restricted his breathing. He gazed at Pamela's delicately painted toes, the diamonds glittering around her ankle. His eyes travelled up to her slender hips and as he looked into her beautiful face, his mind spun out of control. He daren't allow panic to overtake him. Was the photographer her sister? Did Pamela have a sister? Perhaps someone just like her...*onetwothreefourfive*...Pamela might be related to the woman, but when he focused he could see that not only was Pamela taller, he remembered that the photographer had shoulder-length hair.

Relieved, his attention snapped back to the girls below him before returning to the matter in hand.

Control... control...two, four, six, eight...He grappled for his handkerchief – *A gentleman is never without a freshly laundered and ironed cotton handkerchief, my darling* – and pressed it to his mouth to force back screams...*go away you old cow...* catching Pamela's eye, he pretended to cough and looked down into the audience once more.

The two girls were incandescent with excitement, one of them even going so far as to wave to Pamela, whose face lit up with pleasure as she smiled down at them. *She knows them?* The flautist turned to the rest of the audience acknowledging the applause. *Did she see me with Ariel?* A shaft of fear struck him. He forced himself to hide any emotion. He rubbed his hand over his thighs to keep them from shaking.

Pamela Miller raised the flute to her lips. Within minutes, the audience was transfixed by the beauty of the music, swelling throughout the concert hall – mesmerising, magical.

Ariel was forgotten.

CHAPTER 9

Jeffrey Triumphant.

Saturday, 9.10pm.

Deep in Jeffrey's doggy brain lurked a vague memory of something exciting hidden under a pile of bushes at the top of an embankment near the water. 'Jeffrey! Jeffrey? Where *are* you?' Robert Simkins shone his powerful flashlight around the park.

Snuffling his way along, his tail wagged faster as the scent got stronger. Yum. It was almost more than a daffy dog could bear! He snorted his way forward and there it was: the pile of bushes and leaves. Jeffrey wasn't about to let his treasure go. He barged into the centre of the pile, dug deep and tossed his head, sending a flap of old sacking into the air. Branches of every size and leaves flew in every direction. Seeing his quarry, he pounced.

'Jeffrey! Get out of there, you dozy animal!'

Jeffrey held another sandal in his drooling jaws. Torchlight flashed over him, passed on and then veered back and down; behind the dog, lay part of a jeans-clad body. Quaking, Simkins moved forward as though in a dream and gingerly moved aside the top branch to see a still form underneath – a young girl, glossy dark hair hiding her face, arms folded across her chest as though she was asleep.

He had never seen anything like it; he felt sick. Drugs? A recollection from CSI reminded him that a dead person usually didn't fold their arms neatly in front of their body, unless of course, it was suicide. He didn't dare look any further in case he found needles or something, but the unwelcome realisation dawned that someone had covered this person up after they'd died. He shuddered. Dimly, he remembered from some TV program, that he shouldn't touch evidence with his bare hand, but how else was he to take it from the dog?

Shaking from head to toe, he pulled a handkerchief from his pocket, grabbed Jeffrey's collar and, wrapping the material around his hand, wrenched the – thing – from his dog's mouth and dropped it on the grass. He had fastened the leash to Jeffrey's collar and wrapped the end around his wrist, when he remembered: 'Oh no, the other shoe this morning!' His heart sank when he recalled grabbing the mate off his dog and casually chucking it in the bin at the back of his house. Fortunately, the garbage collection wasn't due for a few days. He became aware that the night air was bitter, buttoned up his coat and pulled the hood over his head. Shivering, he took out his mobile phone.

Jeffrey, deprived of his prize, flopped onto his well-padded, furry bum to commence an intimate and vigorous cleaning regime.

CHAPTER 10

Susan

Call Out.

Saturday, 9. 45pm

My mobile cut the conversation in mid-sentence. What else would it be but *work* on a chilly autumn night when I was well fed, sitting in front of the fire in the company of my sister and good friend, talking about our men and our children?

'Susan?' The voice of the Incident Commander from Comco spoiled the ambience of the moment well and truly.

'Yes, sir.'

'The body of a young woman has turned up in West End, down by the river near the old boatshed. Forensics're on the way.' He filled me in on the exact location, gave me command and hung up. Cursing silently, I turned to my sister, Melanie and our friend, Briony. 'Sorry, ladies. A body's been found in West End.'

Guilt assailed me. Someone's daughter, sister or perhaps girlfriend was lost forever, and I was cranky about leaving my friends? I gave myself a mental scolding and tried to switch to professional mode.

Briony looked hopeful. 'Do you want me to come?'

'No, not tonight, but you'll probably end up there tomorrow.'

Briony Feldman was shaping up to be a very fine officer. We had met two years previously when she'd been contracted to write the autobiography of the eccentric, lustful Sir Arthur Robinson, at the country town of Emsberg. A historian, she had been disenchanted by the job, but fascinated with the murder investigations swirling around us. Having bonded over coffee, cakes and a funeral, my suggestion that she join the police force was enthusiastically embraced. Now stationed at West End, she is a uniformed constable.

Dressed in heavy polar fleece pants, boots, a T-shirt and warm coat, I grabbed my shoulder bag and keys and raced out the door. Melanie and Briony would let the dogs out for their nightly constitutional, lock up and troop off to bed when they were ready.

The roads were all but deserted as I sped to town and joined the mainstream traffic into the CBD. The lights from the concert hall shimmered coldly on the river as I crossed the bridge, wishing I could have been part of the audience.

Uniform had set up the crime scene and Forensics arrived as I pulled up. The generator for the portable lighting chugged, a background to the voices of the forensic team. The chilly night air of the river hit me as I stepped out of my car. Zipping my coat, I pulled the hood over my head, hoisted my shoulder bag off the passenger seat and walked to the tape. Jacketless and shivering, the young constable keeping the crime scene log moved to meet me, but I told him to wait and trudged back to my car to get an old gardening jacket of David's. He smiled his gratitude and scrambled into the grubby garment, before inspecting my ID, logging me onto the crime scene and lifting the tape for me to duck under.

A familiar face greeted me. 'What's the "go" here, Al?'

'Ma'am. The call was logged at 21.10 by Triple 0. The body is that of a female person.' He looked at his notebook. 'Caller's name, Robert Simkins. Dog found a shoe –he waved at a bulky, plastic-wrapped exhibit lying on a small tarpaulin – 'and then uncovered the body. Apparently the dog found the matching one this morning, around 0500, but Simkins chucked it in the bin at home thinking it was discarded by a drunk. We've sent a car around to get it. He saw no one anywhere near the body when it was uncovered.'

'Right, thanks, Al. I'll talk to Mr Simkins in a moment.'

He moved away to instruct a search in the grass for anything interesting. I opened my mobile and phoned my partner, Evan, who would arrange for the members of my first team to come in. Fortunately most of them lived within the city precincts. As soon as I finished the call, I walked toward the body, careful not to impinge on forensics. Invisible beyond the spotlights, the sound of the river lapping at the bank made me shiver.

The young woman lay on the ground, arms folded over her chest as though prepared for burial, brilliantly lit by the portable lighting. One leg was straight but the other had been pulled sideways. *Sexual assault?* She was fully clothed, so it didn't seem likely.

I bent down and peered at the graven face, eyes half-open, and opaque. There was no telling what colour they were, but her skin and dark hair spoke of possibly Italian or Spanish descent. Dark marks around her nose and mouth – were they the result of bruising? Or dirt?

I wasn't close enough to be sure. Shadow obscured her throat. I looked at the girl's feet. Had the dog dragged both shoes off or...no, the bottom of the nearest foot was grass-stained, so she'd taken her shoes off before she died. I straightened as Al came back. 'Handbag? Tote bag? Mobile phone? Anything?'

'No sign of a bag or phone. The "perp" must have taken them. Maybe a mugging.' He sighed. 'What a waste.'

A forensic specialist moved up beside me. 'Inspector, I need to get in here.' She bent down, a blue boiler-suited and booted figure, took a pair of latex gloves out of a sealed bag and proceeded to blow into each one before sliding her hand in, flexed her fingers, then squatted down and opened a box of specimen jars. Just then, John Lynch, the government pathologist stopped beside me. 'Hello Susan, haven't seen you for a *long* time!' We'd met over drinks only a week previously.

Ignoring his attempt at levity, I ploughed ahead. 'Have you any idea how she died as yet? Just a preliminary heads-up will do.'

He bent over the forensic officer's shoulder and spoke quietly to her. Straightening up, he drew me away a short distance. A whimper and wriggling movement alerted me to outsiders. Following my gaze, John smiled. 'That's Jeffrey who found the body and his owner who called it in.' A middle-aged man squatted beside the Labrador stroking his head. I turned my attention back to John.

'It appears she's been dragged' – he pointed to a barely discernible track along the ground–from there – and it looks as though the perp piled the bushes over her here. Rigor is full on, so she's been dead anywhere between twelve and sixteen hours, depending on the temperature. We'll need to get her back to base and see what's what. Sorry I can't be more specific, Susan, but I'll let you know as soon as possible. Bruise marks around her mouth and bloodshot eyes. Her sternum felt caved in. No obvious sign of rape, no obvious track marks anywhere but again, we'll know when we do the post mortem. I'd say, off the record, it's more than a mugging. Okay? I'll give you a full report ASAP.' He turned away before I could thank him.

I moved over to Simkins introduced myself. The dog leapt at me, tail wagging, but his owner pulled him back by his lead with trembling hands.

'Do you walk in this area of the park often, Mr Simkins?'

'Quite often. I live at the end of the road at 68. I try to take Jeffrey for a walk before I start work.'

'And today was different for some reason? And what time did you find the shoe this morning?'

He looked puzzled for a moment and then realised my meaning. 'It was around eight o'clock or eight fifteen, I think. I cut Jeffrey's walk short, so I took him out tonight. It's late because I was finishing up some work after dinner. My wife and children are away visiting her sister, so I was on my own in the house. Good chance to work without any interruptions. I'm an architect and work from home most of the time...it was actually a *sandal*, Inspector.'

So, the girl was dead well before eight. 'When you were out this morning, did you see or hear anyone in or near the park? Someone walking along the footpath or boats on the river?'

Simkins stared into the darkness for what seemed like forever. 'It was deserted, Inspector. Not even joggers were out, but they don't often come this far down the park. No footpath, you see.' He wiped the back of his hand across his eyes.

I glanced back down the grassy expanse. He was right. The footpath finished some three hundred metres away. I sighed. No CCTV footage then, something confirmed by a nearby uniformed officer, unless the girl and her companion had walked past the cameras down near the ferry terminus. 'Thank you for your patience in waiting for us, sir, and I must commend you for calling us. Some wouldn't want to get involved. We would appreciate your coming in to headquarters to sign a statement tomorrow morning. It will only be a formality, but where paperwork's concerned, needs must.'

I handed him my card. He responded to the charm I applied to the occasion and with a, 'Come Jeffrey, home,' he left.

As members of my team arrived, I sent them to roust out the nearest neighbours. A chilly night meant that most people would be inside watching TV although a few people, perhaps smokers banished from their homes to puff in isolation, stood in an interested clump behind the checked barrier. A few shouts indicated members of the press, but we ignored them.

'Okay, we'll need to see the tapes from all of the CCTV cameras down near the terminal. Pity about this end...' Evan stood beside me, frowning as he made notes.

Had the perpetrator deliberately chosen this end of the park, with its trees and long grass for his, or her, crime? Most murders of young women are men, and instinct said this one was no exception.

CHAPTER 11

Pam

Glowing Success!

Saturday, 10.30pm

I couldn't believe the concert had gone so well. Not once had I experienced a twinge of nerves – well, no more than any performer would have under the circumstances. Rezanov had been a considerate and expert partner in our combined items; performing solo with the orchestra had been a joy.

I was happy to see the girl from the dress shop and her friend in the audience and from the expression on their faces they'd had a wonderful time. I was puzzled by the empty seat beside them. Goldie had been sitting there at the start of the program. Perhaps she had moved somewhere else, maybe to take photos. *You'd better have a good excuse, madam, and those photos had better be good!*

But the one thing which excited me above all else, and almost made me miss my cue, was seeing my closest friend and "pseudo" sister, Ally and her husband, Briece Mochrie, in the front row of the audience! "*See you later,*" Ally mouthed to me, grinning and nudging Brie.

When I reached the dressing rooms after the concert, Tia and her friend, Rose, arrived at my door first, quivering with excitement. 'So you enjoyed the music?' I asked, as they squeezed into the double seat beside my make-up bench. I placed the huge sheaf of flowers with which I was presented, on a side table, carefully moving the bouquet from Mum and John so it didn't get swamped.

'Ooh yes, and you looked *awesome*!' They ran their hands over the petals of the gladiolas. 'What're you going to do with these?'

'Take them home with me and thank you, Tia, the dress did the trick didn't it?'

I glanced down at my dress, admiring the glitter which looked as expensive as it was, even in the neon light in the dressing room. Just then, someone knocked. Excited gasps alerted me to the fact that Rezanov had arrived. It was with great pleasure that I trapped him long enough to introduce the girls. To his credit, he was charming and patient with their exuberance, wishing Tia a happy birthday. Beaming, they got his autograph and left with promises from me to visit the shop at my earliest convenience.

We looked at each other steadily for a long moment. *God, the man was a work of art.* 'Pam, you were superb tonight. I'm very impressed!' Then he spoiled the moment with an impatient glance at his watch. 'They're waiting for us in the foyer. Better get going.' I spun the chair around and scuffled for my gorgeous, licentious shoes. His eyes widened. I hoped they sent a lying message that there was someone available to appreciate them in private.

He led the way out of the room, holding the door back for me and marched along to the lift where he leaned against the wall, arms folded defensively over his cummerbund, pouting in glorious splendour. A cloud of Rezanov groupies would undoubtedly be awaiting their prey in the main foyer. The large group of musicians waiting before us engaged me in conversation, glancing somewhat nervously at Himself. Unable to join the crush in the lift, I stood back to wait until it returned. I tried smiling at my companion. Receiving no response, I stuck my tongue out at him. A tiny smile twitched fleetingly at the corner of his sublime mouth.

'Oh come on, Rezanov. It would be worse if *no one* bothered to wait for you, wouldn't it? Then you'd have something to *really* pout about.'

He glared at me. 'You love this, don't you? The applause...the...' words appeared to fail him.

'Of course I do. If it weren't for these people I wouldn't have a career and neither would you, mate!'

He was silent for a moment then snapped, 'Are you dating that idiot?'

'Which idiot are you talking about? Is there another one in the building besides yourself?'

'Seymour.'

'Is he an idiot per se, or have you got it in for him because he called your bluff when you threw a tantie this morning?'

He had the good grace to look sheepish and a tinge of red darkened his gorgeous face. 'Ah, no, of course not. *Are* you going out with him?'

'I'll go out with him if he asks me. Not that it's any of your business!' The lift doors slid open and we stepped in. I leaned against the back wall, concentrating on the level numbers – as you do.

'Is what Seymour said about you true?'

'What do you mean?'

'That you could have taken my place in the concert tonight?'

I didn't want to admit just how long ago it was since I'd chosen the flute professionally instead of the piano and that now I only accompanied other musicians or played for fun. 'Well, I *have* given a few piano recitals, but I've heard Seymour himself could have played the concert if he wanted. He plays with an ensemble from time to time.'

He stared into my face for what felt like forever, then grunted and broke eye contact. I thought I saw a smidgeon of relief on his face. Hiding a smile, I stepped ahead of him into the foyer to the applause of what seemed like hundreds of people. Within seconds we were swamped by well-wishers anxious to discuss the performance and obtain autographs.

Ally and Brie arrived at my side and we hugged until our breath left us. Ally was so excited that her words tumbled over each other. They congratulated me and Ally screamed enthusiastically over my dress. Brie rolled his eyes when his wife chortled over my shoes. 'You were wonderful, Pammy! You're still coming to supper in the city after this aren't you? We've been looking forward to it.'

'Yes, of course, I've been looking forward to it too. When did you get here? And why didn't you tell me you were coming to *this* concert?'

'We didn't want to spoil the surprise, Pammy darling.'

'Where's the brats?' I asked referring to their over-active two year old twin sons.

'Oh, Brie's parents have them for the night!'

I thought about that for a moment. Ally and Brie's identical twins are reminiscent of Kipling's Bandarlog – much given to pelting each other with fruit and falling to fighting amongst themselves. Ally's eyes twinkled. She knew me too well. 'Don't worry, Lara's there too. We'll wait for you to finish up here and take you in with us.'

I laughed. Brie's sister is more than a match for the boys. 'I have Goldie's car tonight. I'll just ask her if she wants to come as well,' I said, casting my eyes around the room.

With a cheery wave, the two of them vanished to the bar. Signing what appeared to be the last of hundreds of programs, I was still looking for my cousin, when Goldie materialised at my side. 'Pammy, I'm so sorry I wasn't there. Harry had to leave at the beginning because they found a body in West End in the park near your place. I went with him. Will you forgive me?' *Harry?*

A tiny intake of breath nearby alerted me to something not quite right, but Goldie touched me on the arm to keep my attention and continued. 'A young girl. Harry Brown, my mate on the Courier Mail, got the heads-up from one of the cops that they think she might have been *crushed* to death.' Horror lurked in her eyes, but I knew that Goldie, ever the reporter, couldn't have resisted going with him.

'I hope they find out who did it. Her poor family.' We shared a moment of sorrow, before I was distracted.

'Pam, can you come with me, please? The directors want a photo with you and Vlad.' Bill Seymour was suddenly standing beside me, looking from Goldie to me in confusion. I hastened to introduce them. He was very gracious, but he led me away before I could say anything more.

The directors and sponsors stood with their Gucci-clad, bejewelled wives in the centre of the foyer, beaming with triumph and alcohol-fuelled good will. Rezanov, who had also been rounded up, was standing beside the young conductor, Lance MacPherson; both looked about to bolt. Their eyes latched onto my waist as Bill gently guided me toward them. Rezanov snorted and glared at us; Lance glanced at him thoughtfully and then back at me. The Russian opened his mouth, but thankfully, before trouble could break out, the directors were upon us and we were shunted into position for the official photo, which would no doubt appear in the Sunday paper supplement.

I couldn't wait to get away from the fuss, so when Goldie rushed up to me and said she was off home – she would catch up with Ally and Brie tomorrow – and would catch a taxi I was relieved. Now I could leave too. She was gone before I could suggest she take her car; I would get Ally and Brie to take me back to the house after supper.

Autograph hunters and members of the orchestra distracted me. When I finally came up for air, Rezanov, Seymour and Macpherson had left, presumably womanising in the city.

CHAPTER 12

Dingo

Unravelling

Saturday, 11pm

It was the photographer! He looked closely at the beautiful woman talking to the flautist, a great lump of ice forming in his chest, travelling into his belly. Had she recognised *him*? No, all her attention had been on Pamela Miller. They looked like sisters – perhaps they were. Whatever, Pamela obviously knew the woman well and now he had that to worry about too. Long schooled at hiding his feelings, he kept his expression under control, but before he had decided what to do, she headed for the front doors of the complex. Goldie was her name; at least he'd gotten that much information.

Sliding through the crowd, Dingo hurried after her, trying not to look as though he was in pursuit. What if she had a car? *Out of my way, you old bags!* Restraining the urge to push a gossiping pair of matrons aside, he dashed down the steps after her. *Must keep back, she'll see me.*

That the woman might have downloaded the photos of the park didn't occur to him; all he could think about was how he could get the camera. He realised that he was getting too close, but just as he was about to let her get ahead, she hailed a taxi. Thinking quickly, he held his program up, angled so that the streetlight fell across it, as though trying to read the print.

Her words came clearly through the night. '13A Geroge.' With that, she climbed into the cab and was gone. He couldn't believe it. On the one hand, he'd lodged in Geroge Street as a student. It wasn't far from the hotel and about two kilometres from where Ariel lived – *had lived*. On the other, it was *number thirteen*. Terror swept through him. How could he possibly... *tennineeightseven*...he had to take hold of himself, regardless of the number. It was just a number, right?

Adrenalin pumped through his veins. He saw a bus coming toward him. From living in the area previously as a student, he knew that route would take him to the bottom end of the suburb. He whipped his bow tie off and stuffed it in his pocket, undid the top two buttons of his shirt and ruffled his hair. At least he looked as though he'd been out for the night, perhaps to dinner or the pub.

There were only two people on the bus, but he kept his head down, ostensibly reading the program in his hand. The bus driver had been talking to someone outside the window as he got on and hadn't even seen him use his Go Card. He had to talk his way into the photographer's home and get that camera.

In spite of his compulsive obsessive disorder – or because of it – Dingo was able to compartmentalise his thoughts. He was proud of that. Ariel, as per his therapist's instructions on how to handle problems, was now neatly packaged into a box he called "Grief," to be dealt with if or when it arose again. The foremost box which required attention was the matter of the photos, which would put him with Ariel just before she...got into her box.

Murderers always return to the scene of the crime, he'd read somewhere, but he had no urge to do so. Right then, his concentration was on keeping control of himself and of the situation. *As long as there was an even number of everything in his immediate surroundings, he could cope.* He put his head down and walked as fast as he dared, careful not to attract attention.

Ten minutes later, he stopped a short way from the photographer's two-storey, 'tarted-up' workman's cottage. The street light was out, but he could see the chocolate-box-pretty building very well. Standing in the shadow of a tall shrub on the footpath beside the front gate, he thought about how to tackle his mission. Go straight up and ring the front door bell? Maybe wait until the lights went out and then break in. Did she have a pet? That could be a problem. He didn't know what to do about a dog, because he couldn't bear to hurt one.

Disheartened, Dingo found himself counting to keep his courage up. He'd got to two hundred when all but one of lights went out downstairs, and after a moment or two, the upstairs light went on. He craned his head and checked the height of the balcony against the brick wall on the right hand side. Yes, it was doable, but she needed to settle down first. His heart quailed at the idea of scrambling up the fence and climbing onto the roof. There had to be another way.

He slithered closer and peered along the garden fence, noting there was no gate into the back yard, only straight pathway all the way. A woman's voice nearby startled him. Heart pounding, he shrank back into the shadows, fingering the tiny penlight in his pocket. *Always be prepared, my darling...* He squeezed the barrel of the torch. *Shut up* you old bag.

The voice faded and he realised it was coming from the block of units to the left of the cottage. A light in the downstairs unit went out and silence fell. Could he introduce himself as friend of Pam? Or perhaps as a member of the Pacific Orchestra who wanted to catch up with Pam? No, that wouldn't work. What if she phoned Pam to ask...maybe the best way was just to walk up to the door and enquire if someone else lived there. Perhaps she'd ask him in? No, she wouldn't invite a stranger inside her house at this hour. Then he had an idea. He walked swiftly to the front gate of the units to where rows of letterboxes lined the wall. Cupping his hand over the beam, he shone the tiny light onto the names: Henderson, Wright, Meadows, Matthews – any one of those would do.

He looked up and down the street; no one in sight. Both buildings on either side of the cottage were in darkness and there was no sight or sound of dogs. He was pretty sure that if Goldie had a dog she would have let it out before closing up for the night. Right, Plan B – knock on the door. He placed his hand on the front gate and his heart almost leapt out of his chest. *Number13!*

What to do what to do...? Dingo stepped back and fled behind the shrub. Had to be even or something terrible would happen! And *thirteen* as well...he squatted in the shadows and tried to calm himself. *Surely, he couldn't be so unlucky.* When he felt able, he crept back to the gate. *Number 13A!* Where was 13B? He moved along the footpath keeping to the grass so that his shoes made no sound on the pavement. As he reached the boundary of 13A, a sigh of relief escaped him. Goldie's cottage and the one next to it shared a driveway, so logic would have to indicate that it would be 13B – and twice thirteen was twenty-six! An even number; he was safe. It was okay to proceed.

He hurried back to the front gate and stepped inside the fence. There was a light on in the downstairs front room; the curtains were slightly ajar. He moved to the window and peered in. It was a comfortable room, with what appeared to be a luxurious three-seater lounge, a fireplace over which was the shadowy portrait of a man. A large screen TV stood across the corner near a glass-fronted cabinet full of china. A serving hatch opened into the dark room beyond, perhaps a kitchen or dining room.

His gaze alighted on a table at the far end of the room. A vase of flowers stood to one side and in the middle, a *camera*. He didn't know anything about them, but this one looked very professional; a bag and tripod lay beside the instrument. Quivering with fear and excitement, he watched as the woman came into the room and froze, barely breathing as she gathered up the camera, folded the portable tripod and packed them both into the bag. A swift glance around and she went to a side table and dimmed the table lamp, gathered up the bag and left the room, closing the door after her. Realising she was heading for the stairs, Dingo leapt to the door and knocked.

He sensed her surprise and indecision. 'Who is it?'

He cleared his throat and held his hand up to his mouth to muffle his voice. 'It's Kevin Matthews from the block of units next door. There's been a prowler and I need to speak to you!'

He stood slightly to the side of the door, so she would be forced to come across the threshold. There was a long pause before the latch was unfastened and Goldie came forward to greet her neighbour.

Her eyes widened. 'You're –' *Oh yes, she recognised him!*

Dingo slapped his hand over her mouth with one hand, grabbed her by the neck with the other and propelled her back into the house, kicking the door shut. The bag thumped to the floor behind her.

'I won't hurt you if you keep still!' he hissed. She writhed and lashed at him with her feet. It was like holding a wildcat. He yelped as her teeth clamped onto his finger. Incandescent, all consuming fury exploded in his brain.

All he wanted was the camera!

Give. It. To. Me.

Her strength startled him. Her body swung independently of his hands, her arms flailing as she tried to reach his face. He overbalanced and they fell to the floor, bouncing off the newel post as they went down. Filled with fear and rage, he tightened his hold on her neck with one hand and squeezed her face between the fingers of his other...*tighter... tighter.*

They rolled across the floor one way, then the other. His back slammed into the bottom of the stairs. He scrambled to his knees, dragging her up with him, still holding her head in his hands.

Then, like a bird dashed against a window, a crack of bone under his hand and her head rolled to the side. Her legs stopped threshing, her arms fell, her face slackened beneath his fingers.

He loosened his hold.

She folded to the floor.

Relieved of her weight, Dingo lurched against the wall and then slid to the floor. Propped up by the wall, lungs heaving, he stared at the woman. She couldn't be – *no, it was impossible*! Not twice in one day! His vision went dim. Bile rose in his throat. Automatically closing his senses against the stench which suddenly enveloped the hallway, he levered himself up the wall, staggering as he found his feet and sat on the bottom step, shaking with fear and distress. His finger stung where her teeth had clamped down. He fished in his pocket, pulled out his handkerchief, wrapped it around the wounds and gently cradled the digit, before inspecting the damage. A little blood oozed up. He wrapped it carefully in the handkerchief and tied it firmly.

He found himself trying to count his heartbeats, trying to slow down, to get control of the panic bubbling inside. *How had it come to this?* He knew, oh yes he knew, had known since he was eight years old that one day his life would come full circle – for hadn't mother told him so? And Mother was always right.

Okay, deep breaths...slowly, take a deep breath...

He looked around, trying to avoid the body on the floor. There it was. He stood up, supporting himself on the new post for a moment, then regaining his balance, stepped around the body. Trying to protect his wounded finger, he struggled with the zipper, opened the bag and checked that the camera was there. *It was.*

Dingo put it down and looked into the lounge room. A pile of material lay folded on a chair just inside the door. Had he touched anything? He didn't think so, but then remembered bracing himself against the wall when he stood up. He stepped into the room and leaned forward. It looked like a table cloth. He picked it up and walked unsteadily into the kitchen behind the dining area. An infinitesimal moment of self preservation reminded him to put the cloth over his hand before turning on the tap to wet a section of the cloth and then to wrap the other end of the cloth around the bottle of washing up liquid before squeezing it onto the wet part.

He wiped everywhere – a great swathe of the wall, newel post and banister and stairs – that he could remember touching. When he'd finished, he folded the cloth along the original lines and tucked it under his arm. Camera bag in hand, he stared down at his victim, tears welling in his eyes. *I didn't mean it, but you shouldn't have fought me...*

Holding the front section of his jacket over the knob, he quietly closed the front door and looked up and down the street. Something moved on the fence! He froze and then relaxed as a cat dropped onto the footpath and went in the direction of the park. Nothing else stirred – no cars, no couples walking, not even the sound of a TV coming from the block of units or from the house next door. Sirens wailed in the distance, then faded. Nothing to do with him; already he had boxed Ariel into the past. *No, nothing to do with him...*

He walked down the path with the strap of the camera bag over his shoulder, the material tucked inside his jacket, on through the gate and started back in the direction of the hotel, touching every second fence post as he went.

CHAPTER 13

Pamela

A Shocking Discovery

Sunday, 12.35am

Brie and Ally wanted to follow me back to Goldie's place, but I managed to persuade them that I'm a big girl and don't need protection. Ally teased me about Bill Seymour during the evening but I managed to side-track her. Charming and comfortable, I couldn't see myself in any type of relationship with Bill, though the look in his eyes indicated that he *liked* me. Now, if it was Rezanov...*oh no, I'm joining the group troop!* How could I be so stupid?

We had a great evening discussing everything musical and many things not. My friends perform together as a "husband and wife" duo, travelling across Europe and the USA most of the year round. 'How did you manage when the twins were born?' I asked Ally. The problem was of course, that if you stayed out of the limelight for too long, you could lose your career. Would I ever have that "pleasure"? As things were going with my love life – *not* – I doubted I would have to worry about it.

Ally laughed. 'Oh we had it all sorted. The twins stayed with Mum and Dad for short hops and we had a nanny for the long hauls. How's Aunt Ros?' I filled them in on the latest news, causing Ally to worry when she heard about mum's operation. She announced that she would be in to the hospital to see mum as soon as the staff would let her.

They waited at the parking station until I had gotten safely into Goldie's car and onto the road before waving me off.

Around me, late night revellers were heading out clubbing or, in the case of the more mature such as myself, trundling homeward. Deciding to take a shortcut along the river road past the park, I turned right and then left into the narrow road by the river. As there were only a few houses along there and it was not a general thoroughfare, I was surprised to see flashing lights and a barrier across the road. As I neared, there were police cars and under the trees in the park, bright lights.

A yellow and silver-jacketed figure held up his hand for me to stop, whereupon he peered into my window. 'Do you live down this street, madam?'

'No, I'm staying at Hill End – Geroge Street. What's happened?'

'Have you a specific reason to be in this area, madam?'

'No, I just thought I'd avoid the traffic and take a shortcut home.'

He said that an incident had occurred and the road was closed to all traffic, except the people who lived there. He moved in front of the car and took down the numberplate. 'Can I have your name, please?'

Worried now, and although he hadn't asked for it, I handed over my licence, which was duly scrutinised –

is that a reflex action for cops? – explaining that I was staying with my cousin and using her car.

'I'm sorry Ms. Miller, you'll have to turn back.'

Sighing, I turned the car and headed past another couple of carloads who'd pulled up behind me. Speculating on a probable accident, I turned down the main street toward Goldie's house. The success of the major concert of my tour, coupled with the excitement of being back in Brisbane seeing my family, was taking its toll; I was looking forward to a hot shower and bed.

Ever thoughtful, Goldie had left the downstairs light on for me. I decided to leave the borrowed Nikon 2 in the boot of her car for the time being. It would be safe there and wouldn't be forgotten when I left for Emsberg the next day. I got out and gathered up the bag with my gorgeous dress and my flute case which I placed outside the garage on the pathway. Tempted to leave the flowers in the back seat until morning, I realised they'd wilt overnight,. I heaved out the huge bouquets of flowers and dumped them beside the cases, locked the car and pulled down the roller door. Two trips to the house would do it.

There was no sign of life as I crunched my way up to the front door. I set my bag and music case down on the verandah, then fossicked around for the front door key, but when it turned in the lock, I realised that the door was *unlocked*. Puzzled, I turned the key back and re-opened it.

The stench hit me as I swung the door back. Something large sprawled across the floor at the foot of the stairs just inside the vestibule. I reeled back, heart pounding and squinted into the dim light from the lounge-room to see Goldie, arms flung out, face turned to the side, knees drawn up almost to her chest. Terrified, I dumped my bags on the floor, fumbled for the switch and stood blinking in the light.

My cousin's vacant eyes stared through me. *No. Oh no!* There was no pulse in her wrist, but maybe, just maybe, I was mistaken. I pressed shaking fingers on the base of her throat looking against all hope for movement. Goldie might be alive... her skin was still quite warm. I looked at her chest, but couldn't see any sign of movement. My panicked breathing sounded loud in the silence. Straightening up, my gaze shot around the hall, up the stairs and into the lounge. *Was there anyone else in the house?*

Terrified, I fumbled for my mobile and stabbed 000 with shaking hands.

'What is your emergency?'

'Ambulance, please – *hurry!*' The words stumbled over each as I tried to give the address and tell her that my cousin had fallen down the stairs. Maybe she was only knocked out. *Please, God.*

'Is there anyone else there with you?'

'No, I just came in and found her lying at the bottom of the stairs.'

'All right, try to stay calm and the ambulance will be with you in a couple of minutes.'

There was something I needed to say, but I couldn't remember what it was. My hands trembled so badly that I could barely turn my phone off. Goldie was meticulous about locking the front door and putting the chain on. Had she been coming down the stairs on her way to do just that and slipped? *Hang on, Goldie. Please, please don't be dead.*

Help was on the way. I sank to the floor and leaned against the wall beside the front door. A gust of wind swirled into the house, sending chills ramping up my back. My teeth chattered; my hands felt like lumps of ice.

Suddenly, the road at the front of the house was filled with action. The ambulance arrived, sirens wailing, at the front gate. Two paramedics jumped out and ran around the back to emerge carrying bags of equipment, sweeping past me. They entered the house and sprang into action. Rigid with horror, I stood in the doorway, hanging onto the frame.

'Could you wait outside please?' one asked, as they bent over Goldie.

I grabbed my handbag and cases and staggered out onto the verandah. Pain so fierce that I felt physically sick, welled inside me. Did she slip? Was she...no. No, she couldn't be...*dead*.

It was only a couple of minutes before one of them came to join me, expressed condolences and asked me to stay where I was. They had to call the police to attend a sudden death. I collapsed into a squatter's chair, unable to process the implications of what was happening.

The police arrived in a welter of sirens and glaring lights. Two uniformed officers stepped out and waded through several bystanders who had gathered to rubber-neck. They told them to move back, closed the front gate purposefully and joined me on the verandah. Before they could speak to me, the male paramedic stepped out the front door to meet them and, with a side-long glance and a gesture with his head, invited them into a huddle. Shivers ran through me; I felt sick. *Goldie's dead.*

A wave of shock went through me. How would Fiona handle it? How would *Alex* cope? In spite of his bluff and powerful persona, I had the impression that Fiona was the stronger of the two.

The paramedic went back inside, followed by the two cops who looked at me intently as they passed. A murmur of voices and then the medics both came out carrying their bags which they parked against the wall. The breath left my body. I lurched to my feet. I needed to see Goldie. It just couldn't be real. The young, uniformed cop with a kind manner eased me back into the chair.

'What's happening?' I didn't recognise my own voice.

Behind him, I was dimly aware of the other one talking into his mobile and then going back to the patrol car, from which emerged a steady stream of radio chatter. Lights streamed out of the units and houses nearby showing word had spread; this was just like CSI. *It is CSI.*

Movement along the street revealed spectators, some in coats, pyjamas and slippers joining rugged-up walkers. I ducked my head, feeling vulnerable to the curious stares and whispers.

'Could you give me your name, please Ma'am?'

'Pamela Miller. What happened?'

'We don't know yet how it happened.' The cop pulled over a footstool, one that Parry had given Goldie in their early days of courtship. Painted with fluffy smiling sheep, it said a lot about Parry's sense of humour. The cop sat, pencil poised. 'We'll have to wait for the forensic team. Can you give me your address?'

I just knew there was something he was not telling me, but before I could ask another question, he spoke. 'Ms Miller, take me through what happened. Let's start from the beginning. What's the lady's full name? Is she a relative?'

'Yes. Marigold Jeanette Humphries.' I explained our relationship and that I was staying with Goldie.

'What time did you get home?'

'What happened? Goldie *did* fall down the stairs – *didn't she*?' He didn't answer.

'There's something terribly wrong, isn't there?'

He hesitated a moment then told me that it appeared that Goldie's death was suspicious. Shock ripped through me. '*What? How?*'

'There are signs that she may not have met with an accident, Ms Miller.' His sympathetic concern nearly sent me screaming, but I could see he wasn't going to give me any more information.

'Now, again, Ms Miller. What time did you get home from the city?'

I had to think again before I could give him an estimate of the time I got back from town and then force my scrambled memory to remember my actions leading up to the moment I called Triple 0.

'Are you sure the door *was* unlocked?' Behind him, his partner was tying yellow plastic tape to the low fence separating the front garden from the driveway. It stretched across the driveway, up to the house where he hitched it around a downpipe, effectively blocking access to the house.

Focus. I switched my gaze back to the cop in front of me. 'Yes, when I turned the key the door locked, so I had to undo it to get in.' *I'm not making any sense.*

'At what time did Ms Humphries normally close up at night?'

'As far as I know she always locked up immediately she got in after dark. If it wasn't dark, she left the doors open to let a breeze through. In summer that is,' I added, realising just how chilly the night air was becoming. Autumn had arrived.

'Did you see anyone walking along the footpath or on the street when you arrived?'

I thought for a moment. 'No, but I wasn't looking around. I just wanted to get ho – here.' I dashed tears away with the back of my hand.

'Do you know what time she might have arrived home tonight?'

'Yes, I do. She went to a call out during my concert and came back just as it was finishing. She caught a cab home just after ten o'clock. I don't know what company.' He looked puzzled, so I quickly explained why we were at the Concert Hall.

'All right, someone will be here shortly to take a detailed statement. Does Ms Humphries, have family in Brisbane?

'Her parents live a couple of streets away...I don't know how I'm going to tell them!' Tears welled.

He looked concerned. 'We'll tell them. Has she got a pet? A dog?'

'No, she's away too much.'

'Okay. Will you be all right sitting here? I need to talk to the paramedics.'

'Yes. Don't worry about me. I'll be okay.'

Mind-numbing cold settled into my bones. I guess shock played a part because I couldn't think coherently, let alone process grief. Visions of Goldie tumbling down the stairs kept running through my mind. The cop had said it was a suspicious death. Had someone pushed her? Why? Then I remembered reading that the police are always called to a sudden death...but *murder? Had there been someone else there with Goldie?* She hadn't left the Concert Hall with anyone that I remembered. Harry what's-his-name? I didn't see him after the concert. Could he have been waiting for her? My mind whirled with confusion and shock.

Police cars and a big van arriving stirred me out from my fog. People were donning the familiar, hooded blue jump suits and booties beloved of crime shows and as seen on the night-time news. Others sealed off the yard and the street, across which they put a roadblock. My mind jumped back to the scene along the river earlier. It looked alarmingly akin to the one here. I dragged the squatter's chair further along the verandah and slumped into it.

Two men walked purposefully up the steps and went inside. It wasn't long before one of them – a short, portly man – came out. 'Ms Miller, is it?' He didn't wait for me to answer, but laid his hand on my arm and patted it gently. That led to a flood of tears which reduced me to a complete wreck. He vanished and the next, an incredibly tall, well-built man stepped into my line of vision.

The light picked up his high-cheek-boned features, glittered off his slanted eyes, highlighting his jaw-line. Dressed all in 'assassin' black, he oozed authority. His eyes travelled from one end of me to the other. Then the uniformed cop who had taken my particulars diverted his attention. I slumped back into the chair as though unhooked from a wall. My heart ached. Goldie, my cousin, my sister...my eyes closed from sheer exhaustion...

'Ms Miller? *Ms Miller!*'

A dark chocolate voice slammed me into the present. How could I nod off after the horror of what had happened?

'Detective Senior Sergeant Anthony Hamilton, Ms Miller.' His eyes glittered in the half light. Something warm stirred deep inside me. 'I'd like you to take me through exactly what occurred from the moment you arrived.'

'I've already told *him* everything.' I looked nervously at the uniformed officer standing in the doorway.

'Yes, but *I'd* like to hear it from you now.' His tone was uncompromising.

Sighing inwardly, I recounted the events after my arrival at the house. He turned to his side-kick, whom I hadn't seen come out of the house and gave him a look of enquiry. The colleague nodded; Hamilton's expression folded into Easter Island statue mode. 'Where did you go after the concert?'

I told him about my supper with Ally and Brie, how long we'd been in the restaurant and that we'd taken our own cars home. 'I got here about...half an hour...I don't know, maybe more now I think. I can't remember.' Tears welled up again and spilled down my cheeks. Fumbling for a tissue, I realised I couldn't find my handbag.

The detective reached under the chair, his huge hand brushing my leg. I jumped. He ignored my reaction and dragged my bag out by the strap. 'This what you're looking for?'

I nodded gratefully and rummaged around for the wad of tissues which habitually infested my bag. "What happened to Goldie?' I was determined that this time there would be a straight answer.

'Ms Miller, it appears that someone may have been here with Ms Humphries, because we don't think she *fell* down the stairs. Forensics will be able to confirm the cause of death.'

'You mean, she was murdered?' My voice came out harsh and grim. *Not again...*

I must have spoken, because the detective pounced on it. 'What do you mean, "Not again," Ms Miller?' Piercing blue eyes examined me like a specimen in a lab. My skin flushed hot, my heart pounded. Of all the times to be attracted to a man – a cop for God's sake – and Goldie's *dead?* Guilt crawled deep inside.

'Ms Miller, what do you mean, *again?*'

I snapped back to attention and slowly recounted the details of Jess's death just over four years ago. The cop took the particulars down in his notebook, looking at me from time to time as though to assess whether I was telling the truth. I wasn't responsible for any part of what had happened then or now, but Hamilton's expression tended to indicate he thought otherwise.

'So was Ms Humphries with anyone tonight that you know of?'

Hardly daring to ask in case there was another body in there, my lips formed the words without any help. 'Is Harry here too?' *Don't tell me Harry's upstairs...is he dead too?* My heart pounded. Please God, no more...

The cop's nose quivered like a gun dog. 'Who's Harry?'

'I don't know his surname, but he's a reporter from the Courier Mail. Goldie went with him to another police callout earlier, but I thought she left the concert hall on her own. You mean it might be a robbery gone wrong?'

'We need to establish if the victim brought someone home with her.' He looked at me sternly, as though I should know who and what. All I could think about was what had happened to Goldie. Had she been strangled? My legs started to shake.

'Now I have to ask you some questions about tonight...are you all right?' His eyes bored into my face.

'Yes, I'm okay.' *No I'm not and it's bloody cold...*

The interrogation began: *Who was Marigold Humphries? How old was she? Was she married? What did she do for a living? Did Goldie and I get on well? Had we had an argument? How much did I know of her private life? Did she have a boyfriend, when did I last see her and what were our plans for the night?*

Answering was like mentally wading through treacle, but I forced my mind to focus. Despite the chill in the air, perspiration broke out under my arms and trickled down my ribs, soaking my cammie top. Hearing my teeth chattering, the assassin enquired whether I had a coat in my bag. I shook my head. 'Can someone get a coat from my room upstairs?'

'Sorry, Ms Miller. The house is a crime scene.'

'There's an old duffle coat in the garage, hanging on a hook on the left side just inside the door. Could someone get that for me, *please*? Here's the key to the roller door.'

He despatched a passing uniformed constable to fetch the coat, which I gratefully slipped on, trying not to react to "eau de mouse," watched closely by the detective. Did he think I had a weapon in the pocket? *I'll just bet that cop checked it before he gave it to me.*

Was I a suspect? *Surely not!* My mind squirreled frantically around the hours leading up to my return home. I could prove where I was; Ally and Brie had been with me every moment. Goldie's flesh had been warm to touch. She must have died just before I arrived home...*surely the police didn't think I came back and fought with her after I left the city?* Goosebumps broke out on my arms.

The cop who'd fetched the coat said something to the detective, who turned to stare at me. 'Why are two bunches of flowers lying beside the roller door?'

The flowers! 'They gave them to me at the concert hall. I was going to go back for them after I...' Words failed me. The flowers were the least of my worries. The two cops spoke for a moment and then the uniformed one left. The assassin moved to the front door, where he stood watching the forensic investigators as they went about their business.

Murmuring to each other, the blue-clad scientists moved slowly on their booteed feet, stooping, crouching, collecting seemingly invisible specimens and popping them into what I knew from CSI, had to be test tubes. The bright lights dazzled me; someone was taking photographs of the scene. Like a crumpled piece of material flung on the floor, my cousin's body lay, obscenely distorted in death.

The lights shone onto the verandah and out into the street, trapping greedy spectators in their beam. Some shied away, some vanished and a few avidly contributed what I assume were their less than humble opinions to the uniformed cops moving among them. At the front door, a constable had taken up residence, muffled in a parka, taking the names of those who came and went.

The night air grew colder. I pulled the heavy coat tightly around me, wrapping my arms across my torso. Just as I was thinking that I would be there all night and wondering when they would tell Aunt Fiona and Uncle Alex, the crowd at the front fence turned to watch a slender, attractive woman dressed in a heavy coat, her hair in a long plait, duck under the checked tape and walk into the driveway. She stepped onto the verandah.

Before I could stop myself, I leaped to my feet and lurched forward.

CHAPTER 14

Detective Inspector Susan Prescott

Not Again?

Sunday, 1.15am

Pamela Miller towered over me. As I held her I could feel her muscles shaking deep inside. I gently coaxed her back into the squatter's chair – well, dropped her into it would be a better description. I signed in with the constable and then poked my head through the front door to take a lightning inventory of the action before sitting on a nearby stool to talk to Pam.

Voice trembling so badly that sometimes she had to stop, she told what had happened. I allowed her to ramble a little. Sometimes you can pick up a lot of what someone tells you without realising what they're saying.

As she talked, I became aware that this death was going to explode into the media. Even *I* had heard of Marigold Humphries, celebrity photo-journalist shot and wounded overseas in a war zone, whose articles, interviews and image had appeared in everything from The Australian Women's Weekly to Time magazine. She'd even been interviewed on Oprah Winfrey's show. I wasn't aware she was Pam's cousin, but now I knew the connection their physical similarity became obvious.

I wondered if *Pam* had been the target of what I'd been advised was murder, but knew that Humphries was the more likely of the two, having made enemies in many walks of life – politicians, bankers – definitely animal poachers and abusers. Had one of them tracked her down and done the deed? It wasn't rocket science. Someone had either come back with her, broken in or she'd opened the door to him – or her. From the quick glance I'd had at the victim, the woman had been as tall as Pam, but more muscular. It would've taken a powerful man *or* woman to get the better of her.

As Pam finished speaking, Anthony Hamilton came up to us and suggested that she might go with an officer to tell Marigold Humphries parents what had happened. Pam turned even paler. Seeing the exhaustion in her face, I made an instant decision. 'Anthony, you can take Pam to the Humphries' place and you don't have to bring her back tonight.' "And break the news to the Humphries" went without saying.

I turned to Pam who was snuffling into a handful of tissues. 'We can't let you take anything from the house, I'm sorry. This is a crime scene now, the whole property including the garage, so you'll have to make do. You can stay with your aunt and uncle for tonight? You could be of help to them.'

'I've nowhere else to go right now. My unit's not going to be ready until tomorrow and Mum's got her big operation on Monday. Do you think we can keep this from her until after that's over?'

'I doubt it, but talk to John and see what he thinks. I saw Ros this morning – yesterday morning.'

'You saw mum? How was she?'

'Very tired and longing to get it over with.'

'I have a feeling she's got more of a battle to overcome than she's letting on. John obviously knows but he's not telling,' Pam replied, her posture one of defeat.

Anthony looked from one to the other of us. I felt like telling him to wipe the surprise off his face and that I *do* have friends who are not cops. He hesitated for a moment and then reached for Pam's arm to help her up. She fumbled around for her flute case and bags, but he scooped them up and waited patiently for her to move. She walked a couple of steps and then turned back to me. 'I know this sounds silly, but when they open the garage in the morning can they go slowly?' A sheepish expression passed across her face. 'There's a little possum lives in the roller door. Goldie made a pet of it and she asked me to be careful.' Her face crumpled.

'I'll tell them, don't worry and I'll try and talk to you tomorrow. We'll need you to give a formal statement and come back here when Forensics have finished and see if there's anything missing. We'll have to ask Ms Humphries' parents to have a look as well.'

Pam wiped her eyes, smiled briefly, said good-bye and followed Anthony Hamilton out to the police car. I didn't envy him. If there's one thing a cop hates most it's telling a deceased's family that a loved one has died. Car accidents are awful, but murder beats everything. I hoped Marigold Humphries wasn't an only child.

Turning back to the crime scene, I requested kit and suited up from top to toe, after which I edged into the hallway, trying not to get in the way. Traditional floral sofa covers, plain curtains and mock Queen Ann furniture gave the lounge room a "cottage" feel, as did the fireplace, complete with granite surround and mantelpiece bearing family photos.

I checked them out: Pam and Marigold, arms wrapped around each other, Pam with Ally Carpenter and now deceased Jessica Rallison, a much younger Ros and a woman who was obviously her sister. Would that be Fiona Humphries? I must have met her at Ros and John's wedding but couldn't remember her. David and I were standing in the back row of their wedding photo. Eloise and James had come home from the UK for the occasion. Pam and my niece, Ally Mochrie, were dressed in bridesmaids gear but no sign of Marigold Humphries. Perhaps she had been overseas at the time. A veritable gallery of smiling faces lined the back of the mantelpiece, but apart from Humphries, none was recognisable.

The portrait above the fireplace invited attention. Parry, 1976 -2009. Obviously the man in the painting meant a great deal to Marigold – Goldie – Humphries. *Please God, look after her... and let them meet up.* I wouldn't admit to anyone but David that when I attended a death I always said a quick prayer. My team would probably think I've lost my marbles and invest too much emotion in the case. As for the boss, DS Petersen, his take on it didn't bear thinking about.

The forensics team worked methodically in the background. They would let me know what I needed soon enough. As though he had heard my thoughts, Lynch came up behind me. 'Well, Susan, no rest for the wicked, eh?' He grinned and then launched into a preliminary report. 'Caucasian female, late twenties to early thirties, in good health. Body temperature relatively warm, so she's been dead for only an hour or two. Broken neck and bruises on her throat indicate strangulation, bruising to her legs and scrape marks on the wall. Fully clothed and doesn't look as though there's been sexual assault, but we'll know more when we do the autopsy. It's obvious that the wall has been washed down as well as the bottom four stairs, the posts and railings. Because he – or she – knew enough to do that, then no doubt the doorknobs and any other places the perpetrator touched have been cleaned as well, unfortunately for our friends in Fingerprints.'

Who could she have annoyed enough to actually want to kill her? What was he or she after? Lynch hadn't finished. 'The person who did this was very strong indeed. Her larynx was completely crushed and the hyoid bone snapped. She was no shrinking violet herself and there are indications that she worked out regularly. She would have put up quite a fight.' He ran his hand over his head, blinking. The second of his callouts in one night; his whole team must be stuffed.

So, two deaths in twenty-four hours within a couple of kilometres of each other...*I don't like it*. We made eye-contact, in perfect accord. He nodded and returned to his work. My team had gone upstairs, but so far there had been no indication that they had found anything significant. I tapped out a number on my mobile. 'Any sign of disturbance up there?'

'No, ma-am. Everything's normal as far as we can see so far. Pamela Miller was staying in the guest room. Her bags are here, but no sign of anyone searching. Nothing obvious in Humphries' either, but we'll bring her laptop and files down when we finish. Perhaps Ms Miller will know if anything's missing.'

The sigh in the officer's voice indicated discouragement. I wasn't surprised. My gut said it was personal; the perp wanted something or had a grudge. We had a lot of ground to cover, but perhaps the parents could help. Much would depend on the answers to the questions we asked of her nearest and dearest. It's always the way – quiz the people who knew her and check out who benefited from Marigold Humphries' will.

I wanted to spend time with Pamela, not convinced that she didn't know what this was about. Oh, of course she probably didn't realise what she knew, but if I put the right questions, she would tell me. I was getting incoherent with tiredness. All I'd had time for after the first call out was a shower, before the phone rang again. No sleep and no prospect of rest any time soon, probably not until tomorrow night at the very least.

I wondered what was happening at the home of Marigold Humphries' parents.

CHAPTER 15

Dingo

Terror Unleashed

Sunday, 1am

Dingo rushed up the back stairs to the second floor. His hands trembled so badly, he struggled to get the key in the lock. The handkerchief wrapped around his finger snagged on the key. Impatiently, he ripped it off ignoring the stinging, then unlocked and pushed the door open. He switched on the light and blundered to the bed, where he tore the camera out of the bag and fumbled for the SD card. The looped wrist strap snagged on his finger bending it back until he swore at the pain. He dropped the camera on the bed, and sucked the slight puncture wounds on his fingers. *Keep calm...two, four, six, eight, ten...*

When the pain had eased, he took a deep breath, picked the camera up again and gently pulled the card. It looked like no SD card he had ever seen. He stepped over to the bedside light and switched it on to inspect the strangely-shaped object. CF...*Compact Flash!* It wouldn't work in his laptop! He'd have to get a card reader...which meant he would have to go out in the morning and buy one. Dick Smith, Myers, there'd be plenty of places he could go. He wanted to slam the thing against the wall. No, it had to work. Nothing else would do.

No matter how hard he wished, the result would be the same. There was no way he could view what was on the card that night. Disbelief sent shivers of fear surging through his body. He *knew* she'd taken his and Ariel's photos. She'd even waved to them as they cavorted across the grass, posing for her, laughing. He plopped onto the bed and sat motionless. *Seven...no...six...no, eight...ten... deep breath...slow your breathing...*

Dingo leaped to his feet and bolted for the en suite where he lost the meagre contents of his stomach. Leaning on the edge of the toilet bowl, he grabbed the toilet paper, pulled a large piece off the roll, spat into the bowl and wiped his mouth. Gripped by inertia, some time passed before he hauled himself upright and staggered to the washbasin. His lower back hurt, and he finally remembered falling back onto the edge of the stair while wrestling with the photographer. He rubbed the sore patch and then stared at himself in the mirror. Glazed eyes, gaunt cheeks, white face, hair lying flat against his head. Turning the cold tap on and cupping his hand underneath the stream, he bent to rinse his mouth out. Grimacing, he squeezed a blob of toothpaste onto his finger, rinsed and spat.

A small bottle standing on the shelf above the basin caught his eye. How long since he'd taken the last dose? Dingo couldn't remember. He shook some tablets into his sweaty palm, threw them into his mouth and chased down them with a swig of water. Minutes later, they came back up. He leaned over the toilet, exhausted and sweating. *Have to get control...a rinse, more teeth cleaning. Deep breaths...deep breaths...two, four, six, eight, ten...*

Scrabbling through the zippered side pocket of his backpack, he found a bandaid and a foil pack of codeine. He carefully plastered his finger, after which he sat on the side of the bed and picked the camera up again. Maybe, just maybe...could she have *pretended* to take photos just to make them happy? Resisting the impulse to smash it on the floor, he shoved it back into the bag. Terror had him in its grip. What if the cops found him and he had the bag in his room? He opened the door at the top of the built-in wardrobe, pushed the bag to the back and closed it. He would dump it in the morning.

Disappointment and fear pitched him into frenzy. Hardly stopping for a sip of water, he kept on the move until the first light of dawn seeped through the window, counting as he paced back and forth, long steps, short steps – *as long as they were even numbers he was safe!* Exhausted, he fell on the bed, just remembering to set the alarm on his watch before he dropped into sleep.

* * *

The day his father died, Dingo lost all hope. A stocky, powerfully-built quiet man, his father, Marcus, was helpless to stem the onslaught of obsessive love with which Frances smothered their son, though he did manage, to a certain extent, to protect the child. Marcus and Dingo were a team. When Frances, worn out with ranting at Dingo to practice his music, fell asleep in front of the afternoon soapies, they would take the opportunity to go fishing in the creek, mend machinery or just go for a walk in the bush with the dogs. When he was three, he would wait out by the house fence, listening for the sounds of sheep being driven to the woolshed. As soon as their plaintive tired cries could be heard he would slither down from the fence post and run to meet his father who would pull him up the side of his stockhorse onto the pommel of the saddle. There he would sit, secure in his father's arms as they followed the mob to the yards.

It was a moot point as to whether Dingo was lucky or not that Frances, a former concert pianist and now music teacher, had realised his ability by the time he was three. An old trumpet was discovered in a trunk in the shearer's quarters and the young boy, intrigued, tried it out. To his own and everyone else's surprise, he'd made a pretty good go of it for his age. From tooting a few notes, he graduated within a few days to picking out simple tunes. Flushed with over-excitement, his mother sprang into action, buying "beginners music." An ancient piano, stored in the back of a shed, was hauled out and the piano tuner summonsed to the property. Before a bewildered Dingo and angry Marcus could marshal any defence, the child's future was set in concrete.

'You'll practice until you drop!' His mother's implacable statement was delivered every day through thin, grim lips. Her eyes narrowed to slits as arguments over Dingo's future raged nightly. A driven woman, denied the successful concert career she had given up to marry a farmer, Frances was determined to have it all through her son. '*He's a genius!*' his mother screamed, '*A prodigy!*'

'He's just a kid who likes to play music. He's too young for you to start making a career for him. He's only three, for Christ's sake!' Marcus' voice took on an unaccustomed edge, but to no avail. The raging went on and on. Many nights, Dingo snuck out of the window in his room, across the verandah and out to the nearest dog kennel where he crawled in beside the occupant who was only too happy to comfort the sobbing child.

Then came that dark morning and the child's world changed forever.

The weather forecasters had it right. The storm hit, bringing down a gum tree onto the garage. The crack of the trunk and shriek of the metal roof as it folded into itself was a sound which haunted the five year-old Dingo's dreams continuing until became an adult. Pieces of wood and tins thrown off the shelves ricocheted off fence posts. His father almost threw him out of the shed, where he fell to the ground, screaming and lay there, his arms wrapped around his head until the terrible sounds faded and the dust stopped swirling around him. He stood up and took a couple of steps toward the ruined garage before running, eyes wide with horror, to the house where he found his mother slamming windows shut.

'Daddy's under the tree!' he screamed, pulling at his mother's skirt.

She swung around and whacked him across the head sending him crashing to the floor. *'Can't you see I'm trying to shut the windows?'*

'Daddy's in the garage!' he yelled again, confused. Wasn't she supposed to run out and look?

His mother swooped down on him, arms flailing and he smelled what he knew was something bad, but at the time didn't realise was alcohol. *'Shut up you little bastard! Can't you see I'm busy?'* She rushed from the room. Dingo ran outside into the storm but was driven back inside the laundry, where he curled under the concrete tubs and sobbed, while the wind whipped sheets of iron from the roof and the garden disappeared forever. What was the point of trying anything more? Mum wouldn't take any notice of him.

From then on, life went downhill for Dingo. It was hours before the storm abated and Frances sobered up enough to realise that her husband was missing and went to look for him. The drama after his father's decapitated body was discovered surpassed anything previously known in the household. His mother alternately punished him for 'not telling her what had happened' and smothered him as her 'fatherless child.'

They moved into town after the tragedy. The horses and other livestock were sold and the sheepdogs were sent to new homes – Marcus' dogs were highly prized for their skill. The cat came with them to the isolated mansion which his mother had purchased with money inherited from her husband, his insurance payout and the sale of the farm. Dingo was grateful for the cat. It became his only companion and his mother actually liked it.

Frances kept up the relentless pressure to keep his music up to standard. She would storm up and down his music room, thumping a stick on the floor to emphasise timing, drowning out the beat of the metronome. She drove her son so hard that he frequently fell asleep over his lessons, home schooling being the method which his agoraphobic mother chose for his education. If Dingo thought life was hard then, it was as nothing compared to what happened after he killed the baby.

CHAPTER 16

Pam

Revelations

Sunday 2.15am

The short drive to Fiona and Alex' house was over before I could work out how to tell them that their only daughter was dead, let alone how it happened. Detective Hamilton was no help, staring grimly ahead with not a word. Just as I was on the verge of panic, we drew up outside the house and he turned to me and touched my hand. 'Are you okay? I can tell them if you like. You've had enough to cope with already.'

The skin on the back of my hand felt as though it had been branded. I could barely speak. 'Thank you, I'd be grateful if you would. I don't know how to face them. Only yesterday we were here, Goldie and I, and we were having...such a lovely time catching up.' Tears poured down my cheeks. *Stop crying, Pam, for God's sake.* A white handkerchief appeared in front of me.

'Do you have a secret supply of these?' I wiped my eyes and went to pass it back, but he held his hand up with a wry smile.

'Yes, my aunts are prolific givers of boxes of them and I actually had one on the back seat. It came yesterday.'

'Was it your birthday? My mother said her aunts always gave her soap and face washers for her birthdays,' I sobbed.

'Er...yes, it was my birthday and yes, most of mine do too.' His lips actually curled up at the corners and just for a moment, the Easter Island statue came to life. Before I could say anything further, he'd opened the car door and got out. In seconds he'd handed me onto the pavement, and I still had no idea of how we were going to handle this.

It took awhile before our knocking brought the sound of footsteps. The front door opened and Alex stood there, hair standing on end, tying the cord of his old green tartan dressing gown. I glanced down; his bare toes looked defenceless.

Before he could speak, Detective Hamilton introduced himself and asked if we could come in. My uncle's eyes widened; he nodded and stepped back.

'Alex, who's there? Is it Goldie?' My aunt's voice floated down the stairs.

'No, it's Pam and...someone...'

Alex didn't wait until she came down the stairs, instead ushering us into the lounge-room, sending worried glances in our direction. Hamilton glanced at me. I opened my mouth but nothing came out, so he stepped into the breach. 'I think we should sit down, Mr Humphries.'

Thoroughly frightened, Alex plopped into the nearest chair. Fiona rushed through the door to stand beside him, a hand over her mouth.

Hamilton and I sat opposite on the lounge and he took the initiative. 'We have some bad news and I'm sorry, there's no easy way to tell you.' He took at deep breath. 'Your daughter, Marigold Humphries, has been found dead in her home.'

Alex and Fiona stared at him. Alex sat with his arms hanging down at his sides, helpless in the face of the worst news any parent could hear.

I jumped up and went to Fiona, but just then Millicent came through the door bent on finding her mistress. Before anyone could move, Fiona snatched her up and wrapped her arms around her. For a moment, the cat enjoyed being held, but then Fiona's arms tightened. The cat struggled; Fiona held her even tighter. The animal cried and Alex was galvanised into action. He quickly stood and tried to loosen Fiona's hold, but she squeezed harder. Millicent struggled and raked at the sleeve of my aunt's dressing gown, her cries mingling with the Fiona's keening.

Immobilised by the sight of two adults and a cat struggling, I didn't immediately react, but the detective was made of sterner stuff. He leaped up, clamped his hands around Fiona's wrists and gently prised her arms open. Millicent escaped and fled behind the sofa. Alex, relieved of grappling with his wife, cast a grateful glance at the sergeant and sat her down. Her wails faded to whimpers as I headed for the kitchen to make hot drinks. As I walked down the hallway I heard the hinge of the liquor cabinet door creak above her sobs.

By the time I got back, two glasses of brandy stood on the table, one less full than the other. My aunt and uncle, arms around each other, gazed at the detective as though he possessed magical powers which would bring their daughter back to life. Hamilton's stoicism had been replaced by a kindly demeanour as he told them gently but firmly, what had happened and why the police thought Goldie's death was not an accident.

I laid the tray down on the coffee table and poured without asking what anyone wanted. I figured they didn't care what they got and according to the TV shows, cops would drink anything hot. I passed out the cups and then sat beside the detective, trying to concentrate on what he was saying.

'...so we won't know for sure how she died until forensics have done their work. I'm so sorry but I do have to ask you some questions. Do you feel up to it now?' He made eye contact with Fiona. She nodded slowly. The material of her dressing gown trembled on her lap.

Alex, ashen-faced, took her hands in his. 'We'll be all right, Mr Hamilton, ask whatever you need to know.'

Just then, Millicent re-appeared and leaped onto the sofa beside Fiona who, on autopilot, removed her hands from Alex' and took the cat into her lap. To our relief, stroking the dense fur seemed to calm Fiona. Millicent purred approval.

Hamilton took out his notebook and pen. 'When did you last see your daughter?'

'She stopped by this afternoon. Er, yesterday afternoon.' Alex face crumpled as he realised that was the *last* time he would speak to his child.

'Mrs Humphries?' Fiona didn't reply. Alex spoke gently into her ear and she raised her head.

'This afternoon. She rode her bicycle over. I was watering the garden when she...' She couldn't continue.

The detective made another note in his book. 'What did you talk about?'

'She just said she'd see me tomorrow...and that was it. She didn't kiss me goodbye.' Fiona dropped her head onto Alex's shoulder. The weary movement broke my heart.

Hamilton looked at them thoughtfully for a long moment. 'Have you any idea who might wish Ms Humphries harm? Any people she might have upset lately?'

'Call her Goldie...Mr...er...it's better. Easier. No, I don't know of anyone who would want to harm our daughter. 'Alex pursed his lips. 'I would be surprised if she hadn't made some bad friends over the years though. I doubt if any journalist would have everyone love them, but I can't think of anyone here who would actually k... do something like that.'

'What about that man who kept sending her flowers after Parry died?'

'You mean Adam McIntyre?' Alex's lips folded in a thin line.

'Who's he and where does he live?' The pen was flying across the page.

'He's a fellow journalist, but I don't know where he lives. Goldie said they had a fight over the phone the other day – last week sometime – and he was really nasty. She was liv–id.' Alex's voice broke. He turned his head to look at his wife, whose face was buried in the cat's fur. Silver strands in his dark hair, which I hadn't noticed before, glittered in the light, the furrows of his cheeks forming chasms in his colourless face.

'Do you know what they fought about?'

'Yes.' Rosy colour flooded Alex' face. 'They had an affair a few months ago but Goldie broke it off. He's been – I guess you could say – stalking her – ever since.'

'Did she report it?

'No, we wanted her to, but she said he was – 'Alex' lips curled down'– a right little ferret with no –' he glanced at Fiona, who didn't appear to be listening, '– no dick to speak of.'

I almost laughed. That was Goldie to the letter, but feeling guilty, smothered the second of levity. Nothing had sunk in. Goldie was going to walk in the door at any moment, laughing and ready to party. The coat she'd left behind yesterday was draped over the chair in her 'writing nook' off the lounge room, her spare hairbrush still upstairs in the guest bathroom, along with the toiletries she kept for when she stayed overnight with her parents and the change of clothes in her old childhood bedroom.

The only sound was the scratch of Hamilton's pen as he made notes, his fist twisted into the peculiar angling of the left- handed. I realised, with amazement, that he was actually using a fountain pen. My feeling of floating detachment was surreal. *Had I dreamt the previous couple of hours?* Weariness seeped through my limbs. The ticking of the old-fashioned clock on the wall alerted me the fact that it was almost three o'clock in the morning. I had been up and on the go for almost twenty-four hours. Despite my best efforts, I couldn't prevent myself from yawning. I caught Alex' eye, but didn't recognise the angry man who glared at me. 'Are we keeping you up, Pam?'

Recoiling from the sarcasm in his voice, I clapped the white handkerchief to my face to keep from retaliating. Anger wouldn't solve anything.

Hamilton looked up from his notes. 'Ms Miller found Goldie when she came back to the house from the concert. She called the ambulance and the police and she's had to wait while forensics did their job and answer questions as well. I don't think she's had any rest since she got up yesterday morning, isn't that so?' He glanced at me for a confirming nod.

My aunt looked over at me, shocked. 'We hadn't realised...' My uncle said nothing.

'It's fine. Shall I make some more tea?' I was determined to keep the peace.

Alex declined for himself and his wife. I turned to the detective with an enquiring lift of my eyebrow. 'Not for me, thanks. I'm almost finished here.' Hamilton turned back to my aunt and uncle. 'You say this Adam McIntyre might have had a grudge. Anyone else you know of?'

Fiona looked at him, her white face ravaged with grief, her eyes dark with shock. 'Harry, one of the journalists she knew at the Courier Mail might know. She was pretty thick with *him* and she has several girlfriends she always caught up with when she was home. Alex, get the black and red phone book would you? I know a couple of their numbers are in there.'

He went to get the book and Fiona bent her head over Millicent and resumed crooning. I remembered my bag and music case in the cop car. Hamilton raised his head and looked at me; we spoke over the top of each other.

'I'd better get –'

'You'd better get –'

We stopped together as he got to his feet. 'I'll get your things out of the car while your uncle's looking for the numbers.'

While he was gone, I moved over to Fiona and put my arm around her shaking shoulders. She felt boneless, as though the life-blood had seeped out of her body. For a moment, she rested her hand on mine and then dropped it back onto Millicent who lay patiently, as though sensing her presence was holding her mistress together.

As Alex came back into the room holding a piece of paper, the detective came through the front door with my belongings. 'Where can I put these?'

Alex looked daggers at me, but didn't say anything; Fiona didn't appear to understand what was going on.

'I'd better go to a hotel,' I said, embarrassed.

My uncle, perhaps not wanting to look bad in front of the detective, took an ostentatious look at his watch and said, 'You'd better stay what's left of the night.'

As he left the room, I caught the detective flashing Alex' back an angry glance. 'I can take them. I'll stay in the guest room upstairs,' I replied.

'Which room?'

I hesitated, then told him where. Without a word he took my bags up and was back in moments. Alex came back into the room and handed him the list of numbers. 'I'll try and get Fiona up to bed. She won't sleep, but she needs to rest.'

'Someone will be in touch tomorrow. We'll need you to look through Ms Humphries house to see if anything is missing.' Hamilton turned to me as my uncle shepherded my aunt, still clutching the cat, to the stairs.

'I wouldn't know. I haven't been there for a couple of years.'

'You were there only yesterday, so you might have observed more than you think. We'll be asking her parents to do the same. Can you come outside for a moment?' He opened the front door and ushered me out. 'Can you think of anything else in the light of what they said about McIntyre and the journalist?'

'No, I can't think straight anyway now. Will I see you tomorrow?' I wanted to bite my tongue. It sounded like I was asking him for a date.

His remarkable eyes crinkled at the corners; I think he knew I felt uncomfortable and why. 'Maybe. Someone else might come round to take a statement...how come you know Inspector Prescott?'

A chill wind wafted along the porch; I folded my arms firmly across my midriff. *Here we go again.* 'I met her a few years ago after my best friend was kidnapped. So you can ask Susan – Inspector Prescott – about it or I suppose you could look it up. There was lots of media crap about it when the Esposito's came to trial.'

'I seem to remember that.' He looked concerned. 'Are you over that now?'

'Does one ever get over something like that?' Pain, so long damped down, swept through me as though it had happened the previous week. 'Oh, I forgot! I was going to go down to Emsberg and see my mother tomorrow afternoon. She's going into hospital early Monday morning for a cancer operation.'

The detective looked stern. 'I'll have to check with DI Prescott as to whether you can go after you've made your statement. I wouldn't hold my breath if I were you. Can you see your mother at the hospital before her operation?'

'I hope so. I'll have to ring my stepfather early tomorrow morning and let him know what's happened so *he* can tell Mum.' *If the media doesn't do it for me.*

Hamilton leaned close. 'Try and get some rest. It'll be a bad day tomorrow.

CHAPTER 17

Susan

Preliminaries

Sunday, 6 am.

'Susan...*Susan*!'

The voice came from the end of a paddock.

'Susan! You need to wake up now.'

'Evan?' My head felt like a ton weight on my neck. I squinted at the wall clock. Six. Day or night? It was impossible to tell with the lights on. I slumped against the back of the chair. Dopey and disoriented, I stared at my partner.

'Susan, you've been asleep a whole half-hour!' Evan chided, smiling sympathetically. It was alright for him. He seemed to exist on coffee, biscuits and fresh air. I had known him to only take cat naps over a couple of days and still function efficiently. He handed me a sheet of paper. 'The preliminary forensic report on the body in the park. Do you want to get over to Humphries' house before Fingerprints gets there?'

'Yeah. Just give me a minute to get the team organised. You'll be driving, by the way.'

It seemed such a long time ago since last night and the early hours of this morning. I stared at the squiggles on the sheet. What was...oh yes, my glasses. I fumbled around on the desk and located them under a pile of papers.

Jane Doe had had the air supply to her nose and mouth cut simultaneously. Bruising indicated that she had been held tightly by one hand, the other apparently wrapped around both her wrists, which showed pressure marks. Faint marks showed that her throat had been squeezed, but death had been caused by someone *kneeling* on her chest. Two massive bruises showed where the perpetrator had knelt; her sternum had actually caved in. This had the effect of damaging her lungs, heart and spleen. Poor girl never stood a chance. One good thing for us, there was plenty of DNA on her face. Obviously someone very strong had been involved. A weightlifter? Maybe. *Was he on steroids? Perhaps he went off his head.*

'Lima Astro, Jane Doe's team's in. Do you want to take over?' Evan asked, referring to the briefing and reports to be given. The Incident room next door contained the whiteboard and all the paraphernalia for Limo Photo, the Humphries investigation. If the two cases proved to be linked, we would have to think again. Officers were grouped around the coffee machine, preparatory to briefing.

'Send someone out for breakfast, please Evan.'

David hadn't phoned or text me. Had he called while I was asleep? I paused to pull my mobile out of my pocket. Nothing. Perhaps he hadn't had the chance. Busy with investigations or lurking undercover with criminals? *Too right you are.*

I resumed my path to the whiteboard. The young girl's face gazed down on me, her arms folded across her chest as though posed by an undertaker. Other photos of her body, clothes and her shoes were pinned beside it, close-ups of her nose studs and earrings farther down the board. I sighed and waved the forensic report. 'Are we all here?'

A chorus replied as my tired team sat down with their coffee and notebooks.

'Okay, we'll start. A female person, approximately seventeen years of age, time of death estimated as the early hours of yesterday morning. The killer could have been a female, but the victim is young and fit. There is no indication that more than one person was involved.' I went on to reiterate the forensic report on cause of death. 'Saliva was smeared over her mouth and nose. No skin scrapings under her fingernails, which were surprisingly short, so no DNA there. There's nothing to say that her killer was a young man, but the fact that she was out in the early morning would tend to suggest she had a companion rather than wandering around on her own.'

I paused for a moment. 'No obvious sign of sexual activity, but if she was with a boyfriend they no doubt used condoms. There was no identification – no wallet, no purse, no mobile phone or iPod and no jewellery. The victim has no tattoos or distinguishing marks except for the studs in her nose and earrings. Unfortunately, the stud and earrings are mass produced, but someone might recognise them when they're put in the papers. There's no match with her fingerprints, so she's never been in trouble. Now what have you got?'

There wasn't much in the surrounding area. Some cigarette butts, a child's sock, the girl's sandals of course and a broken dog leash, along with enough used condoms to put a serious dent in next year's population growth. Perhaps there would be more evidence when the search was completed; that was when police cadets came in handy. Breakfast arrived in the form of Maccas which my team fell on like wolves. I waited until they had settled again and continued.

'So no mobile or iPod. How did the house to house go?'

'No one saw or heard anything, Ma'am.' *Of course, they never do when you want them to.*

'Now –' I ticked off the names of two officers who had just arrived on duty. 'Right, you know the drill. House to house is ongoing. So far, nothing. We do the backpackers hostels, hotels, colleges and universities and see who's missing.' Groans rippled around the room. 'Yeah, they come and go from those places all the time I know, but someone may fail to meet up with a friend, not turn up for coffee or for a class. Even for work. Soon someone is going to miss her. Now, who owns the old boat shed?'

'The Western Yacht Club owned it before they disbanded and now no one appears to be responsible for it. We've dug up a clerk from the city council to find out who's paying the rates,' advised one of my team. 'He hasn't gotten back to me yet.'

Just then, my mobile buzzed. I took it out of my pocket and read: '*All good. Love you. xx*' He's safe!

I turned back to the matter in hand. We couldn't allow the media to publicise her photo until her family had been located and notified but, a contradiction in terms, we couldn't find them until we knew who she was. We would have to dig and dig some more, continue knocking on doors. Surely it wouldn't be too long before anxious relatives, friends or if she worked, an employer contacted her parents. If she was a student, she wouldn't turn up for classes. I remember my tutors being somewhat slack when I was doing university night classes, but someone would notice her absence eventually. Surely the girl would have been texting to her friends? I'd yet to meet the teenager who didn't have to be surgically removed from their mobile phone. Someone would know where Jane Doe had been the night before and maybe even who she'd been with.

The team dispersed and I bolted for my cubby hole of an office, the umpteenth cup of coffee for the day in hand. I closed the door, sank into my chair and took a deep gulp of the lukewarm liquid, so tired I could hardly keep my eyes open. David was safe...thank God for that. I shut my eyes and leaned back, letting my mind drift over our lives together.

Images of us in our very early twenties drifted across my mind. Oh we were so darned immature it was sickening. The birth of our twins soon straightened me up, but David was another story. I guess lack of money and our stressful jobs – well, David's job was more stressful than mine. Our daughters were fractious, colicky and seemingly, sleep unnecessary. David, desperate for sleep before night shift, moved in with a mate, leaving me to cope on my own. My Aunt Beryl came to the rescue and moved the babies and me into a house on the bay, where she and her cats looked after us. It was a few years before I met Harry Prescott, an architect and married him. I always wanted to have a child with Harry and it was almost thirteen years before I discovered that the bastard had had a vasectomy before I met him.

David turned up to investigate two murders in Emsberg where Marli and I were house-sitting for Harry's sister Eloise and her husband James. That was the beginning of our renewed relationship and now, well, I had some rather interesting news for him when he got back from the mountains. It wasn't something a woman wants to hear at the age of forty-two. I'd settle for the menopause any day.

Sighing, I hauled myself to my feet staggered out to send my team home. I brought Superintendent, Col Peterson, up to date before meeting Evan to go to the Humphries' crime scene. I phoned my neighbour, explained the situation and thanked her for taking up the slack with our animals. Hopefully, I would soon get a spare hour to go to my sister's house to shower and change into the fresh clothes which I kept there for emergencies and where I hoped to enjoy at least an hour's sleep, before coming back to the Incident Room to tackle the investigation into the death of Marigold Humphries.

CHAPTER 18

Pam

Hostile Territory

Sunday, 11.00am

Shouting woke me. Bleary-eyed, I gazed at the ceiling, trying to work out where I was. Pink curtains, rosewood dressing table complete with Art Deco table lamp. Memory flooded back. I was in my Aunt and Uncle's spare room, lying fully clothed on the bed and Goldie was dead.

Downstairs someone started hammering on the front door. What was going on? Footsteps hurried past the bedroom door and clattered downstairs, Alex' angry voice raised. I could hear Fiona crying. My feet found my shoes in record time. I snatched up my mobile phone and rushed down to the vestibule where my aunt was standing, wearing a red, quilted dressing gown, her hands over her face. She turned and stumbled into my arms as Alex threw open the door. The front hallway lit up with flashes. He slammed it shut and shot the bolt.

I pretty much *dragged* my aunt along to the kitchen, where the phone was ringing off the hook and pushed her into a chair before running to pull the blinds down, shutting out the over-excited faces peering through the window. I answered the phone, but as soon as the caller said the words, "Sunday Mail" I slammed the receiver on the bench top, leaving the caller cheeping in frustration.

I opened my mobile and dialed the number which Anthony Hamilton programmed into my phone, but as it started to ring, there was another ruckus at the front door. I could hear Alex talking to someone, footsteps and then the detective himself, phone ringing, came into the kitchen followed by an older, kind-faced woman. A tiny thrill slithered through me as the detective and I made eye contact. *Pam, what's wrong with you! Of all times to...*

'Mr and Mrs Humphries – Pam – Ms Miller, I'm sorry you've had to contend with that lot. This is Jo Fields, our Family Liaison Officer. She'll be here to answer questions and help with all the things we're going to need you to do.' Hamilton glanced at me, as he closed his mobile.

My uncle broke in. 'Do you know who did it?'

'No, we are just starting our investigations–'

'Well, you should be out there looking for him!' Alex' face turned red with the rage of which the family knew him capable. The detective's expression did not change, but he exchanged a glance with Jo Fields, who sat down opposite them.

'We don't know yet whether Ms Humphries –'

'Well, you should!' Alex wasn't about to let up.

'– knew her attacker. Ms Humphries *may* have known the perpetrator. We are hoping you can give us some leads.'

Alex trumpeted into his handkerchief and Fiona clasped her gown tighter around her body. I started making tea. There followed a brief argument after Hamilton asked Alex and Fiona to come to Goldie's house to see what, if anything, was missing. The spat intensified when he added that they also needed to have their fingerprints taken for elimination purposes.

Dishes piled in the sink revealed that Alex and Fiona had eaten breakfast, but hadn't called me. The sooner I got out of there the better. The contractors I hired to put my furniture and personal effects back into my unit would be busy this morning. I was deeply thankful I had made the arrangement...

'Pam! Wake up! It mightn't be important to you, but you could at least *listen*!' I jumped and turned to face Alex' hostile glare as he continued to berate me. If I hadn't gone out 'clubbing' after the concert, Goldie would still be alive. What right had I to put my social life ahead of my hostess? I was a guest in his daughter's house and I couldn't be bothered even coming home after the concert. 'Chasing after some man, I suppose, like that Russian git.'

Rage started to boil deep inside. It was all too much. The media uproar, the shock of finding my beloved cousin dead, Alex's inexplicable hatred and Fiona's blank grief – exhaustion threatened to overwhelm me. The detective's deep voice pulled me out of my fog. 'Pam, we need to get your fingerprints for comparison with those in your cousin's house and we also need to know if there's anything missing from the house.'

'What about Fiona and Alex? They'd have a better idea than I would.'

'They're coming in later.'

'Can I go back to my own unit?'

'Of course. We have to do this first though.' He took my arm and eased me out of the room and up the stairs to the bedroom. 'Get your bag and music case. Alex doesn't mean what he said. That was grief talking.' He tried to look convincing, but failed miserably. *Oh yes, Alex meant it alright.* My hands shook. I was unable to believe the venom directed at me. *Should* I have come back to Goldie's instead of going out with Ally and Brie? Could I have saved her or would we both have been killed?

'Do you think he's angry because it was Goldie and not me who died?'

'Probably. There's no accounting for grief, Pam, you know that from before.' Anthony Hamilton ran his hands up my arms and squeezed my shoulders gently before stepping quickly away. I realised why when my uncle appeared in the doorway. My aunt and the Liaison Officer loomed behind him.

'Pamela, I think it's better if you don't come back here,' Alex snarled. 'You couldn't even be bothered to get up and be with your aunt this morning. You must have known she needed you!'

I could barely look at him. I loved Goldie too. I snatched up my handbag and flute case and the detective picked up my clothes hold-all. Alex was forced to stand aside to let us pass. I followed the detective down the stairs, hopping over the bottom two, to the front door where he stopped me. 'Let me go first.' He opened the door and spoke briefly to two uniformed constables outside. As I stepped outside, hordes of reporters shouted and surged around the steps. The officers shielded me with their arms as Anthony Hamilton, ploughing through the media scrum, towed us in his wake.

Shouts assaulted me on all sides.

'What happened, Pam?'

'Did you see the murder?'

'Who killed her?'

'Did you have a fight with Goldie?

'*Was it you?*'

'*Are you under arrest?*'

Shocked, I turned back to rip the man's throat out, but the constables pushed me into the front seat of a nondescript grey car and slammed the door. I thrust my head down against the dashboard to avoid the cameras pushed against the windows.

'Your cousin is big news,' Anthony said quietly, as we headed along the street, leaving chaos behind. 'And so are you.'

Tears of rage ran down my cheeks; another fresh handkerchief appeared, as if by magic. 'Here, and I don't want it back,' he said, as we pulled up outside Goldie's cottage, where to my dismay, more photographers lurked. He pulled into the driveway, again dodging media. I was helped out of the car by a uniformed officer and rushed into the house.

I stood silently, my heart pounding. The floorboards and the bottom steps were covered in what I assumed to be fingerprint dust, partially covering stains. I stepped around the spot and moved carefully into the lounge room. Chairs had been pushed aside, cushions scattered, drawers were pulled out of the sideboard with the contents piled on top. Glue and fingerprint dust smothered everything. I could hear someone moving around upstairs.

I reminded Hamilton that I wouldn't know if anything was unaccounted for because I hadn't been there for a long time. 'It's such a mess so how would I know anyway?' I peered past him from the kitchen into the laundry only to see the same kind of chaos.

We moved back to the front room where Parry's portrait gazed at me; I averted my eyes. Anthony

Hamilton watched everything I did. The intensity of his gaze made me uncomfortable. 'How about we go upstairs?'

As we ascended the dusty staircase, a man carrying a folder passed us on the way down, nodding to Anthony as he passed. Was it only about forty-eight hours ago that Goldie and I had been laughing and catching up on gossip as we sipped nightcaps and prepared for bed?

I moved into the guest room where my suitcase had been emptied and the contents strewn over the bed. Nothing was missing. The en suite appeared undisturbed, though fingerprint dust coated all the hard surfaces. Goldie's room was messy, though whether this was her usual chaos or caused by the detectives searching, I couldn't say.

Anthony guided me slowly around the room, peering into the opened drawers and cupboards so I could look without having to touch anything. Knowing technicians and cops had seen the discarded knickers and bras on the floor, I flushed with embarrassment for Goldie. It looked as though she had dressed in a hurry before leaving for the Concert Hall. Clothes lay in piles next to the chest of drawers against the far wall. 'Can you see if anything's missing from the wardrobe?'

I looked at the clothes thrown every which-way on the bed and shrugged. Only a few dresses were left hanging. Her handbags were piled on the pillows, opened. Pens, tissues and money purses lay in a heap on the bedside table. 'I haven't been here for over a year so I wouldn't know,' I repeated. Shrugging, Anthony said that perhaps Goldie's mother would be able to account for everything.

We moved to Goldie's office. I looked around but couldn't see anything obviously missing except for her laptop and tapes and the steel filing cabinet which normally sat in the corner. Her desk, normally strewn with papers and files, was bare. 'We took all that down to the station,' Anthony explained. 'We're hoping her work colleagues can help.' We have to go through her files and notebooks to see if there's anything that might have led to her death.

'You mean a threatening letter or something?'

'It's possible. Your cousin wrote a lot of fiery articles about social injustice and welfare issues. Any one of those groups could be responsible for her death,'

I shuddered, remembering when my friend Jess was murdered. Her computer and files were taken for forensic examination too. I tried to focus. The walls were lined with photos of Goldie and famous people, award nights and photos taken in the field of war...

'What is it? Have you thought of something?'

'Yes, there's something gone from the house, but I can't think what it is.'

'Okay, well we only have to check out the garage and garden shed, so don't stress. It'll come to you. Are you coming back here?'

I explained about my unit and the organisers, so he waited while I packed up my things and carried my other case downstairs for me. The mêlée at the front of the house reached stentorous proportions, the bullying shouts of the media following us down the driveway to the shed and the garage. The bouquets of flowers lay discarded by the roller door, their blooms drooping in the heat of the sun. The golden ribbon tied around the sheaf from the Concert Hall looked garish and overdone.

Anthony asked if I wanted them.

'No. Poor things, they'll be dead by tomor –' *So was Goldie.* Pain rolled through me; I wanted to bite my tongue out. The detective guided me into the garage. 'Anything missing that you can see?'

I looked at the few tools leaning against the back wall – covered in what I recognised as fingerprint dust. A lawnmower was parked in a corner with some oil cans beside it. 'No, but then I've never been in here until last night and that was in the dark.'

'Did Ms Humphries have a gardener? Someone to mow her lawns or did her father do it?'

'She had a mowing contractor, but I don't know the name of the company.'

'No worries, we'll find out who it is.'

Then it hit me. 'Goldie's new camera! It's not in the house!'

'They took several cameras out of the house for testing. *Do you know what it was?*' Anthony loomed, his expression eager.

'Goldie lent me her second camera, the Nikon 2. I borrowed the car yesterday and locked it in the boot for safety. Her new one is a Nikon 4 and it cost a fortune!'

'Okay. So her main camera is unaccounted for. Would she have left it at her parents' house?'

'Oh no, she had it yesterday because I saw it on the kitchen bench. She took it with her when she went to take photos of the river.'

'So someone *has* taken it. Thanks, Pam. Now let's have a look for the one you borrowed.'

He went to the driver's side, opened the door and took the keys out, slapping fingerprint dust off his shirt as he came around the back of the car. He opened the boot and there was the camera, covered in dust. 'It can't have had anything on the SD card or they'd have taken it for examination,' he explained. 'By the way, do you happen to know who Ms Humphries' executor is?'

'No, I don't. She kept all her personal papers in a folder in the steel filing cabinet in the office. Goldie told me once that because of her lifestyle, she keeps – kept– her affairs up to date. Everything will go to her parents. As you know, she had no siblings and the portrait of Parry will probably go to his family.' Anthony looked puzzled so, as we headed for the police station, I told him the story of Parry and Goldie.

After my statement was written and signed, my fingerprints were taken – I was assured they would be destroyed after they'd been matched and eliminated from enquiries – I was allowed to leave. All I wanted to do was to be left alone and process the trauma of the last twenty-four hours. Anthony Hamilton offered to have me taken to my unit, but I pleaded for time out.

Heading for the Transit Centre opposite police headquarters, I hired a couple of lockers for the afternoon and stowed my bags and flute case, after which I bought a packet of tissues, a cheese and tomato roll for lunch and a bottle of water. I had brought Goldie's Nikon 2 from the house, so I tucked it back into my shoulder bag and headed for the Roma Street Parklands behind the station. I would spend an hour there, collect my things from the locker and head home to get in a few hours practice for my next concert.

Did Anthony Hamilton's parting smile hold more than formal courtesy? *Oh yes, you can question me any time.* I pulled myself up, consumed by guilt at having sexy thoughts about a man when Goldie was dead.

Rage flared again, encompassing not only the monster for murdering my wonderful cousin, but for taking my personal triumph away. My concert felt as though it had never happened.

A park bench under the shade of a large tree looked as good a place as any to make necessary phone calls.

My mother's husband, John, answered and in spite of promising myself I wouldn't worry him, my words tumbled over themselves. Understandably, he was shocked. 'We haven't had the radio or the TV on today and I was just about to go into town to get the paper. Your mum had a bad night, so I'm letting her sleep as long as she can this morning. You're not a suspect are you?'

'No, I don't think so.' Anthony Hamilton certainly hadn't acted as though I was, but being first on the scene didn't preclude me from being a "person of interest." Didn't the police always suspect the person who finds the body?

'You'll need to stay up there today, so would be you able to come in to the hospital before your mum goes into surgery?'

'I'll be there first thing and meet you in the foyer. Why don't you bring her up and stay at my unit for the night?'

'Thank you for the offer, Pam. I wanted her to make the trip up there later today, but she refused to leave here because of the animals. Andrea is coming down to house sit.'

'How's Fudgie?' I missed my cat terribly.

'Fat as ever. He's fine.'

'Good. Surely they'd be okay just for the night?'

'Yes, but she's trying to prolong leaving the house until the last possible moment.'

Obviously Mum thought she might not see her pets again. I know the doctors always give you notice of all the things that can go wrong in theatre nowadays, but I felt that maybe the old adage, 'Ignorance is bliss' could sometimes be applied.

'That sounds like mum. I want to come down and spend a couple of days with you both before I start the next tour.'

'Well, you know you can come here any time, love.'

Feeling calmer, I sat back to eat the roll, savour the gardens and try to get my head around everything that had happened. My mind, numb with weary grief, slowly came to life, throwing unwanted images of Goldie as I had last seen her, leaving the concert hall in a taxi...Had she known what was going to happen when someone had struggled with her on the stairs? She had to have let him in or how else would he have been in a position to fight with her? Was it the bloke she accused of stalking her?

Anguish flooded me as I thought about her last moments and the terror she would have felt. I knew now she'd had her neck broken. Hopefully, she wouldn't have felt a thing. How could I face life without her? Goldie – traveller, career-driven, brilliant – rushing in and out of my life, bringing warmth, love and loyalty. I'd had only three short years with her, owing to Alex's dislike of my mother and his alienation of her from my mother. Seemingly Alex and Mum had made up somewhere along the way. Was it John who'd brokered the reunion? He would take no nonsense from my uncle.

If I ever married I would have had Goldie and Ally as my bridesmaids, godmothers to my children...for a moment, a vision of the stoic detective flashed through my mind. *Stop thinking about Anthony Hamilton. This is not about you, it's about her.*

I took a deep breath, leaned on the railing and watched the artificial waterfall cascading into the pool on the edge of the park below. Opposite, tenants of the blocks of city units moved in and out of their balconies. Had they read their papers yet? Would they look at the name Marigold Humphries, and say 'Look! It's that woman who was on TV last month...' or last year, or, 'Wasn't there some trouble in Afghanistan?'

Families walked past, unaware of the shaken female silently staring into space. The saying, "Loneliness is everything it's cracked up to be" rose to mind.

Fiona hadn't shown hostility, but she came from the 'old school' where a woman took her cue from her husband. Would Alex have turned on me if Goldie had lived or was it inevitable? I'd thought they regarded me as a second daughter. The sense of betrayal was excruciating.

I sat on a nearby seat to make some calls, returning Ally's first. 'I couldn't return your calls because of what was happening at my aunt and uncle's place.

'Don't worry about that. Poor Goldie. I didn't know her that well, but you were very close. How are you feeling?'

'Washed out, depressed, you name it! I can't talk about it right now and the police have asked me not to discuss it. I can't even go down and be with my mother today, but I'm going to get into the hospital tomorrow morning and see her before she goes into theatre. I can keep John company.'

She excused herself and spoke to someone.

'Who's with you?'

'Brie and some friends. We're having coffee in Queen Street Mall. Want to join us?'

'Thanks for the offer, but no, I really need to get back to my unit and settle in. The whole day's been...well...you know...' Words couldn't describe it and I didn't try to. We closed off with condolences from both of them.

Gradually the sun thawed my muscles. I started to relax and concentrate on the marvellous landscaping and variety of plant life around me. Goldie's camera was loaded and ready to use so I stopped in front of a bush covered in a blaze of autumn colour to take one photo then another, as the colours in the park slowly awakened me from my fog of misery. Goldie would have loved these scenes. Only three women have been close enough to me to be called 'sister' – Ally, Jessica and Goldie. I missed them so much. Jess dead and now, my cousin. Dare I believe she was with Parry? I've never been overly religious, but I guess I believed *something*.

So I thought about my life and the incongruity of people's appearance compared to what they're really like, and about all the reasons why I shouldn't get interested in a certain cop who looked like an assassin. Wasn't there some law that said cops couldn't get involved with witnesses? Had he looked at me in a decidedly un-professional manner, or was I reading things into it that weren't there?

Below was the fern gully of the parkland, where I remembered some ornamental iron birds standing at the edge of the lake.

I started down a long pathway bordered by bottle trees heading deeper into the shadowed tunnels.

CHAPTER 19

Dingo

Nightmares

Sunday, 11.30am

A riel clawed at him, screaming! He kissed her hard, pressing his body down onto hers, holding the back of her neck –

Dingo lurched upright, fighting to free himself from the sheets, as he tried to switch on the table lamp. His heart leaped around in his chest like a frog trapped in a jar. Had he been yelling? *It was a dream, nothing more.* No sound of footsteps running. Best get control...ten, nine, eight, seven, six – Ariel get back in your box – fivefourthreetwoone...*I didn't mean to hurt you! I didn't mean it. I really didn't mean it. I'm so sorry.*

A car horn down in the street sent a fresh jolt of fear through him. He struggled out of the twisted sheets, damp from his sweat and rushed for the en suite, where he dry retched until he fell, exhausted, against the porcelain bowl. *It was a dream, just a dream.*

His lower back hurt. He twisted carefully to look in the mirror. A faint line of bruising ran from one side to the other where he'd landed across the stair in the photographer's house. Trembling, he rinsed his mouth, splashed water on his face, then cleaned his teeth and took three Codeine. The small bottle of tablets on the glass shelf under the mirror jogged his memory. *Remember your Sertraline, love. You know if you don't take your tablets, you'll go doolally...Get off my back, Mum, or I'll...kill you. She's dead she's dead she's dead.*

It was a cold, dark day on his eighteenth birthday that he'd buried Frances. Only the vicar and the Trustee of his father's fortune attended, his mother having remained a recluse until the day of her death. Strangely, when he left her there on the bleak hillside overlooking the edge of the city, he felt lost, disoriented. The cat had long since died and Frances had refused to get another, so Dingo bore his loss alone. It didn't occur to him until years later that he was a damaged person, but in spite of the women in his life and the friends he had made, he was still alone.

He went into the bedroom and did some gentle stretches. He couldn't afford to have anyone notice the stiffness in his gait or his aching shoulder. What to do? First, the city. And he had to dump the camera that night.

His stomach rumbled. He squinted at his watch: eleven thirty. He pulled the curtains open, flinching as sunlight flooded the room. Below, cars passed silently – blue, white, green, silver – so many silver cars – why did everyone choose silver? Were they cheaper? Was it the latest colour – the only colour – no, there was a reason. Someone had explained it to him once.

Lunch was in progress by the time he got downstairs. He paid the cashier and then helped himself liberally to the buffet, relieved there was only a smattering of what appeared to be tourists sharing the elegant dining room. No one took any notice of him as he wolfed a chicken salad. The digital card reader was his priority for what was left of the day. He had to be at the headquarters of the Pacific Symphony at nine o'clock the next morning. He wanted to get back to his unit on Kangaroo Point and practice his music. He could also have access to his car. He could *walk* it from the hotel, but...he almost dropped the ball on his poise as his mind flashed back.

'I want to go for a walk!'

'But it's nearly four in the morning, Ariel.'

'It'll be getting light shortly and the river is gorgeous when the sun comes up! Come on Dingo, it's the best time of day. We've cleaned everything up. Mum'll never know you were here, so let's go!'

Back in your box.

He wasted no time in getting out of the hotel. Newspaper posters shouted at him from the corner store a block down from the hotel: 'World Famous Journo Murdered!' and 'Vale Goldie!' There photos of Pamela Miller in *that* dress. Just thinking about it made him harden up. He forced himself to dismiss the image and concentrate on his mission to get a card reader. Beads of sweat prickled his torso. He wished he'd not worn a hoodie, but then how could he hide his face? *Don't be silly. No one knows who you are, stupid – except for the rest of orchestra. Put your sunglasses on.*

Unable to help himself, he stopped and purchased a paper. The newsagent was inclined to be chatty. 'Terrible thing, that. Right down near the ferry, too.' He mumbled something vaguely appropriate and hastily allowed another customer to take his place. He walked slowly down the street, heart sinking as he read the front page and realised just who he had fought with and that Pamela Miller was the Humphries woman's cousin.

Why did I do it? They'd be screaming for his blood. He leaned against a lamp post to gather his wits and rest his back. *Oh God...threefoursix...threefourfive...oh God... no...*Now the Humphries woman had broken out again. He forced back the voices tramping around in his brain. Shut up, *shut up!*

'Are you all right, young man?' The elderly voice breaking into his thoughts almost gave him a heart attack. An old woman leading a small dog, who was even older than she, if that were possible, stood beside him, looking concerned.

'Yes, thank you. I'm fine. Rough night out.' Dingo flashed the beautiful smile which had endeared him to women all his life.

Her face lit up and patted his arm. 'You young people, I don't know...' She shook her head, still smiling, and went into the shop.

Feeling he was pushing his luck, he rolled up his paper and strode out for the city, swinging it like a baton, willing his heart to stop pounding. He was glad to blend in with the Sunday morning walkers, some of them hoodies like himself.

The view of the river as he crossed the bridge was lost on him, as he brushed past the family groups dawdling along and stopping to take photos against the backdrop of South bank. The shops would be open in the Myer Centre. He edged his way through the crowd and found a place which sold card readers. It was all he could do not to rip the thing out of the shop assistant's hands as she pointed out the various attributes and then went on to talk about other more expensive brands. 'No that one will do.'

Disappointed, she placed it in a plastic bag and fixed up his credit card. He wandered out of the shop and walked slowly toward the Transit Centre, thinking he might stop at a bar on the way. A drink would be good. Then Dingo saw Pamela Miller ahead, crossing the street, heading for the Roma Street Station. Would she know what was happening at the house? Would she tell him if she *did* know? He hurried after her, wincing from the pain in his back and shoulder. As he ran into the ground floor, he saw her talking to someone at the desk. Uncertain of how to approach her without looking too interested in the murder, he lurked behind a newsagent's stand. She walked to the lockers and started stowing her bags and flute case, before walking toward the back of the station.

Thanking his stars she was so tall, he slunk after her, keeping at least six or seven people behind, debating whether to follow her or go back to the hotel and use the card reader to check the weird Nikon card. He tucked his parcel into his jacket and then, following instinct kept his head down and tracked her into the park where she wandered, seemingly without any purpose, stopping now and then to touch a flower, or read a plaque by the side of the pathway. He stayed well back as she talked on her mobile and ate a snack, after which she got up and strolled slowly through the park. If she happened to see him, he could chat about the concert and the orchestra. *Did she see him leaving right after Goldie Humphries? Wait, just wait and see what she does.*

He thought there was all the time in the world – until she took what appeared to be a professional photographer's camera out of her bag.

CHAPTER 20

Pam

A Walk in the Park

Sunday, 1pm

The realisation that I was the focus of someone's attention wasn't something which leaped out at me, but rather a slow and terrifying understanding that I was being stalked. It wasn't the sort of scrutiny which lets you know a gorgeous hunk of testosterone is eyeing you up, more the type of: 'I'm watching everything you do and waiting to pounce...'

Frightened of being mugged, I stowed the camera into my handbag and tucked it tightly under my arm with the strap wound around my wrist. Nothing happened, so after a while I relaxed a little. Then something moved on the periphery of my vision. Startled, I froze a moment and peered through the tall ferns nearby. Should I step into the inset pathway in front of me? No, I'd be trapped. My heart pounded and perspiration broke out over my body, sending prickles of panic into my stomach. I looked around for a group of people to join – pensioners, school kids – anyone – but while I'd been absorbed in the history of the gardens and taking photographs, the families had momentarily deserted the pathways to picnic on the lawns below. A small group of elderly women laughed as they pointed at something in the distance. I started toward them, pushing through a large overhang of fern.

Something crashed into my head.

Bright pain hurled me to the ground.

My face smashed into the planks of the walkway.

Lights danced in front of my eyes; a large hand snaked under my stomach, clenched the strap of my handbag and jerked violently.

I flattened myself onto the ground, curling my arm under me. *'No. No!'*

A steady stream of warm blood trickled down the side of my face and into my mouth.

The hand pulled away, wrenching my shirt free of my jeans. I grabbed the front of my shirt with the hand around which the strap was twined, and tried to protect my head with the other. *First thing, get your face out of the dirt.*

Bracing myself, I gingerly turned my head, trying to open my eyes before rolling onto my side. A middle-aged man stared down at me, his face creased with concern.

A babble of shocked voices pierced my consciousness. 'Hey! Are you all right?'

Am I all right? Someone has hit me in the temple, blood's streaming down my face, my eyes are full of tears, I'm almost knocked cold with shock, but – 'Yes, I'm fine, thanks. It's nothing.'

'I'll look after her,' said a whispery voice above my head. 'I'm her brother.'

'I don't have a brother!' No one appeared to hear or understand.

'She's a bit confused.'

Someone wearing huge black sunglasses like blow-fly eyes, face half covered by a black hood loomed over me. His breath smelled of mints, his hands encircled my wrists like manacles as he pulled mine from my head. Deep in the inner recesses of my mind, familiarity stirred but vanished before I could catch it. I squinted upward through a haze of blood in my right eye, but the sun was behind him.

'No, this isn't right! Get away from me! I don't know you!' I protested weakly, trying to push his hands away.

A small audience gathered, no doubt bristling in anticipation of drama. I jerked my wrist out of his hand, clamped my own hand over the cut on my head and braced myself against the stinging pain, still clutching my handbag to my stomach. If I closed my eyes tightly enough, he might go away.

Another voice chimed in. 'I'm a nurse. I've called for an ambulance.' I opened my good eye. A floral-perfumed woman with a kind face was kneeling in front of me. *Thank God.* 'You mustn't move until the paramedics check you out. You've got a nasty cut there, love, so keep still and don't turn or lift your head.'

The space where my supposed brother had been was empty. The pounding in my head intensified. My skin felt tight as the blood trickled down my face. Nausea swirled through my stomach, threatening to shoot into my throat. 'He tried to steal my handbag,' I muttered, trying to overcome the metallic taste in my mouth.

'Who?' She paused, glancing around nervously.

'The man who was here just now. Hoodie – green shirt. Sunglasses.'

She looked around. 'He's not here now. Are you with friends? What's your name?'

I tried to focus. 'Pamela Miller. I'm here on my own.'

She glanced at her watch. 'Someone's phoning the police.' She took a wad of tissues from her bag, proceeded to soak them from a water bottle and gently wiped my mouth before squeezing some water through my lips. 'Rinse out, get that blood out of your mouth,' she urged, 'but don't swallow.'

Gratefully, I complied. 'I think he tried to rob me,' I quavered.

My audience faded, no doubt disappointed I wasn't seriously hurt. *Blood-letting is always good entertainment.*

'Can I phone someone for you? I'm Kathleen, by the way. My husband and I were just about to go home when he saw you lying on the ground.'

A witness! 'Did he see that man hit me?'

'No. Someone said he was your brother, but he went away.' She looked puzzled. 'Are you *sure* he was the one who hit you?'

'Yes, I think so.' But *was* I sure? A large hand had shoved under my body, pulled at the strap of my handbag and in so doing had reefed my shirt out of my jeans. I was a woman alone and easy pickings. He'd only to watch and wait for the chance when there'd be no one else around. Why hadn't I left the garden when I realised I was being followed? *Stupid, Pam ,stupid.*

I drifted off for a few minutes, and awakened to the sound of voices and a scuffle of footsteps on the pathway. Two paramedics swiftly unpacked their bags. One medic wiped my face and cleaned my mouth of blood with something soft and wet. Enquiries were made as to whether I was feeling pain anywhere else. Competent hands checked me for injuries, my blood pressure taken and a torch flashed in my eyes. 'You'll need to come with us,' they announced as they strapped a neck brace on and then lifted me onto a flat stretcher, carefully holding my spine and neck rigid. Expertly and swiftly I was trundled to a waiting ambulance.

It was there two checked caps appeared. The elder of the officers took out his notebook. 'Is she up to answering a few questions? We won't keep her more than a minute or two.' The medics nodded, so he took out his notebook with a purposeful air, introduced himself and swung into procedures. Out of the corner of my eye, I saw his colleague talking to the nurse, Kathleen.

I gave my name and address. 'I've just moved back in there. Well, I'm going back there this afternoon.'

Understandably, the officer looked a little confused. 'You mean you're not currently living at your unit, but you're going to be there from this afternoon?'

'Yes, that's what I meant to say. I've been away touring. I'm a musician and I just got home on Friday from Sydney. The tenants only left yesterday and the household organisers are – well, were – moving my belongings back in some time this morning.'

The cop nodded and made notes in his book. 'From the look of the cut you have on your head and size of the lump coming up, you're not going back anywhere today. Do you feel up to answering some questions? You can make a full statement later.'

I nodded gingerly.

'Now, did you see who attacked you?'

I explained the sequence of events and then described the hooded man as best I could. The ferocity of the pain made thinking difficult. The officer pressed a little, but when I was unable to add to my statement, he closed his notebook. 'Maybe it will come to you,' he said comfortingly. 'That's all for now, Ms Miller. Would you like us to ring someone for you? A relative or friend?'

I panicked. Fiona and Alex were traumatised already, my mother was facing her operation and John worried about her. Anthony Hamilton? No, I couldn't ask him to leave his job and chase after me. Then I remembered Ally and Brie. 'Yes, please. The number's in my purse.'

The officer scuffled through my bag and brought out my purse. With a glance for permission, he sorted through the pockets until I identified their business card.

'This it?'

'Yes, please could you ring them?' I closed my eyes while he phoned and then advised that Ally would meet me at Emergency.

'Wait!' The cop turned back, putting his notebook into his pocket.

'I don't know if this is important or related, but my cousin, Goldie – Marigold – Humphries was murdered on Saturday night.'

'Bloody hell!' Shocked, he turned to his partner, who was already reaching for his mobile phone.

I raised my head. 'Tell DI Susan Prescott...' It hurt too much. I flopped back onto the stretcher.

The paramedic looked concerned. 'Can you hurry it up? We want to get going.'

The cop on the phone shot her an apologetic glance and then, apparently being given an instruction, snapped the mobile shut and nodded to the paramedics who immediately trundled me into the ambulance. I raised my hand and touched my right temple. It had swollen to the size of a ping pong ball. My skin twitched and my teeth chattered. The medic who rode in the back with me added another blanket to the foil cover. As we pulled into the forecourt of the Emergency Department of Royal Brisbane hospital, my body started to shake uncontrollably. My stretcher became a trolley again, but I had just enough time to see a tall, hooded man getting out of a nearby car.

No!

I blacked out again.

CHAPTER 21

Pam

The Watcher

Monday, 8am

Overnight stays in hospital are not my idea of comfort and good fun. The endless wait for the CT scan, then the wait for the doctor to stitch my wound, followed by the night-time clatter and laughter of the nurses. The torchlight shining in my eyes, not to mention the constant monitoring of my blood pressure, nearly drove me mad. Of course, I was grateful for the care which was second to none, but exhaustion and grief were threatening depression.

'You can't go home until doctor's been and had a look at you,' announced the nurse, when I whined to leave. I would catch up with my stepfather if I could just get out in time and I was desperate to get home and practice my music.

'That's quite a knock you've had, dear.' The lump on my temple throbbed, the stitches stung. Why would a stranger deliberately hit me with a rock? A mistake? But how could you mistake a 183cm female musician for someone else? Another 183cm musician? There aren't too many of us around. I remembered the hand tugging at the strap of my handbag. Maybe it was 'just' a common or garden mugging. Perhaps Goldie's murder was a burglary gone wrong...just random chance...wrong place, wrong time. I'd tried to put speculation behind me.

After a CT scan was pronounced clear, I was taken on a trolley to a side ward, part of Emergency, and put to bed. Two police officers came to take a formal account of what had happened, taking me through my statement slowly and gently, showing no impatience when I had difficulty remembering details. After half an hour, they left me a card and asked me to call if I thought of anything more...

'Miss Miller? Or should that be *Ms Miller*?'

I opened my eyes, to see a rotund, grey-haired man dressed in a suit, standing at the foot of the bed. I squinted at my watch, dismayed to see that I had missed seeing Mum. John would be upset and wondering why I hadn't turned up this morning before she went into theatre.

'I'm Doctor Phillips. I see you're a celebrity. We've had to ward off the press on your behalf.'

'Really?' There hadn't been any sign or word that my presence in the hospital had become news.

'We like to protect our patients, Ms Miller. How are you this morning?' He frowned and took my chart handed to him by an attendant nurse, who looked at me curiously.

'Fine, thank you. Can I go home today?' I asked eagerly. I would run upstairs and see if I could find John at the Oncology Unit before finding a sneaky way out of the hospital.

'We'll see. You had quite a bump, you know. The CT scan showed nothing damaged, but you're going to be very sore for a few days,' he added, stating the obvious. The doctor peered over the top of his bifocals and prodded gently around the wound with a glove-covered forefinger. I tried not to gag at the fog of cigarette clinging to his body and clothes.

'Hm. The swelling's gone down considerably. Good. Do you have somewhere to go?'

'I beg your pardon?' He made it sound as though I was a vagrant.

'I meant, do you have family or friends who can keep an eye on you for a day or two?'

'Oh yes. I have a friend who will collect me and take me home to my unit.' The night before in Emergency, Ally had told her to call him the instant I was ready to leave.

'Well, I'll let you go if you promise to rest. No nightclubs and carousing!' Carousing? Did anyone use that term anymore? I promised solemnly and he left. Ally promised to come and get me in about an hour and she would text me when she got to the front of the hospital. 'Apparently the press know I'm in here,' I explained.

'Don't worry; we'll get you out in one piece.'

With the dregs of charge in my mobile phone battery, I called my stepfather. Speaking faster than a race caller, I told him what had happened and heard that Mum had gone into theatre around seven o'clock. He refused my invitation to come to my unit, as he wanted to stay at the hospital so he could be there when she came back from surgery. 'I wanted to see her before she went in,' I wailed.

'Don't worry, she was fine, love. You can see her tomorrow. She won't be 'with it' when she comes out of theatre. I'll give her your love, but I'll leave it to you to sort work that out later. You have to look after yourself. Have you got someone to take you to your unit?'

'Yes, Ally will come and get me, don't worry. How did mum take the news about Goldie?'

'Not well. She phoned Fiona and spent about an hour talking to her.'

I knew Mum would have been exhausted after that, so was glad that I couldn't have called her the night before. I had a shower and dressed, just in time to see a text message from Ally who was on her way.

'We've been in touch with the hospital Public Relations department and they're sending someone to escort you.' The nurse looked over my shoulder, smiling. 'Here's Sally to take you out the back way. Give me your friend's number and I'll text her where to meet you and how to get there.'

We turned to see an older woman walking toward us. Having introduced herself, she escorted me through a maze of hallways and tunnels until we arrived at a nondescript door somewhere in the bowels of the building. Outside was a small car park, blessedly empty of reporters. A couple of hospital personnel were smoking over by a hibiscus bush, but they didn't look up as we emerged. Before I finished thanking the woman, Ally's rented car stopped beside us. Within moments, I was helped in and Sally had disappeared.

It was a cool and overcast day and fortunately no one noticed us. Stopped at a set of traffic lights, a nearby newsagent stand had headlines shrieking at the front: *Famous journalist murdered! Concert Pianist in Murder Death!*

Murder death? Puleeeeeeeese. Would the man who attacked me be able to find out where I lived? My phone number is 'silent,' but anyone could find out where I live. If the man who whacked me didn't know who I was *then*, he certainly did now. I kept my eyes down and allowed my hair to flop around my face. Perspiration prickled my scalp and formed beads under my arms.

We stopped on the way home to collect my belongings from the locker at Roma Street Transit Centre and headed off, hoping that the media wouldn't have worked out where I was.

The house organisers were just leaving when we pulled into my park under the building. They stopped for a few minutes and exclaimed over my battered appearance, before leaping into their vans and waving cheerfully as they left.

Arriving home after a long time away, in this case I had been gone six months, it's always a novelty to see one's belongings again. The photos I'd forgotten, the ornaments I hadn't seen, in some cases for years, even the familiar tea towels in the kitchen made m e feel comfortable. The hall stand where I hung my coat was exactly where it should be, the cushions on my lounge suite were slightly askew as though I had just vacated it. I couldn't wait to go through my books again. Several magazines were on the table by the window; my stereo waited patiently for me to put on a CD.

'Do you want something to eat or a drink?' Ally asked, as she shut and bolted the front door behind us.

'No, quite honestly, Ally, I just need to lie down. I felt fine at the hospital, but now I'm stuffed. Then I have to practice.'

'Don't be silly, Pam. You can't practice in your state. At least wait until you feel a bit better.'

'You of all people should know I have to keep it up. I haven't done anything since yesterday. Look, I'll lie down and rest before I do it, okay?'

'All right, off to bed. Do you want a hand to get up there?' She gestured to the three steps up from the lounge room where the bathroom, my bedroom and my music room opened off a small landing.

'No, I'll just take it slowly.'

She galloped ahead of me, carrying my bags which she put on the bench near the balcony door. The familiar pale blue walls, white trim and pretty patterned curtains billowing in the breeze calmed me. My favourite feather duvet, bottled water on the bedside table, bookshelf filled...what more could I want? *My cousin alive for starters.* Someone who would hold me in the night and comfort my wounded self would be nice too...*you're full of self pity, Miller. Shake out of it.*

I dutifully took my medication and Ally turned down my bed. 'Now, rest,' she said sternly. 'I'll bring you a frothy coffee and then make something for your dinner.'

'Are you staying for the afternoon? I don't want to be alone right now.'

'Of course I can stay. The kids are with Brie at his parents place having a wonderful time being spoiled rotten!' She closed the bedroom door and clattered downstairs. Moments later a Mozart Symphony wafted gently up the stairs.

I couldn't sleep. Frustrated, I thrashed around for about half an hour, then got up and moved restlessly around the room, picking things up and putting them down. As a diversion from the horrendous happenings of the last couple of days, it was a dead loss. The Sunday Mail lay on the table beside the books. I fumbled through my bag for my reading glasses, picked it up and looked at the front page. *International Photo Journalist Murdered!* screamed the headline. A photo of Goldie accepting an award was splashed across the front page. Grief squeezed my heart. *Oh, Goldie.* Further down the page, my own photo was set beside a small article explaining who I was and that I had found Goldie's body, inferring that Pamela Miller was a "person of interest."

Hastily turning the page, there was more tragedy. A girl's body had been found in the park where Goldie and I had spent many happy hours walking, just a few streets away from my home and Goldie's house. The police were calling for anyone who'd seen anything untoward to come forward. I recalled the roadblock on Montague Road on the way home Saturday night, just before I found Goldie. While I had been happily playing in the concert and dining with Ally and Brie, the worst had happened.

I turned the page and tried to read a feature about the antics of a minor film star, a right scrubber by all accounts, but it was no good. Tossing it aside, I examined the books, thinking that perhaps reading for a while would make me forget the trauma of the last couple of days. I sorted through them, an eclectic lot from which I chose the autobiography of a somewhat splendidly proportioned woman cook, half of a fun duo, who had been on television a few years ago.

I was about to call Ally and suggest we practice together, when a waft of cool air from the open window sent a chill over my bare arms. As I started to pull the sash down, something attracted my attention across the road.

It was all I could do not to scream the place down.

Heart pounding, I closed and locked it, pulled the curtains across and groped for a robe and tottered down the few steps to the lounge room, clinging to the banister.

Ally ran out of the kitchen, shocked, as I burst in. 'Pam, what's happened, you're as white as a ghost!'

Fighting for breath, I couldn't answer. She hurried out of the room and came back holding a paper bag wide open in front of my face. 'Come on, mate, deep breathe.'

I tried to tell her that's an urban myth, but she persisted, so rather than argue, I grabbed it and thrust my face inside.

'That's it, breathe in...hold it...breathe out. Breathe in...breathe out...I'll get some water, breathe for goodness sake. Keep going Pam, breathe in...breathe out...'

Eventually I was relatively normal, apart from a thudding heart, trembling all over, cold invading my body. Ally looked at me with concern. 'What happened? ' She took my hands in hers. 'God, you're freezing. I'll turn the fire on; you're like an ice block.'

'The man who hit me was in the garden! It had to be him. He was wearing sunglasses and a hoodie.'

She wanted to go outside and look around, but I stopped her and phoned the cops who arrived shortly after, sirens wailing. My neighbours popped out of their doors. Any self-respecting mugger would have long gone, but the police discovered foot prints directly under the lowset balcony in the soft garden bed. As soon as my connection with Goldie's murder was mentioned again, mobile phones leapt into action.

Two grave-faced older detectives arrived. For a fleeting moment, I wished Anthony Hamilton had come and then chided myself. *For goodness sake, Pam, you've got rocks in your head. Don't go there.*

The uniformed officers prowled around outside. The detectives settled in the lounge, with Ally close beside me, holding my hand. My relatives had arrived in response to her phone call, despite my protestations. 'It doesn't matter, Pam. *You* need support this time.'

Alex, visibly aged, sat in the lounge chair furthest from me. Fiona didn't say much, but stayed near the door holding her handkerchief over her mouth. She had moved to kiss me when they arrived but a hard glance from her husband stopped her. *Oh no.*

The older detective looked thoughtfully at the dressing on my temple. 'Miss Miller, do you think the man standing outside was the one who attacked and tried to rob you yesterday in the Gardens?'

'Yes. He was wearing a black, hooded jacket. The sun was behind him and he was wearing a pair of those big square sunglasses that cover half the face. I think he was youngish, though. Oh, and I remember now. He had a bandaid on his finger!'

'How would he know where you are? Could he have been on the same plane from Sydney or at the concert on Saturday night? In other words, could he be stalking you?'

'I don't know. He may have been someone I've talked to, perhaps someone I've met. There was something familiar about him, but I can't work out what it was. I was looking directly into the sun, so I couldn't see his features under the sunglasses. With my face splattered all over the papers, it wouldn't be surprising if some idiot decided to rob me.'

The detective watched me like a hawk, perhaps expecting me to either change or add to my story. Perhaps he just thought I was still disoriented or over-wrought from Goldie's death. Maybe I was just a hysterical woman.

'I didn't see anyone acting strangely on the plane or at the airport, even at the transit centre when I got here. I didn't see anything out of the ordinary at the concert. Really, I just don't know, but the papers are full of Goldie and me.'

'If you remember who it might be, let us know immediately. We'll get the report on the incident. Do you remember which hand?'

'What?'

'His finger. Do you remember which hand had the bandaid on the finger?'

'Er...no.' I felt very silly and small. Why couldn't I remember at least that detail?

They looked at each other, before the younger one replied. 'We've checked the gardens all around the units. You need to make sure the windows are fastened securely and we'd advise you not to go out alone tomorrow. Have someone with you –' he glanced at Ally – 'your sister? Are your parents in Brisbane?'

'Ally's my friend and no, mum's in hospital and John's up here in Brisbane. They live out at Emsberg. I promise I'll stay inside.'

Alex looked thoughtful. I caught something fleeting and nasty in his expression before he finally spoke to me, his voice cold. 'Yes, you need to stay inside where *you'll* be safe.'

The inference was that I was a coward who should have been killed instead of Goldie. Alex wanted me punished for being alive. Hadn't the man been just under my balcony and wasn't there a tree abutting it?

The detectives glanced at each other. No fools, they'd picked up the vibes emanating from Alex. 'We'll put the report in and liaise with Homicide. There's no knowing if this is connected in any way to Ms Humphries' death and you can't positively identify the prowler as your assailant. Can you come into the station tomorrow and look through some photos?'

I agreed that I could.

'We'll leave you to sort it out, then,' said the Detective Sergeant, snapping his notebook shut.

'I'll bring Pam in tomorrow morning,' Ally promised. The detectives left, followed quickly by Alex. My aunt hesitated, but a snarl from her husband had her scurrying from the room with an apologetic glance at me.

'What was that all about?' Ally stared after them, puzzled.

Sighing, I recounted, in detail, what had happened between my uncle and me late Saturday night and on Sunday morning.

CHAPTER 22

Susan

Operation Lima Photo

Monday, 10am

The news that Pamela Miller had been attacked at the Roma Street Parklands hit me hard as did the follow-up.

Briony Feldman had approached me with a slip of paper. 'Ma'am, this came in a few minutes ago.' She gave a brief smile and departed. I gazed at the note in consternation. 'West End advises that Pamela Miller saw a man watching her unit yesterday and she thinks it could have been the man who attacked her in the park. Apparently, this one was about the same height and size, and also wearing a hoodie. Didn't get a good look at his face. Browning and Morse have gone to interview her.'

Startled glances were exchanged and a rustle of comment spread throughout the team. Our new Detective Senior Sergeant looked thunderous. We'd dismissed the possibility that Pam might have been the target and Marigold Humphries had got in the way. Now I wondered if she had been the intended victim after all and *Humphries* had gotten in the way. 'What on earth was she doing at the Parklands?' I asked of Evan and young Jacob, the latest recruit to our team.

Jacob said that Pam had told Anthony Hamilton she needed time out from the aftermath of the murder. 'A friend is bringing her into the station to make a formal statement and see if she can identify anyone. They kept her overnight at the hospital, but she should be home by now.'

'Okay.'

'Ah, well let me know when she gets here, will you? Now, everyone in for the Humphries briefing.'

Assuring me that the team was back, with the exception of a couple still following up interviews around the 'Death Cottage' as the media were calling it, we moved to the Incident Room. The bright face of Marigold Humphries glowed down from the board, accompanied on either side by the stalker, Adam McIntyre and the reporter who had invited her to go with him to Jane Doe's murder site. Above Marigold was her father's name, encircled. Yes, it was most unlikely, but his reported hostility to Pamela could be of interest. Across the bottom Evan had drawn a timeline.

As I waited for the stragglers amongst my team to join the briefing, my thoughts swung back to Humphries' house which Evan and I had inspected early on Sunday morning while Forensics attended to their main business, the immediate crime scene surrounding the victim's body. We wanted to get in there before they moved into the rest of the house and before Fingerprints covered the area in powder and glue.

Originally a 1920s workman's cottage, another storey had been added to it somewhere in its history. The morning light would make it possible to get some idea of the person who owned it. I'd arrived back at eight o'clock Sunday morning, accompanied by an exhausted Evan. We'd logged in, gloved and booteed up, and then entered through the back door in order not to disturb the immediate crime scene and upset the scientists, whose vehicles clogged the driveway. Out the front, the media howled for information. A series of impeccably groomed young women with serious faces were taking turns at reporting from the front gate. Marigold Humphries' death was big news.

The narrow laundry led to, what was for me and certainly Evan who had four children, an abnormally tidy kitchen. Someone had taken the house phone off the hook and laid it on the kitchen counter. The only items on the draining board had been a used coffee mug and a side-plate with a butter-smeared knife lying across it. So, no sign of a late-night guest.

Evan made a note while I visually examined the magnets adorning the refrigerator door – mementos of her travels, lots of wildlife, a plastic yabby waving it's fragile claws at me. I opened the door and peered inside. A half-full pot of acidophilus yoghurt, a square of butter, partially wrapped, Vegemite and couple of tomatoes, strips of bacon and half a dozen eggs completed the inventory. Two bottles of chardonnay – one half empty – stood sentinel by a one litre bottle of Real Milk. *So, not much cooking going on then?*

The freezer drawer was packed with frozen pre-cooked meals. Some were commercial, many obviously homemade which tended to indicate that Marigold's mother must have been aware of her daughter's slapdash diet. Hanging on cup hooks from the underside of the overhead cupboards was a set of crude pottery mugs painted with what looked like African scenes.

'Not much in the food cupboard,' Evan said, as he poked the pantry door open with the tip of his pen and peered inside. Apart from a comprehensive herb and spice rack, the contents of the storage cupboard consisted mainly of packets of biscuits and tinned food. Cobwebs and moths could be seen through a clear glass jar containing muesli. A packet of teabags and half a jar of instant coffee made up the list from there. At the far end were stacked tiers of exotic-looking crockery and wineglasses, obviously party-ware. To say the young woman had been a "non-cook" would have been over-stating the case.

I'd lifted the lid of the garbage can near the sink with the tip of my gloved finger, but it was lined with a clean plastic shopping bag. Evan scooted out the back door and I could hear him rummaging around. 'We'll have to check when the garbage collection came round, but there was only one empty Lean Cuisine packet in there along with a pile of newspapers and magazines. The boys'll be checking it this morning,' he reported. He prised open a cupboard under the bench. 'There's stacks of stuff in here, but the coffee mugs are dusty. Can't have had too many visitors!'

'She mightn't have been home for a long time. We'll have to check with her parents, they'll know.' The usual kitchen drawer with odds and ends had just that – a half empty packet of bandaids, bobby pins, rubber bands, old receipts, several biros, several buttons, a reel of white cotton stained from what looked like gravy, a couple of menus from takeaway shops...the accumulation of things that we women might find useful, know we won't but can't bear to throw away.

So far, it had been hard to get a "handle" on the woman's personality. Anyone who travelled for her work as often and for as long as she had could be forgiven for not accumulating too many possessions, but I was surprised by the lack of bits and pieces which usually surround women.

The photo journalist's body was being removed as we moved into the lounge-dining room. An unprofessional spurt of rage shot through me, as I watched the bagged body of the brilliant young woman being strapped to a gurney. So much talent and so much to offer...all gone, leaving devastation in the wake of the crime. How many times had I watched as husbands, parents, siblings and friends bowed beneath crushing pain. Accidents were bad enough, Heaven knows, but *murder?*

Outside, the media frenzy rose in a crescendo as the loaded gurney was trundled to a waiting van to be transported to the city morgue.

The room was cold and felt spiritually empty, not only because it was, but because the energy of its owner had fled. The lounge suite looked as though the stuffing had shrunk, the papers on the coffee table abandoned. The gallery of photographs stared back at me, blank-faced and meaningless, but the eyes of the man I'd been told was the love of Marigold Humphries' life watched with gentle amusement, privy to a secret which only those in the afterlife shared. Did spirits find each other as soon as the host died?

Evan paused to examine Humphries collection of CDs and DVDs, most of which appeared to be copies of news programs. 'Doubt if any of these are relevant, but we'll get her boss to have a look,' he said, making a note.

A shelf of beautifully carved African animals looked on from a shelf above the fireplace.

Seeing that some of the SOC officers were packing up, I enquired if we could go upstairs. "Fingerprints'll be here any minuted,' advised the young Forensic officer as she packed up her kit.

Knowing the house would shortly be a disaster area, we hastily ascended the stairs. After "cottage" style lounge room, the upstairs quarters were a surprise. Ms Humphries had made up for the Spartan furnishings with bold primary colours in all the rooms. We found Pamela Miller's belongings in the guest room; she had been brought here late the previous morning, but couldn't say whether anything was missing, with the exception of Humphries' very expensive new Nikon camera. Perhaps the parents would know.

The main bedroom boasted an un-made double bed, built in wardrobes, a dressing table and a chair. Painted all in white with multi-coloured curtains and a few pictures of wildlife on the walls, the pile of clothes strewn across the bed, knickers half under the bed and scattered underclothes indicated that the occupant was not the perfect house-keeper. Then, why would she be? Living on one's own means you can do what you like.

The office next door housed a large desk, chair on castors and the walls lined with bookcases, crammed with everything from chick-lit, crime and non-fiction, with books piled on top of each other. Papers were heaped next to the laptop computer, indicating work in progress. Presumably relating to photographic work, they were likely to be outside my sphere of knowledge.

'We've taken three cameras in for examination, Ma'am. I've come for the laptop and CDs, her handbag as well. We got her appointments from her mobile. There's a list of calls made and received.'

I whirled around. A young constable stood in the doorway, eyes glittering with anticipation.

'I didn't hear you come in!'

'Sorry Ma'am.'

'Hm...okay. Let me know what you find, and let me know the contents of the handbag particularly. ' I'd muttered, trying to cover my tracks. It would never do to drop my guard at a crime scene.

So, who would want to kill the photojournalist? Could a former lover or enemy have ambushed her? Perhaps her colleagues would have some ideas. Nothing downstairs or up here had been disturbed as far as we could tell. That suggested that she'd answered the door, let someone into the house and been killed there and then. Was it someone she'd "outed" in one of her investigative articles? We could only assume it was something she knew or had witnessed. I'd officiated at many murders but understanding the psyche of a killer wasn't getting any easier to cope with.

Awakening from memory lane brought me into the present. My gaze ranged along the rows of officers, waiting attentively for me to start the briefing. The new face was missing. 'Where's Hamilton?'

'On his way in, Ma'am.'

'Right, we'll –' I noticed the eyes of my female officers tracking the sublime bum of our newest Senior Sergeant. *I, of course, never notice such things.*

Our resident "assassin," seemingly oblivious to the interest he incurred, took his place at the end of the front row. Evan prepared to adjust the timeline of Marigold

Humphries final hours on the adjacent whiteboard, as Jacob recited her known movements.

'Okay, Operation Lima Photo. Marigold Humphries, aged 33, single, freelance journalist. Parents, Alexander and Fiona Humphries, of 5 Hampton St, West End. So far, we know cause of death was a broken neck. No DNA under her fingernails – apparently she kept them clipped short – but a small amount of blood in her mouth and teeth which was not hers, so she bit him somewhere, but probably not enough to send him to a doctor or hospital, unfortunately, Ma'am. On the other hand, DNA when we catch him.'

'Well, that's *something*. Continue, Jacob.'

'NAFIS reports no matches to any of the prints found in the house.' He paused, presumably to let that sink into our consciousness. 'Ms Humphries travels –– travelled – the world taking jobs, mainly under contract to media organisations. She was in Afghanistan on an assignment for –' He named a leading television station – 'and then in a UK hospital until a month ago, when she arrived back in Australia. She spent two weeks in Sydney partially on holiday and then arrived in Brisbane. For the last two weeks, according to colleagues, she's been doing a series of articles on local politics. They say she's well-liked and were genuinely horrified to hear about her death.'

He paused while the team made notes, and then recounted Pamela's statement of what had occurred that morning. 'Humphries arrived back at her house around seven and they had breakfast together. Miller says her cousin didn't discuss her photographic session and that they talked about the concert. Miller left at approximately 10.30am in Ms Humphries' Golf for the concert hall at Southbank. Humphries' laptop and emails show that she worked on the article for Kings River Life magazine for an hour and sixteen minutes.'

'King's River Life? What do we know about it?'

'An American online magazine, Ma'am. Specialises in local news, the theatre restaurants, concerts, book reviews and it's very big on animal welfare issues, animal shelters and rescue organisations.'

'We know she was into exposing animal abuse, factory farms and puppy mills. It's a bit of a long shot that someone associated with those issues in America would break her neck here in Australia and in her own home, but we'll keep it in mind. Go on, Jacob.'

He turned the page. 'CCTV footage taken at 4am from down at the ferry terminal shows Marigold Humphries walking along the path through the park. She stopped here and there to take photos, but then she heads in the general direction of the top end of the park where the boat shed is. No CCTV.'

'Did we check out the rowers on the river?'

'Yes, Ma'am. The first crews came by at about 4.30 and they said they hadn't seen or heard anything.' It didn't surprise me. That lot wouldn't have heard a cannon going off when they were training and they'd have been in the middle of the river.

'Okay, anything from Humphrey's mobile or house phone?'

'No Ma'am. There's a list here. Nothing significant, just calls to her workplace, colleagues, clients – Pamela Miller and her parents. There was a text from Harry Brown telling her to meet him out the front of the concert hall, that there was a murder in West End. She replied, "OK." That was when she went to the murder scene at the park and that's the last activity on her mobile.

She doesn't appear to have kept her financial records on her iPhone.'

'Right. So that's all we have from the mobile, how about her laptop? iPad? Blackberry?'

'Techs are still examining those, Ma'am. We'll have a record of all her financial and business transactions shortly.'

'What about her handbag?'

'The usual things, Ma'am. Make-up, small hairbrush, receipts, notebook – more about that later – address book which we're following up now. A Kindle with 1230 books on it! Bottle of water, half-full, a nail file set, keys to the house and car. Tissues – unused – purse with credit cards, licence, photos, discount cards from dress shops and camera outlets...' So, the traditional woman's gear. I'd be interested to hear what the notebooks contained, but no doubt the techs would let us know if there was anything significant in them.

As Jacob finished, I advised the team of my connection with Pamela Miller, her mother and stepfather. 'According to Ms Humphries' solicitor, Pamela Miller is the chief beneficiary and the Humphries parents are the recipients of a large separate superannuation. Apart from that, there are a few bequests to friends. Obviously, Ms Miller doesn't know about this as yet and I must caution you to keep it in this room.' I lowered the paper and looked at the team.

'So Pamela Miller is the main suspect?' someone asked.

'Before I could answer, a grim-faced Hamilton piped up. 'There's no way Pamela killed anyone!'

Shocked silence greeted the announcement. Sidelong glances flew around the room. I glared in the general direction of the back row to quell a titter. 'Why do you say that, Anthony?' His angry expression intrigued me.

Just what had gone on after he left with Pam to inform her uncle and aunt of her cousin's death?

'Because she couldn't have killed a woman of Marigold Humphries' physique. There was evidence of a struggle and Humphries was an Amazon. Miller would have been no match for her even though they're the same height.'

There was more to this than met the eye. Could our resident hunk have a little something for Pamela? Did *she* know? *Well, he's not married, but he'll have to be careful.* Hm...I would have a word with my Senior Sergeant after the session and see what was going on. 'You're right about that. It's pretty unlikely –' I turned back to the board, hoping to divert the team's attention away from Anthony – 'but we have to leave her in the mix. SOCO says there was evidence that someone wiped the wall at the bottom of the stairs successfully smudging any prints. However, they are hopeful of DNA and that'll be good if we can only match it to someone. Now, what about the neighbours and bystanders?'

'We doorknocked the whole street, but no one saw anything, heard anything or speaks ill of the dead.'

'Okay, so it's business as normal. What else?'

'There is nothing to show what she did for the rest of the day, though she called on her parents around 3pm and left about half an hour later. Miller says Humphries was not at home when she arrived back from rehearsal at the Concert Hall about 3.30pm. She stopped to buy a dress on the way apparently. Jack Boode Thompson, a fellow journalist, says he met Humphries around 4pm to talk about an African program they were to do together, and then they went to a pub and had a session with colleagues. This is confirmed by the group and there's a list here.' Jacob waved his notebook in the air. 'They said she caught a taxi home at about 5.30pm. Yellow Cabs tracked down the driver, who maintains he dropped her off at 5.45pm. There was no one with her and no sign of anyone waiting for her when she got out of the cab. She went straight in and he left.'

Jacob took a deep breath. He looked about as fresh as we all felt. 'Harry Burke, a reporter from the Courier Mail said he picked Humphries up at home and gave her a lift to the concert hall at 7.30pm. They were going to meet later, but he sent her an SMS at 8.15pm to say that he was going to a murder scene. Humphries insisted he swing by the Concert Hall and pick her up out the front and she accompanied him to the park where the Jane Doe was found and then he dropped her back at the concert just as it was finishing at around 10pm.'

He went on to relate Pamela's statement about Humphries' activities at the concert that night. 'We're getting the tapes from the security cameras in the foyer of the Concert Hall later this morning. Witnesses say that Miller stayed for photographs and to talk to fans, after which she went to the city with a couple –' he named the Mochries' – of musicians. The restaurant confirms they were there and time of leaving.' Jacob closed his notebook and sat down.

'Well, we know one thing. Ms Humphries' main camera, a Nikon 4, is missing so we don't know what photos she took. We now know that she lent her second string camera, a Nikon 2 to Pamela Miller and it had a new card in it. The question is, did Ms Humphries take a photo of something she shouldn't have seen on the Nikon 4?'

We all stared at the timeline and then at each other. Speculation broke out. Something was nagging me...'Anyone check the view of the river and surrounds from the *park* crime scene? Remember, there's nothing to say she was anywhere *near* the old rowing shed and her house is streets away.'

No one had. 'Okay, so what else might Humphries have taken photos of? Would she have gone as far as the shed on foot?'

'Jane Doe?' Anthony Hamilton picked up my thoughts immediately.

My team pounced on the possibility that not only had Humphries photographed the girl but also the man – or woman – she was probably with. There was nothing to say at this stage whether the DNA around her mouth was male or female, but my gut said, "male."

'But if it was connected, how did he get to do the journalist over late Saturday night? And unless he spoke to her, how would he know where to find her? Was he in fact, one of the mob at the park crime scene? We need to ask Harry Burke why Humphries didn't speak to one of the officers at the Jane Doe crime scene and say she was there early in the morning.'

'Perhaps she never went that far. Maybe she saw them further back toward the terminal? She could have given him – or them – a card and said to call her later, perhaps to give them the photos?'

'But there's nothing on her mobile or her emails to show that anyone did. The girl may have already been killed and the body covered up before the journalist arrived in the park.'

Back to the drawing board, literally.

I sent Jacob to trundle the whiteboard in from the Lima Astro Incident Room. He parked it next to the Humphries board. I took a pointer and followed the action through, working along the timeline.'

'Perhaps the couple – Jane Doe and her companion – were people she knew already?' someone asked.

'Even if they did, the girl was killed in the morning and the journalist late at night and by the appearance and age of Doe, it would be unlikely that the women knew each other socially, although anything's possible. As far as we know, the only things they had in common was that it was the same day, they were female and found in roughly the same area. Robert Simkins' dog found the shoe at around 8 – 8.15 this morning and Humphries left her house at 4.30am according to Pamela Miller. Of course, we can't rule out the possibility that this was a random attack by a predator, but there was no evidence of rape and she *was* fully clothed.'

The team were silent for a moment. Predator attacks on women jogging or walking listening to their iPods were more prevalent these days.

'So has anyone anything to add?'

No one had any suggestions. Evan frowned. 'We're canvassing backpacker hostels and hotels. Collins and Freeman are going to the colleges, and Brown and Douglas to the universities. That only leaves workplaces, but if someone doesn't turn up sooner or later a boss will send someone to her home.' Groans rippled around the room. 'So let's get back to Humphries for now.'

Theories abounded, from the traditional random break-in which had gone wrong to the ex-boyfriend out to make up with Marigold Humphries and retaliating after rejection. In the middle of the sometimes excitable discussion, David texted me – 'All okay. Luv u. X.' Refreshed, I entered into the fray, directing a question to the team at large. 'So what makes you think it wasn't a random break in?'

The room stopped talking. Jacob looked earnest. 'Well, why would a perp choose that particular place to break and enter? It's not particularly outstanding. I mean, there's other houses which look richer.' He looked around for support.

'He's right,' broke in Sym, short for Symphony – *what gets into some parents?* – bright-faced and a Jacob groupie. 'There's no *indication* the victim had money or even that she was famous. Surely that shows she knew the perp?'

'Not necessarily. She could have been followed home. The taxi driver could have done it for all we know.' Sym wasn't about to let her theory go.

I thought it unlikely. The skinny, old ferret with nasal drip we'd interviewed didn't look capable of over-powering a big, strong girl like Marigold Humphries, who would be too street-smart to let him even get near her.

'Any known enemies? Apart from this Adam McIntyre who was allegedly stalking her?'

We'd been unable to track him down for questioning. His paper said he'd left Friday morning for a job out west, but as he wasn't answering his mobile and hadn't been back to his motel since Saturday night, we had Roma police searching for him. He could have gotten back to Brisbane, killed Goldie and headed back out overnight, but he'd have to be pretty slick about it. I turned to Anthony Hamilton, who hadn't contributed anything to the debate so far. 'So how is Pamela coping, Anthony?'

'She's pretty cranky, actually. With being attacked on all sides over this, she's not very happy.'

What do you mean, attacked on *all* sides?' The room turned to look at him.

'Well, her uncle, Alex Humphries was a bastard to her the other night and again yesterday morning.

Seemed to think she didn't care about her cousin. I got the impression that if Pam had died instead of his daughter, he'd have been delighted. Of course, that could be natural under the circumstances, but his hatred of Pam – Ms Miller – is over the top, in *my* opinion.'

Hm. Was Alex Humphries looking for a scapegoat or trying to point the finger of blame away from himself? 'How is Fiona Humphries behaving toward Pamela?'

Anthony took his time to reply. 'Well, she's a traditional wife –' we female officers bristled; the males grinned, blast them – 'in that she's under his thumb. She'll probably go along with whatever he says. She's in that age-bracket,' he explained hastily, no doubt realising a lynching party was imminent. He smiled ruefully and we women melted. *I bet he has sisters.*

'Do you think it's possible that either of *them* could be responsible? I know Fiona couldn't tackle Marigold, but what about Alex?'

'Stranger things have happened in families.' Oh yes, we all knew the consequences of domestic violence. I looked at Hamilton. 'What did Pam say about the relationship between Marigold and her family?'

'She didn't talk about it much, but she did say that Alex has a hasty temper and that her aunt is always placating him,' he replied, sheepishly. 'I'll ask her about it again t –' He stopped abruptly.

After handing out assignments for the team, I took Anthony Hamilton in tow. 'Hold everything,' I told one my admin assistant. 'Give me ten minutes?'

She smiled, nodded and went back to her computer screen.

'Come in, Anthony.'

He looked at me warily and stepped into what I laughingly referred to as 'my office.' I cleared some papers off the only chair available, invited him to sit and squeezed into my chair on the other side of the desk.

'So what gives with you and Pam Miller?' I placed my elbows on the desk, fingers steepled.

He wriggled. 'Nothing's going on with Pa – Ms Miller.'

Yet, you mean. 'You could have fooled me! Listen, Anthony, you know she's a suspect, purely because a) she found the body and b) she's the heir to Humphries' will. So tell me why you know she's innocent?'

There was quite a long pause, while my new Senior Sergeant gathered his argument, visibly struggling with what to say. Finally he gave up. 'I don't think she's that sort of person!'

My eyebrows mingled with my hairline. Suddenly his mobile chirped. "Excuse me, Ma'am.'

I watched as Hamilton took a call, puzzled when he broke into what was for him, a huge grin. *Hm.*

'That was West End Uniform. They stopped Pamela Miller on her way home from the city twelve minutes before she rang Triple 0 from Humphries' house!'

Relief swept over me. 'How come they didn't tell us before?'

'I left a message with traffic patrol to check how many people they had to turn back after the Jane Doe was found. There were quite a few, but he'd run all the number plates through the motor registry. Pam's name came up driving Humphries' car. He recognised her in the reports.'

'Good thinking, mate!' The corners of his mouth twitched, indicating extreme pleasure in my praise. 'Okay, so you have feelings for Pamela?'

'I only just met her at the Humphries house.' *Cool as the proverbial cucumber.* 'My behaviour has always been professional and it will remain so, Ma'am.'

'I know you were, are and will be, Anthony. Okay, carry on.'

CHAPTER 23

Susan

Boadicea on the Rampage

Monday, 2pm

Exhaustion hit. I put my head in my hands and closed my eyes. *I'm so very, very tired. How am I going to get through this? At my age? How would David feel about it?*

Thank God he SMS'd me. All police officers know that an investigation – especially undercover – can go arse-up in minutes. Negative thoughts weren't going to help; I didn't have good vibes about David's safety, for all his pretence that it was a normal secondment.

'Susan? *Susan?*'

Evan stood before me, hands full of papers. 'Are you okay? How long is it since you slept?'

'I went to Melanie's to have a shower and change.'

'But you didn't have a kip. Typical. So what's with Hamilton?' Evan plopped himself into the chair. 'Is he going to be a problem?'

'No, not at all, Evan. He's fine. He's doing the right thing.'

'Yeah. Why don't you go home and this time get some rest? I'm here, Hamilton's here. You get some "shut-eye." Peterson and I are going to do the press conference shortly. You don't want to be around for that!'

A cracking headache had started behind my eyes.

'You know what? I think I will...'

No matter how hard I tried, sleep wouldn't come. I'd driven home desperate to dive into bed and pull the covers over my head. Barging past the weekly wash piled in the laundry tub, I tripped over the dog's water bowl, stopped to re-fill it and mop up the mess, then raced into the kitchen intent on a sandwich. The lady we employed to housekeep a couple of days a week was on holidays and her replacement sick. *Damn, I'll have to find time to do it myself.*

The animals were delighted to see me. 'Wow, the pushover's here! Let's eat! Let's play!' For a short time we did, but all good things come to an end. Soaking in the bath with a couple of cats sitting on the end is not my idea of fun. They're always so darned impatient, and they can't help swatting each other. More than once one of them has fallen in. The prospect of towelling off a soggy, angry cat before I managed to dry myself, didn't appeal. 'Well, I've got news for you two. I'm having a shower, so get over it!' *Am I reduced to talking to the cats now? Yep.*

I bolted to the bathroom, threw myself under the shower and out, then pulled across the blackout curtains which David and I had hung especially for when we were on "nights." Even wearing my husband's pyjamas I couldn't settle. *What's David going to say when he hears my news?* My thoughts squirreled around, interspersed with Pamela Miller and our little Jane Doe and the photo journalist, Marigold Humphries. I squinted at my watch in the gloom: 3.30pm.

Then the dogs started barking. I crawled out of bed, went to the window which overlooked the front of the house and pulled the curtains. *Oh no.*

My mother, a modern-day Boadicea, was charging – sans chariot – toward the front door, her expression boding ill for anyone in her path. Well, right now, that would be me. What had I done now, or more likely not done? Sighing, I dragged my dressing gown on, slipped my mobile phone into the pocket and headed downstairs to find out. Mother and I are – to say the least – incompatible.

There is no mistaking the signs of a disappointed woman; my mother was classic in that regard. Her mouth had been turned down with disdain so often over the years it had achieved permanency. A woman who plays favourites as expertly as she plays bridge, mum is a master of manipulation. Set for a career as a classical pianist by our grandmother, her expectations had been cut short by her hand being broken in a car door when she was twenty. That she had been throwing a tantrum at the time and brought it on herself was something our grandmother made known on frequent occasions.

Mother's disgust at what she regarded as our worthless careers, when my sister Melanie and I became respectively a vicar and a police officer, tempers my compassion considerably. My father, ground into submission over the years, took the line of least resistance and kept a low profile, "doing his own thing." An architect by profession, he indulged our mother, because deep down I think he really did love her and supported her in her music teaching and overseas trips.

Melanie's husband had been terrified of her, but David was made of sterner stuff. He wouldn't tolerate her "put downs" and verbal abuse of me or of Melanie. Mother couldn't contain her satisfaction when our marriage broke down. 'It serves you right, Susan, marrying that lout. You might have known a man like that' – she meant so good-looking – 'wouldn't be able to keep his hands off other women!'

Mother's reaction when I re-married David had to be heard to be believed. So this was the woman who was currently demanding admittance. *How did she know I was here?* Normally I would have been at work, but she lived en route to our house and probably saw me trying to "tip-toe" past.

'Susan! David has to sort out our neighbours,' she shouted. With barely a glance at me, she threw her handbag onto the lounge in passing and headed for the kitchen, where she tutted over my crockery and utensils in the sink. 'I do wish you would keep a tidy house!' She swung around to face me. 'Tidy is as tidy does. You should know that, being a *detective*.' The corners of her mouth turned down. 'And that dog shouldn't be in the house!'

She lifted a sensibly-clad foot to boot our border collie, but I caught him by the collar just as his lip lifted and shoved him out the back door. 'To what do we owe the pleasure of this visit?' Mother should have known that when I am using correct English, I'm at my most intractable.

'I was passing and saw your car in the driveway. What are you doing at home? 'Without waiting for me to answer, she carried on. 'The next door neighbours are selling drugs and I want David to do something about it! And they're building a pergola right next to our fence and a swimming pool! I won't have it. They'll be swimming in the nude and goodness knows what else.'

Mother's intense dislike of David could always be overcome when there was something she thought he could do for her. As her neighbours are a young couple with lots of upmarket friends and throw uproarious parties, her suspicions were not as unlikely as they sounded.

'Mum, that's not David's area of expertise. He's Major Crime, not on the Council. You'll have to go there to make a complaint about the pool. The matter of the drugs is the Drug Squad's area of expertise. How do you know they're dealing or doing drugs? Have you seen anything which might be the case?' *Better pass it on if she has.* I ran my hand through my hair, debating whether to make coffee for us both – it would keep mother here longer – or to just get her out the door again as fast as I could. She took a little run at me and I backed into the pantry doorway.

'They have some strange-looking plants in the garden and they've always got people coming to visit. It's not rocket science, Susan. The council won't listen to me, you know that. Well, can't *you* ring them?' Her eyes bulged with excitement.

'Mum, I'm busy. I have two murders to investigate, I've only slept for a few hours since Saturday morning. I'm exhausted and haven't got the time to be phoning the council and arguing with bureaucrats. Put a formal complaint in writing and leave them to sort it out. Is there anything else you wanted to discuss?'

'Yes, they're building a mosque in Hitchins Street!'

I couldn't believe she'd left this titbit until last. '*What?*'

'You heard me, Susan. Those Muslims are planning to build a mosque at the back of us! There'll be thousands of cars coming and going, not to mention that shouting they do. You know, the one where they call everyone and his dog to prayers five times a day. We're getting up a petition for the Council. They just can't do it.'

For once I agreed with Mother. 'Okay, I'll sign it. Goodness knows what David will say about it.' Now I understood her concern. We too would be swamped in cars and traffic. Mother's lips mouéd into a superb cat's bum, but what she would have said next got lost in the ring tones of my phone.

Anthony Hamilton's voice thundered down the line. 'Susan, West End just advised us a couple came in to report their daughter's missing!

CHAPTER 24

Dingo

The Visit

1994.

It was so exciting! Visitors for the first time he could remember and they had children for him to play with. He'd been too young to remember any playmates when Daddy was there and Mummy wasn't so angry. At first he'd been frightened and then so shy that they had to push him into the group, but it wasn't long before he got over-excited. The adults had to calm him down. They made him sit in a circle with the others and play a game where everyone skipped around and dropped a parcel behind someone who had to take a turn to skip. Somehow though he waited, no one dropped the parcel behind him, so he had to pretend it didn't matter even though he wanted to cry.

In the background, his mother and two ladies drank wine while a baby slept in the pram parked in the corner of the room. For awhile everything went well. The children were given cakes and red cordial which tasted so sweet that he could hardly swallow it. He spilled some down the front of his new white shirt, but – apart from a look which he knew boded badly for later – his mother didn't say a word. Then the other children wanted to go outside, but he wasn't allowed. 'You *know* you can't leave the house!' his mother hissed, as she dragged him back into the lounge room by his shirt sleeve. Her guests stopped talking. Something about the way they looked at his mother made him uneasy, but within a few moments they turned back to the table.

She bent down, her breath hot in his ear. '*Go to your room and practice!*'

Reluctantly, he walked slowly down the hallway, upstairs into his room where dark wardrobes, heavy curtain and the little bathroom and toilet closet encompassed his world. One section had been turned into a music room with a grand piano where his mother accompanied him, a music stand, and a cupboard with all his music stacked neatly on the shelves. A violin stand in one corner, with a standard lamp parked at the correct angle for reading the scores. There were no toys, but plenty of reading material. Dingo loved books.

He went to the window and looked down into the garden where the visitor's three children were playing tag. His school work, music – everything had to be done inside. Frances had set up a study area across the hall from his room.

Among the few people who came to the big house, with acres of land behind it, were the delivery man with the groceries, the meter reader and a big bluff man whom he knew to be the vicar from the church down the road. After his father died, and they come to live in town, it took awhile before he knew that he was isolated from other children.

By the time he was eight, he knew his mother was mad. Other mums took their children to school because he saw them walking along the road from his window high above. Sometimes they would look up and wave. He always waved back, until the day his mother caught him at it and slapped him so hard across the face that he lay on the floor crying for hours. After that he didn't dare.

Trouble arrived. Two women came to the front door and demanded to be let in. His mother argued, but when they threatened to call the police, acquiesced and invited them into the lounge room. After a short time, she stormed upstairs to his room. Mouth pursed, she ran to his chest of drawers and dragged out clean clothes. 'Get changed into these. Come downstairs and behave. When they ask if you're allowed outside, you say you go out every day! *Understand*?' As she had her 'or else' expression in full force, he agreed.

Somehow they got through the interview with the ladies he understood later were "social" workers, and it was a while before anyone disturbed them again. His mother pointed out that as long as he kept up to his schooling and the Education Department was happy, no one would care what happened at home. The ladies came once or twice after that and he was trotted out for their inspection. One day he even played the piano for them and they nodded and smiled and said what a good boy he was. The word "prodigy" was mentioned. His mother smiled and smiled until they left, after which he was sent to the rooms his mother had set aside for his studies and bedroom. It was two days before she came for him, smiling and smiling and he was allowed down to the kitchen to eat.

Then came the day that his mother's old school friend found her and even Frances couldn't stop Anna and her sister, June, from visiting. They brought their children and June's newborn baby girl with them. Feigning graciousness, Frances invited them to afternoon tea thereby setting the stage for the worst day of his life.

As he stood watching the children playing in the garden, he was astonished to see his *mother* come out with her friends. Mouth agape, he stared as they joined in the children's game. *Why can't I play too? She won't let me even go outside. Well, I'm going!*

Filled with rage, he ran down the stairs and along the hall toward the front door. As he passed the lounge room, the sound of the baby screaming stopped him. Tiny fists waved above the edge of the pram. He walked over and looked down. Red-faced, angry, the baby roared on. Its legs kicked free of the blanket; he could see runny yellow poo seeping from the side of the nappy. What to do? A large duffle bag was parked by a nearby chair. He rooted through it. Because his mother only allowed uplifting programs and the news on TV, he didn't know what to do with disposable nappies or other baby accoutrements.

Hey baby, don't cry.

The baby's screams increased. Frightened in case something was wrong with it, he yanked the sodden blanket toward him, jumping back as the baby came with it, rolling over the low side of the pram. The tiny thing jerked its arms as it started to fall. He grabbed, unaware that he had the child by the neck as he wrenched it away from the teetering pram. The baby's head felt like a doll's. Surprisingly heavy, the baby dangled from his hands, legs kicking feebly and then slowing.

The screaming stopped.

The body stilled.

Stunned by the suddenness of it all, he stood with the child hanging in his large, powerful musicians' hands. He looked down at yellow baby poo dripping down his bare leg into his sock.

Footsteps thundered into the house toward the lounge room.

'*What have you done?*'

Something connected with the side of his head, sending him crashing to the floor on his back, his hands still around the baby's head and neck, her body bouncing on his chest. His mother was thrust to one side and the child's mother hurled herself at him. '*You killed my baby! You've killed her!*'

The baby slipped through his fingers and rolled onto the floor.

The screaming went on and on. He got slowly to his feet, trembling as tears welled. His mother grabbed him by the back of the neck and threw him through the door onto the wood floorboards of the hallway. 'Get up to your room, you stinking, rotten little shit. *Murderer!*'

He crawled over to the bottom stair and leaned his back against the post, disconnected from the drama, unable to process what had occurred. Somewhere in the dim recesses of confusion, he knew the accident wouldn't have happened if the adults hadn't been outside having a good time.

Sirens sounded outside. His mother rushed out of the lounge-room to the front door to usher in the stampede of ambulance officers, carrying bags. No one told him what was happening. Sounds of frantic activity, combined with noisy crying came from the room. The other children gathered around the bottom of the stairs, with him but apart, all too frightened to make a sound. Another ambulance pulled up at the front gate and two more officers came through, this time pushing a trolley.

After what seem forever to the small boy, they came out of the room wheeling a tiny mound on top of the trolley. No one looked at the waiting children or spoke to them. The baby's mother, held up by her friend, staggered out the door. His mother marched over to the waiting group of four children. 'Your father is coming for you, so go into the kitchen and I'll get you something to eat.'

Terrified, the visitors scuttled away leaving Dingo cringing on the bottom step. 'You get upstairs. I'll deal with you later.' She grabbed him by the back of his collar and shoved him up the first few stairs before turning away. The front door opened and two uniformed police officers spoke to his mother. It was all too much. Dingo ran up the stairs, holding in sobs until he reached his room.

He didn't know how long he waited for someone to come. *Would she kill him this time?* Perspiration gathered in the small of his back and trickled down into his underpants. His shorts and socks were spattered with yellow poo. Too traumatised to make a sound, he slumped down into a corner and buried his head in his hands. Next came sounds of people arriving, voices raised and then – presumably the other children – leaving, followed by car doors slamming. Voices came from downstairs for a long time but finally darkness fell over the silent house. At one time he thought he heard the telephone ring and his mother moving around, but she did not come upstairs.

He must have fallen asleep. Suddenly the light in his room came on and Frances was looming over him. He braced himself to protect his head.

'Come downstairs. Someone wants to talk to you.'

He followed her to the kitchen where two policemen were standing, holding their caps in their hands. His mother steered him, none too gently, to the table and pushed him into a chair. The male policeman, who had to be older than God for the wrinkles on his face, sat opposite; the woman took the seat at the end of the table. Dingo kept his head down, hoping the throbbing in his ear would stop. His mother started making tea with jerky movements, as though she wanted to rip the teapot apart with her bare hands.

'Okay, son. Tell us what happened, in your own words.'

Saying nothing had always been his best defence when things got bad, so he remained silent.

'You do realise what happened to the baby, don't you? What were you trying to do with her, son? Were you trying to change her nappy?'

Soothed a little by the quiet tones and non-threatening body language, he nodded slowly.

'Why didn't you go and get her mummy?'

How could he tell the policeman that he was *never* allowed out of the house? Mum had told him time and again it was a secret and now she was watching him like a hawk, her prominent hazel eyes bulging like they always did when she was about to hurt him. She might get into trouble...*one, two three, four...five...if I get to ten will the policeman be gone?* He shrugged, staring at the table, his fingers twisting around each other. *One. Two. Three. Four...if I count in even numbers, then when I get to... twenty...they might go.* He so wanted to tell the truth, but he knew what would happen when the police left.

No matter how hard they tried, the policemen weren't able to get an answer. He wasn't capable of forming the words, could only just hold back the terror writhing deep inside. Though he wanted them to leave him alone, he was more frightened of being left to the mercy of

Frances...*perhaps if he counted to fifty...give them more time to go or keep them there so she couldn't hurt him?* At long last, reluctantly it seemed to even *his* young mind, the police left after a quiet conversation with his mother at the front door.

He stood up. Perhaps if he got to his room before she did, he'd be safe. Sensing his mother's attention turning to him, he tore upstairs, ran into his room and slammed the door behind him. He threw himself under the bed, trying to shut out the panic which threatened to send his heart leaping out of his chest. He knew something terrible would happen to him when the police were gone. He scrambled out and rushed to the door. Panting with terror, he started to push his chest of drawers across to block it. His muscles cracked, his feet scrabbled at the bare floor boards but he made it, just as his mother's footsteps came up to the other side of the door.

'Open this right now, you little turd!' she screamed, pounding on the panels. He climbed back under the bed and jammed his fingers into his ears as hard as he could, but her voice screeched on and on –'*The baby's dead! You killed my friend's baby! You don't deserve to live.*'

Hours later, he opened his eyes, rolled over and looked up at the window to watch the stars coming out. What was his mother doing? He hoped she was snoring her head off in a drunken stupor. Could he sneak downstairs and get something to eat? His tummy was hurting with hunger. Trying ever so hard not to make a noise, he pulled the chest of drawers back from the door, opened it and peered out. Sneaking along the darkened hallway held no fears. For Dingo, shadows had long been a sanctuary. He stopped at the landing to hear if she was moving around below. *Nothing.*

Feeling it might be safe he inched his way down, pausing every few steps to check for any sound. Knowing where the floorboards squeaked was a distinct advantage. He passed the lounge-room door, yellow police tape proclaiming a crime scene.

Safely in the kitchen, he opened the cupboard and took out the biscuits. There could be no dinner in case he woke her up, though experience had shown that it would take the house falling down to do that when she was drunk.

A soft click almost sent him into orbit, but he relaxed as the cat slithered through the cat door. Moving as fast as he dared, he took her dinner out of the refrigerator, scooped it into her bowl, checked her water and then sneaked a banana from the crisper. Stentorian snorts almost sent him into shock, but when they faded, he was even more frightened. When she was snoring, he was safe; if the sounds stopped she could be up and around. A Big Cat had nothing on Frances when it came to stalking and pouncing on her prey – him.

It was not until he was at university that he looked in the library microfiche files dating back to when he was eight, that he discovered that the police and Coroner's Court had absolved him of responsibility for the death of baby, Lucy Swales. It was then Dingo realised the depth of Frances' madness. She had never told him the outcome of the investigations, preferring to hold the child's death over his head throughout her life.

* * *

Music threaded through with faces sent his body into orbit. *Why did you do it? Why did you do it? Why didn't you let me go? We were having so much fun.' Ariel's face loomed close to his. He pushed her away and then he saw it again – the baby! You're dead you're dead you're dead! He stumbled back, but they advanced, slowly, staring...someone was panting...it was the journalist.*

He tried to run, to catch up, but the women bounded ahead of him, laughing, each holding a hand of the baby, who was running along on fat little legs. Something was wrong...the baby had been only a few days old – but he was running! They looked back at him and stopped. The journalist aimed a camera at him, started taking photos, laughed and ran to join the ...Ariel! Out of her box! He had to catch her but she was so far ahead it was impossible. No, no wait for me! He tried to keep up but his legs moved in slow motion. His arms thrashed, he forced his legs to wade through the sheets. You must always be gentle, darling. They don't all want to play. That was on a good day. Her bad days didn't bear thinking about.

His eyes flew open.

The gorgeous patterned ceiling of the room seemed to be coming down on him. He wiped his face with the edge of the sheet, damp with his sweat and eased his legs out of bed. Light streaming from the window showed the bedclothes half on the floor, pillows thrown around the room. He turned to sit on the side of the bed and tested his feet on the floor before he wobbled upright, supporting himself on the side table. *What am I going to do now?* Pam had the camera all along. No wonder there were no photos in the one he'd taken from the journalist's bag.

He shuffled to the bathroom, bent like an old man where he used the facility and stood gazing at his reflection, holding the back of the toilet trying to remain upright. No one looking at him would guess he'd actually...*killed*...no, not really *killed*. It was an accident. Truly, an accident. Both of them.

He stuffed Ariel and Marigold Humphries back in their box and pushed the baby in after them. *Tennnine... eightsevensixfivefourthreetwo one*...carefully folded his clothes into his bag, taking extreme care to make sure the edges were perfectly aligned, and that blue lay next to red, white next to black – and that the number of garments were even in number. There was no point in staying at the hotel anymore. He could check out after breakfast and go to his own unit after lunch.

Dingo showered and dressed – jeans, black shirt, joggers and a hoodie. Carefully counting the stairs, he went down for breakfast, feeling as though he'd been run down by a Mack truck. *Fivefourthreetwoone*... he placed his backpack against the wall behind the corner table where his back was protected, and headed for the cereal. He had to turn up at the orchestra headquarters soon. He could use one of the practice rooms there and let off some steam before he exploded. Not having been able to play his music for the last couple of days was sending him crazy. No musician worth his salt would miss practice if he could still breathe.

He scooped cornflakes into a dish, gathered up utensils and turned to help himself to milk and sugar, only to come face to face with a pile of newspapers.

"Who Killed Goldie?"

A striking photo of the photo-journalist took up most of the page. Underneath he recognised a smaller one of Pam, obviously taken during the concert Saturday night. He let out slow breath. Those shoes were enough to give a bloke a restless night on their own.

*Five...four...three...two...one...*he took a deep breath, set his plate down, slowly poured milk over his cereal and then sprinkled one teaspoon of sugar on top. Keeping the memory of those shoes at bay was hard work. He moved swiftly back to his table, trying not to make eye contact with the few people still savouring their coffee and newspaper.

In the far corner, a woman in a suit sat at a table facing him, eating her breakfast. He sensed the interest in her gaze and slowly turned his back to avoid any possibility of eye contact. With great effort, he focused on the morning to come, enumerating in his mind the sequence of events in store. Check out and catch a taxi to the Pacific Orchestra headquarters and speak to the manager about the next concert...it would be good to be back there. Then he would head back to the Concert Hall.

The Pacific Orchestra headquarters was built to last rather, but had an elegant entrance with the name of the company embossed on the front. A tall potted plant with thin dark leaves stood in the corner of the modern reception area. On a notice board were lists of names and some flyers advertising forthcoming concerts. *Down Ariel...ten, nine, eight, seven, six...*

A girl with long dark hair, heavily made-up eyes and a t-shirt just skimming the top of her lightly tanned breasts, sat behind the desk. He could see the demarcation line of what was either orangey make-up or artificial tan just above the satin ribbon banding the edge of the fabric. Beaded chunky turquoise earrings dangled from short rounded lobes. His eyes widened as her pointed pink tongue flicked over her bright red lips and disappeared, leaving them gleaming in the fluorescent overhead lighting.

She was the goods, alright. Sensing his presence, she glanced up under her lashes and flicked the tip of her pink tongue over her lips again. Before he could speak, she stood up, twitched her t-shirt down over her slim hips and walked into a back office. Her tiny skirt barely covered her arse.

Initial excitement turned to disappointment and then, a snake poised to strike; rage gathered inside. He placed his backpack on the floor. *One. Two. Three. Four. Five...* if she didn't come back by the time he got to ten... *so what will you do, Dingo? Shut up, Ariel.*

She came back, smiling this time, well aware of the shit-storm she'd stirred. The plastic label on the front of her t-shirt proclaimed "Cynthia." 'Hi, you're back! And –' she looked over his shoulder – 'and if I'm not mistaken, here's our new percussionist. Hi fellas! Mr – ?' She focused on the newcomer who grinned and gave his name, Craig Douglas.

Cynthia ticked it off and glanced flirtatiously back at Dingo as if to reinforce the notion that she was irresistible. It didn't work. He was too busy keeping Ariel and Goldie from getting out of their boxes.

'Come with me, gentlemen. Mr Gregson is waiting for *you*.' Throwing a barbed glance at Dingo, Cynthia turned her attention to Douglas, beckoning him to enter the office through a side door. Swinging her hips and well aware of their gaze on her skinny backside and long, tanned legs, Cynthia led the way down a side hallway to the Human Resources office where two older women working on computers glanced up briefly, smiled and went back to what they were doing.

'Someone will be along to take you on a tour of the building, show you where everything is and then you'll come back here and receive your swipe card for entry into the place. You'll need to read information on the emergency exits and things.' Briefly, she glanced at Dingo, before switching her attention back to his companion.

He fumed. His business with the Pacific Symphony manager was far more important than the orientation of an additional musician. Of course, he realised Douglas was new cannon fodder for her to try her wiles on having been unsuccessful with himself the previous season. He forced himself to relax. *Don't show them you're upset...*

Just then the manager, Gregson, arrived and introduced himself to Craig Douglas, advising that he would be the guide for the newcomer's orientation. 'We're not due to meet until tomorrow actually, but I'm glad I could be here to show you around.'

Gregson's face lit up when he saw Dingo; he moved across to shake hands.

'Pleased to meet you. How can we help?'

'I was hoping to use a rehearsal room.'

'Ah, sure. Cynthia, a rehearsal room available?'

Cynthia's pout and nod indicated just what she thought of Dingo. 'It's free until twelve o'clock, Mr Gregson.' She shot a come-hither glance at the newcomer, Douglas.

Gregson glanced at his watch. 'We have a meeting, so can you amuse yourself for a while with Cynthia, Craig? I won't be long.'

Douglas' eyes lit up; Cynthia licked her lips again.

Chuckling, Gregson flicked an amused glance at Dingo and they headed for the manager's office. Dingo followed reluctantly, counting the steps it took to get there, longing to finish their business and head for the practice room for it was though his music that he could find peace and maintain his equilibrium. After that, he'd have to get over to the Concert Hall and behave normally.

Control was everything.

CHAPTER 25

Susan

Aftermath

Monday, 3.45pm

Hamilton was just pulling into a park when I arrived at West End station. We walked in together, immediately identifying the middle-aged couple standing in front of the counter.

'She didn't answer the phone at home, Roger, and her handbag's there. She wouldn't leave home without it, but her mobile phone's gone.' Judging by the long-suffering expression on the face of the man who was standing beside her, she'd been saying it ad infinitum. Tall and hefty, with silver hair, the husband stood with his hands in his pockets and a belligerent expression on his face.

'Now look here, Jean, you've made your point. She's just being irresponsible, that's all. She's taken her mobile and gone out somewhere, probably with her girlfriends.' He looked apologetically at the desk sergeant with a "bloody women but what can you do?" roll of the eyes. I wanted to punch him out.

'I'm sorry we've troubled you. We'll go home and wait for her to ring. It was a mistake to come in here.' He put his hand on his diminutive wife's arm, obviously preparing to pull her out of the building. It was time to make my move.

'I'm Detective Inspector Prescott and this is Detective Senior Sergeant Hamilton. May we help you?'

The woman almost fell on us, repeating over and over what we'd just heard her say. My heart sank. I had a strong feeling that they were our Jane Doe's parents. Before I could ask for a photo of their girl, the desk officer flashed me a significant look and passed over an A4-sized, framed photo.

Oh yes. Years of successful policing left me poker-faced. I glanced at the sergeant, who nodded. 'Number 4, Ma'am.' *Don't envy me, do you. Nothing but devastation for them.*

I turned to the couple and invited them to follow me through the cattle grid, thankful that Anthony Hamilton loomed behind me, a huge comforting figure. Something about the male Maxwell made me uneasy.

We trooped down the hallway in silence and I ushered the parents into an interview room. Cups of tea were sent for and then we encouraged them to tell their story. It seemed that they had gone to Mackay to pick up their youngest son, whose motorbike had broken down, leaving Ariel at home. 'She's almost eighteen, so we couldn't see that it would be a problem,' her mother explained. 'Ariel was due to get in on the bus from Sydney – she's been staying with her cousin, my sister's daughter – and she was told to stay home on Friday night, no matter what.' Jean Maxwell cast her eyes down. I knew the look of motherly guilt, having worn it myself often enough. An angry movement from her husband alerted me to how *he* felt. 'Forgot to ring *her* daughter, didn't she?' he snarled. The words he didn't say hung in the air – *stupid cow.*

Her daughter? 'Is Ariel not your daughter, Mr Maxwell?'

Before he could answer, his wife explained. 'No, Roger married me when Ariel was a baby but he's always been her father. Ariel's father left me when I was pregnant, but she doesn't know about it. She thinks Roger is her dad. The boys are Roger's sons from his first marriage.'

'I see.' Bristling at Maxwell's smug, self righteous expression, I tucked the urge to take his head off with a well-used "put down" into the "don't go there" basket and concentrated on the mother. 'So when *did* you ring home?'

'The next morning but there was no answer. I got a text message from her saying she was going to stay with Heather.' *A girlfriend?*

Another cranky reaction from her husband almost started an argument between them. Apparently there was acrimony over whether they should have come home from Mackay straight away. Jean Maxwell said she'd thought something was wrong, Roger insisted they stay and sort out his son and the motorcycle. 'No point in worrying about the girl,' he snapped. 'Teenagers are always irresponsible.' He folded his arms in the classic defensive position.

'Wa – *is* Ariel an irresponsible person?' Anthony chimed in, looking from one to the other.

'Not normally, but that's what they do isn't it? I know she sneaks out to clubs and meets up with boyfriends.'

'You never told me!' Jean's voice rose in outrage.

'Stands to reason, doesn't it?' Her husband was taking no responsibility for his misjudgement.

It was time to step in. 'What caused you to think something was wrong? Apart from her not answering her phone, that is.'

Jean leaned forward, successfully blotting him out. 'Inspector, Heather Quinn, Ariel's friend, died in a car accident over six months ago. She wouldn't be going to spend time with *her.*'

'She only said she was going to Heather's, not that she's going to see *her!* There isn't only one Heather in the world for chrissakes!' Maxwell threw us a man's classic 'my-wife-is-so-stupid-what-can-I-do?' look and lifted his hands, palms facing us as though in surrender to the vagaries of Jean's whims. *You total berk. Can't you see she's really frightened? And she's every right to be this time.*

'Did you call her other friends to see if she's with them?'

'Yes and her friend Maggie said she missed a call from Ariel late Friday afternoon, but when she tried to phone back, Ariel's phone was "switched off or out of range. Carol, her other best friend said Ariel phoned in Friday afternoon and said she'd be at home on her own Friday night.'

So, who had she linked up with? A boyfriend? Or was it something more sinister? Knowing how incautious young girls can be, trilling their private business and movements when talking on their mobiles, I wondered if a stray male had overheard her. Anthony and I looked cautiously at each other. Who was going to tell them about Jane Doe? I recognised male terror. *You're right. I should.*

'I'm so sorry to have to tell you that a girl matching Ariel's description was found dead in a park in West End.'

Jean Maxwell sagged over the table. 'It can't be...not Ariel...' Her husband, shocked, tried to get her to sit up. I stepped out the door and ran into Briony Feldman who sped off to get water. When I turned back, Roger Maxwell was confronting Anthony who was on his feet.

'I don't care what you say, it can't be Ariel. She's stupid, but not so silly she'd go off with a stranger!' he ground out through clenched teeth. 'She's not a *bad* girl.'

'Mr Maxwell, I didn't say she was and the person may not have been a stranger.'

He took a step backward. 'But who –?'

'We'll need one of you to come with us to the John Tong Centre and view the body. Perhaps Mr Maxwell?' The husband paled, but insisted that it couldn't possibly be Ariel.

His wife whirled to face him. 'We have to go and look, Roger! *We* know it can't possibly be Ariel, but we have to help out.' She nodded decisively. 'It's our duty to help the police.' *Uh oh, denial.* It would go harder for her when she saw the body.

Gathering her handbag, Jean Maxwell leapt up, glaring over her shoulder at Roger. Anthony opened the door just in time to prevent her smacking into it. Resigned, Ariel's father –for in effect, that's what he was – followed her, shoulders hunched as though to ward off a blow. Anthony murmured that he would get his car from around the back. I led the couple out to the front counter, asked the sergeant to advise Evan of where we were going and ushered them outside. We stood in silence, hunched against a stiff breeze.

I hate going to the morgue. No one spoke during the twenty minute drive from the city to the John Tong Centre where the horrific business of carving up the dead took place. I've never gotten used to the sights, sounds and smells in the always-full autopsy rooms. As soon as the bodies left, more were trundled in. We only had a "preliminary" on the girl we were sure was Ariel Maxwell. It could be a while before the final report was in, but I knew that John Lynch would get her through as fast as possible and keep us up to date with relevant information.

I had phoned ahead so there was no delay after we got there. The Maxwells crept up to the viewing window and peered through. It didn't take the screaming collapse of Jean to confirm what we already knew. We helped the Maxwells away from the window, though Jean wanted to go inside. 'You can't, I'm so sorry. Once Ariel is released to you, then you can see her.'

They cringed. No doubt they had watched CSI and knew what that meant. There were papers to go through and forms to sign in connection with the identification, after which we asked the relevant questions – do you know this woman? What is her name, date of birth...it was a stressful time for *us*, let alone the parents. Then Roger Maxwell asked the inevitable question: 'Was she raped?'

'There is no evidence of that at this time. She was fully clothed when she was found, Mr Maxwell.'

The relief on their faces was followed by the next – how had she died? We fudged over that, saying that until the forensic report was in we couldn't be sure, but after they insisted, we admitted that it appeared she had been smothered while being kissed, but not that her chest had been crushed.

'What do you mean, *kissed*?' Roger leapt to his feet, overturning his chair. 'That's not possible! How can someone be kissed to death?' Shaking violently, he leaned against the wall, perspiration pouring down his face. His wife stood and scrabbled in her bag, coming up with a bottle of pills. 'He's got to take these. It's the stress.' She managed to get a tablet down him aided by a glass of water. Anthony picked up the chair and we coaxed

Maxwell to sit down again. He wiped his face with a large white handkerchief. 'Are you sure that's what happened?'

'We can't be sure. It certainly appears so, but we will let you know as soon as we do.'

I wished I could have given the couple a stiff brandy each, but they managed to cope long enough to give us a list of all Ariels friends, girls and especially the males, plus work mates and her employer. A separate list of relatives was compiled with phone numbers and occupations; we would chase them up on the morrow.

'What relatives are close by?' Anthony asked.

'My sister, my parents. Roger's family, they're all in Brisbane.'

'Now that you've identified your daughter, you need to let the family know or get someone to ring around family and friends. We'll need to release the photo you brought with you to see if we can find someone who saw Ariel on Friday afternoon and if we're lucky, who she was with. We will also need access to your home. We will need to search for evidence in case she brought someone back with her. Would you be able to go to your sister or parents for the night? Tomorrow we'll need to take your fingerprints and those of your sons in order to eliminate them from our enquiries.'

They turned pale, realising that perhaps those of their daughter's murderer would be in their *home*. Roger started to protest, saying that he was damned if he was going to be driven out of his home, but his wife over-rode him. 'No Roger. They'll need to find out whether there was anyone in the house with Ariel.' She was the stronger of the two, for all his bluster. He quietened down, but I was aware of the rage threatening to engulf us all. Jean took out her mobile and made a call, briefly telling the person on the other end that they wanted to call round. 'We can go over there. I'm dreading telling them what's happened.' Her lips trembled.

'Are there any pets you need to have seen to?' Anthony asked her.

She was at the point of collapse. 'No, our old dog died a short time ago and we haven't replaced him.' She drew a ragged breath. 'Ariel wanted to be a vet you know. She always loved animals. She even had pet rats at one time.' She stopped abruptly and scrabbled in her bag to produce a set of house keys. 'You'll be needing these for...' Sobs claimed her.

We stopped at Jean Maxwell's parent's house in Holland Park and told them we would be sending a Family Liaison Officer to be with them and help with the media. We offered to come in with them, but they declined. We also advised that we would need to talk to everyone in Ariel's life including *all* her relatives and that either parent would have to return and look around their home to see if anything was out of place or missing. We waited until they reached the front gate. We would be back in the morning. We got into our car and drove away quickly as the front door opened and the tall figure of a man, probably Jean's father, appeared.

There'd be no sleep in that house tonight, and tomorrow would be even worse.

CHAPTER 26

Pam

An Unexpected Visitor

Monday, 5.30pm.

I've spent my life in devotion to music, to a career which I love, but is it enough to sustain me for the rest of it? When does slaving to achieve the pinnacle of your chosen profession become a habit which precludes a private life? As do most women knocking on the door of thirty, I am starting to wonder if I will ever find the one man – taller than me – who loves me enough to accept my transient lifestyle and work around it? I wondered who would want to marry a professional musician, apart from another musician. I know that to most people I'm rather dull. Music is my whole world, requiring hours of practice and rehearsals. I don't have many hobbies other than walking and reading. I do paint a little, but because of my transient life-style don't often get the opportunity.

Just get over it, Pam. If it happens, it happens.

Coming back to my unit after a hard day's work is akin to vanishing into my shell. This afternoon was no exception. I blundered into the tiny hallway, scraping the walls with my bags of groceries. Some hot soup would be good with the fresh, rich grain-bread which is my passion, followed by...well, I'd soon find something in the freezer. My head had been aching most of the day; Advil and a cup of coffee would go down well. I was worried about my mother whom I hadn't seen yet and needed to ring John. I put Mozart Concerto for Flute and Piano on my stereo and made coffee. I would practice after dinner.

My phone messages proved a mixed bunch. Aunt Fiona's voice came over frail and furtive, asking me if I was alright and apologising for Alex' bad behaviour, ending with a hesitant invitation to join her for lunch in West End to discuss the funeral and Goldie's house. I would bet a million Alex didn't know she was ringing me and was certain he wouldn't know about a meeting between us. I tackled that one first, gently putting her off for a couple of days. *Maybe the heat'll have gone out of Alex' anger by then.*

Friends welcomed me back to Brisbane, some congratulated me on my successful concert and extending condolences for Goldie's death. Fighting tears, I made a list of who'd rung, and played the rest. Lots from members of the Pacific Symphony offering condolences and support, one from Bill asking if he could come over that night – I would put him off, but suggest another time – and another from Rezanov, offering condolences, congratulating me on my performance Saturday night and saying he would catch up with me. Lance Macpherson's voice cut out just into his message so goodness knows what he wanted. Probably condolences as well. The last was from a firm of solicitors asking me to call re a "matter of interest." *Oh God, I hope I'm not getting Parry's photo.*

Feeling less than enthused by any of the men's attention, I cleared my machine and rang Bill. He sounded disappointed, but was pleased to make a date for the next night. 'If you don't feel like going out for a meal, just let me know and I'll bring the food to you.' I agreed and then phoned everybody's lover, the mad Russian. His message service picked up, so I just thanked him for his kind words. I would have expected attention from His Gloriousness might have given me more of a thrill... *perhaps I'm just exhausted from grieving.*

After that, I spent a good ten minutes on the phone with my stepfather and invited him to stay with me rather than camping in a cold, lonely motel. 'My lounge pulls out into a sofa bed, John. You are most welcome, you know.'

'I've already made arrangements to stay with my mate, Pat. We can live our glory days as coppers again over a glass of the good stuff, Pam. Thank you all the same, darling. Your mum's asleep and seems quite comfortable, and she'll be able to see you tomorrow. Visiting hours start at 10am.'

'Please tell her I'll be up there then. Do get some rest tonight, John. You need your strength for Mum's recovery. It's been pretty rough on you too!'

We said goodnight. I was fortunate to have such a lovely stepdad. I have never known my father who was killed before I was born, climbing mountains of all things. I've photos of him of course, but nothing can conjure up a living, breathing man who, I certainly hoped, would have been a good dad.

The seven o'clock news was about to come on and although my mind and heart cringed at the thought of Goldie being on there, it was like watching an accident about to happen – irresistible.

I bracing myself for the usual awful happenings and thinking about what to have for dinner, when the doorbell rang. Cursing, I turned the low on the TV and headed for the front door. My hand was stretched out when I got a hold of myself. 'Who is it?'

'Detective Senior Sergeant Hamilton, Miss Miller.'

All thought fled. *Oh my goodness.* I threw the door open so fast that it gave us both a shock. Dressed in jeans, a T-shirt which emphasised the muscles of his broad chest, set off by a denim jacket, he looked *down* into my eyes. 'I was just passing and wondered how you were getting coping...' His voice petered out. Was that a tinge of red around his cheeks? *It was!*

'Come in!' I jumped back, giving his massive shoulders more than enough room to get past me into the hallway, slammed the door behind him and set the chain across. He glanced back. 'You didn't have that on when I got here!'

'Er...I forgot.' He scowled and then halted, his head cocked to one side, listening. 'Schubert, the Impromptus?'

Speechless, I just gawped at him. He's into classical music? *Wow!* 'You know Schubert?'

He smiled. 'I have five sisters and two of them are at the Conservatorium here in Brisbane, a violinist and a percussionist. It would be more than my life's worth *not* to know! ' I waved my arm in the general direction of the kitchen. *Five sisters? This man knows all about women!*

'What do the other three do?'

'One's a teacher, one runs an Art Gallery in Cairns and the youngest is a secretary at the Concert Hall at Southbank.' Thoughts flew around my mind, like silverfish sprinting from a cupboard full of old clothes. Trying not to witter, I scuttled ahead of him. 'Is her name Joan?'

He looked surprised. 'Yes, do you know her?'

'No, but she escorted me to the dressing rooms on Saturday morning when I went to the rehearsals.'

He grinned. 'She'd be happy to meet you. She reckons meeting the artists is the best part of the job.'

I picked up a mug. 'Coffee?'

'Yes, thank you. I shouldn't be here, but I wanted to see if you are all right. You've been through a lot.' He pulled a chair out and settled down, showing all the signs of a truly practised "kitchen sitter." My heart-rate went into orbit. I fidgeted, unable to concentrate on making the drinks.

He leaned his powerful, tanned forearms on the table and steepled his fingers. 'Come and sit down; coffee's the least of my requirements.' His handsome face creased into what might be construed as a smile. A mouse to his python, I slid into the chair opposite, unaware I was still holding the coffee and spoon. He reached across, gently took them from me. 'You do realise that as you are still technically involved in the investigation I shouldn't be here with you, so how about we keep this visit between us?

'Will – would you get into trouble if they knew?'

'Deep shit. No doubt about it.' Anthony's eyes twinkled and his gorgeous, firm mouth curved into an honest-to-goodness smile. 'I can't stay long, but I just wanted to spend a little time with you.' *Oh blimey!* I felt all hot inside.

'Aren't I a suspect?'

'You have an alibi, remember? Your cousin was murdered before you left the city, possibly even while you were fetching her car to drive to the house.'

'Ah.' I'd forgotten about being pulled up by the uniformed cop on the way home. 'What happened at the park?'

He looked uncomfortable for a moment, and then said quietly, 'A young girl was murdered.'

'What? As well as Goldie?'

'Yes. We believe the girl was killed on Saturday morning. A man walking his dog found her.' He hesitated for a moment. 'We only discovered who the girl is...was... a few hours ago, so we've kept her face out of the papers until her relative could be traced. Your cousin and you have taken over the news, but her death'll be reported in the papers tomorrow.'

Oh my God. The poor, poor parents...

The moment I found Goldie came rushing back, along with all the fear and pain. My stress levels were through the roof, what with Mum's operation and Alex's hostility on top of it. My head throbbed harder.

I stood up.

The room went dark.

'Pam! Pam?' The next thing I was lying on my bed, Anthony looking down at me. He turned and headed for the en suite. I tried to sit up, but then he was back, sitting on the bed beside me, wiping my face with a warm wet cloth. I closed my eyes and submitted to his gentle attentions. Tears welled under my eyelids and trickled down my cheeks. *Stop it, Pam. You can't cry now.*

'Sssh, it's alright.' The Easter Island statue picked up my sweaty hands and gently wiped each one. I opened my eyes and gazed up at him.

'Anthony? I'm sorry.'

' You've absolutely nothing to be sorry about. I know you loved your cousin and we *are* going to find out who killed her.'

'Do you think Goldie's murder is related to the girl in the park?'

His expression became inscrutable, reminding me that this man is a cop, who might want to discuss the case, but couldn't. 'Perhaps, but we don't know yet.'

He drew me into a sitting position and with all the expertise of my mum, plumped the pillows up behind me and settled me against them. The throbbing in my head eased; warm contentment drifted through me. A huge hand came out and gently probed the dressing on my forehead. 'How does it feel now?'

'You know what? I can hardly feel it!'

The gorgeous mouth in front of me stretched into a broad grin. 'Have you had your dinner yet?'

'No, I must admit I'm hungry.' *Whatever you do, don't sick it up, Pam.*

'Great! Do you like "Indian"?'

'Love it! There's a menu in the kitchen under my kindle on the shelf above the bench.'

Anthony pretty much *bounded* down the few steps to the lower level and was back in a moment waving the menu. 'Okay pick whatever you like and I'll ring for takeaway.'

We ordered and then he took both my hands in his. 'They reckon it'll be only about twenty minutes.' He took a deep breath.

He looked relieved. 'Perhaps we could go out to dinner one night soon?' He smiled. 'This visit is a one-off, but when it's all over I want to be able to get to know you and find out where this is going.'

'I understand. I have another concert to perform next week. It's only in Ipswich, so that's practically Brisbane. I told one of your troops the date I'd be away, where and for how long. I hate driving back late at night, so I might stay with a girlfriend who lives down there, if that's okay?' A young detective constable had made a note of them and as I hadn't heard anything, I had to assume that I'd be able to go.

'Shouldn't be a problem, but I'll check it out tomorrow and let you know.'

I took a deep breath. 'And then I fly to London – after that, Edinburgh in Scotland and then London again for a Royal Command Performance in front of Charles and Camilla no less!'

He looked astonished, as well he might. Most people – particularly men – didn't understand that I had to go wherever my agent booked me. There was no choice if I were to have a successful career. I hastened to soften the blow. 'I'll only be away two weeks and then I come back and work here with the Pacific Symphony for a short season. We're doing an outback concert tour.'

Now he would pull back. There weren't enough fingers on my hands to count the number of blokes who had shot through when they understood that my life is one of being on the move – concert halls, church halls, TV studios, recording studios and sometimes, open air concerts in parks. *Pam, what are you thinking? The man's only just met you!*

Remaining cool wasn't easy, but he didn't look about to bolt. 'There's always Skype. I'm thirty-two, mature enough to understand your dreams and that achieving them means you have to be where your career takes you. You've worked long and hard to get where you are now. Besides, I work long hours and any lady who has a relationship with me wouldn't find it easy either.' He reached one hand down and stroked the back of my hand, smiling. 'But we can work something out if we put our minds to it.'

Our eyes met, my heart pounded. He leaned forward, sliding his hand around the back of my neck to draw me to him. His lips felt soft but firm, claiming mine in a kiss so deep, so sincere, that I knew I would walk through fire for this man. I slid my arms around his neck and drew him down onto the pillows with me. His hands slid over my breasts, kneading and gently squeezing. I tweaked his shirt out of his waistband and slid *my* hands up underneath, patting and stroking the sleek, powerful muscles. Breathing heavily, we sank into each other, taking what each had to offer...

Then the doorbell rang.

CHAPTER 27

Dingo

Shaping a Nocturnal Animal

Late 1990s

Dingo had never tasted takeaway food and only homemade hamburgers, ice-cream and chocolate. He had never ridden on a bus much less a train. From the window of his room he would watch until the vapour trails of planes passing overhead vanished into the atmosphere. *One day he too, would be in one of those...one day when she'd gone.*

After the baby died, Frances' drinking rose to new heights. Sometimes he wondered if she had forgotten that terrible day, but then she would go into bouts of smashing things, and chasing him around the house, trying to whack him over the head with whatever she could get her hands on. After one of these episodes she would drink herself into a stupor and then throw up. From an early age he became more proficient with a mop and bucket than any child should ever be.

Counting became his ritual. If he got to a hundred, she would have likely gone to sleep; if he got to ten before she created a racket, it wasn't good. From his window upstairs he counted passing cars, grouping them into colours and bargaining. *Please God, if the next car is blue, I promise I'll be good for the rest of my life...* If there were two blue cars at once it might be a good day, two red screamed *danger*. He didn't realise that he subconsciously incited attacks because his tension levels rose after he saw red cars. His mother, with her instinct for survival, sensed his vulnerability. The beatings were bad times.

There were precious occasions when Frances was forced out to see the Trustees or for medical reasons. It was a measure of her control over him, that even when she was gone, Dingo couldn't mentally bring himself to venture outside. The problem was that the rare occasions when he was taken out to the dentist were spoiled by the crowds of people on the street pushing past. Even the manic grip of Frances' hand around his wrist, so tight that bruises surfaced, was security. The light, heat and smell of exhaust fumes were overpowering, so much so when he was really small that he couldn't wait to get back to the sanctuary of their home. The doctor came to the house to visit both of them, because his mother pleaded her "condition." Agoraphobia wasn't part of his vocabulary until much later.

By the time he turned ten, Frances was forced to concede that his prowess at music had outgrown her expertise. Reluctantly, she found a music teacher who lived on the other side of town and his weekly lesson became another treasured expedition. His mother would bundle them both into a taxi – she said to make sure the teacher was doing the right thing by her prodigy – but also to ensure that he had no contact with anyone other than Gordon Eastwood. Musically, Dingo flourished. It was not long before the man recommended that his mother take him to a professor at the university in the next city. This was too much for her to accept. She remained adamant that her son remain with Eastwood.

Despite Frances' edict that her son not enter any competitions, the teacher held private concerts at his house so his students could play for each other and get experience in performing. When Frances' vigilance relaxed enough to send her son to his lessons in a taxi, Dingo joined in. He knew better than to mention the program at home. It was at one of these sessions that a stranger appeared and Frances never knew that her son had performed for, and greatly impressed, one of the foremost professors of music in the country.

Dingo's musical education continued with Gordon Eastwood, who encouraged his pupil to reach heights that he, Eastwood, could never have attained. The professor remained in contact and it was this connection, along with Eastwood's excellent teaching, which enabled the boy to attain the standard which would see his career assured.

When he turned thirteen, Dingo, aided by rising levels of testosterone, knew he would have to break out, die or kill his mother. He yearned to experience the outside world and managed that through watching TV for his schooling, as per the Distance Education curriculum and from keeping the sound almost off, while he watched programs of which his mother wouldn't have approved.

She watched every move he made...at least he thought she did until he discovered the spy cameras hidden around the house. How she had gotten them there and made them work, he didn't know. He had found out when he sneaked out onto the back patio one day, chasing the cat while his mother was asleep. The beating he received for that minor excursion remained with him a long, long time.

The sleeping pills his mother hoarded in her bedroom were fair game. He wasn't a fool. He halved them and watered the grog. Having a dead mother on his hands was not something he actually wanted. She wasn't an unintelligent woman. There were times when she could talk rationally about the state of the world, the latest drama on TV and political matters from the daily newspaper thrown at the door early in the morning. It was at those times when Frances was relatively sane and approachable that he was persuaded things were looking up. They weren't.

Then he started going out at night. By dint of discreetly working out where the camera was angled to include the back door, he devised a method of crawling against the skirting board. If he squeezed his shoulders together, he could crawl through the cat door, which had actually been made for a dog before the boy and his mother moved in.

On the first occasion, he turned off the outside sensor light, wriggled his way out and, accompanied by the cat, made it past the inner fence surrounding the garden and across the paddock to the boundary line before panicking and running all the way back to the house. He'd squatted against the wall of the laundry for what seemed like hours, counting his thudding heart beats, waiting for his mother to come pounding out of the lounge room to dispense punishment for him even *thinking* about disobeying. Too frightened to push his luck, he stayed inside for the next two nights.

Then he ventured out again. This time, again encouraged by presence of the cat, he stood in the garden, deep breathing and savouring the rhythm of the night. Far away, a dog barked. The houses on the perimeter of the outer fence were mostly in darkness, though here and there a light shone. When nothing untoward happened, he went down to the shed by the garden fence. The door was unlocked. Heart pounding, he stepped inside, smelling the oil and fumes from the petrol tank where the casual gardener hired by Frances kept the lawnmower.

Something stirred in the bushes. Terrified, he got ready to run, only to sag against the fence with relief when a strange cat came mewing around his ankles. It was several nights before he got the courage to venture out of the back gate, cross the three acres of heavily treed land separating the house from suburbia and stand in the laneway behind the fence. He left the gate open and walked a short way toward the main road, where he stood for what seemed like a long time watching and counting the cars going past.

Soon his rising confidence allowed him to venture down the laneway and into the shopping centre. It wasn't long before he met other night creatures, bent on prowling, waiting for something exciting to happen.

"Hey boag, whatcha doin'?'

'Dunno. Lookin' around.'

"Wanna knock off the servo?"

'Nah. That's boring.'

Naive as Dingo was, he realised that robbing the local service station would be a bad idea. The local cops weren't the problem; facing his mother might be fatal. After that, he was more circumspect about who he associated with, not realising at first that his size, black clothes and seeming aloofness made him cool. It was this misleading persona and the fact that his companions only saw him occasionally and at night, which earned him his nickname – Dingo. He liked that. It made him feel accepted.

Regular thieving from Frances' handbag ensured he had ready cash to hold his own in the troop. His sexual life began when, one summer night, a fifteen year-old girl pushed him up against a wall and thrust her hand down his pants. A fast learner with an inventive mind, he soon graduated to being the most sought after of the teenage stallions and his habit of disappearing, seemingly into "thin air," and absence for nights at a time only made him more desirable. Never telling anyone his name or where he lived was, for Dingo, a survival device, but to his companions it was *cool*.

For the next few years, Dingo roamed far and wide under cover of darkness, mostly alone but sometimes with mates who thought he was dead cool. His encounters with girls were frequent, but he never told anyone the location of his home or, more importantly, confided *how* he lived. He would never admit to the dubious friends he made on the streets, that when he was alone he peered through windows into lounge rooms to vicariously partake of family life.

There was one house in particular which fascinated him. An ordinary suburban Federation- style brick house with a verandah all the way around attracted his attention. What Dingo regarded as the quintessential Australian family lived there – mother, father, a boy of about his own age, a small girl, a cat and a fat Labrador who smiled a lot as did the family.

He met the dog first, out for its regular evening constitutional in the nearby park. A soppy animal who loved everybody, it was overjoyed to spend time with

Dingo who made sure he brought a ball along to throw for it whenever he could escape after dark. His next step was to accompany the dog home. He would stand behind a tree on the footpath on the other side of the road, watching the son whose job it was to let the dog out and bring it in again. At first the dog, whose name was Benji, waited for Dingo to cross the road with him, but soon accepted that they would part company behind the same tree.

Then one night, the family went out, leaving Benji in the yard. Greatly daring, Dingo went up to the fence and leaned over to pat the excited dog. The light from a nearby street lamp revealed a half-open window. He longed to get closer, to share just for a few moments the family warmth which emanated from that house. He looked around, and seeing no one, quietly opened the front gate, slipped inside and closed it. Benji trotted helpfully beside him as he stepped slowly onto the verandah and, keeping close to the shadowed wall, worked his way around to the window.

A light had been left on somewhere in the house. The dim glow revealed a single bed against the far wall on which posters of well known cricketers were displayed. A jumble of clothes sprawled across the bed and on the floor he could make out a gym bag with a tennis racket lying half out. A desk with a computer and a backpack stood against the left wall.

Suddenly, Dingo was inside the room. He didn't remember sliding over the windowsill but now he was in he was compelled to explore, his senses alert for any sound of the family returning. He knew he would get into terrible trouble, probably be arrested and Frances would beat him senseless, but the warmth and essence of the family drew him like a hummingbird to nectar. Benji stood on his hind legs with forepaws on the sill and looked on in approval.

He couldn't help touching things – a basket of knitting by an armchair – a blue sweater for someone, a book on the coffee table, bookmark saving the place, a tea cup left on the draining board in the kitchen and stroking the plump tabby cat curled up in an armchair. Moving faster, conscious of time passing, he slipped down the hallway, past what was obviously the little girl's bedroom, pausing at the family bathroom, breathing in the scent of talcum powder, moist towels. A little way along was the parent's room where shaded lamps glowed either side of the double bed.

A man's blue sweater lay on the bed. He picked it up and buried his nose in the folds, drinking in the folds of – a father. He could barely remember Marcus. The terrible storm and collapse of the shed which took his father's life was the most vivid recollection, though he could remember the smell of horse sweat, leather and sheep and the security of his father's arms holding him on the pommel of the saddle as they followed the sheep the last few kilometres to the yards.

A sound outside sent him back along the hallway, running lightly into the son's bedroom and over to the window. Was that a car turning into the driveway? He could hear Benji barking out the front. Terrified, Dingo dropped the sweater on the floor, slid out of the window, crouched and ran for the backyard where he hid behind shrubs near the boundary fence.

Headlights cut a swath across the lawn and what he knew was the family's 4WD pulled up at the front gate. Benji went berserk with joy. Moving faster than he had ever in his life, Dingo raced for the high, wooden back fence, leapt up, caught the top and hauled himself up and over, just before the dog remembered him and rushed down the garden looking for a game.

'Benji! What's the matter, you stupid dog? Come back here!'

'He's probably chasing a possum, Wally. Come and help mum with the groceries!'

Breathing heavily, Dingo ran down the road, praying no one had seen or heard him. At the bottom of the street, he slowed to a walk, thrust his hands into the pockets of his jacket and slouched home, forcing himself not to panic.

He was never so happy to be home than that night, but it didn't stop there. Breaking into *homes* – not houses – to touch, to be part of family life became a secret addiction. When he grew up, he realised that it was only by proxy that he knew how families "worked." That his home life was tragic hadn't occurred to him until he started mixing with the teens after dark. The nights that he managed to sneak out tired him for the next day, but he forced himself to keep up the facade and practice the hours his mother demanded. When Frances had her afternoon nap, her son caught up on his sleep.

He rarely thought about the death of the baby after he'd finally managed to tell the police what happened that day when he was eight. They'd written it all down and his mother had signed in his name. Frances told him that she had to go to the Coroner's Inquest and give evidence. 'You're lucky you didn't get thrown in gaol, you little shit,' she'd roared, shoving him roughly.

A couple of fat women from Children's Services wearing thick stockings and sensible shoes, had come to see them, talked in low tones to his mother while they drank vast amounts of tea and scoffed all the scones she had made. They left after exhorting him to practice his music. He didn't mind, because music was his only relief from the grinding emotional poverty allotted him. By the time he turned thirteen, he'd worked out that the women going into the garden and leaving the baby alone was their own fault. That he was socially inept was the fault of his mother – in fact, everything that was negative in his life was someone else's fault. And as long as he kept counting, he could maintain control.

CHAPTER 28

Susan

No News is Good News?

Tuesday, 8.30am

'Guess who got released yesterday afternoon?'

'Oh no.'

'Yes, Grant-baby's back on the streets and no doubt looking for trouble –'

'And if there isn't any, he'll make some!' I finished for Evan, who was looking less than impressed. Juvenile would be furious.

Sighing, I joined the team in the Incident Room.

'Okay, we've got a name for our Jane Doe, Ariel Maxwell, identified by her parents yesterday afternoon. We've released her photo to the media and as you would all know, it was splashed all over the Courier Mail this morning. We need to intensify our enquiries around the park and it seems Ariel went there frequently.'

We spent the next three-quarters of an hour re-hashing, speculating and cursing the case. Those of us who were the parents of teenage girls felt pressure to chase down the killer, those who weren't, regarded it as one more sad challenge.

'Now, our first port of call is the Maxwell's and then we'll deal with Humphries. Right, Jacob and Sym take the Maxwell's residence. Pay particular attention to Ariel's bedroom. Fingerprints'll follow you in.'

'Yes, Ma'am.'

'Someone *must* have seen the girl when she came in on the bus from Sydney. Check the bus timetable, you might get lucky and the bus driver could be home or at the station. Trains – you know what to do – and Gerry, just in case, find out if she flew up. A long shot, but not unlikely. Now, someone needs to canvas the shops nearest the Maxwells. If she had a bloke with her, then it's likely they got takeaway. The parents say Ariel wasn't much of a cook.' I sent two more of the team members out then turned my attention to my Senior Sergeant, who was writing in his notebook. I had the sense he was hoping to be overlooked. *No such luck, gorgeous.*

'Any more on Pamela Miller?' I could have sworn he blushed.

'No, Ma'am, and no further problems with a prowler.' *And how would you know that? Hm.*

My team scattered in all directions, chattering among themselves. *We're missing something, I just know it.* If Ariel Maxwell's murder didn't tie in with the Humphries' killing, I'd eat my hat. Granted one happened in the morning and one late at night the same day, but until we found the link we couldn't prove a thing. Before I could get a cup of coffee and prepare for a team briefing on the Humphries' murder, I got a message. 'Susan, the Super wants to see you!'

Sighing, I gathered my notes and headed off to give an update on the investigation.

Superintendent Peterson lurked in an enviably large office on the other side of the level, overlooking the river. A tall, imposing man, he looks every bit the avuncular person he is – until you do something wrong.

'Right, Susan, so what's the update on the Maxwell murder?'

I brought him up to speed and then ventured to expound my theories about a link between the Humphries and Maxwell cases. He looked sceptical. 'It's a long jump from a teenager murdered on Saturday morning to a thirty-three year old photojournalist late Saturday night. Apart from them being in the same area within twenty-four hours, you've nothing more to link them.' He stared at me over the top of his reading glasses. 'However, I am aware of the numerous times that your gut feeling has steered you in the right direction and this time may be no exception. I have every confidence in your skills.'

For a man who rarely smiled or gave praise, I was taken aback to be treated to both. He didn't miss much either.

'I believe your new Senior Sergeant is showing interest in one of the persons involved in the Humphries case.'

'Where did you hear that, sir?'

'No one told me, I overheard a couple of your team discussing it outside the toilets.'

'Ah. Well, Pamela Miller is no longer a POI and I've already had a chat with Anthony. He's a very professional officer and won't do anything to sully the case.'

'I'll accept your assurances, Susan. I know you'll make sure everything's on the up-and-up.'

We parted amicably and I headed back out to the office checking my texts. Nothing from David. I went into my cubby hole and picked up the phone. Peter Moffat had better be available or I'd skin him alive. His phone rang out. Frightened, I dialled again. This time it picked up.

'Moffat.'

'Pete, it's Susan. What's happening with David? He usually texts me twice a day when he's away and rings me at night. I haven't had anything since last night's contact. Is he on an assignment?'

A telling silence followed. Then he sighed. 'He's just *busy*. I'm sure he'll get back to you as soon as he can.' His tone indicated I was being a typical hysterical woman and confirmed for me what I suspected. David *was* undercover and Peter his handler. *Damn them.*

I said goodbye, trying not to tell him that I knew what they were up to. Nausea rose in my stomach; I rushed for the washroom.

When I came out, Evan was standing in the corridor holding a clipboard. 'Susan, what's happened?'

Exhausted, I leaned against the wall. 'Nothing desperate. I haven't heard from David today and he's usually in touch when he's away.' Evan was the only officer on my team who knew what I suspected about David's job over the range.

'Well, no news is good news, as they say,' said Evan dryly. *He knows something.*

I allowed myself to be guided back to the office.

'But there's nothing you can do about it. They're not going to tell you anything even though you are a police officer. I know it's impossible for you not to be concerned, but David is strong and clever. Whatever he's doing, he won't let them get him.' Evan looked me in the eye. 'Susan, even crims hesitate to kill police

253

officers. Settle down. You have two murders to investigate and knowing this city, there'll be more to come in very shortly. You need to stay focused and trust in David and Pete, otherwise you'll have to ask Petersen to release you from the case.'

He was right. Reluctantly, I tried to put aside my fears to concentrate on the here and now. 'Okay, so how did the team go at the Maxwells?'

Evan consulted the report clipped to the board. 'Not well. No dirty dishes, everything wiped in the kitchen, but the remains of fish and chip wrapping and squeezed lemon quarters in the garbage. They should be able to get good prints off the wrapping but as you know, unless we have a match...interestingly, the lounge room is pristine, not like you'd expect from a teenage girl. The cushions were perfectly straight and coffee table is as clean as a whistle, so someone, either Ariel or the person with her, was trying to hide his – or her – presence.' He rolled his eyes. Her? *Yeah right, in a pig's eye.*

'They did get some smudged prints under the coffee table and a few in the bathroom under the edge of the hand basin, which didn't match the parents. Of course they could be the sons, but Mackay notified us that the Maxwell boys'll be back here tomorrow. We'll get their's then.'

'Okay, so anything else of interest?'

'Well, the parents said that nothing's missing, but another thing – Ariel's bed was stripped and her sheets in the washing machine. They'd been washed, but not dried.'

We knew what that meant.

CHAPTER 29

Pamela

Surprises

Tuesday, 7am

I'd missed practising Sunday and Monday. Panicked, I'd risen at four o'clock and put in three solid hours. I had my spare room sound-proofed so I could do my practice without driving the neighbours into a stampede. The media, frantic to get a comment on Goldie's murder, putting my block of units under siege on Sunday night didn't help matters. The Body Corporate Chairman was not amused. 'Not something we encourage of our tenants, Ms Miller.' *Old goat.*

I slumped back onto the bed, wishing I didn't have to go anywhere, do anything except "veg out." My drawn face stared at me from the bathroom mirror. Dark eyebrows, very fair skin topped by rather ordinary, wild blond crinkly hair cascading to my waist couldn't detract from the tired lines around my eyes and the bags under them. Events since Saturday night were becoming almost too much for me.

Alex' hostility, the knowledge that I was a suspect and had in fact been attacked was reinforced by the tight stitches in my head. I picked at the Elastoplast holding the small bandage on the wound and carefully peeled it off. A small amount of dried blood had seeped from the cut, held together by four ugly black stitches. Another week before they came out. The hard lump on my forehead had shrunk to a small squishy mound.

Sighing, I prepared for a shower, thinking of all the things I had to do today, before concentrating on the one highlight in my life – Anthony Hamilton. A thrill shot through me as I remembered his visit the night before. My mouth curved into a smile. Then I remembered that I was supposed to go out with Bill that night. Leaving a message on his mobile saying that I couldn't make it left me feeling slightly guilty, but what the heck? Men broke dates all the time.

I've always enjoyed really hot showers – Jess used to complain it took hours for the towels to dry after I'd had a shower – so I turned the tap on further, relishing the heat on my muscles, allowing it to spray gently on the stiches.

Already I felt physically better, but as I got out, dried myself and dressed, reality set in. No Goldie to share my excitement with. In the past four years, I'd giggled along with her and Ally over various blokes, speculating whether they were likely to call and, when I was much younger, hanging around the house with Ally and Jess longing for the phone to ring, always careful to keep our mobiles with us – just in case. The times when we'd had too many drinks and we'd wept together about how lonely we were, how much we wanted to find someone to love and who would love us unconditionally and how that would never happen again.

It was incomprehensible that only this time last week, Goldie was yet to meet me at the air train and looking forward to the future. Maybe someone important had arrived in my life and Goldie was going to miss everything. If Anthony and I – ended up together – *cool it Pam, for God's sake. You barely know him.* Okay, so I was allowed to be excited. Just a little bit, right? The number of times I've met "someone" and been bitterly disappointed couldn't dim my spirits. I was fed up with kissing frogs and hoping this one would be the prince.

Generally, I'm pretty happy with my life, quite content, practicing my music, reading or going out with girlfriends, but like most women, I want to love and be loved and of course, have children. Time is slipping by. Almost twenty-nine, though not over the hill by any means, soon becomes thirty, then thirty one. You always think there's plenty of time to do all the things you want, but now that I'm in my late twenties, I realise what older people mean when they say time goes so fast. Now, having met Anthony Hamilton...*careful*, Pam. Better to expect nothing and if something comes of it, then that's a bonus. Guilt reared. How could I even *think* of being so happy when my cousin was dead? And in the worst possible way.

I wanted so badly to see my mum. John phoned me early to say that she was doing well and longing to have me visit her in hospital. 'She can't talk for too long, Pam, but she's desperate to see you.'

Morning rituals were rushed through, the dressing on my head changed – oh, to be free of it – panadol scoffed down and then the crucial part of my day...what to wear.

Travelling a lot means I don't have many clothes. Jeans, t-shirts, slacks, sweaters, a coat or two, ballet flats and joggers are all I require of my everyday wardrobe and not many people get to see me in the same things. That did not include my performance gear, which comprised three gowns – the inevitable black, the navy blue and a turquoise cocktail frock, all long enough to hide the ballet flats!

Remembering the new gorgeous golden dress and shoes I'd worn Saturday night reminded me that it would have to be dry-cleaned before the next concert. Well, since my next one was Saturday, perhaps it might be okay to wear it once more. My old navy one felt totally passé.

I struggled into my best pair of jeans, a crisp white shirt and denim jacket, tied a jaunty scarf around my throat and, leaving a mussed fringe to hide the dressing on my temple, hooked my hair back with jewelled combs. A pair of suede boots and a dash of makeup and I was ready to face the world. It was only 8.30am, so I figured to do the statement and dry cleaner first and then head for the hospital. I galloped back down the stairs. I had to put in some *more* practice that day no matter what.

I turned on the radio, then hearing Goldie's name turned it off, unable to face the news. Something sprang to mind. I had nothing suitable to wear to Goldie's funeral. *Pam, if you wore black to my funeral I'd come back and haunt you!* Goldie's half-serious words, spoken after she'd been wounded sprang into my mind. Wondering if the shop where young Tia worked would have something suitable, I made a mental note to call in later.

Just as I was about to leave, the phone rang.

'Pam?'

Lance MacPherson had never phoned me before. Curious, I stayed silent waiting for him to state his business.

'How are you feeling? I heard you copped a whack on the head at Roma Street Parklands on Sunday?'

How had he known that? So far the media hadn't discovered the attack, probably because there were two far more exciting things to report. I bet Ally or Brie told him.

'I'm fine, Lance. I have a few stitches, but nothing that won't be healed in a few days.' I fingered the new dressing carefully, feeling the drying stitches through the fabric. 'I'll be able to do Ipswich,' I added, referring to my next concert.

'Good girl! Superb concert on Saturday. You were terrific but I told you that, didn't I?' Oh yes, he'd kissed my hand and grandstanded along in fine form, just like his elegant father, Sir James.

'Listen, a group of us are going to a late lunch at Silver's in West End. Would you like to join us? I know it's a bit soon after...you know...but it might cheer you up.'

An invitation? *What does he want? Gossip?* 'It just so happens that I need to do some shopping so yes, I'd like to come. Who's going to be there?

'Bill Seymour, Charlie Wilkins, Joy Martin...probably the Impaler if I can rake him out of whoever's bed he's currently in.' He went on to name several more musicians whom I knew well and a few I didn't.

'Okay, thank you. What time?

'Around 1.30 or thereabouts. I'll book a table. It's a sort of a welcome to the new percussionist, Craig someone or other.' Typical conductor, didn't know the name of a new musician. He couldn't have that much going on in his handsome head. *In fact, I doubt there's much beyond music and women in there at the best of times.*

That would also give me time to go to the West End police station and make a formal statement about my attack and the man watching me from the street. After that I'd go to the hospital and then call at Goldie's solicitor's office. I'd thought to see Mum in the afternoon, but John had asked me to come in the morning. 'She'll be stuffed by the afternoon. All the carry-on in the morning with the doctors and medicines. She'll probably sleep after lunch.'

I finished up my breakfast, gathered up my bag and coat, and trotted out the door making sure before I did so that the windows, particularly the ones to my balcony, were locked. The thought that Anthony Hamilton might ring me, or that I might actually see him some time that day, sent a warm thrill through me. *Thank God it didn't go any further...well, it might have been nice.*

I pulled up outside the station, grabbed my bag and headed inside. It didn't take long to get the statements organised and I was on my way again to the hospital to see mum. John met me when I got out of the lift and warned me that she was festooned with machinery, but quite bright under the circumstances.

It really hurt to see my mother with tubes sticking out of her throat and great swathes of metal clips in her neck confirming that her throat had, literally, been cut. Her eyes were quite bright, but owing to the patch of flesh taken from her arm and sewn into her mouth, her voice was muffled and weak. John kept dipping massive cotton buds into a glass of water and gently wetting her dry lips.

'Mum! You look great,' I assured her, as I sat in the chair which John pulled up for me.

'Huh, that's a laugh, Darling,' she said slowly, the side of her mouth angling up in a wry smile. She looked worried when she noticed the dressing on my stitches, but happy to accept my reassurances that it was almost healed.

John and I did most of the talking about the events of the last few days but we tried not to go into too much detail. 'Have you heard from Fiona?'

'She left a message at the desk. They said she'd be up in the next day or two, but Ros asked me to ring and tell her not to worry. She's got too much on her plate right now.'

We were silent for a moment, thinking of the terrible arrangements Fiona and Alex would have to make over the next week. I knew that Goldie's body still hadn't been released from the government mortuary. We steered the conversation to Fudge and the other animals at Emsberg, but before long, mum started to show the signs of exhaustion.

'I'll leave you to rest now, but I'll be back tomorrow, Mum. Don't worry, everything will work out in the end.'

John followed me out of the ward. 'Any change from Alex yet?' he asked, his tone revealing just how he felt about his brother-in-law's attitude.

'No, and I haven't been near them for the last day or so. They came around to look at Goldie's house to see what was missing, I believe, but I wasn't there.'

'Good. Stay away from them. I guess you'll have to go to the funeral, but Ros won't. I'll ask Daniella Winslow to stay with her and come myself.'

'That'll be good. We can support each other. I'll have to be at the wake, so please try and come to that too?' I needed my big, comforting stepfather by my side. Even though he's retired from the police force, being with him felt like having a personal bodyguard.

CHAPTER 30

Dingo

Past Mistakes

Tuesday, 8.30am

He was actually going to have lunch with Pamela Miller! Well, with her and a group of the musical fraternity, but that didn't count. Would she have the camera with her? She'd appeared to like – even fancy him – when they first met, but did she still? The police hadn't come to interview him over the attack in the parklands, so she can't have realised who had hit her. He hadn't wanted to. He liked the woman. Under other circumstances...Having had an awful night's sleep, in spite of rubbing his lower back and shoulder with liniment, he lay on the bed and tried to relax.

Nineeightsevensixfivefourthreetwoone...exhaustion overcame him and he drifted back into a deep sleep. His last thought was that he really must go to his own unit in Kangaroo Point, but living in the hotel made him feel as though he was keeping tabs on Pamela and the cops.

* * *

Frances' funeral was held on a cold and misty morning. The wind got up before ten o'clock and by 10.30 – the witching hour – it howled off the hillside and swept up to the mountains nearly taking Dingo and the family solicitor with it. Dingo felt so relieved when her casket was lowered into the grave that he had to stifle a wide grin. *At last he was free!*

His mother had died in her sleep of a heart attack, and her son thought, no doubt undiagnosed cirrhosis of the liver. Dingo had already applied for entrance into the Conservatorium of Music. After acing his audition, he couldn't wait to sell the house.

It wasn't long before he'd set himself up in a lavish unit in Brisbane, so it was with tremendous optimism that he started his studies. Practising for hours, sessions with tutors – every aspect of his experiences filled him with joy. No longer did he have to sneak out at night. He could and did, invite girls home. His good looks, height and physique, supplemented by his mother's training in manners (lightning reflexes with a wooden spoon) ensured he was comfortable in every class of society. Invitations to wild parties and willing women came at him from all sides and he reciprocated. Comfortable in the night – so long his saviour from madness – he relished the darkness. His reputation grew as a musician, lover and wild man.

But then, strangely, the loss of his mother began to bite. So long under her control he hyperventilated at the worst possible moments – in music sessions, while accompanied by an orchestra and once almost whilst giving a recital.

Dingo had lost his nerve and before he knew it, his career was in jeopardy. Realising that his life was spiralling out of control, he crept back into that dark place which he had inhabited nearly since the baby died. Unaware of it at first, he'd started counting again until a measure of control grew and his studies got back on track...

Dingo, do my back for me? He picked up the bar of goat's milk soap and ran his hands over her back to her waist, around her front and up to her breast, kneading, stroking. She leaned back into his torso, reaching behind her to slide her hand around his penis. 'Turn around, Ariel, so I can get at you...'

She turned and – Marigold! No, no! You're dead! I killed you!

Had he been screaming? His heart felt as though it was going to pound out of his chest. No footsteps raced along the passageway outside his room. No shouts or banging on the door. He flopped back onto the bed, too exhausted to pull the sweaty sheet from beneath his sore back. A feeble kick dislodged the top bedclothes.

The darkness in the room prevented him from judging the time. Had he missed the lunch date? He rolled over carefully and reached for his watch on the bedside table.12.25pm. No, plenty of time to shower, dress and get down to Silvers. Even be a little late. That would show he was cool and hide the panic which tightened his chest and twisted his gut into knots.

He couldn't wait to get near Pam and maybe, just maybe, discover where she kept the camera, the one thing that could link him to both *accidents*. He lay on his back and carefully counted the squares in the pattern in the ceiling. His career, the one thing he prized above his comfortable, successful life could all be over.

Everything had gone downhill after Ariel.

CHAPTER 31

Pam

The Good, the Bad and the Very Ugly

Tuesday, 11.30am

I drove to the Solicitor's office in the West End CBD much lighter of heart. A newspaper stand with a photo of a pretty dark-haired girl on the cover: "HAVE YOU SEEN THIS WOMAN?" in banner headlines above it, was the first thing I noticed as I parked the car. A large photo was at the bottom of the page with a small one of me beside it. The caption, Celebrity Journalist's Cousin Says...' *Bloody hell!*

The article went on to say that: "Pianist, Pamela Miller, fresh from her triumph at the Concert Hall on Saturday night stated that she had no idea who might have murdered her cousin. 'I just found her after the concert,' she said.' I said no such thing. I wanted to find the reporter and rip his throat out. All artists like publicity but this was sick. Forcing back tears, I turned my attention to the young girl.

The longer I examined her face, the more familiar it became. Had she been at the concert the other night? Perhaps she'd asked me for an autograph. Somewhere, sometime she had crossed my trail.

The offices of Sytch, Grimly and Sytch were quite a glamorous arrangement. Expensive- looking landscapes adorned the walls; a couple of vases packed with brightly coloured flowers caught the eye. A likely contender for the Miss World title, who didn't look as though she was prepared to finish talking on the phone any time soon, occupied the reception desk. I sat in one of the armchairs and took out my Kindle. When she finally stopped talking, I ignored her, a ploy which didn't go down very well.

'Can I help you?' *If you stop yapping on the phone long enough you can.*

I introduced myself without getting out of the chair.

'Oh yes, your appointment is for ten thirty. I'll see if Mr Sytch is available to see you now, Ms Miller,' she announced coldly. She'd hardly finished speaking when a short, elderly man galloped into the room. A monk's habit, complete with sandals and he could have played Friar Tuck.

'Miss Miller! Come in, come in!'

He rushed me into his office, where he settled me into a comfortable chair and bounced around the back of the desk. Having asked if I would like coffee and how, he pressed a button on the intercom and requested Miss World to bring some in. 'And those nice peanut and chocolate biscuits, too please, Sarah.'

Having offered his condolences on Goldie's death, he opened a folder on the desk in front of him. 'Your cousin thought a great deal of you, Miss Miller.'

'Please call me Pam, Mr Sytch,' I interjected.

'Er, thank you, er Pam. She told me that though she only actually met you three years ago, you'd become as close as sisters.' He coughed, turned a page and after a few more comments, began to read Goldie's wishes. I couldn't believe what I was hearing – her house, her car, all her possessions, including a pile of investments, apart from some bequests to her parents and close friends – she'd left to me. 'But what about her parents?'

'Oh don't worry about them, er – Pam. Your cousin was a very rich woman and she made sure they were very comfortably provided for from her superannuation. There is one special request she makes of you...that the portrait of Parry Reynolds –' He looked over his spectacles at me – 'be given to his sister, Elizabeth. Apparently he was very close to her.'

I almost collapsed with relief. 'Oh yes, I would be happy to do that. I really liked Elizabeth though+ I only met her once. She's lovely. '

Mr Sytch beamed. 'That she is. Right, now we'll get down to business, shall we?'

The coffee, delivered by the sulky Sarah was very welcome, but I hoped she hadn't spat in mine. The solicitor explained that Goldie had expressed a wish to be cremated and that her parents arrange the funeral service and wake, jobs I was relieved to have them do.

Mr Sytch went on to ask about Goldie's and my families, expressing surprise and pleasure when I told him that we had lived in Townsville and the close connection I had with Ally and Master's Island. Thorough, but kindly questioning brought out most of my childhood in minutes. 'Oh yes, my wife and I are great fans of Ally Carpenter. We went to the concert she and her husband put on in London last year.' He took a great gulp of coffee. 'We have several of their recordings. I have a couple of yours too, er Pam. The Tranquillity and Wandering with Schubert.'

To say I was astounded would be an understatement,

'And may I add that Iris and I enjoyed *your* concert on Saturday night very much?' He coughed. 'It's such a pity that the night ended that way. Are you recovering from the attack in the park?'He looked pointedly at the dressing peeping out from under my hair.

'Yes thank you, and I'm glad you enjoyed the concert.'

'Yes, um...perhaps we'd better get on, eh?'

Exhausted by the time I had signed heaps of papers and the arrangements were explained about probate, I was only too happy to leave. Stunned at the generosity of my cousin, I couldn't take it all in.

I drove back along the winding street past the park where remnants of checked police tape hung from a tree, but there was nothing else to show where the tragedy had occurred. In my mind, that part of the park would always be synonymous with death.

I had to circle the block umpteen times before a man driving a Jaguar pulled out of a space. I slid in, narrowly missing the tail-light of a Mercedes, and walked quickly to the dress shop where young Tia worked. Smells coming from the bakery next door almost side-tracked me. I paused to peer in the window, salivating at the gorgeous cream cakes and buns displayed. A particularly succulent-looking Bee Sting glistened under the lights. Knowing lunch was just around the corner, I shrugged and moved on. An interesting emerald garment occupied the display case where my glorious golden dress had flaunted itself.

Loud voices alerted to an argument. I paused in the doorway, wondering whether to venture in but a high-pitched squeal sent me charging inside.

A tall scraggy youth stood over the small shop assistant. As I gaped in horror, he smashed his hand down onto her face.

I lunged for him.

He turned and charged at me.

I whacked him under the chin with my handbag.

He rocked back on his heels, came at me again, roaring at the top of his lungs.

From nowhere came a long forgotten lesson in self-defence: I slammed the edge of my hand up under his nose.

Bone crunched.

He screamed and stumbled back into one of the elegant, Edwardian-style chairs holding his nose. Blood spurted through his fingers and dripped onto the brocade upholstery.

'Do dodding bitch!Doov boken be nobe!'

Tough.

Tia looked at me, aghast. 'Oh no, he's hurt!' Her face bore a livid mark where his fist had landed.

'Is that so?' I snarled, holding my hand behind my back so he couldn't see it quivering with pain. My bones ached, but nothing like the agony the youth was going through. The girl came forward and I got a good look at her swollen eye and the large dark bruise on her cheekbone, signs of previous ugliness.

'*He hit you!*'

She looked frightened. 'He didn't mean it!'

'Oh didn't he just? I'm going to call the police! He should be arrested for assault.' I scrabbled in my bag for my phone, but Tia grabbed my arm, raising pleading eyes to mine and whispered, 'Please Pam, don't tell anyone. Grant gets so frustrated because he can't get a job...he caught me talking to that Vladimir Rezanov down the street. All we said was hello and how's things... but after that the boss's son came in to fix the catch on the fitting room door and Grant caught me talking to him *as well*. Grant's very protective...'

Protective? I latched onto the most innocuous episode. 'Grant *caught* you talking to the bosses' son? You've got to be kidding. What sort of controlling behaviour is that? Of course you had to talk to him!'

I may as well have been addressing the wall for all the response I got.

Tia took a box of tissues off the counter and moved over to the abuser sitting in the chair, holding his nose, glaring malevolently. It was no wonder he couldn't get a job, covered in tattoos with rings in his nose, a silver stud in his cheek and plastic crosses inserted into the lobes of his ears. He needed a good wash and a haircut. But it was more than that. Grant just looked plain *bad*.

We made eye contact. Enraged by the sly hatred in his eyes and aware that only Tia's presence and the fact that we were in a public place prevented him from attacking me, I stretched to my full height. 'Come on, you stinking little ferret, just try something. *Anything.'* I swung my bag within his peripheral vision. *Action girl, that's me.*

His gaze flicked to it for a moment and then, muttering something foul, jumped to his feet and lurched out of the shop. I looked at Tia expecting signs of relief, but was disappointed. 'What did you do that for? Now he'll hate me!' she wailed, tears streaming down her cheeks.

I put my arm around her and squeezed. 'Come on, mate. He'll get over it.' *With any luck he'll step under a bus and save everyone grief.*

She snuffled into a handful of tissues. 'Oh no, he's bled all over the chair!' She flapped her hands, seemingly undecided how to tackle the problem.

'Have you got any stain remover out the back?'

Her expression brightened. 'Oh yes, we keep it for any spots that get on the dresses. You know people *will* touch them when they've been eating stuff.' She made as if to dash out into the back room and then remembered her job. 'I'm sorry, I can do that later.' She picked up the chair and shoved it through the curtain into the back room. 'How can I help you?'

'I have to go to a funeral in a few days and I need something suitable to wear.'

She sniffed, wiped her eyes with the back of her hand and tried a watery smile. 'Oh yes it's your cousin. I'm so sorry, Pam. You've had such an awful time and here I am thinking about myself. Debbie and I are still talking about Saturday night. You were so gorgeous in that dress. I told Mrs Marchant, my boss, and she was really pleased with me.' She looked so happy again that I figured she'd probably received a little extra something for the sale.

Ever the professional assistant, Tia sprang into action. 'I'm sure we have a few outfits which might suit you.' She began skimming dresses along the racks, red, green, blue, the complete spectrum.

As I started every woman's nightmare, or happy hour depending on one's perspective, I forced back tears. Goldie should have been here, sitting outside waiting to inspect each outfit, screaming 'Get it off, it looks foul!' Even thoughts of Anthony Hamilton couldn't comfort me. I finally settled on a dark purple wrap-around dress and toning crystal earrings. Although I was tempted to buy new accessories, I decided to go with my good black pumps and handbag with the silver clasp. Unfortunately, the dress needed the hem raised just a bit.

'When is the funeral?' lisped Tia, through a mouthful of pins as she crawled around the floor, seemingly oblivious to the new swelling on her cheek. I wondered what her employer would have to say about her appearance, realising that Tia couldn't have realised the implications of what it might do to her job.

'I don't know. Probably not until next week.' *Oh my God, I didn't need to get involved in a brawl, today of all days.*

'We'll have it taken up straightaway and it'll be ready to pick up tomorrow afternoon.' She processed my severely strained debit card, still sniffing. 'You *will* come back sometime, apart from to collect the dress? Please?'

'Of course I will. I'll be going overseas soon for a concert series, but I live just around the corner, so to speak! I'll see you again.' I reached over the counter and took her hand. 'And Tia, seriously consider shedding Grant. It's not a relationship which is going to turn out well. He's an abuser and it's only going to get worse. Do you understand?'

She promised to think about it, but I could see I hadn't made much of an impression. Regretting that I hadn't insisted on ringing the police, I drove off to meet up with Lance Macpherson and the group. Something told me that things were about to go downhill for the girl.

CHAPTER 32

Pam

The Luncheon

Tuesday, 1.30pm

I ran my hand over the car, unable to believe that this beautiful piece of machinery – a GTI Golf, something I couldn't have afforded in a fit – was mine, thanks to the generosity of Goldie. How had she felt when she made out her will only a few months ago? Had she an inkling that it would be read so soon and that this vehicle would be the one referred to in her will as "my current car"? No, but a journalist whose everyday life involved ducking bullets, bombs and the Judiciary all around the world, would have been well aware that the next job could be the last.

Goldie's stoic acceptance of Parry's funeral flashed into my mind. As the graveside service ended, she'd taken one last look at the flowers piled beside the casket, its silver handles glittering in the pale morning sun, waiting for the vicar to press the button for the descent into the grave. She'd touched the gleaming wood lightly and then nodded. As soon as the casket with its sad cargo descended into the depths, she turned away. 'Right, that's it then. Let's get through the wake as quickly as we can. I have to catch a plane tonight.'

I knew her bravado cloaked an agony so deep that she couldn't express it, and as I watched her greeting his family and friends – and holding his weeping mother in her arms – without letting her facade crack once, I knew she would throw herself into the first war she could get to. I shivered, remembering a time a couple of years ago, when Goldie talked about that very thing. We'd been to dinner one freezing night in London, come home and sat in front of a roaring fire, talking about everything in our futures and of course, our pasts. Goldie had never spoken about losing the love of her life until then, but her tongue perhaps loosened by a bottle of Scotch she reminisced once about Parry's passing, an event I remembered well.

'I've never regretted my lifestyle, Pammie, but the one thing I wish I'd done was hitch up to Parry and have a child before...well, you know. It's too late now for me to have a baby and I don't know any bloke I'd want to get that close to.'

'But Goldie, you're only thirty-one! You might very well meet someone else one day. You can't discount that possibility, and women are having first babies in their forties now!'

'Oh Pam, don't buy into that myth. We only hear about the successful births. They don't publicise the thousands of IVF treatments that are failures.' I remembered she had written a particularly poignant article which included an interview with a woman who had tried to have a baby in her late forties and left it too late. 'My career was too important to me,' the woman had confessed. 'I always thought I had time.'

'Well, I still say you have stacks of time, mate. You've barely scratched the surface of the men out there,' I said, resolutely.

'Yeah and where's a decent one amongst them? You know I've not been celibate since Parry died, Pammie, but there's not one that I wanted to sleep with twice – well, maybe a couple, but with our jobs it's here today and gone tomorrow.' She'd sighed and poured us another glass of port, making it clear that she didn't want to pursue the topic.

What with our tangled schedules – my career had started to hot up, thank God – and Goldie spending little time in a place where we could meet, there hadn't been many opportunities for uninterrupted time. Now, just when we'd gotten together again, a monster had taken Goldie's life. I knew my cousin well enough to understand that wherever she was, she would be furious that a "common or garden" man had done what the Taliban had failed to achieve.

Meanwhile, there was Parry's portrait to be packed up and that was a priority. That led to another speculation. Alex and Fiona would want access to the house to pick up mementos of their daughter. I would have to ring them and, please God, it wouldn't be Alex who answered. I couldn't cope with him. Perhaps he had always disliked me? But wouldn't I have known if that were so? Could he have hidden his feelings successfully for the past four years? Much of the time I had been overseas and met Goldie at various sites around the world. Only twice had I come back to Brisbane and spent time with her here. *Now I come to think of it. I don't really know him all that well...*

Fiona and I were closer. An image from a couple of years ago flashed into my mind – a bird-leg thin arm with purple bruising around the wrist. 'Caught my wrist in the strap of my handbag, dear,' Fiona had explained, and changed the subject. Having just seen Grant in action and recalling Alex in a rage one of the few times I'd been in his house, I wondered. Would Goldie have known if her father was abusing her mother? She wasn't home much, but domestic abuse goes on for years and if indeed, that had been happening she must have seen something. Had it started later, after she left home? I'd heard victims were good at hiding spouse abuse.

I'd never know for sure now unless Fiona opened up to me and she was unlikely to do that. Would I find any evidence in Goldie's home? Should I let the Humphries' have full reign? No. I'd go through my cousin's papers first and make sure there wasn't anything there that her father could take, like diaries. Unless they already had...

Unless I refurbished it, I would forever see Goldie's body lying at the foot of the stairs, but selling it would be even worse as far as Alex was concerned, as though I was so ungrateful I didn't care what happened to it. Just then, I glanced up. Right in front of me, almost as though Goldie had sent me a message, was a locksmith's shop. Five minutes later, I had made arrangements to meet one of their "smiths" at Goldie's house later that afternoon.

Just then, my mobile signalled a text message. 'Dinner 2nite? AH.'

My brain scrambled to compute who that was, then the "penny dropped."

'Lovely thk u!'

'C u 7.30?'

'G8. Wh 2?'

'Chinese?'

'Y.'

Anthony was taking me to dinner! I wondered how he had wrangled that, aware that anything could change and he might have to cancel. In the mean time, what was I going to wear? Knowing he didn't want anyone, namely his work colleagues, knowing that we were together, meant most likely a suburban restaurant, so warm slacks, long-sleeved blouse and a sweater would be the thing. I shrugged. That was the least of my worries. My intention was to meet up with the group for lunch! I put the car into gear and pulled into the traffic.

Silvers Restaurant is an upmarket, glamorous establishment. Situated behind lattice work to protect its precious customers from the hoi poloi, it features lots of trendy statues which look as though they would be more at home in a cow paddock. Greenery and running water merely made me want to go to the loo. I sidled into the foyer to be greeted by a glamorous twenty-something young woman – is there a run on "Miss Worlds" in West End? – who looked at me as though I was something she'd scraped off the pavement. Before she had time to enquire whether I was meeting someone, I was hailed from behind a jungle of ferns.

'Pam! We're here!' A face from the violins popped through like the Cheshire Cat. I scurried around the Greek urns, passing a table full of what appeared to be office girls, all texting on their mobiles. A hug from Ally and Brie, who looked relaxed – no doubt because the twins were with his parents, who definitely wouldn't be relaxed – a surprising kiss from Vlad the Impaler (perhaps I should be honoured?) a big smile from Bill Seymour and happy hellos from the rest. Some I recognised but one or two were new to me. Lance

Macpherson, looking like everybody's favourite grandson, hailed me from the bar.

Someone pulled a chair out for me and I plopped myself down next to a tall, handsome lad new to the orchestra. He introduced himself as Craig Douglas. On the other side of the table, Vlad leaned back in his chair and bared his teeth in a wolfish smile. *Crikey, the man was not only dangerous but a work of art!* In spite of the fact that he wasn't "into" me, I could tell that my long conversation with Craig annoyed him. Always the little prince, Rezanov obviously thought he warranted special attention. I deliberately let him wait while I checked out Douglas, who you wouldn't kick out of bed for scattering biscuit crumbs either.

Three women whom I'd observed around the music scene giggled and told funny stories about people they'd met. Ally obviously wanted to come and sit by me, but contented herself by wiggling her eyebrows appreciatively at the men flanking me. 'We'll talk later,' she signalled, in the way that only lifelong friends and sisters understand. Finally, Vlad and Craig each got up and went to talk to other people; a woman I had met once or twice moved into the chair to my right. We were happily surprised to discover that we would be in London at the same time and made arrangements to hook up. Bill Seymour joined us and added in some amusing anecdotes from his time playing with the orchestra and then taking up his job as manager of the concert hall, before moving over to talk to a violinist whom I knew had recently joined the Pacific. From the expression on his face, he might be about to make a move on her. *Thank goodness.*

At first I thought I was just being paranoid, but something felt "off." It wasn't anything I could put my "finger on" so to speak, but someone either in our group or nearby, was paying attention to me. A sudden movement nearby felt furtive. Had someone put something in their pocket or said something? I couldn't be sure. A chill settled in my gut. I debated whether to bolt to the restrooms. *No, don't show you know you're being watched.* Should I tell Ally? She was deep in conversation with Craig Douglas. *Careful Pam, be normal. Show nothing.*

I allowed my gaze to roam the room. The girls at the table next to us had given up texting their friends for the time being and were actually talking to each other. Wait-staff rushed to and fro with meals. No one made eye contact. I ducked my head and scooped up the last of my meal, then blotted my lips with my table napkin – the movement was so infinitesimal as to be non-existent, but it had happened! Halfway to my right...as I turned, the configuration of bodies changed. *Damn. Should I tell Anthony tonight?* He might want to charge around and arrest everyone here. More likely he'd tell me not to be so silly.

All appeared to be normal again, but someone was far too interested in me and not in a good way.

CHAPTER 33

Dingo

Getting Closer

Tuesday, 1.30pm.

Dingo's underground life as a child and teenager had long trained him in the art of utilising his peripheral vision to his best advantage. Frances' lightning blows had taught him to dodge like a boxer, her verbal assaults bouncing off him like summer rain. When his mother's death had finally cast off the shackles of incarceration, in spite of – or even because of – his teenage nocturnal lifestyle, initially he thrived.

His fellow students were too juvenile to hide their emotions. In spite of his open and charming public profile, Dingo *knew* how to be a non-person, having learned over the years to cloak himself in invisibility, to vanish into the woodwork merely by being still, allowing others to focus on themselves and their companions rather than himself. The moment when they forgot him was when their secrets came out.

Dingo "did" secrets.

Lunch was a blast. Renowned for its seafood menu, the smell of succulent prawn pasta, great chunks of salmon and hot chips wafted from the plates of his companions. Surrounded by fellow musicians, catching up with the latest gossip and in-jokes served to both excite and calm him. He made sure he got the opportunity to sit next to Pamela Miller during the shuffle of positions between courses.

'Hey Pam, how're you doing? You excelled yourself Saturday night!' He leaned close, smiling into her eyes, trying to ignore the small bandage peeping out from under her riotous curls. 'I know you have a couple more concerts here, but where to after that?' *As if he didn't know.*

'Thanks, I appreciate that.' She beamed back at him, eyes twinkling, as she gave him her overseas itinerary, culminating in a performance before royalty. Clearly excited by the prospect, she was going to keep talking, but he couldn't have that.

'You'll get your photo taken with them, that'll be something to remember! But you're a bit of a photographic nut yourself, aren't you?'

Pam looked puzzled for a moment. 'Yes, I like taking photos but my cousin, Goldie –' she closed her eyes momentarily and swallowed. '– was an expert. It was in all the papers.'

'I'm so sorry. You got my messages? It must be very hard for you.' *And it'll be a lot harder for you if I can't find that camera...* 'I guess your cousin must have taught you a lot about photography then?' He smiled in what he hoped was a beguiling manner and seeing her glass empty, picked up the nearest bottle of chardonnay.

'I'm driving! No more thanks, but I will have some juice. Yes, Goldie did give me some tips, but I'm strictly amateur.'

He stood and leaned across the table for a jug of orange juice. 'Would you like to go out to dinner some time?'

Pam touched his hand. 'Thank you, but I'm actually seeing someone right now.'

He forced a grin. 'Lucky bloke! So what sort of camera do you have?'

Confusion swept across her face. 'I don't actually have a camera, but Goldie lent me hers the other day. I thought I might – '

Just then, Ally Mochrie bounced around the table and inserted herself between them. 'How're you doing, Dingo? Saturday went well for our girl, didn't it?' She nudged him in the ribs and laughed. Rage surged through him. Just as he was getting to the point of the camera, fucking Ally Mochrie had to interfere. *Thanks a lot. Now I'll never know what she's done with the damn thing. Ten. Nine. Eight. Seven...*

'Dingo?' Pam's eyes widened. 'But – '

Ally roared with laughter. Dingo wanted to strangle her there and then. 'Oh, that's his nickname from the UK! So how've you been, mate?'

The moment was lost, but he now knew she had the journalist's other camera, the one that *had* to have his and Ariel's photos on it. He smiled at Ally, to all intents and purposes, carrying on a lively conversation, but a lifetime of hiding his feelings meant his brain was working at lightning speed...there was only one thing left to do.

CHAPTER 34

Susan

Breakthrough

Tuesday, 2pm

Fear sent me into a state where I couldn't concentrate, couldn't focus on anything other than the fact that David was hadn't phoned me. I'd left countless messages begging him to ring. Pete Moffatt wasn't answering either and no one at Toowoomba seemed to know where he was. If they did they were only saying he was busy on a case.

My stress levels were far too high.

I moved papers around on my desk. Reports on Ariel Maxwell and Marigold Humphries couldn't hold my attention for more than a few minutes at a time. I debated whether to call in my Senior Sergeants and confess that I could no longer function as the leader in these murders. I still hadn't spoken to Pamela Miller after meeting her outside the Humphries' house. The perp hadn't ransacked the house. Perhaps the camera was clearly visible after the attack. Maybe he was too scared to touch anything else, or maybe it was just a case of being interrupted.

'Susan?'

Anthony Hamilton loomed in the doorway. I swept aside the reports and swung around, delighted to see he was holding two containers of what looked like hot coffee in his hands. 'Just pop them there, Anthony. How did you guess I was dying for a cup?'

A dark chocolate chuckle burst out of him. 'We're cops. It's in the training manual!' *Oh, you'll go far my lovely. Now, what are you up to?*

We sipped our lattés in silence for a few minutes before he came to the point. 'Pamela Miller would appear to be no longer a suspect, Ma'am.' He looked me straight in the eye.

'We can't be sure of that, Anthony. She has an alibi for the time of death, but she could be acting in collusion with someone.' I didn't believe that, but I wanted to see how far he would go to defend her.

He flipped his notebook open. 'She's genuinely grieving for her cousin and there's absolutely no evidence to suggest that she was involved in any way whatsoever. Her bank accounts are healthy and she has her own unit which she finished paying for two years ago. She sold her car before she returned overseas where she's been for the past year. Musical experts say she's regarded as being the foremost flautist in the country. Why would she want to murder her cousin or get together with someone to do that?'

'Apart from the inheritance, no reason whatsoever, Anthony. I don't believe she's guilty either, but I still think there's a link between the two murders.' I changed tack. 'Are you "seeing" Pamela?'

He looked back at me; I could see the wheels turning. 'I'm taking her to dinner tonight.'

'Okay, well be discreet about it. If it turns out that she's our perp, then you'll swing as well, right?'

'Yes, Ma'am.'

What was the point in pushing my Senior Sergeant? Pam was innocent of any wrong-doing and as far as I knew, possibly still in danger from her intruder. What better bodyguard than her personal "assassin"? And sex has a way of finding its targets regardless of the circumstances. 'Any further news on the Maxwell case?'

'Only the chip shop owner reporting –' His phone chirped. With an apologetic glance, he took the call and then flashed a smile which, had I been younger and single, would have curled my toes. Well, to be honest, a smile like would curl any woman's toes, right?

'Ariel Maxwell came in on Virgin Flight VA 951, landed Friday, 4.30pm, at the domestic terminal. The airport management are making their CCTV footage of the arrivals hall available, particularly the luggage carousel!'

At last we were getting somewhere. No wonder the Roma Street transit centre had been a washout. 'Wonder how they came in from the airport? If they were on the air train from Brisbane domestic terminal we might just get lucky, and then there's the cab rank over the road.' Police HQ is opposite the Transit Centre.

'I'll get on it right away, Ma'am. Oh, and the magazine, Kings River Life doesn't appear to have any connection with the case.' He picked up his notebook and our takeaway cups.

'Good one, mate. Let me know when the tape comes through. And by the way, it's "Susan."'

With a wide grin and a wave of his huge paw, he vanished. At last, a breakthrough and now we might be getting somewhere. On the verge of doing a mental jig, I remembered. *Please God, let David be safe.*

Evan poked his head through the door. 'Hamilton just told me about the airport CCTV.'

'Yes, it's great. Now we'll get somewhere, with any luck.'

'Calls coming in from everywhere, Susan. People reckon they've seen Ariel with everyone from the man in the moon to Santa Claus!' He slapped a file down on my desk and threw himself into the chair. 'I can't leave here without these cases being solved. I'll never forgive myself if I have to go out to Warwick before they're finished.'

Only a week before Evan left for his country posting and the hierarchy would come down on us like a ton of bricks if we hadn't gotten a result, but three days in and we hadn't a viable clue or a suspect in sight for either murder.

'What do you reckon about Alex Humphries? Do you think he knows more than he's telling?'

'No, I don't think so and I doubt he had anything to do with his daughter's death, but he certainly has it in for Pamela.'

'Have you spoken to her yet?'

'No, I haven't had a chance, but I'll ring her tonight.' I leaned back and rubbed my eyes. I gave him the latest news about Pamela being vouched for by police manning the road block at the Maxwell murder.

'Well, that's a relief. I expect Hamilton will be pleased about that!' He adopted his paternal expression. 'You need to go home. We'll let you know if anything breaks. Reports coming in all the time, so there's bound to be a break soon.'

'Well, so far the sod's managed to cover his tracks – the mobile, no airline ticket in her handbag, condoms presumably flushed, sheets washed, dishes done. Do you think he actually planned it?'

Evan remained silent for a while, rubbing his hand over his jaw. 'No. I think it was love play which got out of hand. I reckon the cleaning up in the house was done before they went out, so Ariel's parents wouldn't know she had someone there for the night.'

'Hm. I think you could be right, but I still think the Humphries killing is tied in somehow.'

'Okay, so give it to me.'

'Right. Apart from my gut you mean?'

'Yep.'

'There's something about the broken neck...well, more about the *power* involved in both murders. It would take a great deal of strength to do that. The Humphries woman was incredibly fit, as strong as most men but she got overpowered and her neck broken.'

'Are you basing the connection between the cases on the strength of the perp then?'

'What are the chances of there being two separate strongmen loose in the West End within the same twenty four hours?'

'Still, it doesn't mean squat unless you can marry them up.'

'Trust you to shoot me down in flames!' I laughed and poked my tongue out at him.

He grinned. 'I'm not saying you're wrong, and we all know about your famous intuition, but even for you, this is a stretch. If it was the perp from the park, how would he know where she lived? I'm playing Devil's Advocate here.'

'Well, for a start almost anyone she worked with. Adam McIntyre stalked someone else into bed that night. Roma station has confirmed that, and the only thing missing is Humphries' best camera. Doesn't that say he wanted what was in it? The SD card?'

'Hm. Perhaps he was disturbed before he could look for anything else. He had to come through the front door though, because there's no sign of a break in and it was unlocked.'

'It was a cold night so why would she go outside again? She hasn't got a pet to let out for a pee. No, he must have got her to open it. A simple knock would do it and from what Pam said, the chain wasn't on when she got home, so either Humphries forgot to put it on or she deliberately opened the door to a caller. Easy peasy.'

We stared at each other for along moment and then burst out laughing.

'Look at us! We'll solve this one on our own yet!' I chuckled. 'We know that the last time anyone – apart from the taxi driver – saw Marigold alive, was when she left the Concert Hall. The driver says he waited until she got inside the house and shut the door and he didn't see anyone hanging around. He was probably counting his money and didn't really look, but he maintains that he always checks that his female passengers get inside their houses before he leaves and even though he's a weedy little creep, he's also a grandfather, so I believe that. We can't find anyone who saw someone following her, so the perp had to know where she lived, which brings us back to her workplace or friends.'

This time we both sighed.

Evan looked at me intently. 'Why don't you go home and get some rest, it's almost home time and we've a big day tomorrow. You'll tell me what else you're hiding when you're ready.'

'What do you mean?'

'Come on, I'm a husband and father of four – well, five in six months time. I recognise "the look."'

'Five! Good heavens, mate, don't you know what's causing it?' I asked, trying to sidetrack him. 'Congratulations, to you both.'

'Thanks, Susan. And I'm right, aren't I?'

I contemplated lying through my teeth, but Evan and I had started out as constables together. He was one of the few male officers who had supported me all through the debacle that was my first marriage to David. I owed him. 'Yes, you're right. David doesn't know yet and heaven only knows how he's going to feel about 'double the joy" again.'

'For crying out loud! Really?'

'Yep and at my age. At least the doctor's pretty sure its twins again. I've an ultrasound booked for this Friday. I only hope David's home to go with me.' *Oh, my love.*

'You know Genevieve and I will help all we can, even though we're going to be in Warwick. It's no more than two hours from here.'

'Yes, I know and thank you, Evan. I've always appreciated you have my back.'

'And you mine.' He stood, came around the desk and put his arm around my shoulders to give me a squeeze. 'I'm on call tonight and I'll make sure you hear any excitement that eventuates. You haven't heard from David yet?'

'No, nothing. Pete Moffat is dodging my calls too. But David said before he left, he'd phone as soon as he's coming back. He *promised*. No matter the time of day or night.'

'You know you can rely on David, Susan. If they're flat out on a case up there, then he might not be able to call. I know you'll hear as soon as he can do it. I know it's hard but just sit tight. I have a lot of faith in David and you should have too. Now get home and rest up, mate.'

I got to my feet slowly. Being home on my own didn't appeal one bit, especially with my suspicions about David's safety, but I had to feed the animals, phone the girls and definitely get some rest. Perhaps I would call Melanie and coax her into coming over for the night and if she hesitated, I'd pull the older sister's prerogative and twist her arm. If that didn't work, I was sure I could find something with which to bribe her.

Like chocolate.

And wine.

CHAPTER 35

Pam

A Feast or a Famine

Tuesday, 4.30pm

I rushed out of the restaurant like a madwoman, so eager to get home, shower and get ready for my date with Anthony that I barely said goodbye to anyone. Ally would have loved to corner me for a talk but as she closed in I hissed, 'Got a date, have to talk to you later.' Her face lit up, but before she could fire questions at me I took off, almost running to the car. First stop, Goldie's house to meet the locksmith, then home. *Let's hope the bugger's not going to be late.*

A handsome young rooster was waiting by a tradesman's van as I drove up. Just for once, fortune seemed to be smiling on me! While he changed the locks on the back, front and garage doors, I wandered through the chaotic house again, trying not to look impatient. Even though Goldie had died here only a little over two days ago, I still felt that she would walk in the door at any moment. I'd have to ask Susan about when I could get a firm in to clean the whole place. Whatever, the house didn't feel bad anymore and I was able to relax and make the locksmith, a cheerful youth with the rather odd name of name of Bergil, and me a cup of coffee. Whistling happily, he handed me the invoice, took my cheque and passed me the keys to everything. 'What do you want to do with the old ones?'

'They're no use to anyone. You can take them back and use them somewhere else if you like.' I handed the keys over and he put them into a cloth bag with the old locks.

As I drove home, relieved to have gotten that out of the way, I thought about the luncheon. I'd had a great time catching up with my friends and meeting new musicians. Craig Douglas was an interesting man and I'd enjoyed spending time with him. He was contracted with the Pacific for the next six months, so I'd get to know him when I got back from the UK. Vlad, Bill and Lance had all made time to talk to me. Was I mistaken or had they not only treated me as a "star" but flirted with me as well? They'd *all* asked me to dinner and Bill had invited me to go sailing with him when I got back from the UK. *Woo hoo!* Sailing? I'd never have picked him for a yachtsman in a month of Sundays. Craig Douglas had lurked in the background watching me. Would he make a move as well?

And *Dingo?Who would have thought?* I chuckled. When a woman finds someone she's interested in after a long "man-less" drought, does she give off some sort of pheromone that tells the rest of them she's desirable? No men around for yonks and then you have to beat them off with sticks!

The girls from the orchestra were all friendly and seemed great fun, so the trip out west in two months time boded well and a great surge of happiness went through me. Things were looking up! A new man on the horizon, a thriving career – note in that order! – *and* my agent told me she was negotiating for another CD for Decca! What more could a girl want?

The car seemed to find its own way into my parking spot under the block of units which kind of surprised me as it hadn't been there before. I dragged out my bag, locked up and raced for the lift nearly knocking down my elderly neighbour who was just stepping in, dragging one of those little wheeled trolleys full of groceries after him.

'Young lady, I'll have you know I got here first so you don't have to flatten me to make a point!' *Uh?*

'I'm so sorry, Mr Uqhart, I'm just so excited. Heavy date tonight!'

He peered at me over the top of his glasses. 'Oh it's you, Pam. Hear you did well on Saturday night.'

I punched the button for the first floor. 'Thank you Mr Uqhart, I'm just so relieved it went off well, but now…well, my cousin was killed the same night, so things aren't too good,'

'Ugh.' He shook his head, not meeting my gaze. Some people are embarrassed by death and don't know what to say. 'Goodnight Pam.'

I didn't wait to see him shuffle into his unit, but raced to my door. Keying in the security code, I put the chain across and threw my keys into the coloured glass bowl on the kitchen table. Six o'clock and I had an hour and a half to get ready.

Singing in the shower is not usually my thing, but this time it was different. Squawking merrily, I slapped gel around like it was going out of style, dried myself, hurled powder in every direction and then, wrapped in a towel, examined my wardrobe with a rather jaundiced eye. I threw several pairs of slacks and jeans on the bed, but nothing "grabbed" me. An electric blue wrap-around dress which I hadn't worn for years cried piteously from its position at the very end of the row. Hoping it would still fit I tried it – Hallelujah! – make up and high-heeled sandals. At 183cms, finding a man who was around 195 meant someone "up there" had finally heard my pleas. I could actually wear heels! *Oh for heaven's sake, Pam; it's only the first date.*

I am blessed, or some would say cursed, with a mane of thick curly fair hair, great ringlets of the stuff, which never seems to behave itself. Locked in mortal combat with my "crowning glory" I was less than pleased when the phone rang.

'Pam, it's Susan! Am I ringing at a bad time?'

'No, not at all. I've got a date in about forty-five minutes, but there's plenty of time for a chat!'

'Yes, I know you've got a date. He confessed all to me a couple of hours ago!' She laughed, and I relaxed a little.

'Does this mean I'm not a suspect anymore?'

'Well, I can't discuss the case but no, you have a viable alibi, so unless you're in cahoots with some nefarious individual, then you're in the clear. So where's Fudstuds taking you tonight?'

Giggling at the nickname for the assassin, we settled down for what should have been a comforting chat, but something was "off." I'd known Susan for almost five years and she had become a good friend of Mum and me, so I was pretty much "up" with the tone of her voice. Something was wrong but she was "cracking hardy."

'I can tell from your voice that you're worried about something. Is it the case? Is everything all right with David?'

'I always worry about my cases, Pam, you know that. No, nothing's wrong, David's fine. I just thought I'd give you a call. I spoke to John and he reckons Ros is doing well and should be able to go home early next week. Have you seen her?'

Oh yeah, so nothing's wrong, eh? Like hell. 'Yes, I went to the hospital this morning and I'll go tomorrow. She gets tired pretty quickly and she looks awful, but she's insisting that she's fine.'

We laughed. The women's answer for everything!

'How's John holding up?'

'Just the same, you know him. Quiet and strong.'

'So, Anthony Hamilton? Exciting things happening there? Even the Superintendent knows about it.' I could tell Susan was dying to find out how close Anthony and I were.

'Is he going to get into trouble?'

'No, Pam. Even we cops know that love will always find a way. It's going well then?'

'Well, this is only the first date, so I wouldn't hold my breath if I were you, but...I really like him.'

'Yeah, you and most of the female squad! No, don't get me wrong, he's not showing any sign of even looking sideways at any of them. He goes red around the gills when your name's mentioned though!'

We exchanged a few more pleasantries and gossip before she rang off. I spent the half hour before Anthony was due to arrive in a hysterical flutter. *Just go with the flow and see where it takes you.*

I pinned my hair on top of my head, leaving a bit hanging over the little dressing on my head, then took it down again, plaited it and then ripped that out. Fumbling to roll it into a bun at the base of my neck and still leave the dressing covered, I nearly leaped out of my skin when the doorbell rang.

Sporting a chocolate sports jacket, black T-shirt and jeans, boots and his normal stern expression, Anthony stepped across my threshold and before I could even greet him, took me in his arms, pressed me against the wall and kissed as though he wanted to eat me alive. *Yum.* His hands swept through my tangle of hair, sliding down my back over my derriere while I clung to his coat like a Cobbler's Peg. His gorgeous, muscular body did all manner of things to me...including his extremely interesting package...

Breathless, we pulled apart, grinning at each other like mad things. 'I'm pleased to see you had the chain on the door.' He smoothed my hair back from my face.

Remembering my strenuous and noisy attempt to take it off and let him in, I giggled. 'Well, I have to do what the cops tell me, don't I?' *Pam, could you sound sillier if you tried?*

He gently touched the dressing. 'When are the stitches coming out?'

'They want to keep them in for another week. They're itchy already!'

He grinned. 'That means the wound's healing quickly! Are you ready?'

He jingled his keys in his pocket. *Is that programmed into men's DNA, like toasting their bums in front of a roaring fire?*

As I grabbed my coat and bag and we swept out the door, something nagged at me. Somewhere today I'd seen something which should have been significant.

CHAPTER 36

Dingo

A Little Break & Enter

Tuesday, 7pm

Would she ever leave the damned place? He waited in the park opposite the block of flats, hunched up in his quilted parka, hood pulled well down over his face to hide from observers and ward off the chilly night air. He'd settled into position where he could watch the front of the unit block and Pamela's balcony simultaneously, relieved to see that the branches of the tree were still close enough for him to get across to the balustrade. No one had thought to cut them back after his recon' Sunday afternoon.

He would make his move once she'd gone out and the rest of the occupants of the block had settled down to watch TV. He had a small jemmy under his coat ready to prise the balcony door locks open. He stamped his feet, counting his steps, to keep the circulation working and contemplated going down to the shops for fish and chips – no not that – perhaps a pie. Ariel and Marigold had been blessedly quiet, but he didn't want to wake them. They'd only nag him. Nearby a tree full of lorikeets screeched, preparatory to roosting for the night. They would have irritated him, but if they kept up their racket long enough, they would be blessed cover for any noise he might make entering the unit.

A blue car sped by, then a green one. *Please God, no red ones...* a white one pulled up next to the flats and disgorged a couple of women before the driver turned the car into the underground parking area. Talking animatedly, the women went into the foyer. A group of revellers came out of the pub down the road. As they came closer he counted them: eight. Even numbers and he was safe. They passed, laughing and punching each other on the shoulders, too drunk to notice anything untoward around them.

He looked up at the glass doors leading onto Pam's balcony, remembering how happy she'd been at lunch. Her face glowed, her eyes sparkled – only a man could bring that sort of glow to a woman's face. He'd done it himself many times. He wondered who it could be. A musician? At twenty-eight, rising twenty-nine, Pammie-girl was getting a bit long in the tooth for some men. He knew all about the hangers-on, the corporate types who thought if their company sponsored an orchestra they had "squatter's rights" on the female musicians. He'd been the target of female "corporates" himself, thrusting, controlling women who expected and received the homage of men who relied on their patronage when it came to the arts. He didn't mind the thrusting when they were in bed, but otherwise...he spat on the ground.

His prey's head of wild curls came into view. She looked out of the window and then drew the curtains of what he was pretty sure was her bedroom. He hoped she kept the camera there, but the place was relatively small. He wondered if she kept it in her – no Marigold

Humphries' car, as she'd told him at lunch. That could be a problem but she'd also volunteered the information that she'd sold her car before she went overseas, and wasn't it great that she had a car space allotted to her in the underground car park of her unit block. Unit 8. Wherever it was, she'd be taking care of the camera because it was a good Nikon, he knew that much. Perhaps after he got the SD card, he'd use it himself...no, better to get rid of it straight away. *Pity.*

A sleek, low and extremely expensive car slid into a park at the front of the building. *Why did the rich always get a parking space when they needed it, like the heroes in movies?*

He watched as a huge man got out, clicked the locking remote with nonchalant arrogance and bounded into the building. This one had testosterone to burn and Dingo'd bet everything he owned that this bloke had women coming out his ears.

Normally, Dingo was – in spite of his solitary upbringing – pretty level headed, especially in his work. All that changed after Ariel came into his life for such a brief time. It was as though, with Ariel's death, his public persona was all he had left. Marigold he discounted – she was what the Yanks called "collateral damage' and therefore not important in the overall scheme of things, but the rage simmering inside blinded him to everything but the presence of Macho Man.

Onetwothreefourfivesixseveneight...that's a dark red car...no, it's brown. It has to be brown. Teneleventwelve... red car danger, red car danger...breathe...breathe...that's right. The security light above the door to the foyer came on and lit up the area. It was dark, gleaming blue! *You're okay, it's blue.*

He wondered where the man mountain had gone, but it didn't make any difference where he was headed, Dingo's sole focus was the camera. Having overheard her telling Ally Mochrie she had a dinner date that night, all he had to do was be patient. He shielded his watch with his coat and clicked on the tiny light on the dial. 7.20pm. she'd go out soon and then he could spring into action, up the tree, over the balcony wall and into the bedroom. Ten minutes at the most.

A couple passed him, oblivious to anyone but themselves, but he shrank farther into the bank of shrubs on the edge of the park. A stiff breeze had him shivering. He pulled the hood of his anorak over his head and thrust his gloved hands deep into his pockets. *Not long now.*

The front door of the block swung open and the hulk stepped out, holding the door open for – Pamela! So this was the one she had the hots for. Dingo didn't think much of her choice, but conceded that most women would fling their knickers into the ring for that one. He watched sourly as they got into the sleek, dark blue monster and drove off.

Now!

He slipped a pair of surgical gloves on, carefully tugging them up as far as he could without tearing them. He'd brought two pairs just in case; it paid to be thorough. Looking both ways, he stepped out of the shadows and started for the unit block. Being right at the front with one balcony overlooking the small park, it jutted over the narrow laneway. Just as he started across the gap, someone came around the corner. Slouched in a duffle coat with a tasselled beanie on his head, the young man walked toward him. By his side trotted a stocky, black dog. A Staffordshire bull terrier, it paused as it neared Dingo and growled. Its owner stopped and called it to heel. 'He don't like strangers, mate.'

'Er, well I'm not going to hurt him.' Dingo thrust his gloved hands into his pockets and stood perfectly still. He knew from his nights of roaming the streets of his home town that you never ran from dogs. He had a scar in the back of his leg to prove it.

A sneering laugh, accompanied a smoker's cough. 'Too right, you won't mate. He'll have ya as quick as look at ya.' Eyes gleamed in the periphery of light from the front of the building. 'If I want him to.' After a moment's intense scrutiny, he whistled the dog to heel and they walked off, the animal pausing to look over its shoulder as they reached the back of the units. It knew he was planning something – oh yes, it knew. The sneering youth had a pretty good idea that Dingo was where he shouldn't be as well.

Breathing heavily, Dingo backed up and slid back into the bushes. He'd have to wait until things, namely his heartbeat, settled before trying again. He peered at his watch. 7.17pm. How long would Pam and the thug be out? If they had arrived at the restaurant, then they'd need an hour to eat and a bit of time to talk. If he was any judge of body language they'd be back to her place right after they'd eaten and bouncing around in the bed, but if he was lucky they'd go to her boyfriend's place.

Something crackled behind him. He pressed further into the shadows and peered around. Someone was walking through the trees several metres away. He squinted as a tall woman walked out onto the footpath and into the streetlight. A jogger? She turned away from him and trotted off along the road leading to the river. *Whew.*

He moved forward to re-check the approaches to the building. There was no one in sight, so he slithered across the road, and made a quick run to the tree –

'Harley? Come on puss!' A woman calling her blasted cat. She made clicking noises and banged what sounded like a spoon on a tin can. Dingo raced back across the lane and into the trees again. Something hissed at his feet. He jumped into the air and almost fell as a dark shape streaked out of the trees and across the road.

'There you are Harley, you naughty boy. I wish you'd stay out of the park.' She scooped up the cat and walked back into one of the ground-floor units. Dingo leaned back against the trunk of a rather substantial tree. *Fucking hell. Dogs and cats everywhere...*

He glanced at his watch. He'd been trying to get to the tree for three quarters of an hour already. He glanced in each direction. Nothing coming in the way or cars or people...it was now or never! He pulled his hood further down to avoid security cameras, sprinted for the tree, swung up into the lower branches and quickly climbed to the height of the balcony. The unit next door to Pam's was dark. He paused, waiting for the leaves to stop shaking and assessed the situation while he checked his gloves for damage. Nothing apparent, so no chance of leaving fingerprints. He really didn't expect even the cops would look for prints in the tree, but you never knew.

Only a metre over to the balustrade. He leaned toward it, only to hear someone walking along the laneway. Shit, it was the man and his dog again. Hardly daring to breath, Dingo, froze as the man stopped to light a cigarette and looked up and down the laneway and then over at the park, appearing to consider his options. The dog sat beside him, grinning up at the tree. *Oh God, Jesus no...*

Just as Dingo was sure he'd been sprung, the dog's owner grunted something, clicked his fingers and the dog, with a final glare at Dingo, sloped off with his master.

No more time to waste. He stretched across the short divide and grabbed the railing along the top of the wall. With a heave and a wriggle Dingo tumbled onto the balcony, landing with one foot in a pot plant. Cursing, he stepped out of the crushed plants and bent to try and revive them, but it wasn't going to work. Pushing the pot into the corner of the balcony – maybe Pamela Miller would be too taken up with her man to notice it until morning – he touched the handle of the French doors.

It moved. He grasped it and turned.

She'd forgotten to lock it!

He opened the door and listened. There was no radio or TV on. She'd left a light on in the lower part of the unit, just enough for him to see that the room was tidy, with no clothes strewn on the bed. He moved cautiously into the room, breathing in smell of *woman,* then moving to the en suite, from which emanated the tantalising scent of talc, soap and bath salts.

He stepped over to the door and gasped! Someone was at the far end – *no it was his own reflection in the mirror!* He leaned against the door jamb, breathing heavily, imagining Pamela and her bloke finding him dead of a heart attack on her bedroom floor, and wouldn't she be surprised? Chuckling, he went back into the room and looked around. *Hm*...maybe she'd kept the place tidy to invite the boyfriend up here. The front of his jeans tightened as his imagination took over...he looked at the bed, licking his lips, in danger of forgetting what he was there for. Time was passing. *The camera! Where was it?*

The one thing he could count on was them rushing back to fuck themselves silly.

Drawers, cupboards – he started at the bedside tables – reading glasses, novel, notebook, pens, postcards from friends, loose earring, some M & Ms in a small jar, lip gloss, a box of condoms – *oh you slut, Pam* – and then worked his way through the rest of the room, paying particular attention to the top shelf of the wardrobe. An avalanche of handbags landed on his head. Angrily he tossed them aside and stretched up to feel around the back of the shelf; nothing. Her chest of drawers only held clothes. He liked her taste in knickers, but no sign of the camera. He scooped up the handbags and hurled the whole lot up onto the shelf, jamming the door shut before they could come down again.

He moved out of the bedroom and opened the door of the practice room next to it. A music stand, an old upright, ornate piano, shelves filled with sheet music. He glanced around, noting the "egg-carton" insulation. *Good girl.* He opened the cupboard against the far wall, but saw only piles of music books. The small CD player on top of the unit was of no interest.

The camera had to be down on the bottom level of the split-level unit.

Fortunately she'd left a small nightlight on. Thanking his lucky stars the few steps into the lounge and kitchen area were carpeted, he ventured down, sliding his gloved hand along the wall so he wouldn't slip. Landing with a splat and a broken ankle was something which didn't have any appeal. *Tennineeightsevensixfivefourthreetwoone...*

Think. It's an expensive camera. Where would she put it?

He forced himself to breathe slowly and evenly as he let his eyes wander around the room. Family photos, the piano and paintings...dozens of books...he looked along the shelves where expensive ornaments gazed down on him. Keeping calm, his gaze slid across the comfortable flowered lounge, to the coffee table where a magazine lay open at the page with the crossword. She'd almost finished it – clever girl – and then to the dining room table. He moved closer to where her flute case lay open, the beautiful instrument gleaming in the dim light. *You'd lose that, along with everything of value if it wasn't me here, babe!*

The camera had to be somewhere here. The thought of it in the car made his balls cringe. A noise came from outside the front door. Voices, footsteps! Before he could even think about hiding, they passed. He heard a door opening somewhere. Sweat broke out all over his body. *He had to get out of here!* He looked at his watch. They'd be back any time now.

Dingo went to the kitchen intending to open every drawer, even the refrigerator if necessary, but suddenly there it was, on a small side-table near the door. He scooped it up. *Thank you, God.* His hands trembled as he picked up the case lying next to it and stuffed the camera inside, cursing as the strap caught in the zipper. *Hurry hurry!* Frantic now, he struggled to close the case as he ran for the steps up into the bedroom, unaware that a tiny piece of one of his gloves had torn in the metal zip and dropped to the floor.

He raced across the bedroom to the balcony doors and slipped through, trying to keep below the level of the balustrade. He peered over the railing. Nothing stirred. *Thank you, God.*

He slung the strap of the case around his neck. It was the work of a moment to swing across into the branches. Just as he was about to climb down, the Audi came around the corner; as it swept past, he caught a glimpse of Pamela Miller's wild hair under the streetlight.

He tumbled the rest of the way down the tree, raced across the laneway and into the park. Panting and shaking with fear, he hunkered under a shrub, holding his precious booty tightly to his chest. He could see the couple through the leaves, brightly lit by the lights at the front of the building. The boyfriend got out of the car and came around to open the door for Pamela. They stood for a moment, faces close. Dingo could sense the charge of sexual energy crackling between them. The boyfriend closed the car door, pressed the button on his key to lock it, slipped his arm around Pamela and they disappeared into the building.

A garbage bin caught his attention. Carefully he ripped off the surgical gloves, rolled them into a ball, gently lifted the lid with one finger under the handle and dropped them in, scarcely taking his eyes from the front of the building.

His mind flew into panic. Had he left everything as he'd found it? The handbags! He'd thrown them back into the top of the wardrobe, uncaring of how they'd landed. *Pam wouldn't be looking at them tonight!* With any luck, she wouldn't realise there'd been an intruder until morning. He had to get back to the hotel and crunch that SC card under the heel of his boot.

Stumbling through the park, there tripping over tree roots here and there, he made his way to the road on the other side and walked back to the hotel. He'd check out first thing in the morning; now he had the camera there was no reason to hang around the area. He couldn't wait to get home to the familiar nest he'd created for himself and his music.

He sauntered across the foyer, past the empty reception desk to the lifts, briefly acknowledging a greeting from a staff member coming from the bar, who looked at him strangely. It was only when he reached his room that he realised he was still wearing his hood pulled half down over his face and the camera was bulging under his jacket. It didn't matter. He'd be gone first thing in the morning.

He laid the camera on the bed, wiped his sweaty hands on the legs of his jeans and then opened the case. It was a beautiful piece of digital machinery. He took it out of the case, turned it around several times before opening it and taking out the card which he inserted into the reader and took a deep breath. Slowly he flicked through the photos.

His blood turned to ice as he reached the end of the card.

He couldn't believe it. Only Pamela *Miller's* photos were on the flash card. Roma Street Parklands for God's sake, flowers, trees, waterfalls – tower blocks of units across from the transit centre. The kids fucking playground!

He stuffed his face into the pillows to stifle his screams. *Where are they? Where are the photos of Ariel and me?* The howls echoes around in his brain; his body curled into the foetal position. They'd posed, danced on the grass, grinning. He'd risked his job, his freedom, his safety in breaking into Pamela Bloody Miller's unit – *all for nothing!* His breath came in great gasps.

He felt as though he was having a heart attack. It took a long time for him to calm down and when he did, an idea crept into his mind. Had the Humphries woman only pretended to take their photos? But she'd written their names down – no, *his* name because Ariel had been giggling and doing handstands while he was talking to the journalist. Would the police find his name among her things? They hadn't come to question him, so apparently not – at least not yet.

His bladder threatened to explode. He raced to the bathroom, used the loo then wiped his hands and face with a warm, wet face cloth. Ten...nine...eight...seven... six...five... Even if they did find his name, what would it mean? Nothing at all – unless she'd written something about the photos beside it and his phone number. Did she date the pages of her notebook?

He slumped on the bed, so exhausted that he couldn't think straight. His lower back ached along with his shoulder. His bitten finger seeped blood and serum from under the dressing. He groped miserably in the bedside drawer for the packet of bandaids he'd put there within easy reach. All he wanted to do was creep back to his unit on Kangaroo Point, a wounded animal but safe amongst his own possessions and not be trapped in some alien hotel with women, dead and alive, crowding him on all sides.

Suddenly, he made a decision and flew into action. He packed up his possessions, collected his toiletries from the bathroom and threw the cameras and their bags into his bag. Paid up until the next morning, he left his key-card on the bedside table, hoisted his backpack over his shoulders and picked up his bags.

He was going home.

CHAPTER 37

Pam

A Shower of Embarrassment

Tuesday, 8.45pm

It was the rush to the loo in stockinged feet that alerted me to the fact that my unit had been broken into. We'd come back from dinner, I'd kicked my shoes off by the front door and left Anthony to put the electric jug on for coffee while I scooted up to the bedroom level.... and then...you know how something registers, but it sort of doesn't? When you're caught up in the moment and it isn't until you've settled again that you realise something is different?

I'd washed my hands, tried to do something with my hair and was about to walk out of the bathroom, when I realised I had grit on my feet.

Now, anyone will tell you – especially Ally's mum, Aunt Eloise – that I am not the neatest person in the world. In fact, when I'm not being "Holier than thou," cleaning up in case a new boyfriend, in this case my personal assassin, takes fright and runs, I live in perpetual clutter. But I hadn't had time to turn my unit into Hurricane Hollow and being over-excited about pretending to be the perfect keeper, had actually wiped over the bathroom and swept the floor. So I hadn't picked up grit on the tiles, but there it was, stuck to the fibres of my stockings and feeling uncomfortable.

I tiptoed slowly out of the bathroom and looked around my room. Nothing obvious, but when I turned on the light, I went cold. Small flecks of dirt led from under the curtains across the balcony doors and in a direct line to the bed where they vanished.

I screamed.

'What is it?' Anthony bounded up the steps.

All I could do was point at the particles. Moving carefully around them, he peered down, then at the French door leading to the balcony. 'Did you lock this tonight before we went out?'

I couldn't remember. I always do, but I'd been so excited about my date that maybe I hadn't. 'I thought I did, but...'

He moved over to the curtains, took a pen out of his shirt pocket and moved one aside. The door was closed. Then he took one of his copious white handkerchiefs and placed it over the door handle.

It opened.

Throwing me a stern look, he pushed the door open and leaned out. 'Is there a light for out here?'

'Yes.' I sidled along the wall and flicked the switch behind the other curtain.

'There's more dirt out here. Looks like someone stepped in one of your pot plants. No, don't come out, just stay where you are.'

My skin crawled. What had the intruder touched? Had he been in my underwear drawer? Was it the bloke who hit me and tried to steal my camera – *the camera!* I raced down to the kitchen-dining area. My precious flute was still lying in its case. Where in God's name had I put the damn camera? I couldn't think straight. Anthony came back down the steps and watched as I circled in confusion. 'What are you looking for?'

'The camera! That's what the creep was trying to steal when he hit me over the head and I *know* it was him watching my place the other day. The cops reckon I could have been mistaken, but I'm not that *stupid*.'

Anthony put his hands on my shoulders. 'Now, calm down. Try and remember what you did when you came home today?'

How could I tell him I was so excited to be with him that all I could do when I got home after his text was dance around the kitchen squeaking "Yes, yes, yes!" and punching the air? I closed my eyes and leaned in against him, breathing in his gorgeous smell, his aftershave. He wrapped his arms around me, but true to the cop he is, refused to be side-tracked. 'Think about it. You came through the door and what's the first thing you did? Something you probably always do?'

'Put my handbag down, take off my coat and –' I pulled back and went to the small side table by the front door. 'The camera's missing! It was here. I dropped the bag of groceries on the table and my handbag, and then went to hang up my coat. I had the camera strap over my shoulder so I had to take that off first. I *know* I put it here!'

'Is there anything else missing that you can tell?' he asked, taking his mobile out of its pouch.

I walked slowly around the room checking the books, pictures, ornaments, a money box of small change – it rattled satisfactorily in spite of me robbing it on a regular basis – and the stereo and television were present and correct. My piano looked untouched. 'I'll look upstairs, see if everything's there!'

Anthony, who was talking on the phone, paused. 'Don't touch anything!'

I smiled and drew out a pair of surgical gloves from the box on the shelf under the sink. He grinned as I drew them on. With a wave I headed back upstairs.

Knowing enough from watching CSI not to walk on the evidence, I skirted along the wall to the bed and opened the bedside drawers. Nothing appeared to be missing. The new box of 24 assorted condoms lurking blatantly in one of the drawers made me blush. Bloody hell! Knowing a forensic team would be in here, I whipped them out of the drawer and opened the wardrobe door, intending to stow them at the back of the top shelf.

All hell broke loose!

A squawk as I went down in an avalanche of handbags, boxes of shoes, spare coat-hangers and "stuff" landing on my bottom, the contents of the box of condoms showering me. Mercifully my most of collection of forty-two handbags were obscuring some of the foil packets. Before I could sweep them up and stuff them under the mattress, down my bra or even in my knickers, the object of my lustful intentions burst into the room and threw himself on his knees beside me.

'What's happened? Are you hurt?'

'I'm fine! Just give me a minute!' I muttered, but he was too chivalrous for that, sweeping aside bags and brushing me down. His eyes widened as condoms sprayed around us. 'What on earth...?'

'Er...I was trying to...er...' The blush started around my waist and elevated rapidly until I just knew my face was bright red.

Then he got the message. Grinning, he started gathering them up, counting diligently. 'Where's the box?'

Sheepishly, I scrabbled around and produced it from under the bedside table.

'Coloured *and* flavoured! Were you planning on using them with anyone in particular?'

'Um, well...you never know.'

He started laughing. 'Oh Pam, if you could see your face! Were you trying to hide them from Forensics?'

I nodded, avoiding eye contact. He roared with laughter. 'You can *never* hide anything from that lot! They'd have found them wherever you put them.' He placed his hand under my chin and gently tilted my face up to his. 'I'll be only too happy to help you use them – *when* your cousin's case is solved! Now, let's see what we can do to lessen the damage.'

He kissed me quickly, then grabbed a handful of the wretched things and stuffed them into the inside pockets of his jacket. 'Leave a couple in the box and put the rest in your bra,' he advised, as the sound of sirens, which had actually registered somewhere in the dim recesses of my mind, came closer. 'The troops'll be here any minute. I'll go down and let them in. Leave the handbags and stuff where they are.'

I gathered up the rest of the damned condoms, shoved most of them into my bra, thanking my mum's genes that my generous endowment in that area would prevent them falling out, and put the box with a couple left into the bottom of my chest of drawers. Now it was empty, the techs'd think they had a female sex maniac on their hands. The sound of voices came from the kitchen and lounge room level so, being careful to skirt the faint trail of earth, I ripped off my surgical gloves and walked down to join them, trying to look as if butter wouldn't melt in my mouth.

To say I was shocked was an understatement. Standing in the front row, was Susan Prescott's side-kick, Evan Taylor, and another young cop, grinning like fools. Anthony, looking pink about the gills, came to stand beside me.

'This is Detective Constable Jacob Coops. Well, well, what have we here? I understand you've had a break-in, Pam?'

Evan's eyes twinkled. He was enjoying every minute of our embarrassment. *Please God, if you have any mercy left in you for idiot me, don't let the condoms fall out of my bra...*

'Yes, we were at dinner,' Anthony took over, 'and Pam discovered evidence to suggest that someone came in while we were out. Her iPad, laptop, iPod are all here. Apart from having a good scout around, it appears the only thing missing is Pam's camera, the one which she was lent by Marigold Humphries. Looks like he entered through the balcony doors.'

Instantly, their faces sobered. Evan nodded slowly. 'Was it the same camera your attacker tried to steal from you at Roma Street Parklands?'

'Yes. It only has photos of the Parklands on it though. Why would he want that?'

The three cops exchanged glances and Evan appeared to come to a decision. 'Because it's possible that the murder of Ariel Maxwell and your cousin, Goldie, are connected. Now you've had a break-in and the camera's been stolen, but until you've had a good look around, it appears nothing else. It's not rocket science, love.'

'I can't see anything valuable missing, but as you say, when I've had a good look...'

A commotion outside the front door heralded the arrival of two people carrying what I now recognised as forensic kits. The Body Corporate wouldn't be best pleased. I could see neighbours from my floor clustered behind the technicians. The looks on their faces said it all; I would be persona non grata in the building now for sure. It was only a matter of time before the media landed on us as well.

A uniformed officer arrived, talked briefly to Evan and then stationed himself outside the door after herding the neighbours back into their units. The techs moved in and suddenly there was no place for me there. My confusion must have shown, because Anthony and Evan took me aside. 'You'll need to go somewhere else tonight, Pam. Any ideas?'

'Well, I can't go to Goldie's or to Aunt Fiona's because of you know who.' Anthony nodded. 'I could give Ally Mochrie a ring. Perhaps Brie's mum and dad mightn't mind if I camp there because they've got a big house. Can I take anything from here? I do need my flute and my handbag.'

Anthony took me to the Mochrie's huge house in Kenmore where I was met with so much love that I cried my eyes out. It was all getting too much, culminating in the break-in after such a lovely evening with Anthony and the fact that I was worried about getting enough practice before the next concert in four days time. There was still Goldie's funeral to get through and what about Aunt Fiona and the trouble with Alex? They – well *he* – would *demand* entry – had already been in there – and oh dear, when they found the locks had been changed, my uncle's reaction didn't bear thinking about. I decided to hide behind Mr Sytch. After all he did advise me to do it. Sweet little man that he is, I was sure he was more than capable of dealing with Alex. I fell gratefully into being cosseted by the Mochries parents and thanked God the twins were asleep.

CHAPTER 38

Pam

Heartbreak

Wednesday, 8am.

Something tickled my face. I threw myself on my tummy and ducked my head under the pillow, refusing to face the morning. Perhaps if I played sick I wouldn't have to get up and face the day, or the twins, or the cops, or statements, or the Humphries – anything in fact.

Giggling alerted me to the identities of the little skellums who were disturbing my precious sleep.

'Nam, Nam!' Something landed with all four feet on my back. I was well and truly sprung. The feet disappeared as I rolled over and came face to face with the Mochrie twins, a right pair of scallywags. Their grandmother's cat, which they had hauled into the room and dumped on my back, bolted out of the room. The boys rolled around the bed, shrieking with laughter and punching each other.

Bright and incredibly advanced for their age, although I love them dearly, a little of their company can go a long way. Ally and Brie are fairly strict parents, thank goodness, but their grandparents on both sides indulged Rory and Rulf – *yes, I know –*

abominably. I cuddled them for awhile before Ally called them for their breakfast. Promising to play later, I crawled reluctantly out of bed. So much to do; so much to face. Another statement at the police station, see Mum as soon as I could and I had to pick up my dress at the shop.

When I got out to the kitchen, Angela – Brie's mother – had taken a message from Fiona. 'She was quite surprised when the police told her you were here, Pam. Apparently they went around to Goldie's house this morning to get some things and couldn't get in. Apparently Alex wasn't best pleased.' *Looks like the shit's about to hit the fan.*

'The solicitor, told me to change the locks. Since someone had already gotten in, he said I had to do it for insurance.' Angela threw me a sympathetic look. 'Well, she asked me to tell you the funeral's on Friday, 2pm at the Cemetery at Mt Gravatt. A graveside service.' I was surprised that the solicitor hadn't insisted on a cremation, but figured that as the Executor, he could countermand Goldie's wishes if her parents kicked up enough fuss. I knew she hadn't specified it in the will, but verbally expressed her preference. I pulled out my phone and scrolled through the text messages. Sure enough, there was one from him and about a million from everyone else. The one I really wanted to see, Anthony's, asked me to ring him when I got up. He'd added a string of x's at the end.

Ally and her mother-in-law came into the room with the twins in tow, so we didn't have an opportunity to talk properly until they ran outside to play with the dog. 'So how're you feeling, Pammie? We thought you could do with a lie-in.'

I sipped my coffee and thought about it. 'Actually, not too bad now I'm here with you. Thank you so much for taking me in last night. I was a mess!'

'Of course we would take you in, Darling.' Angela grinned and patted my hand. Ally reached over and hugged me. 'And don't worry, Brie and I are coming to the funeral with you. After all, we knew Goldie too and we're going to support you anyway.'

'John's coming with me too. I'll ring him after I've finished this.' I waved my coffee cup. 'Then I have to get going. Stacks to do and the concert on Saturday as well. Sometimes I even forget about that and I've only had three hours practice since the concert. Fortunately, it's with the Classical Musos.'

We'd played together many times so a run through of the program would be all that was necessary. I'd ring them too and see if we could set that up for Thursday morning. Insurance wouldn't be an issue with the unit. After all, I'd left the doors unlocked so it wouldn't pay out even if anything was missing. The camera wasn't important in the scheme of things, the police would have locked up and Anthony would have the keys.

The Mochrie women headed for the city to shop, the Mochrie men escaped to the golf course and the Mochrie menaces had been taken to Daycare, much to the relief, no doubt, of the resident cat and dog.

Just then, my mobile rang.

'Hey Pam! How are you this morning?'

'Er...Dingo?' I giggled. 'I can't think of you as anything else now. Fine thanks.' I smiled. Even last night's break-in couldn't dim my happiness.

'Want to meet for coffee at ten-thirty?' His tone suddenly sounded grave. 'I really have to talk to you, mate. Can you *please* meet me at the coffee shop across from Silver's?'

Hesitating, I thought for a moment. Even something as innocuous as coffee with another man had no interest for me now that I had Anthony in my life.

'Please?'

Something in the tone of his voice concerned me. 'Okay, but just for a quick cup, okay?'

He thanked me profusely and rang off. *Damn, I didn't really want to do that.*

I put Ally's nightie into the laundry for washing and answered my messages. As I put my mobile into my bag, my hand encountered something unusual inside the lining. I felt around and got it out through a small slit in the fabric. Goldie's USB stick, the one she lent me on Saturday. I'd forgotten all about it, but remembered she'd left it in the fruit bowl on the kitchen counter, me fishing it out and throwing it into my bag. Curious, I fingered it, wondering if there was anything on it. Just then I caught sight of Ally's laptop on the coffee table.

I picked up my mobile; she answered almost straightaway. 'Of course you can use the laptop, Pam. The password's Dandelion88. Oh, I forgot to tell you that Angela's changed the place for the house key. It's now in an artificial rock next to the third pot plant to the left of the front door on the verandah!'

'Got it! See you later and thanks again.' It was the work of a moment to fire up the laptop and put the USB into the port. Leaning back, my thoughts were well and truly away with the fairies – namely, a certain huge gorgeous, scrumptious, heavenly cop – when the last photos on the stick came up on the screen.

I couldn't believe it.

Ariel Maxwell, laughing as she danced, a tiny sprite tripping through the grass against a backdrop of trees and the river! Goldie was a superb photographer. In spite of the soft dawn light, there was no mistaking the face which had been all over the news in the last two days, but it was the identity of her companion which left me gasping.

Numb with shock, I fumbled for my mobile. 'Anthony! I've found the photos! You know, the ones Goldie took at the river.'

'Calm down, Pam. Just settle down, take a few deep breaths. I can't understand you properly. You say you found some photos of Goldie's that were taken in the park by the river?'

I took deep shuddering breaths and tried to control my trembling lips. Tears welled and poured down my cheeks. 'Yes. Goldie lent me a USB stick last Saturday afternoon.' I went on to explain how I found it and apologised for forgetting it.

'You mean it was there all the time?'

'Must have been. Ariel Maxwell, you know, the young girl is on it, posing and dancing and you'll never guess who else!'

I told him and explained that we were meeting for coffee and when.

'Can you email the photos to me?'

'Yes. I'm still at the Mochries and I'm looking at them on Ally's laptop. What's your email addy?'

He gave it to me and I zapped the photos through,

'Hang on the phone, Pam.'

A few minutes later, he came back on the line. 'Got them! Don't go and meet him, and don't speak to him on the phone again whatever you do because he'll hear in your voice that you know about him. Where are you now?'

I gave him the address. 'Should I text him and cancel?'

'No! We'll pick him up when he gets to the coffee shop, but you keep away. A patrol car will be over in a few minutes for the USB. We'll deal with it.'

'Can I go back to my unit then?'

'Yes, we've finished with your place now. No fingerprints, but they found a skerrick of surgical glove on the lounge room floor. I've left your keys with the reception desk downstairs. Talk to you later. Take care.'

I sat down, shaking all over. Of all the people I would never have guessed. Grief and disappointment that someone I knew, liked and admired for his brilliance could do something so terrible not once, but twice – for I had no doubt he had killed my cousin as well – overcame me. Heartbroken, I put my face in my hands and wept.

It wasn't more than ten minutes later there came a knock on the door. I wiped my eyes, blew my nose and peered out of the window. A uniformed police officer was standing outside, so I opened up and handed over the USB, after which I sat for a few minutes, silently trying to get my thoughts in order. *You've not only murdered two women but you've ruined the lives of those people and our family, hurt me beyond belief and destroyed your own. How could you?* My family and that of the young girl would never recover from the loss of our loved ones.

I called a taxi to take me back to my unit to collect my car and change my clothes. After that, I'd see mum, then go and collect my altered dress from Tia's little shop. It wasn't far from the coffee s hop where I was supposed to go, but I figured far enough away to not be seen, especially if I raced in and out before...*Dingo*...arrived to meet me.

The fingerprint dust and chaos in my unit was a real turnoff. I scrabbled amongst the pile of my clothes on the bed, found something that wasn't creased and got out of there as fast as I could. I knew the Body Corporate would be waiting with a tiger net for me. Luckily I owned my unit, but things would get ugly. My lovely home had been violated and I just didn't know what to do. My pleasure in living there had gone. Probably I'd sell it, but living in Goldie's house was not an option.

Mum was sitting in a chair when I got to the hospital, John by her side. They were drinking tea and laughing when I walked in. Their smiles disappeared the moment they laid eyes on my red swollen eyes. I told them about the break in, but not what and who was on the message stick. I knew enough to keep quiet about that, even though John was a retired copper. *Would it be all over yet? When would they go for him?*

Not wanting to be near the action, I cut my visit shorter than I'd intended, and went to collect my dress. Finding parking spots has never been easy for me, but this time there was actually one a few doors down from the dress shop. I locked the car and glanced around to make sure the coast was clear before I headed up the street. As I reached the door of the shop, Tia came out of the back office, self consciously touching her battered face. 'Hi Pam. Come for the dress? It's ready but you need to try it on again just to be sure it's okay.'

She ushered me into the dressing room. I stripped off my top and jeans and took the dress she handed through the door. It looked just the right length but I wanted to check the hem length in the long mirror. I smoothed it over my hips and backed up to the door. Not far enough to gauge the length, I opened the fitting room door and moved farther away, but when I glanced at Tia.

My heart started to pound.

Her pinched little face and terrified eyes, staring at the shop front window rang alarm bells.

Wild-eyed, hair standing on end, he looked as though he had slept in his clothes for a week. Dark circles under his eyes, ashen faced, he rushed into the shop, panting. 'Pam, *please*. I saw you coming in here, but I couldn't wait. You must tell me – *the camera –*'

A figure burst through the door behind him and launched itself at us.

As I went down over the brocade chair, my last sight was of Grant's vicious face, lips drawn back. Screaming invectives, he threw wild punches, hitting Dingo anywhere he could land them.

I fell heavily on my shoulder. The chair legs tangled in the curtain covering the doorway to the back of the shop and my weight pulled it down. The pole whacked the stitches in my head and I wound my arms around it to protect myself from the bodies crashing around me.

They rolled off me, grappled and fell through the dress racks. A manikin went flying and crashed through the glass shop-front. Grant was being choked when I saw something glitter. The two men collapsed onto the floor, rolling over and over, smashing against the counter, knocking over the hat stand, surging into the dressing room and out again. A long way off, someone was screaming.

A heavy grunt flowed into a long drawn-out moan.

Deathly silence.

A rivulet of blood flowed from under the bodies, spreading and seeping into the carpet fibres.

I tried to sit up, but my legs were entangled in the broken chair. I could hear shouting in the distance. Tia had disappeared.

I have to get of here.

Before I could work out how to do that, the tiny shop was flooded with police. Grant was dragged off his victim, howling like a wolf. One of the cops told him to shut his mouth or he'd do it for him. They rolled him onto his face, handcuffed him, hauled him to his feet and bundled him out the door.

My head swam; my limbs wouldn't unlock from the wood. I couldn't remember why I'd even come into the shop.

A forest of highly polished black shoes, long, dark blue legs topped with male backsides and cop hardware stood facing away from me. Then a pair of jeaned legs arrived just as paramedics carried in their bags.

No one appeared to have noticed me lying in the broken chair, half covered in curtain. I was about to shout for help, but then I heard Anthony's voice:

'Vladimir Marcus Rezanov, you are under arrest for the murder of Ariel Maxwell and Marigold Humphries. You have the right to remain silent. Anything you do say may later be used in court.'

CHAPTER 39

Susan

Promises

Thursday, 9pm.

I'd been right all along. The two murders were connected, but it didn't give me any joy. Two beautiful young women dead, their families and friends devastated. The police prosecutor would collate our evidence; the solicitors and barristers would work up the case. What a pity such talent was going to waste, but maybe he'd teach music in prison and rehabilitate a few.

After Rezanov was delivered to hospital under guard, suffering from a knife wound in the top of his thigh, the scientists had taken over the shop, much to the disgust of the owner, who roundly berated the young assistant and had to be forcibly restrained from throwing her into the street. Finally, the woman contented herself with sacking the girl, publicly and with relish.

Statements taken and paperwork done, hours later I dropped Pam into the more than eager clutches of my Detective Senior Sergeant. She'd talked about putting her lovely unit on the market. 'I'll never feel comfortable there again, Susan.'

No prizes for guessing what the future held for her. Rumour had it that Anthony Hamilton had a rather nice stone cottage in New Farm, just large enough for two and a couple of pets. She'd offered to get me four tickets to her Saturday night concert in Ipswich, promising to wear the fiery dress and golden shoes about which we'd heard so much in the media. Apparently, Pam would be asking our Anthony – awash with sisters, one of whom works in the Concert Hall office – to help her talk the manager into giving Tia the job of junior office assistant.

The fallout from Rezanov's arrest for murder was immense. The world of music – classical and otherwise – had been rocked since his arrest and social media fizzing with disbelief. Current affairs programs analysed ad nauseam, each "talking head" having a different spin on his motivation, ranging from a thwarted love affair with either woman, Marigold Humphries being the prime candidate, to insanity. I favoured insanity.

Earlier, I'd watched the TV news on which the whole drama was played out for the umpteenth time. There was the team, including Evan, Anthony and myself, with our two prisoners. Vladimir Rezanov, renowned concert pianist, pitifully dazed and disoriented, was surrounded by paramedics, after *sweet*, *gentle* Grant Winslow, was handcuffed and dragged out, screaming with rage. Waving her arms in the background, was Pam's young friend and fan, Tia from the dress shop, sporting a great black bruise down the left side of her face and a bleeding nose, crying her eyes out.

Pam had told us that Grant had previously beaten Tia up for exchanging a few words with the pianist in the street, as well as talking to her boss's son. When he'd seen the man go into the shop, although he was trying to talk to Pam, Grant had jumped to the conclusion that young Tia was cheating on him. At least the little monster couldn't get to her again – for now.

Still no word from David, but I was too exhausted to stay up waiting for him to call. Deciding that I would apply in the morning for a week's leave, hopefully effective immediately, I let the dogs out and waited for them to finish their business. 'Bedtime, you lot!' I poured myself a hot drink, checked that the rats had been fed, made a mental note to pay the kid next door for her work and buy more food for them. Then, ordering the dogs to their beds in the laundry, I tottered off to my own, where Fat Albert and Genevieve lurked, plotting to push me out to whichever edge they could manage.

I was out like a light the moment my head hit the pillow.

* * *

It was the sound of footsteps which alerted me to someone in the house. Fearful, I sat up and reached for the bedside phone, surprised the dogs hadn't barked. I heard the laundry door open. 'Susan?'

'David!' I scrambled to get out of bed, but suddenly he was there and the light was on. He bounded over to the bed, sat down and swept me into his arms.

'You're safe. Oh thank God you're safe! And you didn't ring.' My voice came out scratchy; tears ran down my cheeks.

'No time.' His cold face pressed against mine. As he squeezed me, something squeaked. He stepped back and reached into his pocket to pull out a minute ginger kitten. 'Got left behind after the RSPCA cleaned out the animals at the dog fight. One of the blokes found him in the grass! I know I promised to phone you, I'm sorry.'

What...?

'You *were* under-cover. And what am I? A repository for unwanted cats?' I gathered the tiny animal to my chest...

My eyes snapped open. It was pitch black. Where was David? The kitten? I wriggled across the bed and switched on the light. The cats raised their heads to look at me in disgust. My heart pounded; nausea welled. It had been a dream! Did this mean that he had appeared because...*No no!A dog fight?* Terror shot through me; perspiration broke out over my body.

Imprisoned in the sheets, blankets and cats, I couldn't get close enough to the bedside clock to read the time without my glasses. I rolled as close as I could. 4am. *He still hadn't phoned.* I picked up the receiver to check that nothing was wrong with the line. The dial tone burred in my ear. Disgusted, I slammed it back into its cradle. If he'd called my mobile it would have rung downstairs on the charger and when it didn't answer, he would have dialed the phone in the bedroom.

I cupped the growing mound in my tummy. Panic swept me into a maelstrom of fear for my husband, my lover, the father of my soon to be four children. *Please God, I promise never to doubt you again if you just let him come home safely.*

The future stretched ahead, barren, empty, without hope.

And then the phone rang.

THE END.

If you enjoyed AFTER ARIEL, please take a
moment to leave a review! Thank you, Diana.

A DARK AND LONELY PLACE

With just 24 hours left to live, Gerry Haines drew up his bucket list. It was done with much laughing and good humour around a roaring fire, quaffing good wine with a group of five friends. He wouldn't have laughed quite as loudly or long if he had known that one of those friends would cut his list lamentably short.

If you asked anyone who knew Gerry well, they would have said he was a meticulous worker, a good friend and a good listener.

In fact, Gerry was more than a good listener. He was an avid one, a trait which would prove to be his downfall.

(To be published in 2015)

* * *

BIOGRAPHY

Diana Hockley lives in a Queensland country town, with her husband, Andrew and six pet rats. She and her husband once owned a mouse circus which travelled throughout Queensland and northern New South Wales. The Hockley's bred Scottish Highland cattle until their retirement seven years ago and are dedicated animal welfare supporters of the Animal Welfare League, Destiny Donkey Farm/Rescue, RSPCA, SPANA, Animals Australia and Animals Asia

The Hockleys have three adult children and three grandchildren.

Diana is an avid reader, and produces and presents a weekly classical music program on community radio. She has written a considerable number of short stories and articles some of which are available on Amazon. Her work has been showcased in Australia, the UK and USA, and she edits, writes and reviews for the Californian online magazine, Kings River Life, and has had work published in Mezzo Magazine, Honestly Woman (Australia) the Highlander, Austin Times (AUS & UK) It's Rat's World, Solaris (UK) Literary Journal, University of Michigan (USA) Foliate Oak (USA) and children's website, Billabong. In 2006 prizes in Scenic Rim Arts Festival for Poetry and fiction.

The first in the Detective Senior Sergeant Susan Prescott trilogy, The Naked Room, is available worldwide. Her next crime novel, The Celibate Mouse, was developed during the last year of writing Naked Room, and is available on Amazon USA, Canada, UK, Europe and worldwide. All three books are available in digital and paperback. The fourth is in the process of procrastination!

Diana lurks from time to time on Twitter, Facebook, LinkedIn, Google + and Quora.